Kelly Gardiner is a writer of novels, poetry and
nonfiction. Her poetry has been published in
journals including *Going Down Swinging* and
Southerly and she is the author of the young adult
novels *Act of Faith* and *The Sultan's Eyes*, and four
books for younger readers. *Act of Faith* was named
by the Children's Book Council of Australia as one
of the Notable Australian Books of 2012 and was
highly commended in the Australian Society of
Authors' Barbara Jefferis Award in 2012.

This book is set in Historical Felltype, which takes its name from John Fell, Bishop of Oxford from 1676 until his death in 1686. Many of the original Fell types were cut by Dutch craftsmen and purchased by Fell in the early 1670s for use by the Oxford University Press, of which he was an early promoter. The Fell types, characterised by a bold irregularity, were revived in 1876 and adapted for digital typesetting in 2000.

goddess

Kelly Gardiner

FOURTH ESTATE

Fourth Estate
An imprint of HarperCollins*Publishers*

First published in Australia in 2014
by HarperCollins*Publishers* Australia Pty Limited
ABN 36 009 913 517
harpercollins.com.au

HarperCollins*Publishers*
Level 13, 201 Elizabeth Street, Sydney NSW 2000, Australia
Unit D1, 63 Apollo Drive, Rosedale Auckland 0632, New Zealand
A 53, Sector 57, Noida, UP, India
1 London Bridge Street, London, SE1 9GF, United Kingdom
2 Bloor Street East, 20th floor, Toronto, Ontario M4W 1A8, Canada
195 Broadway, New York NY 10007, USA

National Library of Australia Cataloguing-in-Publication data:

Gardiner, Kelly, 1961- author.
  Goddess / Kelly Gardiner.
  ISBN: 978 0 7322 9888 3 (paperback)
  ISBN: 978 1 4607 0249 9 (ebook)
  Maupin, Julie de, 1670-1707
  Biographical fiction.
  Historical fiction.
NZ823.3

Cover design by Darren Holt, HarperCollins Design Studio
Cover images: Woman by Daniel Murtagh / Trevillion Images; all other images by shutterstock.com
Author photograph by Rebecca Michaels
Typeset in 12/17pt Historical Felltype by Kirby Jones

For Susannah

HEREIN, THE FINAL CONFESSION of Julie-Émilie d'Aubigny, known as Mademoiselle de Maupin, late of the Académie Royale de Musique.

As related to Father Fabrice, Confessor, parish of Saint-Pierre.

Avignon
July 1707

Prologue

DON'T HOVER IN THE DOORWAY like that.

Come in or piss off—I don't care either way.

Who in Hell are you?

Prophet of doom, by the look. First man I've sighted in two months, and what do they send me? I'm not entirely sure it was worth the wait. Still, I like to see a new face, and you're handsome enough. For a priest.

What a waste.

But then, you could say the same of me.

Did the Abbess send you? That'd be just like her. Can't they let me rest? *Requiescat in pace,* as it were.

I suppose they've told you to take my Confession, have they?

I must be dying. I thought as much.

Sit down, then. Sit down. Let's get this over with. I'm afraid I can't offer you a glass of cognac, but you look more like a mother's milk fellow to me.

3

Did they warn you about me, Father, before they pushed you through that door? Have you heard all the gossip—in the cloisters, in the kitchens, all over Provence? I know what they're saying. I know what you're thinking, too. The oldest story of all—scarlet woman turns her face from sin at the end of her days, takes the veil, finds humility and salvation.

Pig's arse.

I'm sorry to disappoint you but I'm not really a nun. I'm only here for my health—fat lot of good it's done me. So this won't be a nun's Confession you hear. If I can get up out of this damned—sorry, Father—this bed, I'll go to Mass, like everyone, but for the beauty of it, the wonder—for that moment, when they hold the chalice aloft, of connection with Heaven. For the drama of it, you might say.

That's the point, isn't it? Otherwise nobody would bother, surely, week in and week out. Don't scoff at me like I'm some kind of heretic. We all need a little music in our lives, the touch of *tragédie*—mysteries and soaring voices and a shot of sunlight through blue glass. It's a spectacle, more like the old days at the Palais-Royal than you'd care to admit, Father—a reflection of the moment the orchestra begins to tune up and the house falls silent, ready to believe anything that happens on that stage. There's magic in it, in the ritual and the riches, that I love. It has nothing, unfortunately, to do with faith.

That's why I like it here. It's comforting. My city friends would laugh their hats off if they heard me say that. If I could laugh myself, without coughing up my entrails, I would. Here in this white cell I have found comfort. A chair. A bed. Treetops through a high window. Bells calling everyone to Vespers. The soft sounds of sweeping. It's not comfortable, but it is comforting. There's a difference, do you see?

The heart—perhaps the soul, I'm not sure—is at rest. Not peace. Oh no. My body, faithless thing, aches and rumbles and twists in pain in the cold hours of the morning. But the essence of me is soothed. Here.

Or at least it was until you turned up.

So. Brace yourself. What shall I confess? Over which of my many sins would you like to salivate?

Good grief, man—suck those lips in any further and you'll swallow them. You've a mouth on you like a hen's backside.

Not quite what you expected, eh?

Good.

Now, then—how old do you think I am?

I beg your pardon?

If I wasn't dying, I'd kill you for that. How absurd. I'm no older than you—thirty-three or so. No older than Christ.

Do I look that bad? I have no idea. They don't go in for mirrors much here, I'm afraid. I must look a fright.

Death's door. Heaven's gate. Maybe. You're all so certain. But my life has been a series of slender escapes. I am famously elusive. Are you listening? Famous, I said. Elusive. Pay attention. I might elude you all—elude death—yet again. I've done it before, many times, you know. Although I agree it doesn't look likely.

I've always managed to escape somehow, but never without a scar or two. Some wounds have been mortal—that's obvious now—deeper than I cared to admit, bleeding away quietly inside so that nobody notices except, of course, me.

And God. Yes, if you insist.

Are you writing this down? All of it? Very good. It's about time somebody did. Here, nobody listens to a word I say. Perhaps they think I'm making it up. But I couldn't. Nobody could—not this life. It is known throughout Europe, if I say so myself. The duels, the stardom, the Opéra triumphs, all the escapades. The escapes. You can read about me in the pamphlets, any day, on the streets of Paris.

At least you could—then.

I was a star, once. Did they tell you that? I was a goddess.

Or am I just another sinner to you?

I was a monster, once. That was my real sin. That was my downfall.

Well, shut up and I'll tell you.

Act I, Scene I

Recitative

WHERE DO YOU WANT ME TO START? Do I have to confess my entire sordid life, or do you just want the highlights?

Very well. We begin at the beginning. You're a stickler for detail and process, I can see that. You sure you're not a Jesuit?

So. I was born—

Eh? Yes, all right, if you insist. I was born, like all women, with the stain of Eve, with the Original Sin imprinted on my body. From that moment I was doomed.

Is that what you want to hear, Father? Is that why they sent you?

Always please the audience, that's my motto. Give them what they want, or they'll tear you limb from limb. You think you're special—appointed by God to be my audience today, whether you like it or not. But you're no different to the standing-room crowd at the Opéra or the punters in the cask-room at the Saint Nicholas tavern. Perhaps a little less forgiving, and certainly more sedate—but I'll put on a show, if that's what you're after. If you want a doomed heroine, you have found her.

I digress. You wish to start with Original Sin, pedant that you are, and so I shall, though the original sin was not mine.

I was born. Don't ask me how, since I have no mother. Don't ask me why that is, either. Perhaps she ran off. Perhaps it killed her, bringing me into the world. I have no idea, and nobody ever bothered to tell me. There was just the old man. He was hard, my father. No harder than most, I suppose, but possibly drunker and a little too free with his hands. In every sense.

But, by God, the man had such a way with the blade. People mistook him, in an inn or in the street, for some kind of oaf, and in a way he was. Face like a pudding. I get my looks from my mother's side, obviously. He was big, with fists like ham hocks. But I've never seen anyone with a faster counter-riposte.

He'd been a *mousquetaire* in his youth, always off to the wars, with the odd month in prison after tavern brawls and early-morning duels. He was of the old school, of Viggiani and Grassi and the Italian thrust, long after it had gone out of fashion. Too shaky and too drunk for duels and fine sword work, of course, by the time I came along, though he still loved a mêlée and could stop a horse from bolting with a fist between the eyes. I saw him do it once. Mind you, he ended up flat on his back. By then he worked at the palace—the old palace, that was, until we all moved to Versailles.

He was a clerk, a dogsbody, really, for Comte d'Armagnac, the King's Master of Horse. God knows why. They detested each other. They loved each other, too, had been through wars together. Men are like that, I've noticed. So are opera singers.

Papa spent his life slapping and shouting at grizzling little boys until they were fit to wear the King's uniform as he once had. He flogged them until they were strong enough to hold a musket or wave a fan over the royal forehead, to be a page, a flunkey, in the presence of our Lord—Louis, I mean, not ... Sorry, Father. You see what a sinner I am?

Where was I? Ah, yes, Louis.

O, how the Sun King illuminated every corner of our lives. Hard to imagine it now, I know. But then—ah, then—those boys would have killed to enter his service, died for him, given anything to wear his *fleurs-de-lis*.

I dressed as a boy, too—except on Sundays, you'll be pleased to know. I trained in the dust and the mud with the lads until our toes were bruised, our thighs shuddered, and our arms could barely hold the blade straight. They taught us our letters and our Latin. They read out grand poems from the ancients and stories about Charlemagne and Philip the Fair and Louis the Fat—or was it Francis the Feeble? I don't recall. The chapters turned endlessly, that's all I remember. They bashed us if we fell asleep.

We rode every morning and every night, and in between I trained the horses on the long lead, running them into a lather. The boys learned dressage—I never did. Waste of a good horse, my father said, although he did teach me to ride as if for battle, with blade in hand and a short rein. We drilled and drilled, weaving in and out—stopping, turning, charging. That was my favourite part. Sword high, full canter, shouting.

Everyone else's horse was from the King's stable—mine was a clapped-out cast-off that kicked like a fury. When we raced to the Trianon in the dawn light, that poor old horse always came clear last. I didn't mind—I rode alone along those lines of coppery trees, with only the odd statue for company. If I close my eyes, even now, I can see it. Smell it. Damp earth. New clipped grass. Horsehair. My own sweat. My own breath.

Papa stood in the school courtyard waiting for me to come home, half an hour after everyone else, and he'd lash me for being late. On that soft skin behind the knees, so tender it tears and bleeds under the whip. Never whipped the horse, mind. Just me.

But otherwise I was just another face. The schoolmasters didn't mind. Perhaps they were scared of my father. They taught us how to bow and dance a gavotte and keep our muskets clean. At night the boys learned other, rougher, lessons in the darkness, and I—well, I learned I had to be tougher and faster than them all.

We fought with fists and knives and blades, bleeding from slashes and blisters and the odd swipe of Papa's knuckles. We ate like soldiers, squatting on the ground, and occasionally we slept like that, too. Occasionally we wept.

They wept.

Not me. I don't cry. Ever.

There were other children in the palace—other girls—daughters of equerries or guards, girls who worked in the kitchens or the laundries and came in from the township on horseback before dawn. But I wasn't like them. I lived in a kind of purgatory. You see, I have been there all my life. It holds no fear for me. It's an in-between kingdom, sometimes a wasteland, never dull. I was neither page nor servant, neither boy nor girl, provided with all the education and grace of nobility but without the title or riches.

Papa was harder on me than any of the boys. But I learned early that I was scum and hid in the crowd—just one more body to toughen up, among a dozen court pages and would-be *mousquetaires*, another soul to be bullied into a little learning. Except, of course, that I was a girl and never going to be a soldier. But what else was he going to do with me? Pack me off to a convent? Not him. He'd rather see me dead at his own hands. For who else was going to feed him gruel when he was too drunk to chew his bread, or drag him into his cot when he couldn't stand? Who else would lie to the Comte when Papa was too hungover to face drill, and polish his boots and sharpen his sword and mend his damn stockings? Instead, he made me what I am—whatever that is.

Good thing he can't see where I've ended up.

I can't imagine, now, what future he saw for me. My life has been impossible. A fantasy. He didn't envisage any of it. Nobody could have. This life—my life—has never been lived before. No woman has ever soared to such heights, circled the planets as I have done, nor sunk to these—O Father, look at me, pity me—these utter depths.

I couldn't imagine it either. The boys all teased me, told me I'd end up married to a cattle farmer in the Dordogne. Or somewhere, anywhere, miles from the palace. While they, needless to say, would bask in the King's light and tread the paths of his garden, carry his chamber-pot and empty his precious piss.

By the way, what do they do with royal piss, d'you know? I've always wondered. I can easily imagine the courtiers lining up for a swig, so serpentine and sycophantic are their minds. Big wigs; little brains. All of them.

But maybe not. Perhaps it's the secret behind Louis's famous *potager*. If he is the sun, then surely his piss is rain from the gods.

What?

Very well, I proceed. But you can't expect to follow a direct path to my downfall. The way ahead is never so clear. Like Papa, I couldn't predict the orbit of my life, nor even, in those early days, the first step—the first hint of destiny.

But one day it just rode into the courtyard and stood before me.

Act 1, Scene 2

Divertissement

HE IS A PUNY THING, this harbinger, standing in the forecourt next to his equally nondescript horse.

He gazes up at wild stallions, trumpeting angels, swords, gods—majesty—carved in stone above a doorway. The gracefully curving colonnade. Shade. Light. An overwhelming stench of straw and sawdust and manure. A cart circles the courtyard, heavy with hay, metal wheels screeching against the cobblestones. He can hear swordplay and shouting beyond the archway, scrubbing, shovelling, boys' voices chanting in Latin.

Servants, courtiers, dogs, coaches—people rush everywhere, stand about laughing a little too loudly. Gentlemen in silk strut, ladies stroll, everyone glances at each other. It's too much, too many—too loud.

The man's gaze shifts to a child of nine or so, in riding breeches and a shirt that must have once belonged to someone else—someone larger.

'You! Boy.'

The child stares back at him. Grubby face. Polished boots. Chestnut hair tied back.

'Can I assist you, sieur?'

The man brushes specks of pale mud from his sleeve. 'I am Antoine Le Bal, here to see d'Aubigny.'

'My father.'

'He's a secretary of some sort.'

'That's right.' The child nods, blue eyes still staring. 'Wait here. I'll fetch him.'

'Are these the King's famous stables?'

'Yes. You are standing before the Grande Écurie. Over that way is the Petite Écurie.' The child waves a hand vaguely in the direction of the road to Paris. 'You can't see it from here.'

'I must have passed it on my way. It looked just like these buildings?'

'Yes, sieur.'

'The great and the small appear the same size to me.' Le Bal lowers his voice. No one need suspect that he's new here. And possibly lost.

'They are.' The child sniffs and spits in the dirt. 'But the great stables come under the dominion of the Master of Horse, Comte d'Armagnac—you must address him as Monsieur le Grand.'

'Of course.'

'Although Papa calls him the Old Goat. But that's a secret.'

Le Bal nods, pretends that he's quite at home at court, although in fact he cannot quite believe that this enormous building is one—just one—of the royal stables. It's as big as the old Louvre Palace back in the city.

Bigger. And the chateau of Versailles itself, the King's new home—he can see it from here, glistening on the hilltop, but it's too immense to comprehend. God only knows how vast—how incredible—the whole palace must be.

He feels, for the first time in his life, that his King must be truly godlike. He swallows, his throat thick with dust.

'And your father is in charge?'

'Not exactly.' The child glances around, checks to see if anyone's listening. 'There are a lot of men in charge of a lot of different things. It's confusing.'

'I see.'

'But not for me.'

Le Bal smiles. Indulgent.

The child smiles back. For just a moment it's as if the sun had torn a hole through the clouds. Le Bal blinks, dazzled. An unsettling child. Odd.

'Perhaps you should inform your father of my arrival,' says Le Bal. 'He'll be expecting me.'

'I doubt it.'

The child ties the reins to a bollard and darts inside. Le Bal hears the shout.

'Papa! Fellow here to see you. Come from the city.'

There's grumbling and a slamming door. The child reappears, followed by a man who limps towards Le Bal, rubbing his eyes. Motions at the child.

'Julia, see to the horse.'

'Julia? But I thought ...' Le Bal blinks again.

'Water it well. Our friend has had a long ride from town, by the looks.'

The child doesn't move.

'A girl?' Le Bal laughs. 'Why, I could have sworn ...'

15

D'Aubigny yawns. 'Your business, sieur? If you don't mind.'

'I am here to prepare the way,' says Le Bal.

'For what?'

'For the Opéra, of course.'

'I beg your pardon?'

Le Bal draws a sheaf of papers from his saddlebag. 'Surely you know to expect me.'

'Papa, there was a letter.' The girl tugs at her father's shirt.

'Silence, child.'

'Remember, Papa? From the Académie.'

'Yes, of course.' D'Aubigny squints at the stranger as if his head hurts. 'Don't mind my daughter, sieur. She's nosy.'

'I have a list of our requirements.'

'I see. So you must be ...'

'I am Le Bal, the *surintendant*'s assistant. I wrote last month. Weeks ago.'

'There are so many letters, you see,' says d'Aubigny. 'Every day.'

'I understand. You are, after all, a secretary. To one of the great men of the kingdom.' Le Bal reaches out to offer the papers, but d'Aubigny seems not to notice.

'People,' he says. 'Always writing.'

'As did I, and now here I am. The others follow in a few days.'

'The others?'

'All of them.' At last Le Bal sees a glimmer of interest—perhaps panic—in d'Aubigny's grey eyes.

'Your pardon, Monsieur Le Bal, but if you could just refresh my memory ...?'

Le Bal flicks a glove at the thick layer of dust on his breeches. 'The Opéra is to perform for the King. Next weekend.'

'At Trianon? Very good. I will escort you there myself.' D'Aubigny turns away and shouts at a stable-hand to fetch his horse.

'No, no,' says Le Bal. 'The performance will be staged in the palace courtyard. Comte d'Armagnac has promised the King an extravaganza. We will use the stables as our headquarters. Surely he told you?'

'Yes, yes, he tells me everything. Everything.'

'We will present *Persée,* one of Lully's masterpieces, for the first time in a rustic setting. You can see the appeal?'

'Undoubtedly.'

'We ordered orange blossom. It's one of the King's favourites.'

'Orange blossom?'

'*Persée.*'

'I see.'

'Master Lully is worried it might rain,' says Le Bal. 'He has seen it in his dreams.'

'It won't, not unless the King wishes it.'

'But just in case …'

'Do not fear, Monsieur Le Bal. We will ensure the King's opera is the most stupendous anyone has ever seen.'

'That's just as it should be.' Le Bal flicks through the papers until he finds the sheet he needs. He has to hold it close to his face to read his own handwriting. 'The machinery arrives by wagon tomorrow. The scenery. We are bringing all of it. They will load it at dawn. The orchestra will come a day early. They are rehearsing in town already. I was sent on ahead to make sure the preparations here are underway.'

'Of course. All is in order.'

Le Bal cannot help but notice the tremble in d'Aubigny's hands.

'But you seem—'

'Everything will be perfect,' says d'Aubigny, summoning what he hopes is a reassuring smile. 'For the King. For Comte d'Armagnac. As always.'

'There is much to do.'

'I will see to it.'

The girl stands on one foot, balancing on a paving stone with both arms outstretched. She looks up at Le Bal. 'Will there be dancers?'

'Quiet, Julia,' says her father.

'I can help if you like.'

'Shut up.'

'Can I watch, Papa? Can I see the dancing?'

'I will not tell you again.'

'But, Papa—'

'Enough!' The girl is silenced by a fist to the side of her head. Le Bal winces—he hits his own children, of course— who doesn't?—but not that hard. The child, the sprite, staggers backwards under the blow, but doesn't cry, barely flinches.

D'Aubigny clenches and unclenches his fist. 'This way, sieur, if you please.'

The King's will is done. Always. It helps when there's a small army of pages and servants to arrange everything. Dozens of carpenters arrive to build a stage, a dais for the throne, benches for the court. Trees are delivered in pots from the *orangerie*. Wagons roll in and out again, bringing trunks full of costumes, crates of feathered headpieces, two harpsichords, canvases painted with clouds and wooden thunderbolts and winged chariots.

The apartments above the stables, the kitchens, the galleries, the palace itself, all throng with people from Paris—dressers, musicians, clerks. Le Bal stomps about shouting at everyone. Every moment is an emergency. It will never be ready in time. Heads will roll.

D'Aubigny's daughter is everywhere—carrying crates or trays of food, showing people their rooms, listening, running errands, keeping her father out of mischief, joking with the musicians, bringing tobacco to the carpenters. Singing quietly to herself.

D'Armagnac's chef is in a foul mood. He's normally calm, happy in his work and his steaming world of predictable aromas and regular rosters and recipes passed from father to son. But not now. This is uncomfortable—like working the spits at midsummer. The kitchens are too new, built by madmen, with every device known to humanity but no sense to it. The fireplaces are too large to set decent coals. The benches too far from the sinks. And the cool room a furlong away down the corridor. It's as if giants had designed the whole palace with no thought to how mortal men might cope. Uncanny.

Not like Paris. There, in the Hôtel d'Armagnac, everything was worn by the decades into familiar patterns. Everyone knew where everything was, the stokers managed the fires so that the roasters knew how long each joint would take, to the minute. The pastries rose as expected. The ices were as frozen when eaten as when they left the cool room. The meals were as hot as if they'd been removed from the ovens a minute before. As indeed they had been. None of this dashing for miles from kitchen to supper rooms. Cold food is the work of the Devil.

Reheating it is worse. Instead of giving him these special rooms with tables and pie stoves for warming perfectly good food, they should make sure it doesn't get cold in the first place.

Stables. Call these stables? Ridiculous. Dozens of people everywhere. God knows what they all do. Run about looking frazzled, mostly. Equerries and footmen and secretaries and schoolmasters and priests and pages—and everyone seems to have an assistant or two. Even the blacksmiths. It wasn't like that before.

Here, d'Armagnac's stables are an entire world. The King's palace, across the forecourt, is as enormous as the sun.

Here, he's just one of dozens of cooks and sommeliers and quartermasters. He doesn't even know how many apprentices he has. Their names are jumbled in his head. They all talk to him. Get in his way. Under his feet—like d'Aubigny's girl, buzzing about like a dragonfly, hoping for a choice end of the roasted lamb or some leftover pudding. Another nasty purple bruise on her face. Standing, staring at him, waiting. Watching. She's always watching.

He tries to take no notice but then it's as if she knows when she's worn out her welcome and he's ready to shout.

'What is it? What do you want today, wretched child?'

She smiles.

He falls for it every time.

How does she do that? The smile is so rare, so fleeting. So overwhelming.

She's practising on him, sharpening her abilities with face and voice just as she works on her grammar and her swordplay every afternoon. It's all she has. She knows it. He knows it. But for God's sake, she's only—what? Nine? Ten? And already scheming, already impossible to resist.

'Here.' He gives in. As always. 'Take this and get out of my way!'

The girl grabs a brioche and races outside. Her father is sober this week, at least until the evenings. She stands in the great forecourt and watches magic evolve. Men hoist the painted clouds up above the stage. Great curtains hang from scaffolding, their corners flicking and slapping in a quickening breeze. Hammers. Shouts. Whistles. The sky is crammed with fat grey clouds.

D'Armagnac and her father stride about, pointing, flourishing sheafs of paper, worrying.

Julie runs along behind them. 'Looks like rain.'

'It will not fall here.' Her father doesn't bother looking up.

'But what if it does, Papa?'

'The King will not allow it to rain,' says Comte d'Armagnac.

It rains.

Not a summer shower but a blast from Heaven—wild, splattering rain that drenches the carpenters. D'Armagnac rushes from his apartments, waving his arms at God. He's forgotten his wig. The girl laughs. Just a little.

Her father runs out into the rain after his master. 'Your Grace, what would you have us do?'

'Cover the scenery! All of it. Before it's ruined.'

Men dash from everywhere. Red dye from the curtains runs in rivulets across the paving.

'You'll have to tell Lully.' D'Aubigny picks up the King's gilded bench with one hand. 'We must cancel.'

'You tell him.' D'Armagnac shouts it over the noise of the storm. 'Tell the King, too, while you're at it. I'll wait here to see your head returned to us on a platter. Bleeding. Do not fear. I'll pay for your funeral.'

'But, Your Grace—'

'I have a better idea,' d'Armagnac says. 'Move it all inside. Now.'

'Where? It's impossible.' D'Aubigny wipes the rain out of his eyes. He notices his daughter dancing, face lifted up to the sky. She'll be sorry. Later.

'The stables. It's the only place big enough.'

'Not very dignified.'

'Rubbish,' his master says. 'Lully wanted it to be rustic. There's nothing better.'

'But by tomorrow, Your Grace?'

'Arrange it.'

'If you wish.'

'It's perfect.' D'Armagnac gazes across the forecourt at his beautiful stables. 'I don't know why we didn't think of it before.'

'We can't seat as many, Your Grace.'

'Nobody matters but the King, the Princes of the Blood, and their families. The rest of the court can stand outside for all I care.'

'Perhaps if we line the benches up along the walls?'

'An intimate performance?' D'Armagnac smiles in spite of the rain and the panic and the ruined velvet. 'Even better. It will be a triumph, d'Aubigny. Man against the elements. Almost operatic.'

They turn away from each other and both yell at once.

'Take it down! The stage. Everything.'

'To the Écurie!'

The great stables are swept and mopped clean three times.

The stableboys move all the horses, one by one, across the cobblestones, to the Petite Écurie. It feels as if the entire palace staff, perhaps the whole of France, is in motion, trundling chairs and banners and cushions and sprays of white flowers, lugging benches and instruments and scaffolding, laughing now, singing, as if the opera has already begun.

The orange blossoms, the benches, the King's dais, even the painted clouds and damp curtains, are carried into the Grande Écurie and arranged, just so, until the place of Julie's childhood—of stone and hay and horsehair—is transformed into a sylvan dale, a mirage, a miraculous world just like those described in the romance novels, the old sagas, of midsummer magic and deception and young women in breeches riding through the Spanish hills in search of adventure.

The performers arrive that evening. Their carriages pull right up to the door and the child waits and watches closely as the groups of girls, boys and old men climb down, stretch, glance around the forecourt, and sweep upstairs to their chambers. One man, a pudgy mountain of a fellow with thin ankles, screams at the footmen, the drivers, the bumpy road, the blinding rain.

Julie watches as he strikes a porter around the head. 'My wig is ruined!'

'Forgive me, sieur.'

'Let me past, you oaf.'

D'Aubigny appears, offers an arm. 'Here. Let me help you.'

'Get your hands off me.' The stranger shoves him away.

Julie watches closely—if Papa has had a few ales, this could get interesting.

But no. He bows. 'Welcome to the Grande Écurie, sieur.'

'My God,' says the mountain. 'I thought we were performing at the palace, not in a stable.'

'A stable was good enough for our Lord.'

'He didn't have to sing.'

The rain keeps splattering—the horses, the cobblestones, the fat man's silk stockings.

Julie tugs at the sleeve of a ballet dancer. 'Who is he?'

'Nasty piece of work,' the dancer whispers. 'You stay out of his way, dearie.'

'Is he a singer?'

'Aye, God help us. An *haute-contre*.'

'A what?'

'It's a high tenor voice—almost like a woman's.' The dancer bends down so his face is level with hers. 'His name's Duménil. You won't forget what I told you? Stay away from him.'

'I won't forget.'

She never does.

One carriage arrives after all the rest, just on supper time. It carries a woman, alone. Comte d'Armagnac rushes out to welcome her, to offer his hand. She walks past Julie, past the musicians and the dancers, smiling graciously. Julie stares after her. They all do.

'Who is she?' she asks.

'She is our star in Heaven, that's who,' says a man with a drum slung on each hip. 'Le Rochois. Our Marthe. Blessed be thy name.'

'Never heard of her.'

'You're too young,' he says, though he doesn't look more than fifteen himself. 'If you knew anything at all about music, you'd worship her like the rest of us.'

'Truly? She sings?'

'She doesn't just sing. She consorts with the angels.'

'Now you're exaggerating.' But Julie's eyes dart to the door through which Le Rochois has vanished.

'Perhaps a little. But you'll see. Or at least you'll hear. If you're lucky.'

That night, Julie tucks her skinny body in between the orange trees, where the King and d'Armagnac and—most fearsome of all—her father will never see her. The King and his brother Monsieur arrive, surrounded as always by women and feathers and tiny dogs, trailed by courtiers and architects and distant cousins. Julie barely notices. She's seen the mistresses and the sycophants and the royal brothers many times before. Instead, she watches the show.

Afterwards she wonders if she really did hold her breath for the entire three hours, but doesn't recall breathing at all and her lungs hurt like blazes so maybe it's true. But who could possibly breathe in the presence of such glory, such beauty, such fire and misery and power?

Power. She feels it swirling through her veins like quicksilver.

The machinery, the trees, the thunderbolts and silks and feathers and King don't matter. She sees none of it. Only the faces, the tongues of the singers—the spit in the corners of their lips, the teeth at the back of their mouths when they reach for a long note—their eyes flashing at the audience, their feet striking the newly shaved pine, their painted faces white in the torchlight. They are all that matter. They are everything. Music is, theatre is, Le Rochois is—everything.

Majesty is on stage, not on the throne.

She sees that now—the truth.

She knows. Decides. She will possess that power. She will make others feel this wonder, glimpse this Heaven. One day.

Act 1, Scene 3

Recitative

FROM THAT MOMENT ON, it was all I wanted. Not much. Grandeur. Passion. Immortality. Music.

I didn't seek fame as such, you understand. Adoration. Wealth. I was never ambitious in that way—not me. But to some people greatness comes naturally, just as inevitable as autumn after a brilliant summer. We must accept it. It's our burden.

I didn't know all that then, of course. I knew only that those sounds, the thousand tallow candles, the gold feathers and long white stockings, the rapture, were to be mine. They had to be.

So from that night I prepared. I had no idea of the path that lay before me, of the things I would have to do to get onto that stage—to be like her, like Le Rochois. To re-create myself in divine form. To sing. But everything I did, everything I learned, some of the men I fucked—oh please, it happens—it all led me to that first moment on stage, many years later, that blast of heat and applause I carry in my heart to this moment.

Did I know what would come of it, then, standing in the stables, holding my breath? Not really. Did I plot my course to glory? Obviously not. If I'd been sensible, I'd have apprenticed myself to the Académie in my early years, instead of—well, instead of everything I am about to tell you.

We'll get to it, by and by. There is still time.

I sift my memories, my pleasures, my agonies, for you, winnowing them all—sometimes I remember everything, sometimes very little. I will keep nothing back—not on purpose, anyway. Not now.

But then. Then. I stuck to what I knew. The palace. The stables. The sword. I sang only for myself. But my body, my brain, my heart, composed themselves for greatness in whatever form it should come. The life. The role. The performance.

You think it's about fame? About admiration? You're wrong. In one sense. I prefer to be alone. No. That's not true. There are a few people—five, at most—with whom I could happily spend days at a time. Otherwise I've always been a creature of solitude. Not an outcast—not always. But I am not at home as part of a throng, the way some people are.

The crowds, the audience—that's different. I am their mistress, I reach out to touch their sweating hands. I can bend them to my will. On a good night. I learned that from Le Rochois, by watching her gestures, listening—really listening—to her breath, to the silences between the notes. She was a woman alone, too. Alone, on a stage, in the midst of thousands.

That's how it has always been. When I was little, Versailles was like a carnival. Every day. People everywhere. Dogs. Tiny *ducs* and *duchesses* on ponies. Footmen and guards and pages. Peasants, tradesmen, Princes of the Blood, pickpockets. Thousands. All of them shoving one another out of the way, clamouring, desperate.

There's so much need in the world. It turns my heart to granite. They are beggars out there, every one of them—from the crippled soldier crying on the corner to the street sellers and crooks and landlords. The bewigged crowd is no different. Better dressed, but desperate nevertheless. Especially at the palace. It's pathetic, really.

I am one of them, I admit it, but also I'm not. I perform for them, but they don't touch me, not the way I touch them.

It's all a show, isn't it? Life. Faith. Music. Pulling on your boots and your sword every morning. Walking down the centre of a street, picking your supper from between your teeth. Smiling at a serving-girl. Bowing to the audience in the *parterre*. It's like Easter Sunday—like the changing of the guard at the palace gates—like a *fête* at Versailles or a holy day Mass in Notre-Dame, with a great choir of a hundred voices. A sermon, a song, which both chills and warms the soul at once.

Have you ever actually given a sermon, Father? Do they trust you to do that?

Then you'll know what I mean. Candlelit, expectant faces, eyes wide in wonder, the hush, the gasps, the sighs. The unwavering—or at least one hopes so—attention of hundreds of God's creatures all falling upon you, upon your bare arms, your throat, even your teeth. Well, the latter doesn't apply to you but do try to imagine it.

Or perhaps you're among those unfortunates who look out upon a congregation of yawning, slumbering faces— open mouths, instead of open eyes. Some people do have that effect on others. You may be among them. I see it now. I imagine you whining on about sin and moral rectitude while the masses fidget and snore and think about what they'll have for dinner, or let their minds wander pleasantly across their more memorable transgressions. Not the impact you intend to have, I know, but we cannot all be stars in the firmament. Someone must be the earth. Dense. Unyielding. Very few of us soar as I have. Very few of us are granted wings of angels.

Icarus?

Very witty, Father. I'm proud of you.

You weren't joking?

A cautionary tale, then. A fable? A moral lesson. How tedious. Do you really think me so feverish? I'm fully aware, I assure you, of the heights to which I ascended, of the machinery and faith—ignorance, whatever you wish to call it—it took to keep me there, of the angle and speed of my descent. Nobody feels it more keenly than me.

So don't trudge in here with your grubby sandals and your fables, Father. You are talking—listening—to one of the few enduring goddesses.

I do not transgress. I transcend. I fly, with coronet and sceptre, over the heads of mortals. I amaze them. They worship at my bare feet, gaze up at me tentatively, as if the glory of my eyes might blind them.

Ah! The wonder of it!

The squalor.

Act I, Scene 4

Ensemble

T HERE ARE DUSTY MILES behind the horse's hooves—
long summer miles through hamlets and across
rivers. The horse is weary. The rider is desperate for
a drink and a roasted hare and maybe a woman's mouth on his
noble cock. In that order. Perhaps twice.

He reaches the gates of the Grande Écurie. Reins in to let
the sentries see his face. They bow and wave him on, announce
his name to the messenger who will race ahead of him to the
palace, pass the word of his arrival through the pavilions, the
kitchens and the galleries.

'Comte d'Armagnac!' The guards bow again.

'Jesus save us, it's hot.'

He hates Versailles, the fusspot orchards, the galleries,
the mirrors, the godforsaken countryside. Hates the weeks
wasted here, standing about in hallways, fussing with wigs and
peacocks, royal mistresses and gardeners and orchestras and
endless bloody *fêtes*. Miles from the city. Never understood

the appeal. The King should be in Paris. Paris is everything. The King is everything. They belong together. Not here. Nowhere.

Into the courtyard, through a gateway and into the inner court, scattering young boys and dogs, twisting in the saddle to check the stables, the hay store, the tack rooms, before his staff has a chance to put things to rights.

All in order. For once. More or less. Raised voices inside the offices—that drunkard d'Aubigny shouting at someone or other.

'He's here! A day early.'

A girl's laughter from upstairs—the daughter, no doubt. No reply, just the big man yelling.

Equerries run out of the shadows and pretend they've been at their desks all along. Stableboys furiously sweep the morning's horse shit out of sight. They'd eat it if they had to, to get the paving stones clean. Lick it up. Swallow it. Anything.

A horn sounds. There's a rush of footsteps from the drill room. The boys form up into ragged lines, pushing the little ones back out of sight. A pathetic lot. He doubts any of them will ever become pages. A waste of time. Years spent drilling and coaching and they'll all end up with their brains spattered on a battlefield somewhere in fucking Flanders. Pages are for peacetime, for courts where nothing happens.

But Louis likes to keep up appearances.

The fool d'Aubigny appears, trying to look nonchalant. He fails. He struts across the courtyard, one look enough to silence the whole line of boys. He reaches for the reins, bows at the same time, tightens a lace on his shirt, tucks a wine-soaked sleeve out of sight.

'A welcome to you, Your Grace.'

'Rode on ahead of my vanguard,' says d'Armagnac. 'Thought I'd surprise you.'

'A very pleasant surprise indeed.'

D'Armagnac doesn't believe that for a moment. 'I'll stay here tonight, go across to the palace in the morning.'

'As you wish, Your Grace.'

'Is my apartment ready?'

'Of course. It is always ready.'

Doesn't believe that, either.

D'Armagnac dismounts, stretches, straightens his sword belt. A woman's voice soars from one of the upper windows. Some girl singing a Lully air. Quite well. He listens for a moment then turns to his secretary with a grunt.

'Let's get on with it, then.'

The inspection is over in an hour, thank God. Things aren't as bad as he'd feared. The accounts are in order. Perhaps someone's taken d'Aubigny in hand. The stable floors and walls are as clean as one of the galleries in the palace. Cleaner.

D'Armagnac offers a prayer of thanks that he's Louis's Master of Horse and not the Grand fucking Chamberlain. Horses are much less trouble than courtiers—or kings, for that matter. His stables smell better than the palace. Horse piss on cobblestones is a decent, hearty scent. But you can never get courtier piss out of carpet, and never convince a courtier to leave the room for a minute, even to relieve himself, if the King is present. They might miss out on something. Pigs.

He'd never cross the great forecourt if he could help it. He has everything he needs here. Apartments, kitchens, gardens, ballrooms. Quiet. Horses. Food. Women, if necessary.

The equerries bow and explain, the procurators and undersecretaries all have something urgent and nonsensical to report. Everyone chatters at him.

'We are glad to see you home safely, Your Grace.'

'The siege is lifted, I hear,' says some fool who's never been anywhere near a battle.

'A great victory for France, for the King, for you.'

'We heard that ...'

On and on. As if he cares. As if any of it matters.

He shouts at d'Aubigny once or twice just to make them both feel better.

'You're supposed to be my secretary, not my mother! Stop fussing.' D'Armagnac stomps towards the stairs. 'Enough.'

Julie stands in the shade, just outside the door, waiting to take his hat, his gloves, his spite. She's breathing hard—since d'Armagnac rode in the gate, she's run clear across the forecourt to warn the cooks that the great man is here, piled a week's worth of paperwork from her father's desk into a cupboard, brushed her hair, winked at a stableboy, raced to her position. She is ready.

D'Armagnac stares.

She is ripe. Thirteen or so—more than old enough. Her mother must have been a beauty, because the filly is astonishing. Creamy skin and her eyes clear, unflinching, even under his gaze. She seems at once softness and steel. He sees it now—never noticed before; that foul-mouthed scamp in breeches and baggy cadet jacket has suddenly become—

He will have her. Must. It's only right. The father is his slave, his creature. She must be, too. Tonight.

Sooner.

She sees the decision flicker across his face.

Sees the ermine trim on his riding gloves, the soft leather boots, the greying hair and the wince at pain in the base of his spine, the dust gathered in the wrinkles of his neck.

She knows she should smile. She does. This is the smile that matters. He looks at her breasts, nods, walks on, not noticing the blush that speckles her throat.

So. It will be him.

The one man in all the world with whom her father cannot argue—our Lord in Paris, as he says. Someone has to carry her out of here. Someone has to be the first. She has known that since she was nine years old. She will die here, a laundry maid or a whore. Or she will fly. Must fly. Somehow.

He will do. D'Armagnac. Who better? He has the King's ear, runs half the palace, his own chateau near Nancy. The Hôtel d'Armagnac near the Louvre, so they say, is finer than the cardinal's residence. She will have new clothes, perhaps a horse of her own.

He is old, it's true. Ancient. She shrugs away the thought. That is the price. His price. Hers. And there are mistresses already. She's seen one or two over the years—paid women who come and go, and a chambermaid last summer who was sent home to Picardie to get rid of the lump in her belly. But she can deal with them—with him.

There's no fear: not now, not later when her father knocks on her door for the first time in his life and stands, pale, in the hallway, staring as if he's never seen her before.

'I'm ready.'

She's washed her hair, changed into clean breeches. She'd wondered about a dress, but then realised there must be something about the boots, the jacket, the ambiguity, that stirs him.

Perhaps he prefers boys, after all. No matter. She'll be whatever he wants. For a time. It's the first step on the only possible path away from the stables.

She leaves her father standing in the hallway.

Act 1, Scene 5

Recitative

I DON'T KNOW WHY they call it deflowering. There's nothing floral about it. It hurts. They should tell you that. Someone should warn you. Perhaps if you have a mother—but I never did. I wasn't ready. I don't suppose you ever are.

Still, let's face it: d'Armagnac was an excellent choice to be a trespasser upon my virginity. Rich as Croesus, foolishly generous to his women, almost as powerful as the King. If only I'd felt content to be a rich man's mistress.

I'm no peasant. We were luckier than most—we had an apartment overlooking the great courtyard. An attic, certainly, but in the world of Versailles a cupboard was a chateau. It's true that when I was a child, my clothes had always been worn by someone else before me, but there's no shame in that. It's how most of the world lives. Papa couldn't bear to see me looking tatty. I grew up bearing the best-wrought blade at my belt. I was used to fine linen against my skin, blouses and breeches left behind in the Grande Écurie by young noblemen who escaped my father's grasp or graduated to the Guards.

My boots were always well-heeled and shiny with pig fat, but it wasn't until d'Armagnac took me into his entourage that I felt the joy of sliding my feet into boots meant for me, into leather not already moulded over the years into another's shape—boots that needed no mending, without loose nails and creases made by someone else's foot. I can remember the feel of it, even now.

The softest leather imaginable—they seemed almost too soft for riding and perhaps even for walking, but they pinched like blazes. Gold breeches, especially tailored to my legs— dear Lord, what a sight I must have been. Can you imagine? Like some creature of the darkness, escaped from a country fair—or a fool from the Comédie-Française. I thought I was gorgeous, in the same way that a peacock imagines that the tail is the bird.

La.

I can laugh now. At the time, the cut of my cuffs, the lace on my blouse, were matters of great importance to me— and to d'Armagnac. In my defence, lest you think me one of those trivial women who worries only about her wardrobe, I grew up in a palace where good tailoring and statecraft were indistinguishable, where courtiers believed that a misjudged earring might lead to exile and ruin. And occasionally they were right.

None of that mattered to my father, of course, who simply believed, as soldiers do, that so long as your boots and belt were polished and your sword sharp, you were fit to serve God Himself.

D'Armagnac was a different matter altogether. He thought nothing of spending hundreds of *louis* on collars or stockings, which I suppose is reasonable if you're as rich as Cardinal Richelieu.

His horses were the finest in Europe—besides the King's, of course. His carriages were made by the greatest master coach-builders. His shoes were always crafted by the same old cobbler from his chateau in Lunéville who knew every wrinkle on his noble feet, in leather from his own herd, specially bred for the purpose. He carried Toledo steel and English linen kerchiefs, and a fan made from the tail feathers of some monstrous Egyptian parrot.

So his mistress—yes, even one more accustomed to stable muck than salons—must dress like a *duchesse*. Or a *duc*, in my case.

D'Armagnac moved me into his Paris mansion near the river—my own apartments, no less. I was grateful to get away from Versailles, I admit—just a half a day's ride, but a world apart. I lived once again in the centre of the city I remembered from my earliest years, and had always loved, often missed. Where Versailles was all silk and strutting, a walled garden stuck out in the middle of nowhere—a dragon eating its own tail—the city was my pathway into the world.

He gave me everything I desired and quite a few things I hadn't known existed. There were finely stitched breeches cut to my own measurements, for days when I was riding or fencing or being a boy, as well as a satin gown, and one of green linen, and embroidered petticoats, for the evenings we spent together.

I had silks, a hat with peacock feathers, earrings of garnet clusters, fruit from the garden that I didn't have to steal.

Act I, Scene 6

A duet

SHE LETS SÉRANNE IMAGINE he's seducing her. It makes him happy. He's gorgeous. Strong. Fine ankles. Still has all his teeth. He dreams of riches, of velvet breeches and a fine sword, of the King one day noticing his talent—his face—and begging him to become a chevalier, a gentleman of the chamber, an adopted son. One day.

He wants her to move to Versailles with him, where he will sit at the right hand of the Sun King. Heaven.

To her, Versailles is a hellhole, a place of dust and horse shit and old men. She insists she will never return. Even Paris starts to feel like a prison. The whole city is there, waiting for her. She knows it. But she's not permitted to wander the streets, to go to the Opéra, to ride alone.

She has to get away. From d'Armagnac. Everything. She whispers about it in the dark.

'Run away with me.'

Séranne settles back on the bed, his hands behind his head, grinning. 'Where would you like to go?'

'Who cares? We'll be together.'

'Are you serious?' His smile vanishes. 'I'm not going anywhere, Julia. I only just arrived. My destiny lies here.'

'How can you know that?'

'I was born for it—for this.'

She considers that unlikely. He wouldn't last a month at Versailles. She won't last another month here in Paris.

'But if you love me...'

'Can you doubt it, my darling?'

'Then?'

He sits up. 'No.'

'We could go south, to Marseille. Your home.'

'Especially not there.'

She slides a hand slowly across his chest. The skin is tight against his rib cage. Something stirs inside her. She blinks it away. Concentrates.

'Your family could hide us. In the castle.'

'I'm never going back,' he says. 'You don't know what it's like.'

'No. I want to see it for myself.'

'You don't understand how lucky you are, growing up at Versailles, living in Paris.' There's a whine in his voice. She's never heard that before.

'You think so?'

'Where else would you want to be?'

'Almost anywhere. Away.' She tries to slide off the bed but he holds tight to her wrist. 'I'm sick of being locked in this house. It's like living with my father. Worse.'

'But you have everything you want here.'

'Do I?'
'Silly girl. Let me kiss you.'
She does.
For now.

Act I, Scene 7

Recitative

THE MISTRESS TOOK A LOVER. What of it? Why is that judged more harshly than the Comte taking a mistress? Or two? Yet it is.

D'Armagnac didn't look too fondly upon it, as you might imagine. I didn't hide it from him—how could I? Everyone in the house was paid to serve his needs, just as I was, and that included telling him my every word and action. There were arguments—threats. Voices were raised. But I was used to fighting with my father, when only a fist to the face would end the debate, whereas d'Armagnac, bless him, was only used to arguing with his fellow courtiers, who can play a nastier hand than me, but do it in whispers. I was expected to grovel, of course, to weep and beg forgiveness. But it's not in my nature. Instead I stood my ground.

He dismissed Séranne immediately. I was locked in my bedchamber for two days until the great man was summoned elsewhere to deal with affairs of state, rather than a raging girl with a sword in her hand. The house fell silent again. I thought I had won. Ha!

The next week a Monsieur Maupin presented himself at my door. D'Armagnac had sent him. La, you've never seen such a man. Clammy and stitched tight into a coat far too small for him, stockings much the worse for wear. One of those strange little men that grow up in the city and work until dusk and live with their mothers and never see daylight. I couldn't for the life of me understand what he was doing there, sweating in front of my door. Eventually it came out—I frightened the truth from him; he was not much more than a mouse, really.

D'Armagnac had told him to marry me.

To be more precise, d'Armagnac had paid him to marry me.

Yes, Father, for once your horrid little scowl is justified— imagine it. What could I do? A prisoner, cast upon the cesspit like an old—

Yes, perhaps I am exaggerating just a little, but nevertheless it did seem to me at first like an infamous plan. Marry me off, but keep me there, like an apple in a cool store, for the Comte's pleasure whenever he felt the need.

But after a while, I admit, it didn't seem so ridiculous. Monsieur Maupin was infinitely malleable, not at all interested in me or what remained of my virtue, cared only that he'd been offered a job and a purse full of gold coins and could tell his friends—if he had any—that he was on intimate terms with the King's Master of Horse.

So I married him.

What of it?

He's lived off my glory all these years, demanded money when I was rich, pretended he'd never heard of me when it suited him. Fair enough. I was no kind of wife to him, and he was purchased for me by d'Armagnac like a dray horse at market. It suited us all. Maupin was packed off to some dull job in some dull province—something to do with taxes, I think, God help him. D'Armagnac had the better of the bargain—a respectable married mistress. Even my father got some kind of pay-off.

And I got—well, to be honest, I'm not sure what I got out of it besides a new name, but it all seemed terribly clever and grown-up at the time.

But perhaps, now I think of it, it was me who was bought and sold. I was fourteen years of age. I had a husband and two lovers and a fine sword. I believed at the time I was buying my own freedom—that's what they all told me—but a few weeks of married life and I was ready to fly.

Act I, Scene 8

A duet

THE KNOCK ON THE DOOR is so soft Séranne thinks at first it's a rat in the ceiling. He doesn't answer. So she shouts.

'Let me in, you idiot.'

'Julia?'

'Of course. Who else?'

The door crashes open. The chambermaid who shares his bed screams and grabs at the sheets.

A girl—is it?—in breeches strides into the room. 'Get out. Now.'

The maid scrambles down the stairs, all pale buttocks and whimpering.

'Julia, what are you doing here?' Séranne looks as if he hasn't slept for days. 'It's not safe for you.'

'I don't care.'

She kisses him. Urgently. Pushes him back against the mattress.

'I've missed you.' She tears at her cloak, her blouse, fumbling with laces.

Séranne pushes her away and sits up straight. 'I came to the house. They sent me away, told me not to come back.'

She hesitates for a moment then whispers, 'D'Armagnac knows about us.'

'What?'

'He has guessed.'

'But how?'

'Never mind,' Julie says. 'That's why you were dismissed. Now he seeks retribution.'

'How can he possibly know?' Séranne scrambles out of bed, reaching for his breeches, his sword. 'We've been so careful. Sneaking about like hunters.'

She shrugs. 'It's Paris. There are no secrets here.'

He runs to the window and draws the shutters closed. His sword clatters to the floor. 'He will not find me.'

She watches him peer through a crack in the shutters out into the street below.

'You're afraid?'

'Of course not,' he says.

He's not looking at her, doesn't see the slight smile.

'We could disappear.'

'No.'

She wonders whether all young men have such soft, dark hair on their shoulders, such strong thighs—wonders what Monsieur Maupin looks like without his grubby linens—decides not to mention the fact that she is married just yet.

'Can you think of a better idea?' she asks.

'We'll lay a false scent,' says Séranne. 'I'll take another mistress.'

'An excellent solution—for you, at least. The mistress's lover takes a mistress. You would be willing to suffer that—for me?' She smiles. 'Ah, but it looks like you already have.' She waves in the direction of the stairs, the maid.

'Very droll, Julia. You think of an alternative.'

He's angry now. This isn't how she planned it. She climbs onto the bed, draws the quilt around her.

'I can't think,' she says. 'I'm afraid. D'Armagnac's anger is terrifying.'

'We'll deny everything.'

'You don't understand. You've never seen him in a temper.'

'I'll protect you, pet.' He comes closer, sits on the edge of the bed.

'You?'

'Have faith in me, darling.'

'D'Armagnac is the most powerful man in France. And you are...' She pushes herself up and away from the bed, laces up her blouse.

'My blood is as noble as his.'

'Of course.'

Séranne breathes in slowly, glancing down at his scarred belly, his wiry arms. He is strong. His blade is sharp. He will not be shoved around—not by her, not by d'Armagnac. 'I'll need money.'

'How much this time?'

'I don't know yet. I'll send you a message. You should go.'

She is already at the door. 'I shouldn't have come.'

'Don't worry,' he says. 'I'll devise a plan of some kind.'

'I know you will.'

But he doesn't. Why should he? He fears no man, can beat anyone in a duel—well, possibly not his mistress, but any man, certainly.

Which he does. Inevitably. Stupidly. One dark night behind the convent of the Carmelites. Some fool who insulted him at the dice table, called him a southern catamite or some such thing, and he doesn't know exactly what that means but it doesn't sound noble and he challenges and they fight and it's over fast but not without a great deal of screaming as his opponent dies at his feet and the seconds come running, shouting at him, and it's never like this in the fencing *salles*, where people get back up after a bout even if a little scratched, but they never scream and certainly never die.

The seconds don't honour the dead or the sacred duelling ritual, not for a moment. They clutch at the body and weep and threaten Séranne with assassination, with vile poxes and plagues, with the law.

Next morning, the news swirls around the city. The police are alerted, the Lieutenant-General himself—La Reynie, the mysterious, dread lord of Paris—takes an interest. He sends his dogs out. Issues orders.

Julie plays her card.

'There's nothing for it. They're calling you a murderer, a criminal. We'll have to leave the city.'

'Never!'

'But my darling ...' She knows she is pleading—for his safety, for her life. 'The dungeons.'

'They can't hurt me.'

'Oh, they can. Believe me.'

'It was a fair fight,' he says.

'The King has issued endless decrees against duelling,' says Julie. 'You know that. The police turn a blind eye only if nobody gets hurt. And you—'

'He insulted me.'

'He's a nobleman. They do that.'

'But I, too, have noble blood.'

'So you keep saying.'

'Do you doubt it?' One hand is on his sword. 'Do you dare?'

'Darling, be reasonable.' She slides her hand up his arm.

'I mean it. I'm not going anywhere.' Séranne pushes her away and crosses his arms. Pouts a little.

They leave the next night.

Julie chooses horses from d'Armagnac's stable that nobody will miss much, packs a few clothes in one bag, buckles on her fine sword, and rides out through the city gates at dusk without looking back. They head south. She wears men's clothes and a great cloak, a chevalier's hat that used to be her father's, feather and all—a disguise, she says. Nobody will be able to trace them. D'Armagnac will send men out, of course, and La Reynie will, too, but they'll be searching for a man and a woman. Lovers eloping. Not two men, perhaps brothers, perhaps not. Safer on the back roads, anyway. There are bandits. Rapists.

She laughs as she rides—sometimes softly, sometimes a full-throated roar with her head thrown back.

Séranne's not laughing. 'What's so funny?'

'Everything.' Her hat nearly flies off onto the road behind her. 'All of it. Not funny, exactly. Just—'

'What?'

'We're free.'

But he was already free. He mutters it to himself, softly so she won't hear. Before. Thriving in Paris and now look. Fuck

Marseille. Never even been there. What would a village boy from Languedoc find in Marseille? Fuck the entire fucking Midi and its fucking hills. Nothing but olives and dust. Paris was the place. And now? Fuck. Back on the roads, penniless and hungry, and what the fuck are we supposed to live on? All right for her. She has no fucking idea what it's like. Used to eating from the kitchens all hours of the day and laundry women and soft beds and good wine aplenty. Never known hardship. Never had to be tough. Three weeks of this and she'll be begging to go home.

He's wrong. He's always fucking wrong.

Act 1, Scene 9

Recitative

YOU WON'T BELIEVE how content I was those first weeks on the road. How gorgeously, voluptuously happy I felt. I'd never experienced the like, and have rarely done so since. It had nothing to do with Séranne, I'm sorry to say, though I never let on. He was hopeless. All his talk of castles and titles turned out to be rubbish, just as I'd suspected, and we were more often hungry than not. He was worse than an old woman with his whimpering and whining, and he was hardly a god of love, either, if you don't mind me saying.

No. It wasn't him that made me happy. It wasn't romance. Far from it.

It was the riding, the country lanes, the fields, the olive leaves and poppies and cornflowers. It was the air. The late-afternoon sun in the treetops. It was suppers at tables in village taverns. Singing at the top of my lungs to anyone who would listen. It was the breeches and my father's hat and my boots. I imagined my life would be like that from then on—wine-soaked summer fruits, and tired muscles, and raindrops sliding down the back of my neck. A new place every morning—a cooking fire in a forest clearing, a village fair, snow on distant peaks. I swore to myself then that I would never again allow myself to be trapped, to be cornered—to be pawed at or punched or enslaved. Nobody wants that, do they? But I'm not like other people. I've chosen, many times, to do anything—anything at all— rather than be enslaved again, even if it meant harm to me or those I love. So I have kept my oath, more or less. But at such a price. Dear God.

I stray from my path. What was I saying? Those weeks—ah, yes! It was my first time abroad in the world dressed as a man. I relished every moment. Women's clothes are annoying, let's face it. All those petticoats. Skirts that catch every draught— honestly, Father, you have no idea.

Or perhaps you do. Look at you. You ask me why I dress as a man—I could ask you why you don't. Look at that cassock. Your hem is muddier than a milkmaid's. Why do you priests insist on hiding your legs from view? Do you imagine one glimpse of your spindly calves is going to send us all into a frenzy of desire? What must you think of us?

Don't you long for the freedom of breeches? To be able to ride a horse like a soldier, not a maiden? To sprawl by the fire at the end of a hard day—boots on the hearthstone, sword at your side—without a care for your posture?

You call me vain, Father, and yet you disparage me when I say that I longed to cast aside the fripperies of womanhood and embrace the liberty of men.

Anyway, my ankles are much finer than yours. I cut a dashing figure, as they say in the romance novels, in my stockings and waistcoat. The wealthiest dandy and his wig-maker can only dream of hair as fine as mine. I never disguised myself as a man. Ever. I'm far too beautiful for that. Granted, it works at a distance: two horsemen against the sunset look less like prey to a bandit than one man and one woman—or, as it has so often turned out, a woman alone.

I'll confess to having something of the dandy about me. Write that down, Father—I confessed to being the most handsome rake in Paris. I'm guilty of the sin of gorgeousness. I was fabulous.

I weep to think of it now.

Oh, don't look so alarmed. It's a turn of phrase, that's all. I'm not actually going to cry. You should know that by now.

What would you do—O sole comfort on my deathbed—if I wept? Would you hold my hand in yours and whisper consolation into my ear? Would you tell me that I am loved, that I've done nothing wrong, that my life has been blessed?

That's what people need to hear on their deathbeds. Believe me. I have sat by such a bed—a rather better-appointed bed, mind you—and held a hand and whispered and wept, yes indeed, sobbed and murmured assurance, knowing all the time there would be none for me. Nothing for me.

I'll have to tell myself all those things, then. You go ahead and mutter darkly instead.

I will ignore you and go on with my story.

Where was I? Ah, yes.

So by this time, Séranne fancied himself as a professional duellist. He believed he could make his fortune showing off his prodigious skills. And me. He pictured himself as an adventurer, a glamorous Parisian chevalier who had narrowly escaped death and imprisonment in order to enable the good people of the south to enjoy his skill, his good looks and, of course, his freakish woman duellist.

He presented me as a fair-day folly—a sideshow—a once-in-a-lifetime chance to see a woman dress like a man, fight like a man, drink like a man.

Which I did. If I felt like a whore, so be it. My body was his currency, to be sure, but not in the usual way. None of that. Not with those hairy farmers' sons.

No, no. It was all quite innocent, I assure you. We would ride into town, attracting as much attention as possible, which in my case has never been difficult. He'd announce an evening show, wherever we could fit a decent crowd—in the tavern or the square. We'd offer them a few bouts, maybe a song or two. The men would all come and sometimes even bring their wives. We always made enough to pay for supper, for stabling, perhaps a night in an inn. We'd spar a little, he'd challenge the local lads to a bit of a brawl, and off we'd go.

There's no such thing as a friendly duel, let me tell you. No matter how they begin, they always end in fury. Even if you pretend otherwise. Even when it's all for show.

My father told me that if you take a blade in your hand, you take your own life and someone else's life in your hands, too. Haven't forgotten.

But it's more than that. When I take a blade in hand, I know what has to happen, what it means. I understand my opponent's intention and my own.

Everything is clear to me—outline, details, future, emotion. Not like the world, where everything is muddy and messed, and nothing ever works out the way you mean it to—no matter how skilful or how honourable you are, no matter how vile your enemy.

When I was a child, we had the finest teachers: the Rousseau brothers, Monsieur de Liancourt—you'd hardly credit it, would you? The finest swordsmen of any age and there they were, drilling us all day, sitting by the fire with Papa of an evening, recalling every bout, every mistake each opponent made.

That's how I learned that fencing is like mathematics, like the logic of Socrates, the art of the ancients. There's no luck, only genius and memory and slashed knuckles. It's like music, with its own patterns and rhythm and inevitability. So is the body.

Art, music, fencing, love, mathematics. All genius. All lyrical.

Most of the men I've ever fought had no inkling of this— the deep mystery of it, the science of it, the intricacy—the intimacy—the knowledge that lives in your veins and muscles and soul.

The fencing masters adjust your pose, your wrist, just as singing masters try to rearrange your throat and tongue, as concert masters order the notes, the cadence. I've had many masters. I hear their voices. I don't need to, anymore, but they still speak to me, through me. Always.

'Your only enemy is fear,' Master Liancourt used to tell me. 'The man before you is simply a pretender. Measure his impatience with the blade—slide it, tap sharply, test his reserve, his courage.'

'All your stealth rests in your fingertips, all your power in your thighs,' Papa said, over and over. 'The strength comes only from your mind. Fingertips. Wrist. Thighs. Brain. These are your weapons. The sword is merely a beautiful accessory.'

On Saturday mornings, Master Liancourt paid a string quartet to play in the corner. Our footwork drills pounded in time with the beat. If they played a long jig, our legs would be ready to fall off by the end.

'Lunge, retreat, retreat, lunge, *flèche*, *en garde*.' His voice loud over the music, me humming along.

'Lunge, lunge, and again, hold it there until I say, until the end of this gavotte. Straighten your back, d'Aubigny, head high now. Strong. That's right. Hold it. No trembling. No falling.'

No trembling.

'Straighten your arm—the movement is only in the wrist; your wrist is liquid, your wrist is steel.'

And look at me now—at my hands.

'My dancers.' He'd laugh. 'My ballet. Let's have a little divertissement. A minuet!'

Off we'd go again, grinning like madmen, groaning after a while, and eventually, one by one, we'd give up, legs gone to water under the intense pain, the boys all furious, despairing.

Not me. I don't crack. I outlasted them all. Until now.

My father used to say, 'Never let your guard down, never turn your back.'

Never did. I remember a time just outside Marseille. Séranne was there. Do you remember? The man with the scar and the missing teeth. Shouted out for me to show my tits. So I did. Shut him right up, didn't it?

You weren't there?

No, no, of course.

I forgot. My mind slips between now and then, you and him, me and ... me and ... I'm confusing you, Father, I see it in your face. You want a register of my sins that you can tick off—penance for that one, absolution there, eternal flame for item number seven. There is no time-beater here, marking the notes, keeping us to pace. There's no such clarity, not here—

you'll have to learn to live with doubt, though it's probably not part of your repertoire.

Bad luck. The only certainty I've ever known lies in the purity of the blade. I always understand exactly what to do and when—what will happen next and how to respond. I don't think. I know it—in my fibres, in my blood and my bowels.

Just like the great masters, I remember every movement of every duel, as if they were all preserved in amber—frozen, perhaps, like trout in the Seine—but animated by memory. Every twitch of the blade, every parry—the foot tap, the blink, the drop of sweat on the end of a nose, the slight widening of the eyes just before pain makes itself properly known—a sleeve damp with blood, the howl of fury and defeat.

And, yes, hatred.

I never met a man who was delighted to be bested by a woman, except, of course, my darling d'Albert. Some laughed about it later; many became friends. But every one of them believed he would be the one to master me—even to kill me—and they all clenched disappointment in their teeth, no matter how chivalrous the handshake or how gracious the smile.

I can't blame them. Disappointment has a horrible taste—I've never liked it myself—the way it burns on the tongue like sulphur and turns your belly to acid.

I can admit now that I made the most of every victory. I strutted like a courtier, always made sure my smiles were the more munificent. I love winning. Who doesn't? Only fools or those who've never beaten anybody.

But I never saw duelling as a game. A duel is more like a very small, personal war. Nothing exists but the blades, blood pounding in your ears, breath and anticipation. Strategy and skill are all that matter—in fact, now I think about it, they are your weapons. Those and the reflexes honed by painful hours of training, the unbeatable instinct, and always the mind that remembers every word—every move—ever studied, discussed or witnessed.

I had my favourite strategies, but never a signature stroke. Too predictable, d'you see? It's all very well being famous for a certain move—the La Maupin Manoeuvre, if you like. But your opponents always know it's going to make its tired old appearance, like a Lully *tragédie*, every season. The crowds clamour for it, which is all very well unless you are fighting for your life.

As I so often did.

Act 1, Scene 10

Divertissement

I N A DARKENED CORNER of a country tavern, the girl sniffs at the air—at the blood and the sawdust and the sharp whiff of sweat, damp wool and brown ale.

Dull light from a dozen lamps hanging in a low line from the beams. A cleared space. The crowd pressed close.

The first bout did not go well. Séranne pricked the youngest son of the local vicomte and he squeaked like a piglet. Now, disgraced, he sits bleeding and cursing in the corner. Hurls complaints of cheating, but this crowd's never seen anything like Séranne. They can't believe a sword can move that fast without witchcraft or treachery. And that was just the warm-up.

Wait until they see her.

She steps into the lamplight.

Peach skin, chestnut hair in a plait down her back. And there—look! Breeches. Ankles. Breasts. Here in Provence! Never seen such a—

Sword in hand, point trailing lazily on the floor. The other hand on a definitely feminine hip.

The men stare, silent, stranded somewhere between lust and distrust. Someone's wine splatters on the floor. There's muttering.

Séranne strides to the centre of the *piste*. 'Gentlemen!'

Now silence. The gazes of fifty or so pairs of eyes slither over her body. She doesn't flinch. They don't matter.

Séranne takes a breath and shouts into the rafters. 'The prodigy of Paris, the marvel of Marseille, the world-famous Madame de Maupin!'

She told him what to say, how to say it. She likes the sound, the symmetry of the words.

The demonstration bout is with Séranne, as always. She tries to make it seem dramatic, tightly fought, but the truth is that it's months since he could get anywhere near her. The men won't believe that, though. They need to think he can beat her—that they can beat her, any one of them. Or else they won't play, won't pay.

They'll see Séranne as some kind of pigeon, when in fact he's rather good. But she's great—she knows it now; she truly has the glimmer of genius inside, a destiny beyond this moment, the beer, the sawdust, the blood.

But they can't know that. Not yet.

The final score is five to three. Séranne winces on the last point but there's no bloodshed, not this time. She salutes him, takes a step back. Séranne, panting a little, sends around the hat. It comes back empty. They don't offer a single *sol*. He throws out the challenge. They stare.

Séranne is no salesman.

'Come, brothers.' He can't keep the plea from his voice—feels it, too. Weary and plaintive, sick of the life, sick of losing every fucking evening, of pleading for a copper or two from men who witness his nightly defeat at her hands.

She stands still, waiting, staring back at the crowd, unsmiling—daring them to touch her, to try; hating Séranne for his pathetic shallow parries and the way he moans in his sleep. She will leave him in the morning, before he wakes up, farting and grumpy.

It doesn't look like there's anyone worth beating in this room. As usual.

Someone shouts. She can't understand it—some southern dialect. She focuses her eyes, pinpointing the man who is still muttering—an old fellow, toothless, but big, a blacksmith maybe. Under her gaze, his friends back away from him.

He stands, enormous, looking at the floor, sorry now he ever opened his mouth but he couldn't help it, thought everyone would laugh and they did but now here he is, alone and no escape. The girl is looking right at him, and that's what he wanted, but now he's changed his mind because it isn't anything like he imagined.

'What did you say?' It's a female voice, for sure, which makes his joke even more stupid.

The point of her sword rises from the floor.

She wouldn't. Surely.

But she smiles at him. She knows what he said now—it's somehow translated itself in her mind.

'Tell me.' Her voice is soft. 'What did you say?'

He gulps. She watches the fear collect in his throat. But he's brave enough, this old fellow, give him that. He says it again, right out loud.

'Show us yer titties.'

Nobody moves, not for ages.

Then she slides the blade slowly, silently, into its scabbard.

She's still looking right at him.

Her hands, those long silvery fingers, move to her throat, untie the cravat, drop it to the floor where it curls like an asp, and unravel the laces on her blouse.

Séranne's mouth opens slightly. She wouldn't. Surely.

She shrugs her shoulders and the blouse slides down her arms, rolls off her hips, nestles around her boots.

Séranne doesn't move. Nobody does, nobody can, except for the girl. One hand on her sword, she circles the *piste* in bodice and breeches, shoulders and arms, staring into their faces. They can't look away now—they all see how the muscles move under her glistening skin, how a strand of hair has escaped its ribbon and now caresses a collarbone. She is perfect. She is a golden statue come to life. A goddess within reach. She breathes softly—they don't. They can't. The old blacksmith is close to tears. Every man in the room is hers, all of them, all she need do is hold out one exquisite hand, except—

'I'll have her,' the vicomte's son, bandaged up and seething, shouts from over near the bar.

He has to challenge her—she sees that. He lost the first bout to Séranne, who in turn lost to a woman. He has no choice. He doesn't see it that way, of course. It must be—has to be—some kind of carnival trick, some crooked set-up to fleece the village of its harvest takings. There's no way the girl can be that good.

The crowd applauds politely. As he pushes through, the men touch their foreheads to him, as they always do, but this time they mean it. Everyone feels something tremendous is at stake—but what?

He doesn't bother saluting her. Why should he?

She takes her time lacing up her blouse, then salutes him graciously, exaggerating the downward stroke so everyone can hear the blade slice the air, the power in her arm.

It doesn't take long. He's a slasher, trained by some old foot soldier in his father's stables. She knows the sort. They think strength matters.

It doesn't. It helps you endure, that's all. It doesn't win bouts, just causes needless wounds, mostly your own. He's all over the place, open wide on every stroke. She toys with him a little until he yells at her.

'Yield, whore!'

That's enough. She nicks him gently on the cheek so he won't forget her—ever—and then responds with a *croisé* so deft he doesn't even realise for a moment that his sword is no longer in his hand and her blade is prickling at the base of his throat.

She looks into his eyes, searching, but sees nothing of interest there. He's bewildered. Later he'll be furious, humiliated, convinced he's been cheated, will make up some excuse, some lie, that everyone will pretend to believe. It's always the same.

She takes two steps back, salutes again, just as her father taught her, and walks away. Séranne can deal with the heaving, hollering crowd, with the coins thudding down onto the *piste*.

She steps through the door, into blessed darkness, and sighs.

Act 2, Scene 1

Recitative

HAVE YOU EVER SEEN the ocean, Father? Here in the south, I mean. You're from Normandy. I can tell by that wretched accent of yours. The ocean is a different beast altogether up north. I've seen it. It thunders. It's grey and wild. I don't know how anyone ever has the courage to set sail on it.

But in Marseille the sea sparkles. There's no other word for it. Really. You can stand on the cliffs and look out towards Africa, towards paradise itself, it seems. You can see through the depths—in the inlets, in the harbour—to the sand and the seaweed and the fishes. Mermaids, even; I wouldn't be surprised.

You should go. Feel the sun on your face, the sea breeze. It'd do you good.

Or I should. That would be better. Let the Mistral clear out these festering lungs, this grieving soul. But it's too late for me. I should have tried. I should have kept going. But I got only as far as Avignon, and here I stopped.

I returned to convent life, at the end. Perverse though it may seem to you, to my friends, this is as close to a home as I know now. It's appropriate. Strangely. I was drawn here. I don't know why. God knows, my last appearance here was not a success.

I'll get to that. All in good time.

But first, Marseille. I was free there. I loved it, felt the sea in my blood from the first time I saw it. Mercurial. Unknowable. Like me.

The sea, the forts, the Opéra, the city. The women. We loved each other, Marseille and I. The city embraced me, celebrated the wildness in me, saw the woman in spite of the breeches—it heard my voice. For the first time, someone saw me, heard me. But I can't go back there, ever. I'll never see the ocean again. It's a city of shadows to me now, of threatening ghosts and regret. I'm sure she doesn't miss me, Madame Marseille, but I miss her.

But then—ah, then—Marseille and I were in the throes of first love. I fenced when I needed to pay for a room, a meal. I sang in cabarets for a few coppers. Séranne followed me there, traced me somehow, turned up on my doorstep like a spaniel. I took him in. More the merrier. We didn't pretend that he was in charge. Or even that we were together. Although some nights, after the show and a bottle or two of wine ...

But I stray from my tale.

They let me sing real music in Marseille. At last. I wasn't a star there, I admit. I knocked on the stage door of the Opéra and begged for a spot in the back row of the chorus. I suspect they employed me for my face, not my voice. But by the end of the season I had a few airs to sing on my own—nothing too taxing.

The first time I sang by myself, to a crowd, it felt like—impossible to capture it now—like leaping from a cliff top—like the wildest passion—like giving birth to a god. Apollo. No! Eros. I played Nyx, goddess of night, surrounded by smoking candles and gold cloth, layered in white paint and sweat-soaked silk, raised up by a heavenly chorus of drunkards and whores and angels. Dear Lord. I feel something thumping in my broken chest just at the thought of it, even after all these years.

You open your mouth—your throat—your soul—and let beauty escape. That's all there is to it. Everything else is craft. But the essence of singing—the point of it—is that freedom, the song-thrush taking flight in your heart and winging its way to life. Can you hear it?

Ah. I can't sing now. I don't have enough breath. But then—then, I could sing notes as pure and clear as ice, as ocean. My voice was a fledgling, although at the time I believed myself a genius. We all did. Séranne sang, too, or at least he did a very good turn standing about; he was always Fifth Guardsman or Peasant Waving Scythe. He was a fine-looking fellow, so why not?

It was still early days for the Opéra there—Gautier was the *directeur*, even then, and struggling to make a go of it. They had only local voices and second-hand costumes sent from Paris. It didn't matter. The crowds loved every performance, every tattered thread of the company—perhaps treasured it even more because it was their own. They felt less provincial, I suppose, as if Paris had shifted south for the winter.

It's a city of knives and tempers so we understood each other's dangers and delights, Marseille and me. I appeared under my old name, my real name—Mademoiselle d'Aubigny.

Opera singers are always called mademoiselle, you know, even if they've been married for forty years. Don't ask me why. I suppose the men prefer to think we are available. As, indeed, we so often are.

They welcomed me, noticed me. The Marseillais. They'd never seen anything like me. But who has? They seemed delighted that I dressed as a man, that my voice sometimes wavered out of my control, that my real fame was derived from the blade and the cabarets. They forgave it all. I don't know why. Perhaps they are used to foreigners, to exotic delights, to sprites and storms and warm winds. They understand the elementals as well as the Muses. I sang like an angel, I appeared on stage as a deity, and I understood—we all understood, without words, without acknowledgement—that my role was to be worshipped. At first I was a clumsy, unfortunate goddess, missing my cues and straining for the higher notes. But I worked hard and they were patient, and I learned to flirt and laugh at people's dull jokes, and to gaze into the audience each night as if I loved them. Perhaps I did. Perhaps I still do. After a time they hailed me as their Amazon queen, beloved of the ancients, like one of those old marble statues hauled up from the bottom of the sea. So they bowed low in my presence and waited in line for a smile or a nod—simple gifts I was happy to offer them. In return I adored the city and the sea. We should have known the infatuation wouldn't end well. Such things never do.

They threw lavish parties and endless salons and we singers appeared on cue, like concubines, to provide a little titillation. Séranne seduced the mayor's wife. I had suitors lining up at my door—men who asked permission before they slobbered all over me. Sometimes I told them no, and instead of hitting me they just looked sad and went away. It was my first taste of the sweet wines of the south, touched by summer—my first glimpse of the power of infamy. It went to my head. I sang and slept and feasted and screwed and then—

Then I saw the girl.

She was a merchant's daughter. An Italian family, fresh from Naples, with ears and hearts full of Monteverdi and Scarlatti. Her father was a patron of the Opéra. Spent all his time trying to convince Gautier to produce Venetian music. Her mother hosted a salon on Saturday afternoons. Everyone went—everyone who mattered. I didn't. I was usually asleep. But one afternoon Séranne picked me up and forced me into a carriage and up the front steps of this stupidly ornate mansion, so new you could smell the paint and sawdust, and there I was—standing in the centre of a Turkish rug in my breeches and boots, with a glass of wine in one hand and my heart in fragments.

She was beyond beautiful.

Fine blonde curls tucked behind her ears and falling softly against the skin at the back of her neck. Unruly hair. It betrayed a wildness of which her own family had no idea—she had no idea, until she met me. Until she was mine. My pardon, Father, I see I am making you blush, but you wanted the truth and so here it is.

Her father showed me off to the ensemble as if I were the latest addition to his stable, or an exotic piece of jewellery he'd brought all the way from Constantinople for his wife—or his daughter. I bowed. Everyone giggled.

Except for her. She sat by the fireplace on a gold chair—you see, I remember every detail. A lace shawl. Emeralds. A gaze that told me that all I had to do was reach out one

70

hand, one finger, to her and she would be mine, she would be everything, and everything would be over.

Séranne led me away to the other side of the room, and I tried not to stare at her but I couldn't help myself. He chattered away, entertaining the ladies. I confess they must have thought me surly. I wasn't. I was simply trying to breathe.

Her name was Clara.

Clara. The sound is like a sigh. Even now I hear it.

She left the room—she told me later that she couldn't keep her composure—and I stood there like a fool, waiting for her to come back, for the door latch to open, for the sun to appear from behind the clouds. She never did—not that day. In the end, Séranne had to drag me out of there, just as he'd dragged me in.

On the way home, we had an argument about her, such a fight—I could have killed him.

I wanted her. Nothing would stop me. Not her father, not Séranne, not the Opéra nor any force in the world. I knew she wanted me.

But Séranne kept it up. It's not possible, he said. Not natural. Not right. You're mad, he said, you're evil.

I wanted to stab him in the street and leave him dying in the gutter. I wanted to ride with her to Paris, to Moscow, to the East Indies.

So that is my sin. Wanting. Too much.

I threw him out of the carriage. We didn't speak to each other again.

The next night she came to the Opéra.

I sang for her, and she knew it. Her father knew it, too.

I went to the salon every Saturday. I stood outside her house every afternoon. Waited in the city, near the dressmakers, in case she appeared. Gazed into the audience every night, searching for her face.

We never met, not alone—always in a room full of people. We never spoke.

She sent an envelope and a ribbon from her hair. No letter, no sign. But I knew it was hers. Then one day, a purple velvet pouch and inside—a gold chain.

I've worn it ever since, on the wrist of my sword arm. D'Albert used to say it would be the death of me—an opponent's blade would slide inside it, catch, and rip off my arm. I always thought it'd be quite fitting if it—if she—was the death of me.

After all, she very nearly was.

But just in case, I always wore gloves, and tucked the bracelet inside, just so. You see?

Yes, of course I could have worn it on the other wrist, but that's hardly the point, is it? This thread of gold has brought strength to my arm when I feared it might fade. It guides my hand. That's as she would wish.

They tried to take it off me when I arrived here. I'm afraid I lied and said it was a gift from Cardinal de Noailles. I can't be without it. It reminds me of … of lost things.

Of her. Perhaps me. We were both lost. Are.

I sent poems declaring my love, my desire. She never received them.

That's probably just as well, because they were dreadful. I blush to think of it now.

But someone read them. Someone knew.

I waited. Watched.

Then she was gone.

I heard a rumour in the city. Some wit composed a ditty

and soon everyone was singing it—about a pretty Italian maid seduced by a female demon and sent into God's care.

After a few days of this, a drunken trumpet player told me the truth.

Her father had sent her away, to a convent. In Avignon. Forever.

Yes. Exactly. This convent.

Now, you may be shocked to learn that this habit you see me wearing is quite familiar to me.

You assume that my life has been entirely worldly, until now, but no—as a young woman I, too, once entered into a holy contract with our Saviour to serve Him all my days. Just like you, Father, although with a somewhat different motive. A few weeks after Clara vanished, I found myself dressing in veil and tunic and prostrating myself in the dark hours before dawn, on the floor of a chapel—right here.

It's always dark, our chapel. Always was. I wonder why that is. Then, and now, the sisters are miserly with the candles. And the firewood. So, yes. I have been here before.

Avignon. The silent city. When I first arrived, it seemed as if a muffling cloak had settled upon it, stifling all noise but the bells. After the hubbub of Marseille, of Paris, of Versailles, it seemed almost frightening. I was too loud for the city, too big. I still am, but now I don't fear the silence. I take it into me like air. I hear the music within it.

But then—oh, then—I blustered and banged on convent doors, seeking everywhere for Clara and the place I imagined to be her prison.

A convent in Avignon—that's what the trumpet player had said, but the idiot didn't tell me how many convents there are in Avignon. Perhaps it was his little joke. There's nothing but convents in Avignon—and monasteries; pale stone walls and bell towers and shuttered windows and firmly locked gates. Glimpses of fruit trees over high walls. No wonder that it's quiet. It's like the hush of a great cathedral—Saint-Roch or Saint-Eustache—in the early morning.

The normal people, the working people, the silk weavers, guards, washerwomen, go about their business as if a little song, the odd joke, would bring down all the punishments of Hell. The waterwheels in the canal barely splash. Even the pigeons keep their beaks shut. Sometimes you hear children calling to one another, but you rarely see them. In these narrow alleyways, a whisper carries for miles. You hear it, but you don't know where it came from. There is a laden donkey—a handcart—straining over the cobblestones, someone clipping a hedge, an argument—or it's flagellation day over at the Pénitents—and the whole city can hear it, or, at least, those who listen and those who are not behind walls three feet thick.

So I quickly realised that banging on doors and shouting was not the Avignon way. The Avignon way involves the pretence of piety and an exchange of silver. I found a man who knew his way around, who had heard all the gossip—you wouldn't believe the things he told me. Even I was shocked.

But never mind.

He found her, soon enough. It's a small city, after all, and there are people with eyes enough to notice a rich merchant with fine horses—a foreigner—delivering his daughter to one of the less austere convents. A serving-girl said the daughter cried all night and was the most beautiful angel ever seen. Who else could it be?

So I knew where Clara was. But what next? It will amaze you to learn that I had no idea. I had come here imagining I'd scale a wall, rescue my damsel and carry her off on horseback like a chevalier in one of the romances. Faced with these endless walls, these massive bolted doors, the watchful eyes from above—no, not Him, I mean the snooping brothers in the upper floors of every monastery in town—my courage failed me for the first time.

I can't tell you how I felt. It was very strange. As you know only too well, Father, our chapel looks daunting from the outside—a high building in a narrow street, all the more imposing when you're a lost soul. It seemed to me then the sort of place from which you might never escape once you entered. I'd seen portals more grand, many a time. After all, I grew up in a place ten times as big. But this convent—for some reason it scared me—then, now. It was as if I could get lost in here, as if the life within was a labyrinth in which a girl, or two girls, might be forgotten, imprisoned, ignored. I felt—what? Fear? Perhaps revulsion? That sensation you get at a crossroads when everything depends on the next action you take—the twitch of the reins, the word of a passing stranger, your hand as it reaches up for the bell-pull.

But I couldn't let any of that be known. So I was meek. Penitent. Desperate. Part of that was even true.

What else could I do but stand before that gate, haul on the rope and politely ask for acceptance into the fold?

Even as the door was opening, it felt like a fraud, like a trap—like a dreadful error. I could have run. I didn't.

They took me in. Didn't cut my hair, thank the Lord, but they took my clothes, my boots, my gloves. I told them my name. I don't even remember what it was, now. Any old name. It didn't matter, at that point, who I was—not to me, not to them. My first few days were spent locked in a cell, with the odd hour prostrate on the chapel floor; they called it a spiritual solitude, to allow me to reflect on my past sins and my vocation. Which I truly did. I felt as if my life had been wasted—as if every moment of every day had led me to that perfect hour when I first saw her face—as if my destiny might dwell in that place. As perhaps it did.

I saw her on the fifth day. They released me from my room—not a moment too soon—and sent me out to work in the orchard. It was cold by then and my fingertips ached, but I remember the air on my face and the scent of turned earth.

She was feeding the chickens, calling to them. I'd never heard her voice. I stood there, with dirt on my hands, listening—gazing at her—willing her to look at me.

She turned. Slowly. Saw me. And smiled.

Someone spoke to her and she walked away, not looking back, and it didn't matter because I knew she would come to me.

Act 2, Scene 2

A duet

THEY MEET—SPEAK—FOR THE VERY first time that night after supper. In the dark. In a corner of the cloister, where even whispers seem to echo off the stone walls, they both talk at once.

'I knew you would find me—'

'When they sent you away—'

'Somehow.'

'I searched everywhere.'

'I thought I'd never see you again.'

'And yet here I am.'

Clara breathes for what feels like the first time in hours. 'You must be careful.'

'Clara.' Julie smiles at the music in it.

'Please. Say it again. Just like that.'

'Clara,' Julie whispers. And then, 'I love you.'

The breath shivers out of Clara's body. 'And I ... but it's ridiculous. Isn't it?'

'Not at all. It just is.'

'Whoever heard of such a thing?'

They've never been so close before. They wonder at each other—stripped of jewellery, satins, even hair tucked away, naked under the rough linens. And yet they are glorious, glowing. Julie marvels over every eyelash, the tiny wrinkles in Clara's lips, the flecks of agate in her brown eyes.

'You're trembling.' She takes Clara's hand—the skin silky against her own—and trembles a little herself at the touch. 'Are you scared? Don't be.'

'It's not that. Perhaps a chill.'

'I'll warm you.' Julie presses the precious hand between her own palms. 'Come with me. We'll escape.'

'Impossible.'

'Not at all.'

'Where could we go? How will we live?'

'It doesn't matter, Clara. I'll find a way. I always do.'

Clara shakes her head but can't stop smiling. 'My father—'

'He banished you here.' Julie says it too loudly, as if she's on stage.

Clara flinches. 'Shhh.'

'You owe him nothing.'

'But God—'

'God is love, remember?'

'Yes. But this—'

'Is perfect. You are perfect. Clara.'

'And you ...'

Julie strokes the soft skin inside Clara's wrist. She shudders. They both do.

'I am yours.'

They meet every evening in the poultry house, after Vespers. The chickens snicker and shuffle. The girls sit in the dirty straw, fingers entwined, not speaking, sometimes smiling. They kiss once but it frightens them so they stop.

At other times, in hallways or behind the kitchens, they whisper to each other. There are secrets. Desires that can only be spoken in daylight. Plans that can only be discussed in darkness. Fears. Memories—little things—mere moments.

'Yesterday, I watched you in the chapel.'

'Julie, you mustn't.'

'I can't help it.' Julie's cheeks hurt from smiling wider than she's ever smiled.

'But God will see.'

'He sees us already. He knows.'

'Don't say that!' Clara glances around to check that nobody's watching.

'It's all right. No need to blush so.' Julie draws her down onto the stone bench next to the kitchen gate. There are no fathers here to stop them, curse them, beat them. Only Him, and Julie is willing to risk even His wrath. For this. For Clara.

'There's a story,' she says, 'written down by one of the old Romans, about two girls who are meant for each other. Iphis and Ianthe, they were called. Iphis grew up as a boy, just like me, and they fall in love, by accident almost. I know the poem—every word.'

'Tell me.'

Their heads are close together, their breath mingles.

'Love came to both of them together in simple innocence, and filled their hearts with equal longing.' Julie quotes the old Roman, but leaves out parts of Iphis's story: the despair, the longing, the excoriation of the soul. Instead she smiles. 'You see?'

'So we are not alone?'

Clara's eyes glitter in the moonlight. Julie wonders if perhaps she is an angel. If perhaps she is crying. She moves a little closer until their thighs touch.

'Iphis and her mother pray, all night, to one of the pagan goddesses.'

'Blasphemy.'

'Never mind,' says Julie. 'Let me finish the story.'

'They are cured?'

'No, of course not. They don't want to be cured. Do you?'

'Sometimes.'

'That's not the right answer, Clara.'

'Forgive me, but it hurts, to think of it all.'

'Then don't think. Just hold my hand and listen.' She does. 'So they pray all night, Iphis and her mother both.'

'You can read Latin?'

'Yes. But I read it in French. In a romance. Some fellow had rewritten it.'

'You are a wonder.'

'You're not concentrating.'

Clara giggles. Julie has never heard such divine music. Her chest aches so much she needs to take a deep breath before she can go on.

'They pray to Diana or one of those old naked goddesses—'

'Now you're being wicked.'

'She grants their wish so Iphis becomes a boy, after all.'

'Really?'

'Would I lie to you?'

Clara leans back against the cold stone wall and stares up at the stars, the outline of the chapel dome, the palm trees.

'But it's just a story,' she says at last. 'It didn't really happen.'

'You never know with those Romans.'

'We can't pray to their goddess.'

'We could try Saint Jude.' Julie nudges Clara's shoulder with her own. 'Or Saint Catherine.'

'You're teasing me.'

'Perhaps.' She grins.

Silence. The half moon is now high over the convent wall. Clara shivers. She has always been good—even her mother said so, during the violent family tempest that brought her here. She'd always imagined herself godly and pure. But she was wrong. Inside her was a demon—red with black eyes, like those painted in her Book of Hours. She feels it writhe; it warms her skin, makes her breath shudder. Perhaps it's been there all the time and she had no idea. Perhaps it arrived with the Opéra. Now it claws at her, pinches her cheeks, leaves her aching. She tries to cast it out—with herbs, with prayer, with tears of repentance. It won't go. She won't let it.

It's worse, and much better, when she's with Julie. She despairs in the demon's delight, quivers under its touch, nearly weeps with fear. She won't listen to its whispering, to its promise. She will not let it touch her.

It's not Julie's fault. The red demon is hers alone. She will pray for them both, like Iphis, unsure what she'll do if God answers.

'Would you like to turn into a boy, Julie?'

'No, not really. I'd rather be as I am. But somewhere else. With you.'

Act 2, Scene 3

Recitative

HERE YOU ARE AGAIN. Well, well. Here we both are—me in the sunlight, bare feet in the grass, for possibly the last time.

Couldn't stand lying in that room another moment. It smells of death ... of me. I never used to smell like this. The stench alone is enough to kill me. And I'm sick of staring at that dying man hanging over the door. I'm sure he's sick of me, too.

So I had the laundresses carry me out here after morning prayer. Now they're scrubbing out that foul room, burning sticks of rosemary and changing the bed linen. About time. They grumbled, the Abbess objected, but a few *sous* can buy you almost anything in this place. It's one of its charms.

Dear God, I'm frail. I didn't realise how fragile I'd become until they lifted me out of my cot. I'd imagined I'd be able to walk, at least a few steps. But no. As it was, I felt as if all my bones might snap. Or crumble into dust. But not yet. Not quite.

I'm not entirely sure I'll survive the trip back up the staircase, but it's worth it, to be out here.

Can you feel that? Winter sun, but it has healing powers, the light, the air. The Provençals understand this. If I was in Paris I'd be locked away in some dark room in a hospice, but here, in the south, people trust the sun. It's so much more obvious here, after all. There's always a scent in the breeze—lavender and olive wood burning, the far-off sea—even in the depths of winter.

And look! These palm trees have grown so tall since I was last here. They're doing better than me, that's clear. Grown from dates all the way from the Holy Land, so I'm told. The Abbess is terribly proud of them. There she goes now, off on some serious Abbess business, the others in her wake like ducklings. Oh, I do like being out here. There's Sister Angeline—a bit mad, that one, but so good with the bees and the sick. She's gentle with my poor bones, too.

Listen to me. I sound like an old woman. That's how I feel. Incredible, isn't it? That I should be brought to such an end. From such greatness, such majesty, such sublime beauty. I don't look it—nobody knows that better than me. I feel this coarse linen against my breasts, all these flaps and folds of wool—it always seems damp with lanolin and the sweat of generations of sisters. I am, once again, clad in someone else's cast-offs. Shoeless. How did it come to this? Have I sunk or risen? Or are they the same thing?

There was a time, many years in fact, when I never wanted to see another nun in my life. Hilarious, isn't it? Now all I see from Lauds to Compline are nuns. The only sounds I hear—the only music—nuns.

Until you came.

With your scratching and your questions, your quiet tut-tuts, the odd sharp intake of breath at particularly interesting moments in my story. You never look at me. Why is that?

Actually, I don't want to know. Forget I asked. Just mind your own business and write. Think of your readers. My readers. One day they will marvel at me, at my life. To them you are nothing. A barrier they must overcome. An interference. A cipher. So scribble, little man. Tell them how I was brought out into the courtyard, brave and unrepentant. No, weary but resolved. No. Unravelled. That's what I am. Unravelling. No. Write this: she was frail but courageous. Yes.

Now we go on. Now we come to it. The telling. That's why you're here, isn't it? To find out the truth of that night? The Abbess knows, of course she does. She's no fool, not like you. It may even be that she genuinely fears for my soul, hopes for the best—thinks that if I unburden myself to you, the better fragments of my soul will be free to ascend.

I doubt it.

I had hoped for a clear blue sky today, for this moment, but any sky will do. God makes the clouds, too, after all. God and that lovely little man with the red hair—what's his name again? A painter, one day to be famous or so he tells us. In the meantime, he makes the sets and the machines for the Académie. Such clouds as you never saw. I know—I have soared among them. Such details. When I played Pallas Athéna—a triumph, naturally—he painted tiny suns all across my chariot, so small that only I could see them, but he knew, and I knew, and God knew, they were there. He wants to paint for the King, desires nothing more than a little room at Versailles and a stretch of ceiling to decorate. He doesn't realise there isn't a square inch left bare in the entire chateau.

But he lives in hope and will never be content. Odd, isn't it? Yet he paints skies and clouds almost as beautiful as God's own.

Contentment. Life. That's what you see before you, here in this courtyard. The fruit trees. Fallen leaves. Ants in the lawn. Sister Marguerite's herbal garden—hear the bees? Even the wasps are singing for us today, or so it seems. I can watch everyone coming and going, instead of merely marking the passing hours by the bells and the sound of feet on gravel.

These are not the words, you may feel, of a woman preparing to leave this world. You're right. I'm not. I may be leaving—we will know soon enough—but I'm not prepared. Why should I be? How is that even possible?

I've read of people making peace with the world before they die. I've seen it on stage, sung the eulogy over their sprawled bodies and grieving lovers. But seriously, you can't tell me it happens in real life. People are struck down, fall dead. People waste away. Death stinks. It hurts. There's no peace in it. So I prefer to sit out here in the world, in the light, even in the cold, as long as I can.

Hear that? The choir—in the chapel. Funny thing, in this city of convents—you wouldn't think of it this way unless you lived here, behind the walls, but it's a city of music. The air is full of it. It floats on the silence. How many choirs must there be? Dozens. Bells. Organs. Even the odd cornet from the guards' barracks. I think of the Mass as music, too, of tone and repetition, recitative and chorus.

Yes, yes, I'm getting to it. In my way. Patience. It's the choir that takes me back, more often than not. To this place, in another time—to other places, sacred places, moments, lives. To the day, so many years ago now, I took the first steps to becoming a sister of the Visitandines.

I didn't receive much of a greeting. In fact, you could say I was grudgingly accepted into the service of our Lord. Lay sisters were plentiful at that time, but only those who bring with them a handsome legacy are truly welcomed. Poor girls like me, with a mere calling to God and no other assets, are a burden on any convent, even here, where the sisters' hearts are unusually kind. I understand that.

It was a different story this time round, let me tell you. Over the years, I've donated hundreds of *louis* to the coffers and it paid off handsomely. This time, when I turned up, coughing and retching, you never saw such a welcome. That's why they put up with me here. We are old friends. Or, at least, my penance for previous sins—heinous as they were, I'll confess that now, before you start with your sermonising—has been lavish and willingly received.

But in those days—nearly twenty years ago—I had no worldly goods to renounce, besides my sword, and I wasn't silly enough to offer that up to the Abbess. I would have sung in the choir, but that's only for the real nuns. Still, I was strong and they needed an extra pair of hands in the orchard—let's not pretend it was anything else. I didn't care.

Look around us. This is a place of peace. I didn't realise that until now. Then, I thought it was a prison—of course, I'd never actually been in prison at that stage; there's no comparison, in reality. But freedom had come to me so suddenly, so completely, I despaired that I might never feel it again.

I confess, I felt its loss like a knife between my shoulder blades at times, or the ache of a rotten tooth. All of my romantic ideas of following Clara, of finding her, hadn't included early mornings in a dim chapel and autumn harvest until my arms felt like they might break and homespun wool scratching the back of my neck. Or, in fact, spending my entire life in a convent. But there I was. Here. Then. Fighting for breath, for air. Failing. Before I got here, before I found her, all I wanted was Clara. After a week or so, all I wanted was to run.

It's not like that now.

There are worse places to live, let me tell you. Here there are berries and peaches every summer, mushrooms and roast boar in the autumn. Jasmine in the air. The worst of the Mistral passes us by. The old bishops don't bother us much, nor the city fathers. We mind our own business. The choir is mostly tuneful, the Abbess kind in her own rough way. The sisters are serene without being silent, devout without boring the crap out of you. They look after me even though, God knows, I give them no reason to love me. Apart from the gold.

There are only a few who are old enough to remember the last time I was here—my perfidy, my crimes. A splendid place to die. Lucky it doesn't burn easily, eh?

Act 2, Scene 4

A duet

CLARA WAITS IN THE POULTRY HOUSE one evening, in spite of the dark, in spite of the spiders. She waits for her—friend—soul mate. Love. Although she will not say that word. Not ever. It's wrong. And yet, she is. Listening for her footsteps, now—every moment of the day. She can't help it. Here they are. Running. The door creaks open.

'Come.' Julie holds out her hand.

'What is it?'

'It is our moment—our escape.'

Fear clutches at Clara's bowels. 'Not yet.'

'Yes,' says Julie. 'Tonight. Now. Sister Carmella is dead. I just found her in the hallway—laid her in her room.'

'Oh! Did you tell the Abbess?'

'Not yet. She'll find out soon enough.'

'Poor Sister Carmella.' Clara tries to remember her face but it's one among so many. 'We must take her to the Chapel of the Dead and pray for her soul.'

'Let the others say the rosary. Tomorrow. I have a plan.'

The body is still, soft, with the bones of a bird, easily carried to another bed—Clara's bed.

'This is wrong,' says Clara.

There's a candle by the cot, burning down to a pool of yellow fat and smoke.

'It's marvellous,' says Julie. 'We'll be long gone by the time they work it out.'

'But Sister Carmella—'

'Has gone to meet her Saviour. She's happy. So shall we be.'

Clara drops to her knees to whisper a prayer over the body, lays the back of one hand on the nun's cold cheek.

'It's a sin. All of it.'

'Don't say that.' Julie grabs Clara's arm and pulls her to her feet. 'Listen to me. I will set you free.'

'I never asked for that.'

'That's only because you don't understand how it feels, but I do. Believe me, once you have been freed, you can never go back. I can never go back.'

'Why, you sound so fierce. You're scaring me.'

'I'm sorry, I don't mean to. But whether you like it or not, I will free both of us.' Julie gulps a breath. 'Or I will die.'

Clara stares at the bed. The tumbled linen, the chamber-pot, the stone floor. The scarecrow body, eyes and mouth open. Was Sister Carmella surprised by death? Even at her age? The red demon shouts in Clara's ear. She will not listen.

'They'll know …' She casts around for reasons, obstacles, anything.

'How? One burnt body is much like another. They'll think you're dead.'

'For a while.'

'That's long enough.'

At home in Marseille there were servants in green coats who brought hot milk and eggs on a tray. Housemaids who mopped the stairs and set kindling in every fireplace even if it wasn't cold. Clara had a harpsichord of her own and a parrot. She had never visited the poultry house or even the kitchens. Never scrubbed a slate floor or washed her own underclothes. Never chopped wood or picked apples until her fingers blistered. Never even saw anyone do those things.

'I want to go home.' The plea in her voice is almost too much to bear—for her, for both of them.

'You can't.' Julie shoves a blanket into a satchel. 'Not ever. Not now. This is the only way.'

'They'll never forgive us.'

'I don't need forgiveness—not from anyone.'

'You will, Julie.' She is close to tears. 'One day.'

'Forget all that. Listen. We'll need horses—one will carry us both for a few days. You weigh less than Sister Carmella and she's been starved for forty years.'

'They'll come after us.'

'We'll travel by night.'

Clara stands still at the foot of the bed with prayer beads wrapped around her fingers, trying not to look at the cross above the door. Julie covers Sister Carmella with layers of cloth. Both of them whisper, urgently, fearful of being heard or of being wrong or of what happens next.

'My father will not let it rest.'

'I'm not afraid of him.'

'We will be damned.'

'We are already.'

'In God's name—'

'Clara, we must go. Now. The city gates will open soon. Take my hand.'

She does.

The candle flickers when it touches the sheet. Almost splutters out. Then the linen smokes and catches, the flames shimmer in the gloom. The bed is alight. The red demon laughs, triumphant, and Clara laughs, too. She has lost, is lost, was always lost.

They leave by the gate in the garden wall, closing it soundlessly behind them. There's smoke in the sky now. Soon the bells will ring.

They run in the dark, through the orchard and rows of purple cabbages. Clara trips and gasps. They race between the stone fences and through narrow lanes that protect monasteries and tiny chapels and merchants' houses full of sleeping children.

At the city wall they slow down, try to appear calm, and slip through the Porte Saint-Lazare at dawn—two virtuous postulants off to pick herbs on the hillside or visit the sick. The guardsmen on the gate wish them a good day.

At the first bend in the road, they rip off their veils and fling them into the bushes. Julie thinks of the chaos left behind them—the burning bed and foul smoke and nuns with buckets of water and the screaming—and smiles. She and her love breathe the air of liberty, of the countryside, of autumn in Provence, and race across the fields towards the coast road, towards the morning, towards freedom.

Act 2, Scene 5

Recitative

DON'T WRITE THAT DOWN. I never meant to tell a soul. I swore I would not. It must have been the fever talking.

But now. I have begun, here, at the end. Or was it?

Sometimes I'm not sure where I am. Or when.

The story? Yes. I'm sorry. I'm just so tired. Always. Perhaps sitting outside for hours wasn't the best thing for me. Perhaps it will hasten the end. Perhaps that's for the best. I'm weaker. I feel it.

But I know my job, my role, my lines. So I will go on.

We were—somewhere. Everywhere. Running. Hiding. Together.

We waited for the metamorphosis. It never happened. Each night Clara prayed I would wake up as a man, and each morning she was astonished to find that I was exactly as I have ever been.

I don't care what Ovid says, the gods don't bother

themselves with such trifles—such human dilemmas. They let us figure these things out for ourselves. Otherwise we would be less than human and much less than holy.

Clara wanted to believe it, and I suppose a small fragment of me did, too, if only for her, if only to make it easy for us to be together—to take her as my wife, to be husband, lover—to feel a love that was blessed in the sight of God.

I have had such a love, since, in spite of my unchangingly female body.

But still, every night, whether in a shabby tavern or a hedgerow, she slept wrapped in my cloak and in my arms. Chaste. But ever so close. Every dawn I woke to feel her eyelashes tremble against my skin.

I remember her eyes and a freckle on her neck. She had a slight limp—you'd never notice it under her skirts—from a childhood riding accident, or so I was told, but it never slowed her down, until we had to run.

And run we did.

Through the dark. Around in circles. Through villages that never even knew we were there, through muddy days on the road to Aix. There we stopped.

There they found us.

Strange as it seems now, we had no idea how many men were hunting for us, how righteous and driven was their anger. Clara's family, of course, and the Abbess, and every other stickybeak in the papal city—filled with wrath and shame. We sparked a fuse of fury that ignited across the south. La Reynie heard of it in Paris and sent men and dogs to trace our scent. D'Armagnac—perhaps it was an order from my own father's pen—dispatched riders and guardsmen. Dozens of men on the King's finest horses rode through the nights in search of two bedraggled girls. Priests in every town denounced us at Mass. The doors of convents all over France were twice-locked each night in case any other sinners were possessed by similar thoughts. The Parliament in Aix passed sentence on me—me, alone—in a secret hearing, as though my crimes were too horrible to describe in public.

We knew nothing of this at first.

All those men scoured the country lanes and villages, all those notaries argued the case for days, the countryside was up in arms, but they couldn't find us; and we—we were together and free.

Strange, really. We were hunted all over Provence and yet I was completely at peace. With her.

Clara. The name of a saint. Face of an angel, too. She had the disposition of a saint, for that matter. Trusting. Faith such as you've never experienced, Father—yes, even you.

Faith enough to renounce her family, her finery—her whole life. Faith enough to make her reckless—foolhardy, even—she who had never so much as disagreed with her mother or teased a baby sister.

That faith was her only flaw. You think faith can only ever be perfect?

Pig's arse.

I can think of a hundred examples of faith that has destroyed people, cities, even whole civilisations—their faith or others'—it's all the same. The fall of Constantinople. The Massacre of the Innocents. The destruction of the Temple— of the Huguenots—of the King of England. That's faith at work in the world. For every miracle, there are a hundred lives lost. More.

In Clara's case it's quite simple. Her faith was misplaced. She had faith in me, an unworthy recipient if ever there was one. She believed that I would save her, protect her, hide her.

She was wrong. There was no escape. No more contentment. No metamorphosis. Dear God, if only I'd learned the truth—from d'Armagnac, from Séranne, from all those books and all those boys. I thought our passion— for that's what it was—was fruitless. I didn't realise that a metamorphosis was unnecessary, that I might have made her happy as a lover, as a husband—or a wife—or both. I was not much more than a child—it's my only defence—and my lovers had only ever tended to their own needs. I didn't know that romance and sex were different creatures—one of the soul, one of the body. I had no idea that two souls can feel as if they are joined in one body, as it were, no matter the shape of the bodies involved.

Clara believed that I would love her as long as I lived. In that, at least, her faith was justified, although she will never know it.

But me? Did I really commit such wrongs as to deserve this fever, this interminable dying—and you appearing at my bedside like an avenging angel every morning?

What do I regret now? What do I confess?

My crimes against people, against the law—yes. Utterly. The arson. Of course. I still smell the burning bed—the burning flesh—in the night. It was foolish. Unnecessary. Vicious. Madness, really, since it made them all the more determined to find us, to punish us. Without that, we might have got away, stayed free. We might have lived together, happily, for years—as sisters, perhaps, or lady companions in some little village in the Var or by the sea, not bothered by anyone except the odd meddling priest, for all our days. I might even have been content, living like that—in peace—incognito—you never know.

But nobody was abducted. That charge I reject. Totally. Those crimes still hang over my head, here, where they began. The King has pardoned me. You may not—I don't care. But I have paid for them. Then. Now. Ever since. Paid through the nose. For years.

My crimes, my transgressions. You think they are legion, but no—they are few. People say I've killed dozens of men, deprived children of their fathers. That I'm a whore, a libertine.

In truth I am marble. I am flame. Fever. I am still and the world swirls around me. I am sea and the great shark. I am caught, dying. I am here. Back here.

The memories sear my flesh, my heart. I still see Clara's face, my last glimpse of her, asleep and trusting.

These are my sins, Father. Those, and loving too much, too violently. But I am reformed. You believe me?

It's true. I won't commit any further crimes, you can be sure of that. Not with this cough, this wasted body, these trembling fingers. I have run out of time, it would seem, but if by some miracle I am granted another year—another ten—I swear to you I wouldn't live my life any differently.

I won't love again. That would be impossible, after ...

But everything else—no—I have regrets, but I will not recant. No matter how much you threaten and scowl.

I'm the way I am because this is how God made me—God and my own father—and that is how I will die.

Act 2, Scene 6

Duets

'JULIE, I'M HUNGRY.'

'You're always hungry.'

Clara's feet slide sideways in the mud. She picks up her hem, already filthy, and walks on. 'We should stop somewhere soon. Beg some supper. Or you could steal another chicken.'

Julie strides ahead of her, looking around at the trees, the sky. 'You told me theft is a sin.'

'I've changed my mind.'

Julie glances back. 'I love it when you smile.'

'I love it when you steal chickens.'

In the villages, everyone watches them. The eyes of every farmer's wife, baker, parish priest—especially the priest— follow the steps of the two strange girls in grubby white robes.

It's impossible to steal an apple from a stall or a loaf of bread. They need a market town. A city. Not Marseille. Not Avignon.

Aix.

It takes weeks to walk there along mule tracks and across hillsides. Julie steers them clear of the high road, the taverns, the toll gates, the guardhouses. They eat raw mushrooms dug out of pine needles, a fish left in someone's trap, bowls of porridge begged from a ferryman, rosemary leaves and birch bark. One day they steal a hare hanging outside a huntsman's cottage. Most days they go hungry.

As they walk, they hold hands and imagine the world.

'Tell me again, Julie. How will we live?'

'A goat farm? I always liked goats.'

'Roasted?' Clara can almost taste it.

'Not for eating, silly. For milking.'

They talk about food constantly. It doesn't help.

'Can you make butter from goat's milk?'

'I don't know,' says Julie. 'But at Versailles the children have little goat carts and race each other across the forecourt. They're very dainty.'

'The children?'

'The goats.'

'I don't think I'd be very good at farming,' Clara admits, after several days of planning a future filled with goats. 'Animals scare me a little.'

'A tavern then?' says Julie. 'An inn. In the mountains. In Italy.'

'Naples?'

'Why not?'

'My grandmother lives in Naples.'

'That's why not.' Julie grins. 'Somewhere else. Venice? I could sing in Venice.'

'Sing for me now.'

She does. Something Italian, for her Neapolitan love. A

duet. She sings both parts, weeps dramatically, falls to one knee in the mud to declare her undying devotion. Her accent is appalling. Her Neapolitan love applauds and helps her up. That night they sleep under a tree. It rains.

Clara weeps into her sleeve, silently, but not silently enough. The red demon has nothing to say on the subject of hunger or blistered feet. It has abandoned her. Sometimes she misses it. Sometimes Julie wishes Clara would shut up.

By the time they reach Aix they have only one pair of sandals between them. They hitch a ride on a cart through the city gates and head for the market.

Clara holds tight to the edge of Julie's robe. 'So many people.'

'Have you forgotten how noisy a big town can be?'

They wait at a crossroads while an old man shepherds his flock across the square towards the market.

Clara flinches at the noise. 'I like it better when it's just us.'

'When it's just us we don't eat much.' Julie throws her satchel on the ground, arches her back and stretches. 'You wait here. I can sneak around better alone.'

Clara doesn't loosen her grip on the robe. 'You'll come back?'

'Of course I will.'

'Promise?'

A sigh. 'What's wrong with you, Clara?'

'I'm scared.'

'Don't be.' Julie attempts a smile, but she's too hungry to make it work properly. 'I'm going to come back with a roasted chicken. You'll see. Or better still, a purse full of silver. But I can't do it with you holding on to me like that.'

'I'll wait. I'll be brave.'

'That's my sweet. Stay here by the fountain so I can find you again.'

The city is not as old as Avignon and not wild like Marseille, either. It's a town of shopkeepers and bakers, of markets and coffee houses, of sober buildings and stonemasons hammering. A flock of ragged sheep pours through the avenue towards the saleyards. It takes until midday for Julie to find a man willing to pay in silver for a few moments in a quiet alley. And then another.

On her way back to the square she sees a warrant posted on a church door. It's tattered but she can read it. It has her name on it. And other words. Arson. Body-snatching. Abduction. Corruption of an innocent. Sentenced to death. To be burned alive at the stake. Reward for capture.

She reads it again. Sentenced to be burned alive at the stake. The words drip ice into her chest until her heart freezes. She will die, here, now. They will catch her, kill her. Kill them both.

No. Wait. There's no mention of Clara on the warrant. Clara is safe. Could be safe. Clara alone.

Her love waits by the fountain.

'Is everything all right? You look odd.'

'I'm tired, that's all.'

'Did you steal a chicken?'

'Better. A few coins.' This time she manages a convincing smile.

'Such an accomplished thief. I'm proud of you.'

'It's enough for a night in a real bed and a hot bath. And a chicken.'

The inn is in darkness. There's a shadow by the fireplace. It stands. Kicks a log further into the coals. A knock at the open door—soft at first, then more insistent. The shadow looks up.

'What is it?'

A man steps into the room, looks around, and closes the door behind him.

'Monsieur d'Aubigny? Or should I call you Madame de Maupin?'

Silence. A sigh. Then: 'Perhaps. Who knows? It depends.'

The man moves closer to the fire, to the shadow. 'Where is she?'

'Who?'

'The other girl—your captive.' He sees her now: thin face, hair pulled back. Not the famous beauty he was expecting.

She grimaces at him. 'Who are you?'

'An emissary from Comte d'Armagnac.'

'A ghost. Or is that me?'

'I beg your pardon, madame?'

Julie stares at the man's face. Dark beard, a scar over one eye. Never seen him before.

'What do you want?' she asks.

'I have come to make an offer.'

She sits down heavily on the chair nearest the fire. 'Make it.'

'You cannot escape. That much is clear.'

'They're not looking for me,' she says. 'I saw the proclamation. So unimaginable are my deeds that the Parliament has accused someone called Monsieur d'Aubigny. Because, let's face it, no woman could be guilty of such crimes.'

'The gendarmes know the truth. If I can find you, La Reynie will certainly track you down and hand you to the Parliament.'

Julie laughs. 'Monsieur d'Aubigny. The metamorphosis at last.'

'Whatever you had hoped, madame, it cannot be.'

'Me? I hoped for a clear road—a life free of despair. And look at me.' It is over. She knows it. Clara will know it soon enough. Perhaps she already does. 'I'm weary. We both are.'

'Where is your prisoner?'

'Upstairs. Asleep. But she's not a prisoner. She is free. We left together. Nobody was abducted.'

'The Parliament will not believe you. They will never even hear it. You will be sent straight to the stake.'

Julie glances up at him. 'What does it matter to you?'

'It doesn't. But it matters to the Comte.'

'Why should he care?'

'I can't speculate.'

Julie looks away, deep into the embers. 'What will become of her?'

'She'll go home. She has done nothing wrong.'

'That much is true.'

'It was a flight of fancy, at most,' he says. 'She'll recover.'

'Is that it? Fancy? I suppose you're right. No woman would love another so deeply that she would risk everything, do anything, to enable them to be together. Would she?'

'Surely not. And you—'

'I ...' Julie shoves a log further into the flames. 'I am the villain.'

'So you will burn. Publicly, shamefully. These provincials make a feast of such occasions. Unless ...'

She turns to look at him and he sees it now—hunger has worn away her beauty but it's still there. No. It's not mere beauty. It's something else, something fierce in her eyes, something so powerful that all at once he can hardly speak.

'Yes?'

'The Comte, in his wisdom—'

'Never his strong point.'

'In his wisdom offers you this—a horse, a disguise, a thousand *livres*.'

Her eyes narrow. 'What is my part of the bargain?'

'Leave. Leave her to her family. Go north, anywhere, away from here, and never return.'

'Why would I—why does he want that?'

A shrug.

A smile.

'He's embarrassed?'

'Perhaps.'

She chuckles. 'That's priceless.'

'No, it's not, madame. It's worth one thousand *livres*.'

'And a horse?'

'Exactly.'

Julie stands slowly and takes a step towards him. 'If you harm her, I'll kill you.' She moves back into the darkness and waits for him to speak.

He nods slowly. 'She will be safe.'

'When?'

'Now.' The soft clunk of gold coins. 'Take the black mare at the second trough. There are clothes in the saddlebags. Be gone.'

'I should—'

He has to remind himself of her crimes, her sin. His master's wrath. 'No farewells. Just go. Now.'

'But—'

'The gendarmes will be here by midnight.'

The woman in the shadows moves, takes the purse from his hand, a cloak from the hook by the door, and vanishes. It's too dark to see the tears on her face.

Act 2, Scene 7

Recitative

WHAT WAS I SAYING?
   Must have drifted off.
   I forget, sometimes, what I'm saying—what I've come to be.

Forgetting is quite pleasant, although I only forget *Now*, which is relatively dull anyway. I don't forget *Then*. Not really. But I find I remember moments completely differently from day to day—my mind wanders back along its familiar paths but sometimes takes unexpected and possibly completely imaginary turns. Odd.

Oh, yes. I was telling you … that's it. The bleakest time of my life. Or so I thought, then.

What happened? There were tales all over the country of a great confrontation—of me fighting our way out of an inn near Aix, killing three men, wounding countless others.

All rubbish.

The truth wasn't nearly so heroic.

You asked for a confession. You want to know which events—which sins—make me sick to the stomach with bile no herbs can soothe; make me want to tear my hair from my skull, the flesh from my face with my own fingernails.

This is one of those sins—one of those few memories that pierce my skin, burn my eyes, all through these long nights.

Cowardice? Perhaps that's what it was. I don't know. Pragmatism, I called it then. Exhaustion, perhaps. I was weary to the bones, it's true, but I'm strong—I could have kept running. I could have kept Clara safe for at least a few weeks more. I could have fought my way out or died trying, since that's the story they made up anyway.

But I didn't. I sneaked away in the night in exchange for a horse and a bag of gold. I left her there and took to the hill roads once again.

If I hadn't, of course, I may never have become the great Mademoiselle de Maupin. I might never have got as far as Paris, certainly not onto the stage of the Palais-Royal. But what would my life have been?

We used to talk about it, plan our lives together. I'd say we could run an inn somewhere up north, and Clara would laugh at the idea of me polishing goblets and throwing drunks out the door. A little farm, I'd say. A goat or two and some hens. Fruit trees.

Can you picture it?

I couldn't. I admit that now. I'd imagined I could be loved, even me, like the women in the old stories. Foolish. We had come to an end in the road, encircled, ambushed. I felt like one of those horses at the Écurie, walking around and around in proscribed arcs, unknowing. Powerful, but held back. Wild but always restrained. You know?

No. Silly question.

But even if there had been a way out of town, where would it lead? To the goats or the drunks? Impossible. Either way. Clara's faith in me was betrayed: trampled under the dusty hooves of d'Armagnac's cadets; bashed and bruised by La Reynie's gendarmes; squandered in the taprooms of countless inns; and finally—pathetically—bribed into insignificance by a comte with a hysterical temper and a tarnished reputation.

I told myself at the time I had no choice—that I was protecting her—that nothing lay ahead of us but despair and hunger. But despair lay ahead of me anyway, wherever I go, whatever I do, and she ...

I've dreamed ever since of telling her that I only wanted to save her, to see her fed and warm. Of course it's true. But ... but I was sixteen years old and sentenced to death. To burn. What would you have done but run? Did I sacrifice her? Us? My own heart? Perhaps. Well, yes. But I lived. I went on. Such guilt, such despair. You can't imagine. It has almost undone me once or twice. It may yet.

They packed her off to a different convent—Carmelites, I think—miles away. Can you imagine how it would have been for her? The punishments, the judgement, the loneliness, the spying, the meaningful looks along the supper table—a prison. Always.

So we have ended as we began, both of us—she a nun, and me pretending to be. She faithful and pure, I have no doubt, if she's still alive, somewhere.

Forgive me.

No, not you.

I can't recall what happened next. I rode back to Marseille—that's right. Stupid. Not sure how I got there, but I did. Then I lay low for a while. Very low.

I'm not ashamed to admit now that I curled up on a bed in a dark room somewhere. I have no real recollection of the details, but it was weeks, surely, spent without moving, without sleeping or eating or walking in the light.

I can't explain it even now. I should have been relieved, even joyous—free of the convent, free to enjoy the city I had once known.

I must have been ill, feverish, just as I am now; for that time and this are the only days I have spent so worn out, so diminished. You see? I recovered last time, mostly, though there has been a part of me unwell—damaged, perhaps— ever since. Nobody could touch me, not really, after that. I wouldn't let them. Until ... much later.

But slowly, almost imperceptibly, the days seemed more bearable. I washed my hair, my clothes. I ate a little meat. Some bread. Opened a window. Breathed. One day, I heard someone singing: one of Lully's airs—from *Thésée*, if I recall. Something I knew. Something I could sing. So I did. Quietly, to myself. Then louder, standing at the window, singing into the evening air. Someone shouted at me. I didn't care.

The next day I saddled my horse, retrieved my sword and my father's hat from my old landlord, and set off.

Nobody noticed me. All my bruises were invisible.

I headed north, away from Marseille, Avignon, Aix, never to return—until now. It was like being on the road with Séranne, but without his annoying presence.

Imagine it—my first time on the road by myself. I had d'Armagnac's money and a good horse. I rode through the countryside, singing at the top of my voice. I can see it, even now. Feel it. One leg dangles over the horse's neck, the other foot loose in the stirrup. I tilt my head back so that my half-closed eyelids, my face and my throat feel the gentle wash of sunshine filtering through pine branches.

I stop singing long enough to listen to the wood thrushes. All the rustles and creaks of the forest. My own heart, still beating. My horse's hooves thudding in the mud.

I breathe pine and stale sweat. Thyme crushed on the trail, horse blankets and leather. Last night's campfire smoke in my hair. Perhaps rain.

I feel. Everything. The ache in my chest that will never heal. A blister on a toe from new boots. The horse moving beneath me, its tired muscles and even gait. The burden of the gold, hanging in a purse around my neck. Heavy. So heavy. Forgiveness. Sorrow. The never-knowing. Clara will never know.

I will never know.

The weight of time, of infamy. The curse of solitude. The joy of it.

Now I think of it, it was the first time in my life that I was really free, though I didn't feel it. But slowly, mile after mile, I unwound the bandages, let my wounds, my scars, crust over. They didn't heal. But I learned to live with them, as you do. Learned how to move, talk, ride, sing, so that the pain wasn't visible to anyone else, so that it hardly seemed to bother me. So that I seemed to be someone else. As indeed I was. No longer a nun, no longer a mistress, no longer the girl page. By then I was a singer.

I sang in cabarets and taverns in any cities and towns I passed through. The crowds, I admit, were uncivilised, but I didn't let them faze me. Oh, no. All good practice, you see.

I learned the hard way how to captivate and touch an audience. Some singers go through an entire career never bothering to learn that. They just stand there and belt out their assigned notes with no pathos, no love. They don't even look around them to see if anyone's watching, if the crowd's entertained, if it is awestruck. Then they wonder why at the end of the evening all the flowers fall at my feet.

I composed lyrics and music for some little songs, and tried them out. They were received kindly. I treated the world as my own open-air auditorium. I sang from horseback, on tables, in little stone churches. I stormed onto stages at local fairs. I hung from the rafters in taverns. Singing absorbed every moment, every thought. When I couldn't live by my voice, I lived by my sword. But I knew by then that the voice was my future.

Act 2, Scene 8

Pastorale

POITIERS. LATE AUTUMN. A countryside heavy with harvest. Wood smoke in the evening air. The forest floor spotted with mushrooms. Far off, the sound of an axe. In the old cabaret on the road to Paris, there's a girl singing.

Nobody's heard the song before—she wrote it last week, humming it to herself on horseback on the long track north. She sings of Marseille in summer, of love lost and the ocean, of crocuses and irises on the hillsides, of the coast road and darkened villages. An old fellow down the front taps his pipe on the table. Someone smiles.

A man sits alone at a table in the centre of the room, one fist clutching a bottle, the other—trembling a little—holding a glass that never seems quite empty, no matter how much he drinks. He drinks a lot.

He watches her. Julie pretends she doesn't care, but feels his gaze on her face, her throat.

She notices the battered slippers, the waistcoat that might

once have been blue velour, might once have fitted properly, might have been beaded, embroidered, perhaps even freshly washed. Long ago. She sees the slight nod of his head in time with her song, the tears that collect in a corner of his eye.

There's one note that worries her. She feels it approach—takes a breath—reaches for it—almost gets there.

Ah, well. Perhaps tomorrow night.

The drunk laughs at her.

But when she's done, he applauds louder than anyone else.

She wipes her mouth with the back of one hand. Reaches for a pitcher of ale. Drinks as much as she can in one gulp. It tastes of the forest. Of hard riding on a hot day. Of summer.

When she passes his table, he grabs at her arm. 'Sit with me a moment.'

'I'm a singer, not a whore.'

'Did I ask you for a fuck? No. I'm too old and too drunk. Sit down.'

She does. He puts his hand over hers and whispers, 'Listen to me. I can tell you things.'

'What do you want?'

'Nothing,' he says. She can smell the wine, stale in his mouth. 'I'm an old soldier in the field.'

'Touch me again and I'll slit your throat.' She pulls her hand away from his.

'Do not doubt me,' he says. 'I know about voices and talent.'

'And?'

'I'll give you lessons. I don't have anything else to do. It will amuse me.' He smiles, all rotted gums and yellow teeth. 'If you want it, little girl, in four or five years you'll be the *prima donna* of the Opéra in Paris.'

'Yes,' Julie says. 'I know.'

Act 2, Scene 9

Recitative

OR SOMETHING LIKE THAT. At any rate, I accepted. Gratefully.

It turned out Maréchal was an actor from the provinces. The city theatre had just thrown him out on his arse. You should have seen him—poor old fucker. He still wore his old costumes from years before, when he'd been famous—when he'd been paid—I suppose to remind himself, and others, that life had once been very different. Who can blame him for that? He was a good musician and a passionate actor. Dear God! Nobody knew the craft like he did—low-brow comedy, high drama, from Lully to Molière and back again. How could a man of such intelligence become a mediocre opera singer in some dump in the country? I never understood it, and nor did he. But that's why—I see it more clearly now—he was a little mad, and more than a little drunk.

He taught me brutally, just like my father, just like my fencing masters—but during his lucid moments, when he shook off drunkenness, he gave me such an education. It was, for me, a revelation. He taught me about the breath, and how to hear the essence of the notes in each song. Most of all, he taught me about acting—how to find the spirit of a song and let it shine in your face, no matter how shitty your life, no matter how minor the part. He taught me to be a goddess, a sprite—to be Cupid one day and Pallas Athéna the next—to appear regal or playful or savage or pure. How to look into the audience and feel their heartbeats; how to bind them to me; how to astonish and amaze; how to be remembered.

But it didn't last long. Three months or so, that's all, we worked together—purely platonic, I can assure you, too, in case you were wondering. He was distinctly not to my taste.

Maréchal understood me, knew every crack and quiver in my voice. He was a madman, and that helped. He and I clung to one another as if we were—and I see now it was true—each other's best hope. I absorbed him into me, or at least as much as I was able to stomach, although there was so much I still had to learn.

One day he didn't turn up to practice. I went to his house. He was slumped on the floor, in some kind of stupefaction. He stayed that way. All of a sudden, he was an idiot, a fairground mutterer. I cleaned him up. Wiped off the vomit and the spittle. Found an asylum where the sisters were used to that kind of thing. It was an act of generosity to leave him there. I still tell myself that. It's true, too, don't you think?

Maréchal always told me to move to Paris and to attempt, at whatever price, to get hired at a small theatre. He'd say he was certain that, once I got in somewhere, and if I kept working at it, even if it took years, I would end up making a name for myself. So I left Poitiers for Paris—earned my keep by singing. What happened, who I met along the way, is the stuff of legend now. People sing about it in the taverns, just as I once sang of Roland and the old heroes.

Act 2, Scene 10

The ballet

ANOTHER TAVERN. ANOTHER TOWN. Villeperdue, or some such place.

The courtyard is busy—a mail coach just arrived, people everywhere. Chickens. A mottled black pig. Hay waiting to be baled up for winter. Weak sunshine. A group of young men near the stables fancy themselves as chevaliers. Perhaps they are. Their swords are bright in the daylight, hung low on their hips. Their voices are too loud, their hats on a rakish angle—so fashionable in the city just now.

A man rides in—or is it? A woman? Who knows? Slides from his—her—black mare and hands the reins to an ostler. A few copper coins, a quiet word, a grin.

The young men watch carefully.

He—she—can't get past them—tries to push through. They elbow each other, snigger, shout out.

'Hey! You there!'

No answer.

'I say. You!'

The newcomer turns. Sighs. 'I'm tired. What do you want?'

One young man, golden as Adonis, pretty as a maid, smiles and saunters forward. 'What kind of creature are you, my pet?' he says.

Julie knows his sort. Swaddled in silk and lace at birth, so certain the world is his—that she is his.

'Not your pet,' she snaps. 'Not a creature. Leave me alone.'

'A girl. Indeed!'

'You are mistaken.'

'I think not.'

The golden boy flicks back his cape so she can see the hilt of his sword. It's golden, too. Red leather wrapped around the grip. No scratches, no dents.

'Let me pass.'

'Forgive me, mademoiselle, but I can't. Not until I have the pleasure of an introduction. Such a creature—'

'Stop saying that.'

'Oh ho! A firefly, too.' He laughs and his friends laugh with him. He looks around to make sure they are listening. 'A girl in breeches, riding alone, picking fights with strange men. Who could have invented such a character?'

'I have invented myself,' says Julie. 'Several times. Now stand aside. I want only my supper.'

'All in good time, pet.'

'Enough.' The blade is out of her scabbard before he can even flinch, its tip at his throat. 'Stand. Aside.'

He takes a few steps back and draws more slowly. 'My dear, you really must be more careful. You shouldn't unsheathe a blade unless you know how to use it.'

Julie wonders if this will be the moment when she kills for the first time. It could be worth it. 'You shouldn't unsheathe words unless you're willing to die for them. Any remark may be your last—at least make it worthy of the effort.'

'My speech offends you?'

Perhaps she should just slap his pretty, sarcastic face. 'A fine word for paltry blather.'

'Then there is nothing else for it but to teach you a lesson.'

'You may try. *En garde.*'

Everyone stands back. The pair salutes. The young men laugh and shove each other sideways to make a clear space. Laugh even more when the woman assumes a duelling stance.

'You're in for it now, d'Albert.'

'Watch out, Joseph! She looks fierce.'

Only one of the men notices that her stance is like that taught in the palace *salles*, in the Grande Écurie—the classic approach devised by Liancourt and devilishly tricky to master. His smile disappears. A memory from his days as a page—the girl—d'Aubigny's daughter. It could be …

'D'Albert, perhaps you shouldn't—'

'*En garde,* my pet!'

It's too late. There is no retreat now.

The young Comte d'Albert is a genius with the smallsword. All his teachers have told him so. He knows it. Five duels so far, and only one wound. That scratch on his arm from the Englishman doesn't count. This will be amusing.

He begins, as is customary, with a simple glide. She parries. It feels strangely gentle against his blade, although it was so fast he barely saw it.

He attacks again. And again. Laughs.

She doesn't even smile.

He is used to being adored, to women who tremble under his gaze. But this!

'My firefly has been taking lessons. Oh ho!'

The firefly waits.

He lunges, tries to slip under her guard but there's no space there, somehow she closed it off without him noticing; her wrist barely moved and yet the gap—that exquisite target— vanished and instead he is off guard and low down and if she riposted right now he'd be dead.

But she doesn't. He regains his feet. Laughs again, though not quite so convincingly.

'Your name, mademoiselle?'

'Shut up.' It comes out as a snarl. 'Fight.'

'You are something of an Amazon, perhaps?'

There's no answer.

She waits for him to try again.

He does. Of course he does. They always do. They can't help it.

He tries a flashy *enveloppement* in mid-lunge that she sees coming as if it was hours in the making. She disengages, ripostes, he counters, she counters, he, she, he, she parries and attacks in one smooth movement to *septime*—and he feels the blade enter his body before he knows she's thrust.

He smiles wide, joyful, with the blood pouring from his side. 'You're a genius, mademoiselle.' Attempts a bow. 'Allow me to ... forgive me. Louis-Joseph d'Albert de Luynes, honoured to make your—sorry, I can't—honoured to witness such a formidable *croisé*.'

She looks into his eyes as she always does. There is humility, laughter, the beginning of love. Her smile fastens on to his.

'Come on,' she says. 'Let's get you bandaged up.'

He's pale. Still smiling as his knees fold beneath him and he falls into black, into her arms, into a friendship that will never falter. Even unto death.

Act 2, Scene 11

Recitative

H E ALWAYS SAYS THAT CUPID pierced his heart in the same moment.

Well, well. Glorious words. It may be they're even true.

Ah! Listen to me. I do him a disservice. Yes, I slept with him many times over the years, to seal the deal as it were, but that's beside the point. D'Albert became my dearest friend. I'd never had any sort of friend before—freaks don't, as a rule—and I wasn't very good at it at first.

Yet we have loved each other all these years—sometimes like man and wife, sometimes like brother and sister, sometimes like Christ and the Magdalene.

Not faithfully, no. Not in the sense you mean. Far from it. What would be the point? We're not married—never could be. Men of his lineage don't marry the women they love. Certainly not if the women are common. Mind you, I'm not common in any other sense, but I am of ... how shall we put it politely? I am of more humble origin than he—not just born of the common people, but of the drunken, battle-scarred grotesques. Of the fairground and the romances. Of those pages of the Old Testament that you skip over late at night. Of the edges and dark corners.

And he—well, he will be a great man of France one day, almost as grand as d'Armagnac. He'll be a *duc*, you mark my words, living in one of those whopping chateaux with a puffy wife and a good hunting stable, going to Versailles for the season, keeping a mistress or two in Paris.

But at that time, he was a silly boy, a love-plundered, moon-gazing romantic—his head crammed with tales of pale young noblemen swooning over maidens disguised as men. He's the only man I've met, besides the King, who's read every word of *Amadis de Gaule*.

Books—I blame books. They create nothing but folly in men's brains. I've seen it many times. D'Albert was the most feeble-minded of all when it came to epics and fairy tales and endless romances. He rattled on and on about destiny, about lovers' paths crossing, about guiding stars—oh, I can't tell it all without blushing.

I had to kiss him, in the end, to shut him up.

I admired him—of course I did—but I didn't love him at first. My heart had so recently been damaged; my mind was elsewhere, miles away, in a convent in Provence where my other, finer self lay prostrate on cold marble begging for forgiveness from the likes of you, though God in His wisdom knows she'd done nothing wrong.

But d'Albert knew nothing of that, nothing of her—nothing, it must be said, of me. That didn't prevent him from dedicating his life to my happiness and a whole lot of other nonsense he'd learned from books. You see? The damned things are downright dangerous.

Eh? Yes, yes. I'm getting to that. You want to know about d'Albert—everyone always wants to know about d'Albert, as if—though perhaps it's true—he is the best part of me, and no matter what happens we return to each other, always.

He's allowed himself to be engaged to some cross-eyed simpleton now—rich and hideous, no doubt, though I've never actually laid eyes on the woman. Needless to say, I won't be invited to the wedding banquet. None of his old friends will be there, at the bride's request, presumably in case we help him escape. So the finest of men will live out his life in rural stupidity somewhere near Compiègne, well out of reach of bad influences like friendship.

He writes every month, mind you. I write back, silly letters full of nonsense about our youth. I don't send them. The Abbess has rules about that kind of thing. I keep them under the bed, in a satchel, tied up with bootlaces.

Could ... if I'm unable, for any reason, if I don't get to see him again, to talk—would you send them for me? The Abbess need never know. But to d'Albert—if I'm ... It would mean the world to me. To him.

Father, I will not beg you for absolution. Or forgiveness. But I do ask this of you—one small gift—a gesture.

Please?

He would reward you, if that's what you're after.

Of course. Your position. I understand. Ridiculous of me to ask. A moment of weakness, of madness—blame the fever. I thought, for just a moment, you were of humanity, not the priesthood.

My mistake.

So. D'Albert. Yes.

He hates me being here. He wrote me the most monstrous, hilarious letter months ago. Listen—I have it by my side.

Pay attention. I won't read it all, just the good parts. You will see what a fool, what a prince, I have for a friend. I asked him for advice—should I take the veil? I threatened to do so when I first arrived here. I'm not sure who was more horrified: the Abbess or d'Albert. I wondered if I should abandon my city life and offer myself up completely to the Lord, or just take a few restful months here as a guest, to recover my wits.

I may yet take the veil. Would you like that? Another soul gathered to the good?

Joseph, I fear, would not approve. He responded—listen to this.

Is it my religion, is it my heart, is it my kindness that you want to put to the test?

Ha! Poor boy. It's always he who is suffering. I am half dead, half mad with grief, but it's his poor heart that is tested. That was always his style. Born a brat, and never grew out of it. Bless him.

Don't you know that you can only achieve the happiness to which you aspire at the expense of my own, and that it will cost me my peace?

Doesn't it make you weep? With laughter, perhaps. But now we come to the point.

To consent to your plans, I have to detach myself from myself, must stifle all sense of sensitivity and delicacy; must finally speak to you what is quite opposite to the movement of my heart, and so immolate myself to please you.

Never has Reason so taken on Nature. So consider whether this sacrifice is worth the price. This is the greatest thing I've done, and could do, with my life.

Nicely put, don't you think? I was supposed to drop everything and rush to his side—or, at least, to some inn halfway, where we could meet in secret.

I wonder, sometimes, why I didn't do what he so clearly wished. But my heart was weakened, my soul so worn, so nearly threadbare, my body frail, and there was nowhere, nothing, for me but here.

All those people, all those lovers. But only one cares if I'm here, or alive, or not. Only one—or two or three—will sob, uncontrollably, for hours when he hears the news. Won't go out that evening, and possibly the next. Will flinch if he hears my name, my death, discussed in the salons.

Do they even hold salons in Compiègne? I imagine that so far north the repertoire only extends to pig shows and harvest dances. Nobody else there will know my name.

I should go to him. He'd look after me. I know it. I'd feel better. I nursed him once—twice. Then. He'd do the same for me. I'll get out of this bed and then it's only two days' ride—or a carriage—yes, I think so. Takes longer, of course, but I'm a little unwell. Call a carriage for me, would you? Ring for the maid. I must get dressed. My hair. Where are my riding boots? No—a carriage is better, that's right. Forgive me, Father, for I have sinned. I have. I confess everything. Now may I go? Where? Yes, a carriage. Tomorrow.

First I need to sleep.

Act 2, Scene 12

A minuet

D'ALBERT IS FEVERISH. THE wound has festered slightly. He's so wan now you can see the blood pulse sluggishly under the skin on his throat, his wrists. His friends won't come near him, except one. The young Duc d'Uzès, as dark as d'Albert is blond, stands by the bedside—loyal, bored witless and praying for a surgeon, for the coach expected to arrive any hour from Paris—anyone—to sort out this mess.

D'Uzès watches the dust float through a shaft of light. He offers wine, ale, a little broth.

D'Albert turns his head away. 'I want her. I need only her.'

It has been this way for hours. It's extremely tiresome.

'She's a sprite, Joseph,' says d'Uzès. 'A chimera. Long gone by now. Don't wear yourself out thinking about her.'

'She's a goddess.'

D'Uzès sighs. 'You're deluded. She almost killed you.'

'Yes!' D'Albert manages a smile. 'Have you ever seen the like?'

'Drink something,' says d'Uzès, holding a glass to his friend's lips. 'Please. Just a little.'

'Why? Oh, why?'

'You'll die if you don't, you fool.' He gives up, places the glass back on the tray, and slumps against the wall.

'What of it?'

'In the name of God!'

A knock on the door.

D'Uzès barks a welcome; hopes for the doctor—or one of the others to take a turn at this infernally stupid conversation. He jumps to his feet and opens the door.

It's her.

D'Uzès shifts so Julie can't see into the room. 'What do you want, mademoiselle?' he whispers.

She peers over his shoulder at the golden boy. 'I hear your young friend is ill—suffering.'

'Thanks to you.'

'Thanks also to his own insolence.'

'Did you come here to mock him?' D'Uzès notes her rough breeches, her homespun cloak. Some harridan from the provinces. How she managed that winning thrust he will never know. Luck. Sheer luck. 'Be off.'

'On the contrary,' Julie says, 'I came to enquire after his health. To see if there's anything—'

'You've done enough.'

The man in the bed cries out. 'Is it her? Has she come?'

Julie pushes d'Uzès aside. 'Yes. I am here.'

'At last.' D'Albert raises a thin hand towards her.

'Is there anything you need?'

'Only you,' says d'Albert. 'To know that you are close.'

'That I can offer.' Julie moves to the side of the bed as if she's known him all her life. He tries to rise but falls back.

D'Uzès is still standing by the open door. 'I've sent for a surgeon,' he tells her. 'From Paris. He'll be here today. Should be. Soon.'

But nobody's listening.

D'Albert stares up at an incomprehensibly beautiful face. An angel come to bear him to Heaven. 'Your name, mademoiselle? I beg you.'

'I am Julie-Émilie de Maupin.'

'What do your friends call you?'

'My friends? I don't know. My father calls me Julia.'

'Then I shall call you Émilie.'

She laughs. The sound is the music of paradise. Of summer. Of flowers. 'As you wish.'

Even smiling hurts, but he can't help it. 'And I am Joseph.'

'Enchanted.'

The woman places her hand on d'Albert's sweaty forehead, says something low and soft, and he closes his eyes.

'Thank you, d'Uzès,' he says. 'You may go.'

D'Uzès slams the door. They don't care.

Act 2, Scene 13

Recitative

WE SPENT TWO WEEKS in that room. Together. The surgeon bustled in and out every so often. The maid brought meals and wine. Good wine, it was, too. Hadn't eaten that well since—since before I met Clara. Great haunches of beef, dripping with fat. Whole loaves of bread. We were insatiable, d'Albert and I. Always were. Always will be. That's just how it is.

He healed quickly. He claimed it was my nursing but I suspect he only wanted to get better so he could—well, never mind.

You don't need to know that.

I know that's the part you secretly want to hear, everyone does, but I'm not in the mood. All you need to know is that after a couple of weeks of being shut up in a room with one person I grew restless. Needed air. Sunshine. Music.

D'Albert says I dumped him by the side of the road. It's a nice story, but it isn't true. He was happily tucked up in his bed, smiling in his sleep. I sat by the fire, watching him, wondering if that was it—if he was it—if I should just allow myself to be … I don't know. Adored. Pampered.

Like a mistress.

Before I even knew I'd done it, I'd packed and saddled and set out on the east road. Two days after that, I met Thévenard.

Yes, indeed. The great Thévenard, the legendary Thévenard. Gabriel-Vincent Thévenard, the voice, the star. Except he wasn't—not then. He was just a boy on the run, on the road to Paris.

He was big, even then—huge, with a booming voice—a fine voice, really fine. He has great depth of tone but absolutely no depth of expression. I've told him this. He can't whisper. Ever. It is impossible for him. He shouts, or sings, and laughs. He declaims. Always has, as long as I've known him, and it's been many years now. On stage, it doesn't matter—in fact, the crowd loves it—loves him. But up close it can get very tiring. He wears us all out.

When we first met, I found it amusing. He made me laugh and—you can imagine the state I was in, what with Clara and the law, and then d'Albert wanting me within arm's reach every second—laughter was both rare and comforting. He had the shiniest hair, I remember, and a moustache that he twirled into points, and he fiddled with it when he was thinking. Which wasn't often. He was as swarthy and strong as d'Albert was pale and wiry. Chalk and cheese, as they say. Yet I met them both within a few weeks and have loved them both, wholeheartedly, ever since. As they have loved me—do love me, still, to this day, though we've led each other on many treacherous paths and wild rides over the years. They hated each other for most of that time, but that's another story.

I was seventeen or so when we first met—so young! And I had already endured many of my greatest trials by that tender age.

You should feel sorry for me. But you don't.

Scribble, scribble. Scratch, scratch. In God's name, if I had the strength to snatch that pen from your hand and dash it against the wall, I would. Even that is beyond me now. For the moment, at any rate. But you never know. Be on your guard, Father, at all times. You have been warned.

Now. Thévenard. Bless him. We met in Rouen, late in those crazed and dusty weeks. He'd stormed out of his father's cookhouse in Orléans, vowing to make his mark on the world. And me—well, I hardly know now where I wandered and what I did, and yet in that short time I met the three men who would alter forever the course of my life: Maréchal, d'Albert and, finally, Thévenard. Who can say there is no such thing as fate? Had I not fled Avignon, had I not abandoned my love to her own destiny, had I not sold my soul for a thousand *livres*, I might never have met any of them. I might have been a nun all my life, instead of just pretending, then and now, to be so.

You see? Now I think of it, perhaps I was right, after all— or, rather, perhaps I was not as wrong as I have always thought myself.

No. No. Stop.

This is a conversation I've had many times. Although usually there's nobody listening. This is how it goes. I am in anguish. I am riven by remorse. Then slowly I talk myself out of it, convince myself that destiny took my life in its hands, until at last I feel as if Clara would have wished to be left alone in that inn near Aix, as if she must have forgiven me many years ago for any imagined slight, as if my conscience was clear—has been, all this time.

But not now. Not at the last.

I can't hide it from myself, nor from you.

If I was lucky enough to meet my mentor and my two dearest friends in the following months, then that is all it was—luck. It was a good grace, a gift I did nothing to deserve. Quite the opposite. I should have given thanks on my knees every day for that providence, but I haven't.

I should've sought her out and begged for forgiveness. Instead I'm telling you, and what good will that do me? You write it down, yes, yes, scribble, scratch—but nobody will ever read these words—she will never read them, and that's all that matters.

I should have told Thévenard how grateful I was for his companionship, for those long evenings of drunken laughter, for the songs and the stories—but instead we fought like tigers—or maybe kittens—on and off for years. But he knows I love him. I'm sure of it. Only friends as fast as we are could scrap and spat the way we have. We have nearly come to blows many times—we would have, except he knows I will beat him, and he is, among his many charms, an utter coward.

But there were times—my God! I could have picked him up and shaken his teeth from his skull. Or thrown him through a wall—I've seen it done to someone once, by a drunken *mousquetaire* in Saint-Germain-des-Prés. He was upset. You can't blame him. A gaming dispute, I think. An allegation of cheating. Cards. Although the man he threw came off worse. Dead.

Yes, unfortunate. The *mousquetaire* was in all sorts of trouble over it, too, even though it was the other fellow who had been cheating.

You see? I never did that to anyone, tempted though I may have been. Mind you, Gabriel was a heavy man—it might have taken two of me to throw him anywhere at all. But sometimes fury lends you unimagined strength.

Once—*Thésée*, I think it was—I was Minerve and he was annoying. Can't remember why, but there was always something. We niggled, that's the word. Played tricks on each other. Invented new and nasty names. Spread vile stories backstage. That sort of thing. We laughed ourselves silly afterwards.

So we met in Rouen, as I said, got drunk, sang a hundred songs until the night watch threatened us with the dungeons, and so we fell into bed. From that moment we were friends— lovers, yes, briefly—get that look off your face—but mostly we were comrades. As my father used to say of his old *mousquetaires*, comrades in arms. Truly we were. We made a pact—to sing in Paris, just as Maréchal had wanted. We promised each other we'd light up the city from the Tuileries to the Bastille.

So we did.

But before I could keep that vow, I had to attend to some business.

Act 2, Scene 14

A duet

D'ARMAGNAC'S ASLEEP. ALONE. THAT'S NOVEL.
She walks in. Just like the old days. Wrenches aside the silk curtains around the bed.

'You!' He loves to shout. She'd forgotten.

'Yes. Me.'

'How did you get in here?' D'Armagnac reaches for his bell but she knocks it out of reach.

'The usual gate. I thought you'd be pleased.'

'On the contrary, I thought you'd be dead by now.'

'Wishes don't always come true.'

'Burned at the stake.'

'Let's talk about that.' She perches on the edge of the bed, long legs dangling down.

'A fitting end for you.'

'Now, now. I did what you wanted. I left her—there, in Aix.'

It's the first time she's said the words. It sounds like

someone else's voice. Perhaps it is. Can't say the name, though—maybe never again. Instead she grabs the bed covers and pulls them back.

D'Armagnac scrabbles for a robe and pulls it around his shoulders. 'You're a sorceress.'

She snorts. 'You're hilarious.'

'A seducer of innocents.'

'You taught me well.'

'You were never innocent.' He laughs, but there's little humour in it.

'You were always deluded,' she says. She notices for the first time his mottled skin, his thin hair, the blue veins in his calves. Older than her father. Always was. And more brittle. Since she saw him last, she has grown used to the feel of younger skin, to the thick black hair on Thévenard's chest, to bodies free of battle scars and sun spots—to Clara's hand soft in hers. To people with teeth. She looks away.

'You are still hunted all over France,' d'Armagnac says, spittle in the corners of his mouth.

'Not me. Some poor bastard called d'Aubigny.'

'So I heard.'

'But thanks to you, I have a married name, and it is finally of some use to me. Mademoiselle d'Aubigny may as well be dead.'

D'Armagnac leans forward. 'They will chase you, no matter what you call yourself.'

'I'm Madame de Maupin. And I'm alive.'

'So far.'

She grins. She's forgotten what it's like to talk to a clever man. 'Make sure of it.'

'Me?'

'Speak to the King. Ask him to call off La Reynie and his dogs.'

'Don't be ridiculous.'

'You will do it,' she says in a soft voice. She won't beg. Not him.

'Why?'

'Lie back, you stupid man, and allow me to remind you.'

He does.

Act 2, Scene 15

Recitative

D'ARMAGNAC DIDN'T WANT ME. He simply couldn't bear the shame of being known as the man whose mistress preferred a woman.

He had a quiet word to the King, who probably laughed himself silly, just as d'Armagnac feared. But no matter—it worked. We heard no more of that nonsense about burning me at the stake, though at the time, in some ways, it might have been a blessed release.

Since Monsieur d'Aubigny never really existed, there was nobody to stand trial—you can't prosecute a phantom. The whole affair dissolved into vapour.

Except.

There are some scars we carry that nobody ever sees. I believe that. Do you?

We all have them, I'm sure. Sins that can never be forgiven. Hurts that will not heal. Pains that plague us in the dark hours—that mark our souls forever.

And scorch our hearts? Yes, perhaps.

It's true that mine was a little scalded. But not in the way you think.

I kept my word—no man could claim otherwise. No matter how great the temptation—how utter the agony.

I can't tell you how many letters I've written and thrown away, how many nights I spent planning another escape. With her. Whenever I had a little cash. Whenever I saw a blonde head covered in black lace. Every spring.

Every autumn.

But I had promised d'Armagnac and, in effect, the King.

I knew, too, somewhere deep in me, that she would never ... Will she forgive me in the end?

I don't ask for atonement. How could I?

You misunderstand me, Father. Those things I don't repent. Those crimes you list in that horrified whisper aren't sinful to me. Have you understood nothing?

You, with your dirty hem and your hands clutching the Bible to your chest as if I'm about to eat you. Don't flatter yourself. I'd spit you out, bones and all, skull sucked dry, and not even notice. I'd tread you into the ground, little man, under my boots. I'd crush your spine with one hand and throw you aside. Or I might have—once. Now, God help me, all I can do is raise an eyebrow and enjoy the spectacle of you blushing and spluttering at every second word.

You make it worse for yourself. You know that, don't you?

Don't distract me. In fact, don't speak. Write it down, yes, just as I say it. Don't alter a word, or God will strike you dead. I swear it. If he doesn't, I will. Don't stain these memories— they are sacred, in every sense of the word, to me, and I hope, I pray, to her. Still. I hold her face in my mind like a painting, like a statue, a church window—the weeping Virgin, perhaps. I hear her words, feel her hand in mine.

O, how it aches.

I didn't know, then, that she would haunt me all these years.

No. I'm lying. I did know—even then—even as I left her there, to her fate, and rode off to find my own. Of course I did. But did the weight of guilt, of knowing, slow me down?

Not for long.

But there was no going back. Until now.

Never retreat. That's what the great masters teach—the finest swordsmen never take a step back.

But where's the skill in that, eh? Where's the play? Fencing isn't jousting; it's gambling. It's war. Sometimes a strategic defeat in one battle can win you the empire—entice your opponent into a blunder, into a show of arrogance that leaves him open.

Wide open.

That's the only secret to my success, in case you were wondering, though, to be honest, you don't look like much of a sportsman. But there you have it. Otherwise I am merely a fine fencer—one of the best in Europe, of course, and the greatest swordswoman in history, but my secret is simple. The men all think they can defeat me. Often they refuse even the most basic courtesies due to an opponent. In their arrogance lies my strength.

One or two steps backwards at a critical point and they think they've got it won.

Then I strike.

Time after time. For years. It worked so well I got tired of winning, tired of their complacency and mine. I promise you, I have never sought anyone's death but my own.

I tried to make things more interesting. Let their blade a little nearer to my precious face or my vile heart.

D'Albert said I wished for death. Perhaps it was true. He'd know better than me. I'd certainly have preferred a blade through the eye than these festering night sweats.

There were times, indeed, when I might have welcomed it, when it might have been worth the ignominy of losing—just to feel the burn of the blade and then nothing.

But somehow I never quite managed it. Some fragment of pride refused to allow a clumsy brute the honour of taking my life, or some sudden panic would wrench me back into the moment just in time.

What?

Rubbish. The hand of God had nothing to do with it. It was my hand—this true, genius hand that now trembles and plucks stupidly at the bedclothes—that saved me. And perhaps a nascent cowardice. Pride. That's all. Sin saved me, in other words. Ha!

Eh?

Who are you to tell me what I can or can't say? Never mind about my blasted soul. Eternal life—what good is that to me? You can't have it both ways, Father. Your Church ignored and—at worst—vilified me all my life. You can't expect reconciliation now, not without forgiveness.

I'm not asking God for forgiveness, you fool! Though the time for that is near. I'm talking about my own. Shall I forgive you and your kind for the trespasses against me? For the blasphemies against love? The pettiness, the pomposity? Will I ever forgive you all—forgive myself for believing a word of it? That's the question here.

It's not yet clear to me.

But I'll sleep on it, as they say. Or, in my case, lie awake and stare at the darkness and wonder about it—all of it.

Thank you, Father, I feel quite myself again. This talk has done me good, although you—if you don't mind me saying so—look a little the worse for wear.

Until tomorrow, then.

Act 2, Scene 16

A duet

THE ROOM IS AS FINE as the drawing room in the Hôtel d'Armagnac but much more tasteful. Windows that stretch from floor to ceiling. A view to a garden. Orange trees on a terrace. Walls the colour of egg yolks. A gilded harp in one corner.

The girl is announced.

'Madame de Maupin.'

There's a woman in a chair by the fireplace. She stands, takes a few steps forward.

'Thank you, Alphonse. Some wine, I think.'

A nod of the head. Almost a bow.

'Certainly, ma'am.'

The Comtesse is no longer young. But still beautiful—everyone says so, even her enemies. Still brilliant. Still—it's undeniable—alluring. A little vicious, perhaps, but who isn't nowadays?

She raises a perfect hand towards her guest. 'Thank you for coming.'

'You left a message.'

'Indeed. Please, come in. Take a seat.'

Julie doesn't move. She's trying not to be impressed by the room, the woman. Blue silk. A soft blonde wig. A little rouge. The gleam of a pearl against pale skin. She blinks away a sensation too fleeting, too exquisite, to be borne.

'Did you want something?'

'I'm enchanted to meet you at last.'

A pause. It's awkward. The Comtesse isn't used to that. For some reason all her usual pleasantries elude her.

The girl crosses her arms. 'How do you even know who I am?'

A smile. 'Don't be silly, my dear. Everyone has heard of you.'

'I hope not.'

'It can't be helped, I'm afraid. You are famous—or, at least, you soon will be.'

'I don't think—'

The door opens. They say nothing but watch while three footmen pour wine and put some cheese and sweet grapes on a table.

The girl sits. At last. She even allows the Comtesse to sit beside her. Fiddly, uncomfortable furniture. The men in the tight silk breeches and the gold braid leave. Silence.

The Comtesse smiles and tries again. 'I understand you have been accepted into the Académie?'

'Yes.'

'They must work you hard, there. Francine, I've heard, is a monster.'

'He's all right,' Julie says, though that's not entirely true. 'He wants us to be successful, that's all.'

'He is exacting.'

'So he should be. He is a master.'

The Comtesse tilts her head to one side to gaze more attentively at her guest. It is, she has been told, her most becoming pose. 'It must be difficult—so many new things to learn.'

'There are harder things in life than learning to sing.'

'Of course.'

The girl senses the fragrance of honeysuckle, of face powder, of desire. She takes a breath and hears it shudder in her throat. Holds her glass up to her lips. She thinks she might be blushing.

'This is good wine.'

'Thank you.'

'Lovely house.'

'I'm so glad you like it. I hope you will come to visit me often, come to think of it as your home.'

The girl laughs. Her teeth are perfect. 'Comtesse, this is nothing like any home I've ever had.'

'But you grew up, I understand, at the palace.'

'You understand an awful lot, don't you?'

It's the Comtesse's turn to laugh. 'I admit I have made it my business to find out as much as I can about you.'

'Everything?'

'The important matters. Your escapades are many and—'

'I hope not.'

'Fascinating.'

'Not to me.' Now Julie takes a gulp of wine—too much. A drop splashes on her breeches.

The Comtesse pretends she hasn't seen it. 'You are a remarkable creature, my dear. I wonder if you have any idea how extraordinary you are?'

The girl shrugs. It seems not.

'Comte d'Armagnac is very fortunate—more than he realises,' says the Comtesse. 'I hope he treasures you.'

Another shrug. She's been told to say nothing—to anyone—about d'Armagnac. She owes him that, at least.

The Comtesse goes on. She can hear herself trying too hard but it's impossible to stop. 'I hear you have already made a conquest or two?'

'Is that what it is? Conquest? As if we are at war?'

The Comtesse's laughter tinkles like a rich man's purse. 'Of course, my dear. You are a fighter. You should do very well.'

'And after the battle?'

'Ah. The peace negotiations.' She smiles. 'Often the loveliest phase—and the most lucrative.'

'I've never been good at that part. I'm not a diplomat.'

The Comtesse moves imperceptibly closer. 'Perhaps that is something I could teach you.'

'I tend to follow my heart,' says Julie.

'How successful has that proved—forgive me if I extend the metaphor just a little—as a strategy?'

'Sometimes it has gone very well.' Julie pauses. 'But as a strategy, it could do with a little tweaking. It has led, sometimes, to an unfortunate state of affairs.'

'You have suffered?'

'Others have suffered. One other. Someone dear to me.'

The Comtesse knows when to be silent. Waits. A few breaths. There are so many ways to make a conquest, after all. They do not all require words. She shifts slightly so that her bosom—still so attractive, even at thirty—can be more readily admired.

'The wonder of it, really, is that we haven't heard about you earlier. D'Armagnac must have kept you well-hidden.'

Julie tries to keep her gaze on the windows, the paintings, the rug. Anything. 'I've been out of town.'

'So I hear. But now you are back among us and readying yourself to appear on the greatest stage in Europe. Are you nervous?'

'A little.'

'Are you ready?' The Comtesse turns away for a moment, and Julie's eyes flicker over her shoulders, her throat, that soft place inside her elbows.

'Not yet,' Julie says. 'But I will be.'

'I have no doubt of it. You will be a sensation.'

'That, Comtesse, is the plan.' She grins.

'In some circles, you already are,' says the Comtesse. 'There are rumours, surely you've heard them, that you are descended from the ancients—the most perfect being of all: part man, part woman.'

'A hermaphrodite?' Julie splutters into her wine. 'That's what they're saying?'

'You deny it?'

'Of course.'

'But you understand it is the ideal, the wonderful twinning of every good aspect of male and female?'

'I've read my classics, Comtesse. I have seen the statues in the palace. But that is not what I am.'

The Comtesse clasps her hands. 'How delightful. How utterly—'

'I grew up with men.'

146

'Even in your heart?' She leans forward, her eyes on Julie's face, but Julie will not look at her.

'I know nothing but men,' she says instead. 'I'm not very good with women—or so I have learned.'

'Then it is time you knew more about your own kind. I shall speak to d'Armagnac.'

'No. Don't.'

'But he would want you, I'm sure, to know how to wear a gown, how to do your hair, on occasion.'

'I don't need—' There is something like panic in Julie's voice.

'Please understand me,' says the Comtesse in her most soothing voice. 'Nobody wishes you to be anything other than your delightful self.'

'Comtesse, I am grateful, but really—'

'Nonsense. I am only too pleased. Truly. I feel as if I am but another of Francine's assistants, helping to prepare you for your debut.'

'I already have enough to learn.'

'I can teach you simple pleasures—the world of a woman,' says the Comtesse. 'I promise it will not be onerous. I think—I am very certain—you desire to know about certain matters, even if you do not realise it.'

'But—'

It's a thing of wonder to Julie—the silencing effect of one warm hand placed gently on her thigh.

'I promise you, my dear, you will not regret it.'

Their eyes meet for the first time. Something inside Julie softens—hardens—cries out in recognition—collapses in tears—laughs aloud.

'Very well,' she says. 'I am yours.'

'I knew you would be.'

Act 2, Scene 17

Recitative

SHE WAS AS GOOD AS HER WORD, you'll be pleased to know. She did speak to d'Armagnac—no doubt in that subtle way she had, that I grew to know so well, although I could never quite master it. Nobody could refuse her slightest whim.

So we met every afternoon in her boudoir. In that sweet room, heavy with the fragrance of tuberoses and jonquils, she brought me into the embrace of womanhood. She taught me—ah! So much.

Yes, Father, that's right. She was a corrective influence on my young soul. Exactly so. D'Armagnac approved. So do you—I can see it in your face. Good, good. For some strange reason, I want you to think well of me—of her. My Comtesse. Bless her. I'm satisfied, then. So we are all content with that story. That's something. We're making progress, you and I. At last.

I was initiated into a new world of women—of sensation. She did teach me about fabric and slippers, and all the latest hairstyles at Versailles, and how to make conversation—to laugh like a courtesan instead of a stableboy—and ... la! She taught me many other pleasures we need not dwell on just now.

But don't imagine it was all civil intercourse—wigs and corsetry. Oh, no. It was training, no less exacting than that of a postulant in one of these great houses of God—although, I grant you, a lot more fashionable.

All the time—every morning, every evening—I rehearsed for the Opéra, and for the world. She prepared me, just as Francine did, for my debut—for my ascension. I was plucked and primed, dressed up and fussed over, powdered and polished. Between the two of them, my voice grew hoarse and rough from use, instead of finely tuned and refined. The Comtesse ordered tailors and bootmakers and jewellers to attend me in her boudoir—I believe, to this day, that d'Armagnac paid for it all, bless his sentimental soul.

She invited a few friends for supper once—all women, all young and pretty—but I could barely speak. Ever since, I've had a policy of smiling a great deal and appearing nonchalant under such circumstances. It usually works. After all, most people prefer to hear their own voice above anyone else's, and a silent listener is surely the best company. Don't you think?

Be quiet. Who asked for your opinion?

Now you've interrupted my thoughts.

What was I saying?

Yes, of course. The Comtesse. Once I grew a little more accomplished, she escorted me to a salon, to practise my arts—or so she said, but I realised a few moments after we arrived that I was merely the curiosity for the evening, presented like a bonbon on a platter, to be admired and somehow—I couldn't shake the feeling—possessed.

Not like that, Father. Don't shudder so. I was simply trying to describe a sensation. Although there were times ... but that's beside the point. The salon. Don't try to distract me again.

D'Armagnac was there, with his wife. He pretended he didn't know me, but stared at me a great deal. I saw, for the first time, how deeply everyone bowed to him, offered him a seat, a compliment, a pretty face to admire. To me, he'd always been the boss of the stables, then later the old man in bed slippers. But there he was, in great state, pompous as the King himself, powdered and posing like a maiden at a court ball.

And the Comtesse? She watched it all. Smiled. Knew, I think, that I had left him and his bed and his benefaction well behind me. Knew, I'm certain, that I was now her creature, not his. Perhaps d'Armagnac realised it, too.

I don't know.

But I felt, that night, that Paris would be mine; that the city—I don't deny it, even if it sounds like conceit—would adore me.

That's what she told me, my Comtesse. She would stroke my hair and hold me to her bosom and whisper it to me. I believed her, too. I could feel it.

One day, the city would be mine. Yes.

But in a way, it always has been. It's my blood. My bones. How I miss it.

Have you ever been to Paris?

Seen the moon rise beyond the city walls? The fishing boats set sail in the river? The markets? Heard the tinkers and oyster girls crying out their wares? You should go, once in your life. You should die there. So should I, come to think of it. Everyone should. No better place.

In Paris, you are surrounded by people. Old women wasting away before your eyes. *Mousquetaires* brawling in the taverns. Everyone living their lives in the streets, in the courtyards. To this day, I'm as curious as I was as a child—I peer through windows in the evenings, after the candles are lit, into gardens, through half-open doors. I watch the flower-sellers tying nosegays. The wreckers pulling down old buildings. The stonemasons building the new.

Don't get me wrong. Like my father, I don't approve of some of the latest developments—all those new mansions, those triumphal arches. Not at all. We are great, it's true, but we are not Rome. Louis is not Caesar. We are not gods—not even beloved of the gods, or how could there be such plagues of sweating sickness and typhus and the children dying of hunger in the streets? I've seen them. Many times. Fed them, too—not out of any sort of piety, but because we are bound together, the orphans, the misfits. We recognise each other. Although they are disgusting little creatures.

Yes, the city is filth and sickness. But still, I love to wander the streets just before dawn. Always have. The city is a different world at that hour. Night noises give way to day—babies cry, mothers sing to them, bakers pound dough, dogs and pigs rifle through refuse in the streets; you can hear roosters, the night watch on patrol, the ferrymen. Notaries take breakfast in the coffee house. Drunks wake up. There are carts filled with fish or geese or apples from up north. Shutters creak open. Church bells.

Without all the people, without horses and wagons, you can see the poetry in the buildings, glimpses along an alleyway of ships in the Seine. If you look up—it astonishes me how few people do that; they're all too anxious about stepping in something foul—but when the morning light reaches the rooftops of Paris in the autumn, there is no place closer to God. Look up, away from the rats in the gutters and the puddles of horse piss, and you'll see, instead, the silhouette of Notre-Dame de Paris against the stars. The sublime rising from shadows. Just like me.

You may think me sacrilegious, even corrupt. Well, well. Time will tell. Not long now. But that cathedral, that holy place, that is where my soul belongs. There was a time—one moment—when just the sight of it stopped me from throwing myself in the river. If the city was my stage, the cathedral is my mother—or, at least, the only one I've known. Even now, if I could, I'd crawl back there, into its dark corners, like a whipped dog—it beckons me, hides and comforts me in its immensity, its stained-glass glory, its candles and statues.

For a part of me is pure. You must believe that.

A part of me is just like Jeanne, Maid of Orléans. She is my saint, my own icon, she of the sure arm and the pure heart. I've done nothing so worthy with my life—I haven't saved France or fought in battles or led the people to hopefulness. But there are the visions. She whispers to me. Yes, she does. I become her, and she enters my heart, this fragile heart. I carry her likeness around my throat, always. It was my mother's. See? Don't tell the Abbess. It's all I have of my mother. Whoever she was. One of the few truly precious things, now, that I possess.

Here's Jeanne, her hair about her fine face—look at the determination in those eyes—the sword raised high. I pray to her memory, and I believe one day she will be sainted by the Church, recognised by the people of France as the saviour she tried to be, just as she is my refuge now, in the darkness.

Since I was little, she has been my strength—Jeanne, and that cathedral on the island. She rallies the hearts of the misbegotten, the queer, the sons of the soil—a pinprick of light in the French soul.

For we have had our dark moments, Paris and I.

What am I doing here, so far from home? God help me. I can almost see it, smell it, hear it. The coffee houses and pickpockets, the alchemists' shops and the crowds and the tailors' apprentices smoking on the quay. Students crowding around the booksellers' stalls near the Sorbonne. Windmills on the hill. As if—almost as if I was there. As if I could reach out and touch the stones of the cathedral, the bark on the trees in the Place Royale. As I once could. Then.

Then—as I was saying. Yes. Sometimes I do need to be guided back to my story. But you are really quite relentless, do you know that?

Very well. I learned so much in those first few months back in Paris. In the Comtesse's boudoir. At the Académie. In the streets and the salons and the fairgrounds. It was as if the world had been made anew. The city seemed to be overflowing with perfume and enchanting women and magic. Filled with music—with songs. And, oh, how I sang.

Act 2, Scene 18

Divertissement

THERE'S A NEW SINGER. An old song. The crowds are always huge for *Cadmus et Hermione*—it is, after all, Lully's first, greatest, *tragédie*. But now there's this new girl, this Pallas Athéna.

It's dark inside the Palais-Royal. People mill about the theatre, shout to their friends, wave over everyone's heads, bow, gossip, drink a toast or two. Cutpurses work their way through the crowd. Someone hails an oyster seller. There's a cheer when the music begins, but nobody listens to the Prologue. They never do. The guards near the orchestra thump their spears on the floorboards for silence. Nobody listens to them, either.

They like new blood, the Paris crowd, in the same way a butcher admires a herd driving through town to the market. They call out, hoping for an off note, a nervous waver in the upper register. They pray for a missed cue, a dropped flower— even better, a crooked wig.

But most of all they wish for that rare, heavenly moment—that thud in the chest, that prickle of the scalp, that glimpse of perfection that brings you to tears, to laughter, to worship.

And then she appears. Descends. A creature from the heavens, from a fresco, from legend. A goddess. An Amazon. A statue come to life—but not marble, not bronze. Auburn hair and majestic bearing. Fine wrists, strong arms, her throat the colour of cream, her voice dripping like nectar from Olympus—rich and pure and certain.

The goddess smiles, she weeps, she storms. She sings. Oh! She soars above mortals, looks down on their perfidies with disdain. She changes the world. Forever. And that's just the first act.

The voice is not a true soprano. There's a little more depth, more emotion. The range perhaps slightly lower than is usual here in Paris—it takes a few moments to get used to it, but then—its beauty, its sheer power, carries them to the heavens—beyond. She is immortal—she is Artemis, she is Aphrodite, she is—who is she?

As she leaves the stage for a scene or two, murmurs sweep the theatre. The other singers can barely make themselves heard over the din. In his box, the *directeur*, Francine, smiles to himself. She may be worth the risk, after all, this wild child of the gutters. That magnificent voice is surely a lesson from God to never, ever, judge the voice by the clothing.

Consider his crew of misfits and angels: Le Rochois, Lully's greatest ornament, still as beloved and graceful as ever; Duménil, the fool, the lazy, sly prick—a cook, for God's sake, but such a pure high tenor; pretty Fanchon with her suitors and her reliable soprano; and now this new fellow, Thévenard, and his low tones that tremble with pathos and authority; and the girl—the tall girl with the breeches and the sword, with her majesty, and her smile, and her range matching any of those Italians.

His wife nudges him. 'Who is she, your new Pallas Athéna? Everyone wants to know.'

'She, my dear, is the future of French opera.'

At the first interval, the foyer is filled with men shouting, laughing, a little light-headed and they're not sure why, but something is different here, now; something has changed forever tonight, in this theatre—something to do with the new singers—Thévenard, the baritone ... and the girl. Who is the girl?

The men elbow each other out of the way to get closer to the young Comte d'Albert, who, it is said, is her lover. A rumour washes from one side of the theatre to the other— they fought, with bare blades. She nearly killed him. She dresses as a man. She slaughtered four men in Avignon. Or in Marseille. There was a girl. A nun. But surely not? She was d'Armagnac's mistress. One of the many. She is the protégée of the Comtesse. Or perhaps the baritone's wife. Or perhaps the illegitimate daughter of the Duc d'——. All over the Palais-Royal there are young men who grew up with her in the stables, in the dormitories, who have lost to her in bouts in the fencing halls. They boast now of her wit, her skill, her legs.

The King is not present tonight—nobody expects him; he rarely leaves Versailles nowadays, such a pity, though at least you don't have to behave—but his brother, Monsieur, is here, in the royal box, as always. Wouldn't miss it for the world, even on a normal night—with the tight press of silk-clad bodies and the candles and the shouting and the piss buckets and the painted scenery and all the world present—but tonight, he knows, he feels it, is not a normal night.

Something is happening here. Something strange and marvellous. The birth of a new world, a new star—two of them. The baritone is sensational, but the girl—the girl is a creature such as nobody has ever seen—heard—before. Everyone talks at once, not bothering to whisper—asking her name, her history. She sang in Marseille—she fought with d'Albert—that one? The swordswoman? Can it be possible?

When he has heard enough speculation from the gorgeous young men around him, Monsieur sends to the *directeur*'s box for an answer.

'Is it true, then? This new girl? She is the infamous duellist?'

Francine bows low to his patron. 'I cannot vouch for her history, Your Grace. She does wear a sword to rehearsal, but I have never seen her use it.'

'And breeches?'

'Yes, Your Grace.'

The young men further along the bench snigger.

'Extraordinary.' Monsieur silences his entourage with a look. 'And her training?'

'With Gautier in Marseille.' Gautier can take the blame if required.

'The tone is unusual.'

'But not unpleasant?' asks Francine.

'Not at all.' Monsieur smiles at the memory of her first few notes.

'She is an authentic *bas-dessus*, Your Grace—what the Italians would call contralto. Although, as is the case tonight, she can sing as a soprano if required.'

'I am familiar with the contralto, of course.' He waves a hand at the crowds in the *parterre*. 'But I fear many of these barbarians are not.'

'They are shocked,' says Francine. 'It's only natural. But I hope they will come to appreciate it. Indeed I hope one day to showcase her true range.'

'Nothing Italian, I hope.'

'Of course not, Your Grace. But we will have to find—or write—something appropriate.'

Monsieur nods his assent, without which nothing so radical, so innovative, could occur. The King, they both know, would never agree to such a thing.

'Her name?'

'Madame de Maupin, Your Grace. Julie-Émilie de Maupin.'

'She is married?'

'So I understand, although I have never sighted the husband.'

'A lucky man.'

'Perhaps. Or a lonely one.'

Monsieur nods. Francine is dismissed. He thinks in retrospect he should have asked her more questions about her life—her real life. His guts lurch—he has no idea what secrets she may have, what crimes she may have committed with that damned sword, and now everyone will want to know everything about her. Perhaps he should locate the husband. Buy her a few gowns.

He listens to the whispers, the gossip.

Mystery, he decides, may be the most dignified option. And the safest.

On the short walk back to his own box he is stopped a dozen

times. The same questions. The same answers. He gives them nothing more.

He decides that tomorrow he will start a dozen conflicting rumours and spread them across Paris. By nightfall the city will be in confusion, and long may it stay that way. Or perhaps—he listens to the uproar—perhaps he will not need to.

Back on stage, the great Le Rochois is fighting the crowd, the noise—they are always silent for her, but not tonight. Now she feels what the others must experience every evening—struggling to make her voice heard above the chatter, the movement of bodies. Nobody is listening to her—to her!—Le Rochois! They are waiting, restless, for something—for someone.

They are waiting for the other one.

The girl stands backstage in her goddess's gown, breastplate and helmet. She will reappear, flying in from the painted clouds, near the end of this act. In the meantime, she watches the others sing. She notices how Le Rochois stands with her chin up and one foot slightly forward—each tilt of the head, every movement of the fingers, is precise and graceful. She sees that lovely blonde soprano wink at a dandy in the crowd. The chandeliers drip wax on the canvas. Ballet dancers stand in lines in the wings, stretching their calf muscles, ready for the next *divertissement*. Fans flutter in the dark like seagulls. People whisper. Hop from foot to tired foot. Push each other out of the way. A fight starts up the back. A flower-seller in the corner sings along, a few beats too late. Hundreds of faces upturned, lit, expectant, just beyond the pit.

Thévenard, bless him, sings like a man possessed, like a man in love, like a god. He stands a head taller than everyone else on stage, distinguished even in sandals and a blue turban, his muscles oiled. Eye makeup dribbles inky tears down his face.

She watches everything—Le Rochois winning back the crowd with her voice, her eyes, her majesty—Thévenard storming onto the stage as if he was born to it. She grins. Loves him for just a moment. No. He's trying too hard. The crowd does not yet worship him. But they will. One day. His gestures are too wild, the voice stupendous but not quite disciplined enough. He has a great deal yet to learn.

He knows it. So does she. That is their strength, perhaps. They have failings, rough, untrimmed edges, and yet—raw as they are—they are both magnificent. And this is only the beginning.

Someone touches her arm, gently, pleading. It is time. They help her up onto the machine—only a real goddess could be comfortable in all this drapery, this armour. She holds on tight as the stagehands winch her up high into the flies, as if she was nothing but a piece of scenery.

The stagehands all adore her. She is like them—has won them over with bottles of wine and lewd stories. She knows them; they know her. They motion to her. She kisses a gold chain around her wrist and mutters to herself, to God, to a lost girl at the other end of France. Nobody hears her. She holds the sword of justice aloft. Raises her chin a little. She is ready.

The clouds part. The goddess descends. The world will never be the same.

Le Rochois watches her through narrowed eyes. Fanchon stops singing and blows her a kiss. The whole world applauds. Everyone shouts at once. She has to wait a few minutes to hear the music above the racket. The orchestra stops playing. There's no point.

She waits. Regal. The other players wait, too, less happily, except for Thévenard, whose character is supposed to be looking stricken at this point but instead has a silly grin on his face. He loves her. Forever.

She raises a hand—waits for complete silence. Nobody—not even Le Rochois—not even Francine—has ever seen such a thing. Then she waves to the orchestra and they begin.

It's her moment, the zenith, the minute or two in all eternity that will remain golden and dazzling no matter what lies waiting in the years ahead. She feels the paint on her face melting, pain where the armour has blistered her skin, fear in her bowels, the old scars, the bruises, the despair. She breathes the black smoke of the tallow candles, the stench of sweat and piss and unwashed costumes.

She watches it all, feels it all, breathes it all in, and spits it out as a song.

Again those glorious, warm tones fill the air and she is reborn. She flies across the stage and everyone in the place is on their feet—even the people with seats—even Monsieur—even Francine—even—especially—the Comtesse and d'Albert and d'Armagnac and an old *mousquetaire* down the back of the *parterre*, who wipes tears from his face and leaves before the Epilogue so that his daughter never knows he was there, never hears him whisper that he always knew she would conquer Paris, somehow, and now she has.

Eventually the orchestra stops playing, and the ballet and chorus take to the stage for their bows, and the players, one by one, line up to be adored, but not her—not her—because she is different, she has always been different, and just this once she will make the most of it.

In the final moments, just when the crowd looks like it will tear down the theatre if she doesn't appear, the painted clouds open again and there she is, the goddess in the chariot, racing down from the skies as fast as the stagehands can manage it, and she pauses in mid-flight—stands.

Everyone stands. Again. For her.

She tears the helmet from her head and lets the chestnut hair fall to her shoulders.

There's a roar. Somewhere in the crowd a woman screams. It's too much. Le Rochois's mouth is open—she—even she—is shouting, applauding, although later she will wonder why. Thévenard sobs with relief, with pride.

Nobody can remember such a night, such a woman, such a goddess.

Act 3, Scene 1

Recitative

I WAS FAMOUS.

Rich. Beloved. All in a moment.

From that evening, my life altered—again—as it has done so often since. Dramatically. Irretrievably. Can you believe it? I barely do myself.

I worked hard, no doubt about it. I'd been hungry many a night, rode many a mile in my life. I was seventeen years old and was the most reviled, and most beloved, woman in France—as, to be sure, I have been ever since. All the world's a stage, according to that English playwright. My world was, from that day on—the salons and drawing rooms, the *salles* and duelling grounds, the ballrooms and avenues and coffee houses. They were my stage. Even here, even now.

I don't care whether or not you trust my word on this. It is what it is. I am. I'm telling you, in that moment—those hours—on stage that night, I became a new being—a creature of the city, of the Comtesse and the Académie—of my own making. Complete. Untainted by my birth or my past crimes. Not exactly reborn, it's true. Certainly not innocent. Of course not. I make no claims of that nature.

A woman. More than a woman. There's a word for it, you know. For me. *Travesti*. The maid in breeches. The one who crosses over. I'm not the first, nor the last. I am probably the finest—the most interesting. In Italy, I've heard, and on the English stage, there are plays written about us—heroines who go about dressed as men—comedies and romances where girls are mistaken for boys, just like in the classics. I saw one once, in Spain. But this isn't one of those stories. Perhaps if I had lived a thousand years ago, with the ancients, with the Amazons or the poet of Lesbos—or a thousand years in the future, when Louis is forgotten like all the other kings, and Versailles has fallen into rubble.

But there is nobody like me—at least, not in my lifetime. I wonder sometimes if that's all I was—all I am—a *travesti*. Not an Amazon. Not a chevalier. Never a queen. But somewhere between man and woman, fool and monster.

That's my fear. In the dark hours.

I'm not speaking of the woman in the riding boots and fine feathered hat, sweeping low in a courtier's bow. Or the deity with breastplate and sceptre. No, no. I mean the stable girl inside me, clamouring like a street urchin—hiding like a thief.

She's always with me—within me. I've always known her, even if at times I ignored her existence or, in my weak moments, lied about her less attractive traits. I don't forget her, though. I seek her out, sometimes, in the crowd at the Palais-Royal or in the streets around the Louvre, even, I admit, in the ballrooms and parlours of the Comtesse and her world. But she doesn't belong there.

Neither do I.

Just as well. I never really cared for the court, for the salons. Not really. I am partial, I admit, to good wine, to a chandelier ablaze with light. I like the company of beautiful or brilliant—preferably both—people. And it is true that it's much easier to be brilliant, and very much easier to be beautiful, if you are wealthy. Or at least well-fed. So I go to the salons and *levées* and balls—not anymore, obviously. Why would I? Now I have you for company instead, scintillating conversationalist that you are.

But then, I watched, admired, scandalised a bit here and there if only to keep my name on their lips. How can I say this without sounding presumptuous? I floated above them, like Pallas Athéna on her machine observing the ballet corps. I smiled and nodded, drank their wine—just a little; drunkenness has only rarely been one of my vices, I assure you. I sampled the roasted meats and ices, danced if I wished, stood in the light so that the shape of my ankle, the curve of my breast, were seen at their best—even sang if I was implored.

Still, I wasn't one of them. I never imagined that they wished me to be. That's a trap. Thévenard, even Fanchon, thought they were so beloved they would be clasped to the aristocracy's naked bosom; so enveloped in the glow of Paris high society that they would become noble themselves. It can never happen. They delude themselves, even now, and they wish it to be true—that I can't understand.

For I've seen the court in its undergarments—in some cases, literally. I've glimpsed the pompous mistress with no teeth, the whining marquis without his breeches and his secretaries. I have seen them all—wigless, brainless, humourless, soulless. I would rather be me.

Yes, even now. You think it odd? It's true enough. I would rather die here, undefeated except by death, than live the vapid life to which so many aspire.

I know that now. I didn't before.

You may think of me, if you will, as a martyr to beauty, to love, to my sex. See me, if you can, not as this pathetic wreck of a woman before you, but as a heart halfway to Heaven—perhaps closer; as a soul not in torment but in repose.

Whatever I have become, I'm not a hypocrite. I've seen those men. They strut about Versailles like bitches on heat, squealing and squawking—peacocks in every way but one. It's they who are the hens, who present and promenade and wait for Louis, for the Dauphin and, yes, for Monsieur, to notice them. To pay just a moment's attention. It's pathetic, really.

They fling their wives, their daughters, even their sons, in the path of men just a little more powerful than themselves—for a title, a position in the royal bedchamber, or some fragment of fortune.

I learned early on—not from Papa and the masters, but from the pages—that the truly noble soul does not need ostentation. The gentle body is distinguished from the common not by gold braid, but by soft silk. Those peacocks at court are often not of the old blood, and you can see it in their mediocre wigs and hear it in their every shriek and giggle.

Dress richly, but simply. That is my motto. For extravagance promotes greed and disdain. The truly noble souls recognise each other by their bearing (and mine has always been regal), by their soft step and intelligent countenance and—this is the most important thing I will tell you, so pay attention—by their tailors.

This applies, you understand, only to men—and to me. It's hard to imagine now, I know. You see me in this plain linen, this habit that scratches and crumples, my hair covered, the veil a little grubby. You've never seen me as I truly am.

But then. Then I would buckle my sword belt over breeches of the finest wool. My blouses were washed every week and dried on lavender bushes. My hair was glossy as chestnuts. I dressed not as a man, not as a woman—just as myself. As a chevalier who happened to be born female. I wore the clothes and the sword of a gentleman, but I wore them as a woman. I never let anyone forget who I truly was—am. Julie-Émilie. Mademoiselle d'Aubigny. Madame de Maupin. *La Travesti*. Nobody else. Me.

I never forgot it, either—who I was, where I came from, and where I might have ended up if it hadn't been for my friends, my lovers, my protectors. I've been very lucky—not so much lately, I grant you, but I haven't given up hope.

I've played many roles, many great women, queens, goddesses. But I am my own greatest creation. La Maupin.

It had to be that way. I swear. I could never have been one of those pretty sopranos—a wife, a mistress. I just don't have it in me, though I've never quite known whether that's a blessing or a curse. It's just how it is. I've never been able to comprehend their rules, and never really believed they applied—not to me. When I was a girl, I wondered how could they stand it, those women? All that bosom-baring and whimpering, all those petticoats and pearls, and never being allowed to leave the house unescorted.

Now I understand that if you have the will and the money, you simply do what you want. Even if you're a woman. It's not so easy, of course, but it's possible.

You don't believe me?

Do.

I'm telling you, it's the truth. The two most powerful people I've ever met in my life—truly powerful, I mean, rather than merely entitled—were women. My Comtesse. And my soul, my twin, my La Florensac. But it's not just them. Doesn't matter whether you're a baker's wife or a whore or a princess—if you have the strength, you can take a lover, write a motet, lead an army, rule a country. Women have. Not all, granted, but some. And we adore them, don't we? In theory. We make statues of warrior women, paint them on our ceilings—goddesses with shields and togas and one fair breast exposed so there can be no doubt. The palaces of Europe are covered in them. The Opéra stages, too, for that matter.

Yet most women I know—no matter how clever, no matter how strong—are dragged down by husbands or fathers or titles or too many petticoats, or priests clutching at their hems, telling them, 'No, you cannot do that, you cannot be that.' I never listened. That's rare. Even a woman like the Comtesse pretends to pay attention to the sermons and the instructions, but then does whatever she wishes.

I don't bother waiting to hear your words—any of you. You'll only tell me what I know to be lies: *you cannot do that, you cannot be that.* Such words are wasted on me, as they are wasted on all women of ambition, of intellect, of power—and there are more of us than you know. I've even known women who write books.

Don't gasp. It's true, I swear. Plays and romances and poems and *tragédies.* Honestly.

How little you people know of my world, my life. Well, well. I know little of yours and have no desire to learn any more.

It's my story that matters.

Act 3, Scene 2

Divertissement

BACKSTAGE, THERE'S A FRENZY. The stagehands laugh as they drag down the machines and set up for tomorrow night. They can't sweep the stage, though—it's crowded with people—shrieking, clamouring people all pushing one another out of the way so they can get closer to the goddess, the nymph, the new ruler of their hearts.

Comte d'Albert and the Duc d'Uzès shove the ballet corps aside and make their way through the crowd. To her.

D'Albert bows before her, tries to take her hand. 'My love,' he says, loud enough for everyone to hear. 'You were magnificent.'

She stares down at him, suddenly impossibly regal, as if the swordswoman has been reborn as a deity.

'I thank you, Comte. I had not imagined I'd see you again. I understood you had rejoined your regiment.'

'I did.' His smile falters. 'But I came back to town. For this.'

'Then I thank you again. Both of you.'

'Madame.' D'Uzès swallows his disdain and bows, too, but not quite as low. 'Had we only known, all those months ago in Villeperdue, that you were ... as we see you now ... we might have—'

'Been more polite?'

Before he can answer, before she can say anything more, the big baritone appears at her side and picks her up in an embrace.

'Ha ha! Julia. We did it. Didn't we?'

Now she can't help smiling. Her arms slide around his neck. 'We certainly did.'

'My darling girl.' His face, close up, is a mess of paint and sweat, his grin wicked. 'They adored you.'

'And you.'

It's a lie. They both know it. But they know that will change, that one day soon he, too, will hold the audience by the throat. But someone's tugging at her sleeve. The pretty, pale young man.

'Shall we see you later, Émilie? There's a party—a dance. Everyone will be there.'

Thévenard releases the goddess from his grip. His smile vanishes. He bends down and hisses in her ear, 'Who is this?'

'A friend. From before.'

'Pah! What sort of friend?'

'None of your business.'

Thévenard shoves d'Albert out of the way with one shoulder. 'Is he your lover? Your protector?'

'I don't need a protector. You know that.'

True. 'Your patron, perhaps?' He can't decide which is worse—his goddess loving someone else or being paid for favours.

'Please, Gabriel. Don't be pathetic. I hate that.'

'I hate him. Privileged little—'

She looks at them from afar, as if she was still flying over their heads in her chariot—the golden boy, the black-eyed giant. Her lovers. Her past.

'Enough,' she says. 'I need to get out of this armour. Let me go.'

They scowl at each other, d'Albert with one hand on his sword, Thévenard's beard dripping sweat onto his chest.

She walks away from them all. Everyone steps aside to let her pass. They feel like bowing, like prostrating themselves before her, but it's insanity, surely. Or passion.

D'Albert dodges around Thévenard and runs after her, calling out, 'Émilie, is he your lover? That singer? Surely you haven't forgotten our sweet days together?'

Thévenard follows him. 'Peacock! I could crush your pretty blond skull in one hand.'

She doesn't turn around. Doesn't wait. 'In the name of God, is there anyone in this city who is not a jealous fool?'

The Comtesse appears before her, as if conjured. D'Albert bows curtly to her. Thévenard looks as if he has been struck by lightning. Or love.

The Comtesse smiles, notices it all, understands it all, and bows herself, deeply, before her protégée. 'My dear Julie.'

She holds out one gloved hand. Julie grasps it, relieved. Grateful.

'We are all in awe,' says the Comtesse. 'You were magnificent. There is no other word for it.'

'D'you know what? I think I was.' Julie grins.

'The city is yours, darling. Anything, anyone, you want. You have only to stretch out your hand.'

So she does.

It all comes to her in the hours, the days, that follow. Wine. Baskets of flowers. Lovesick bachelors with family crests on their calling cards. Letters from breathless girls. Ball invitations. A splendid chestnut mare from d'Armagnac's personal stables, selected to match her hair. A note from Monsieur, delivered by a ridiculously handsome young man. A three-year contract with the Académie, promising twelve hundred *livres* a year. A bowl of plums from the gardeners at Versailles. A tatty bunch of violets with no note attached, delivered, she is told, by an elderly man with a face like a pudding.

Act 3, Scene 3

Recitative

I'D NEVER HAD ANY TRAINING. My father could knock out a march on the fife but he couldn't sing to save himself. D'Armagnac, of course, was officially Master of the King's trumpeters, so I grew up listening to their squeaking and blustering and banging as they got ready for some pageant or other.

The first time I'd heard a string orchestra, all those years before, tuning up in the Grande Écurie, it frightened the life out of me. It sounded for all the world like a pack of wolfhounds.

When I began with the Opéra in Marseille, it took me weeks to comprehend that an orchestra is, instead, a complex, growling, lyrical menagerie. Complete chaos it is, orchestral music, if you think about it too hard.

The truth of an orchestra is heard when they try to find their common notes before the show. All those strings and tubes and odd plunking things straining in different directions;

an orchestra is merely a mob of single-minded maniacs who every so often condescend to work together, and then, mostly, they soar—they ascend—they give us wings.

Then they finish and bow and grumble and stomp off to their grotty little hovels muttering to themselves. Honestly, music is a miracle. You have no idea.

At any rate, I had only ever been used to singing alone, or perhaps with a lute. Not with the entire zoo. Certainly not with other female voices. The training in Paris was a shock, I don't mind telling you, nothing like the days in Poitiers with Maréchal. I wrote to him for advice, but he hadn't lasted long in that madhouse—was dead within weeks, apparently. I don't know if he ever knew how completely I surpassed all his predictions.

Still, I was in a different class to those beautifully trained divas who graced the Opéra before I arrived. Le Rochois was still there, all those years after I first saw her in the Écurie. She was the greatest—is. Even now, though she is long retired. I was no Le Rochois, never tried to be. I had to learn by listening, memorising each note from the sound and the word. But I could do things with my voice that nobody else could do. I astonished the crowds. I winked and they laughed aloud; smiled and they'd nudge each other in the ribs. I certainly made them gasp. But her—they simply adored.

You've never heard of her? You're joking, surely. Marie le Rochois?

Really, Father, even you should have heard her name. Ignorance is as much a sin as vanity or gluttony, you know. She sang at the Écurie, when I was just a child. I've told you that. Didn't you write it down?

Don't expect me to help you keep track. It's complicated. Life is. Keep up. If I can remember these things, with my heart torn from my chest and my brain in a fever, then you ought to at least try. I can barely breathe. Yet here I am, talking. So listen. It's the least you can do.

Le Rochois. And there was a new girl, Fanchon Moreau—blonde, pretty and with a lovely voice. I'll tell you all about her in the fullness of time. Be patient.

Then there were the two Desmatins sisters, both tarts. A whole corps of lesser voices and bit-part players, as well as the chorus. No matter how lowly paid, how ugly, how precocious, they all knew more of music than I did.

To them the *directeur* or his *surintendant* could suggest a slight change of tempo or emphasis, and they would respond immediately. They knew what he meant, and what adjustments they could make—sometimes, of course, they flew into a rage or burst into tears of frustration, but at least they had a point of view.

I had none. In spite of Maréchal's coaching, in spite of all my hard work, my voice still only possessed four options: loud or not so loud, French or Latin. Everything else—all the subtlety, the light and shadow, what the Italians call *dolce* or *agitato*—was an absolute mystery to me.

Humbug it was, too. I figured that out, eventually, and came to understand the effect they wanted and how to shape my own lips and throat to deliver it. Or something like it.

Thévenard and I were upstarts from the gutters: him a cook's son, me the spawn of an ageing *mousquetaire*. They treated us like rubbish at first, and I suppose we were. It was only later I found out that weasel Duménil had been a butcher or some such thing, and the glamorous Desmatins sisters were concubines.

But then even Lully had been a kitchen boy—yes, indeed, in the house of Mademoiselle de Montpensier. His father was a miller. So you see how we have all climbed to great heights.

We had to prove ourselves. It's like any club, any army battalion. There are initiations, humiliations, fights, tests and long nights of hardship. And that was just between me and Thévenard. We brawled like sailors, drank like soldiers, swore like fishmongers. In the end we simply wore one another out until there was no passion, just the sort of holdfast comradeship you share when you've been to war—or rehearsals.

Act 3, Scene 4

Ensemble

THE CURTAIN RISES in less than an hour. Again.

Each night, the singers sigh with relief after it's all over. Before the applause has even finished, they kick off their shoes, start unpinning their wigs. Thévenard kisses Julie goodnight, his moustache damp on her face.

The women of the Opéra crowd into the dressing-rooms, shouting and laughing at the evening's mistakes and glories, wipe their faces clean, throw sweaty costumes on the floor, and sweep out to get good and drunk or laid or rested before they have to do it all over again.

The next day, they're back. Every time. Except once, when they all came down with the squits and had to cancel. Something in the water. Or the air. Francine was furious, but then he wasn't squatting over a pot somewhere shitting out his gizzards like everyone else.

They arrive one by one, even the sisters Desmatins, and assemble slowly. The noise in the dressing-room builds as each woman arrives. Le Rochois and Julie arrive first. Le Rochois always has, through her whole career. She arrives on time, leaves immediately after the show. Julie watches how Le Rochois behaves and tries to do the same. Everything Le Rochois does is correct. Always. She greets the dressers by name, asks after their health, their children. She brushes her own hair—always fifty strokes—and smooths olive oil on her skin so that the face paint will come off more easily.

Julie does the same. The paint is thick and greasy as goose fat. A layer of powder on top, black rims around the eyes, perhaps some colour in the cheeks. For one show, Julie is painted gold every night—face, throat, arms. She glimmers in the candlelight. But it takes an hour to scrape off.

But not tonight. It's the third week of *Didon*. Julie is not playing a goddess this evening, but a magician, a sorceress. White paint will do.

Le Rochois sits alone before the looking glass and paints her lips a deep red, not the carmine shade favoured by the younger women.

Fanchon Moreau arrives next, with an entourage, as usual—four young men and some woman they picked up near the river. Fanchon waves them away at the door, but they won't go; they hover and giggle and stagger a little, until Le Rochois turns in her chair and stares at them. They vanish. Anyone would. Tonight she is Didon, Queen of Carthage. She will not be crossed. She maintains her regal face until she's sure the drunks have gone, and then the three women, the three singers, laugh until their paint cracks.

Julie loves these times, these sisterly moments in front of the mirrors, when the rest of the world is a hush outside, and the Palais-Royal is filling with people, filling with anticipation, filling with noise.

The Desmatins sisters and all the others—dancers, chorus—arrive eventually and crowd in. There are other dressing-rooms, but they prefer to be together in the hour before the curtain. It's a tradition.

Julie teases Marie-Louise Desmatins about her dancing. She watches as Fanchon seeks out a young dancer who is crying softly into her cloak, puts an arm around her shoulders and whispers, 'He never deserved you. Forget him, the bastard.'

Julie watches for a moment longer than is tactful then looks away, to listen as Le Rochois advises her dresser on how to avoid catching a cold in the coming winter. Garlic. Swallowed whole. Swears by it. As nobody has ever known Le Rochois to lose her voice for a single performance, they all take note. Garlic it is.

By the time they hear the first notes of the orchestra tuning up, they are in costume—mostly—squeezing blistered feet into dance slippers, and ready for the wigs to be pinned to their hair. Fanchon slumps in a corner, fanning her face with peacock feathers. Le Rochois pins paper flowers in a dancer's hair. The younger Desmatins tells a long and complicated story about a ball she once attended in Lyon.

Julie sits and watches them all—her found family, her rivals, her friends.

She wanders out into the wings. The smallest boys from the ballet corps are being hoisted up into the flies, where they will wait, hanging, for a quarter of an hour before they swing down at the climax of the Prologue. She's not sure, exactly, what they're supposed to be—sprites, perhaps, or messengers from Jupiter—but the audience loves it.

Two men clatter past with armfuls of gilded pikes and swords. Then another, with a stuffed peacock for Act Two.

The stagehands light the candles. The orchestra is almost ready. The runner clatters down the stairs to fetch the cast.

Julie glances across the empty stage to see Thévenard standing there amid sandbags and coiled ropes. He's not in this show, shouldn't be here. But he can't keep away. He winks. She grins.

They are the masters of Paris.

Act 3, Scene 5

Recitative

YOU MUST UNDERSTAND, the Académie in those days was still fuelled by the brightness of Lully, the incorruptible genius, the King's favourite. He'd only been dead a few years—died the year I ran away with Séranne. I remember the fuss. Louis, they said, was crazed with grief. The whole city went a bit silly.

Lully, dead. And what a way to go. You know the story, I'm sure.

Eh?

Save me, Jesus, from ignorant priests. All right. Pay attention. It's an instructive tale for musicians everywhere. One evening, poor old Lully was happily banging away on the floor with his conducting staff, as they do. His *Te Deum*, I think it was. In the church of the Feuillants in rue Saint-Honoré. People still leave flowers there in his honour. But on that day, he flew into a fury with the harpsichordist and flattened his own toe with a thump of the staff. Gangrene set in and off he popped. Embarrassing, I know, but people have died of simpler things. Look at me.

Mad bastard he was, and greedy, but his was the only music Paris wanted to hear, the only performances the King would attend. New composers came and went, some of them dogs, some of them could have been better than Lully if anybody had ever given them the chance. But no.

Instead, we trotted out the old master's work each year and the crowds wept with happiness. Knew every word—some nights we couldn't hear one another over the audience singing along happily out of tune, even during the heartbreaking arias.

There's nothing like trying to inject a spirit of compassion and pity into a death scene when you've got a thousand punters bellowing at you from the *parterre*. Maybe that's one reason they liked me. I simply sang even louder. Some of the others couldn't do that, you see. They didn't have the lungs for it. But it turns out that a military education is quite good training for a singer. People don't realise—you don't need to pretend that you care about music, Father, just look interested, please—it takes a lot of strength just to wear the costume sometimes, let alone have enough puff to make yourself heard above the mob.

Le Rochois, of course, could calm them with the slight lift of one eyebrow, without missing a beat. Thévenard once stopped singing—in the middle of *Psyché*, I think it was—and shouted at a man in the closest box: 'Shut the fuck up, you imbecile!'

Of course, everyone roared with laughter, including the imbecile, who sang even louder.

Even I, divine as I am, got fed up one night and climbed out of my machine, jumped right out of it—can you imagine? Nobody knew what was going on. I can picture Duménil's stupid face even now. I'd had enough. Really, what can you do? I'm an artist. Above interruptions. I could hear some fool shouting out the words—no tune at all—and all kinds of insults and trying to make a joke of everything. Of me. Of Fanchon. Even of Le Rochois. Nobody had come to listen to him. Then he whistled at Fanchon. Called her a whore. Threatened—

I know! Incredible, isn't it?

So it had to stop. Someone had to teach him a lesson and it was, inevitably, left up to me. I imagine it was a lesson he will never forget. Whoever he is. Some people are just … Anyway, I leapt off the stage and up over three benches to the Cardinal's box, grabbed a cane out of some fellow's hand, and clobbered him across his loud mouth. Not the Cardinal, you understand. Some young drunk.

Everyone cheered and bellowed until I got back into position. The wonder is that it didn't happen more often.

That was the marvellous thing about singing a new work— nobody knew the words but us. They had no choice but to listen, to follow the story, to be surprised. At least for a few weeks, until they'd all bought their copies of the book and knew every word—if not the notes.

To be sure, sometimes they felt a little too surprised. So did we. I could never predict which new music would meet with their approval. Too derivative? Too new? Too outlandish? Too staid? Too Italian? Too English?

I heard about a glorious piece I would've loved to sing: a *Dido and Aeneas* by an Englishman whose name escapes me now. Couperin dug up the score from somewhere. Lyrical. Gorgeous. Pathos dripped from the page. Apparently. I never did master the reading of music. But I was assured it would have been perfect for me, for my tone. Fanchon would have been brilliant, too, but I'd have wrung every tear out of the eyes of Paris. Those words!

'When I am laid in earth ... with drooping wings.'

I can see it now. Hear it, almost.

We talked about it, planned a three-week season. A preview at Versailles. But you can't present something with only three acts. They'd tear you limb from limb. None of that English muck here, none of that Italian nonsense—unless, needless to say, your Italian is called Lully.

Pity.

I did play Dido once, in Brussels—not that English work but another, beautiful and sad, by a German fellow. They are much less parochial about these things in Brussels. They have to be.

I won't pretend I ever approached the majesty of Le Rochois or the versatility of Fanchon. But I can stand there, rigid as a statue and dressed like a goddess or a magician or a river nymph, and belt out an air as fiercely as any old slapper. I can act and sing at the same time—so can Thévenard. You wouldn't think it'd be so difficult, but plenty of the others can't manage it at all. They can do one thing or the other—not both at once, let alone anything complicated. Like walking. Or smiling. Or pretending to weep. They just sing and make all the prescribed gestures as precisely as possible.

But you remember, Father, what I told you—that my singing apprenticeship had been in the taverns and the fairgrounds, among the drunkards and the freaks, a tougher crowd than ever crammed into the Palais-Royal—more exacting, and more intimate. I learned to feel the temperature of the audience, if you like, its mood, its fever—Thévenard was the same—and in time we learned to adjust not only the noise that came from our throats, but also the emotions—the rage, the sorrow—whatever our roles demanded. Well, I did. That, I realised, is as important as the voice and the air in your lungs.

The idea of the *tragédie en musique*—Lully's idea it was first, and we've been regurgitating it ever since—is to excite pity and terror. If all you bring to your audience is wooden faces and stolid singing, there will be no pity, no terror, no consorting with the gods, with the angels. That's what Le Rochois does—did—what I do, and a handful of others in the entire world. We feel. You feel. We stand on the stage and wail and weep and are not ashamed. You—well, not you perhaps, but other, normal people—take us into their hearts, and in comforting us, they find comfort themselves. That, truly, is my gift. My other gift. As I am blessed, so is—was—all of Paris.

They loved me, the people in the streets. That's the only way I can explain it. Perhaps they knew me as one of them, always only a misstep away from dry crusts and smallpox. The others, the nobles in their wigs and their pretty, sharp-faced women, they dared to love me as well.

For years I believed they loved me for my voice, my stage presence, my courageous life. 'Incomparable,' they said. 'Divine.' I am the goddesses on the ceilings of the antechambers at Versailles, the statues in the gardens. That's what they see in me. The huntress. The peacemaker. The Amazon. The Muse. Victory. Glory. War. I am divine.

But now I wonder if I was anything more than some exotic creature in the King's pleasure gardens—not a lion, and surely not a baboon, but perhaps—yes—a giraffe. Unlikely.

Ungainly. Unique. Beautiful in parts but not particularly attractive as a concept. Alien. But compelling, nevertheless.

You have no idea what I'm talking about, do you, Father? I don't suppose you've ever seen a giraffe. Or a lion. Or a baboon. Or even a pleasure garden.

Hell's teeth! Why did they have to send me some dolt from the provinces? How can you even begin to comprehend me?

Be that as it may, I will resume my recitative.

Where was I? Ah, yes. That's right. I was loved.

They loved my voice and my face. They hated, I realise now, my body and its desires. They thrilled at my adventures, cheered my duels, but despised the essence of me. No doubt they tittered and gasped behind my back. I didn't notice it in those early years—I thought I was surrounded by people who wished me nothing but good. I heard the whispers and shrugged off the notoriety, the half-hidden glances and smirks.

I felt as if I had taken in all of Paris—the whole world—with my talents and charm. I read about myself in the broadsheets and believed it to be true.

I was the sun.

I was a monster.

Both were true.

I am a goddess.

I am a sinner.

Both are lies.

They never loved me—not really. They wanted to be close to me; perhaps they envied me. The women envied my freedom, my sheer nerve. The men were jealous of my women, my skill with the blade. But there's not much difference between envy and hatred. In the end.

They cheered at my high notes—oh, the clear sustained

thrill of that tender A minor; the astounded applause exploding out of the dark—and especially the low. They'd never heard the like.

I was light. I was a tiny pool of candle-glow and all around me there was darkness, waiting.

They whispered it in the night—into my ear when they thought nobody was watching, or behind my back when they were sure everybody was. The blade of slander between the shoulder blades—that secret, noisome assassin—was the only wound I suffered at their hands.

Otherwise, they flung flowers at my feet and, if they were very lucky, I would stoop and pick up the stems in one perfectly gloved hand. They shouted for me, revered me.

I was an idol.

I was an iconoclast.

I never took it seriously, any of it. How could I?

So I contradict myself—what of it? Consistency was never my forte. Believe what you will of me; change your mind every hour, every minute. God knows, I do.

You wanted to hear my story. Naturally. It's fascinating. But whatever made you imagine there would be only one version? All of the world's greatest myths are told and retold—there are patterns in the telling, but sometimes the dénouement differs. We all long for Médée to stay her hand, for Hector to survive his wounds—just once.

In opera there are rules. Conventions. The gods never speak with lesser mortals. We—they—intervene in human affairs only through our instruments, the lesser deities. Say, Cupid. Always willing to meddle.

There must be a happy ending. A wedding is best, or perhaps a triumphal march. Deliverance. Redemption. Not in *Phaëton*, I grant you, but in most other works, we end on a high, happy note.

Quinault, especially, always wrote such lovely endings. Juno turns Io into a goddess. Minerve unravels the evil wrought by Médée. Renaud escapes Armide. There may be torture, poison, war, sorrow. But in the end, justice is done—divine or otherwise.

This is not one of those. Perhaps it never could be. Not my luck.

The *tragédies en musique* are stories of legends, of the great myths, on occasion the stories of mortals—of history—of those romances Louis so dearly loved. Even then, there is a divine intervention—a metamorphosis. Salvation.

All horribly pagan of us, isn't it? But it gives hope, after all, that Heaven hears us, that those saints who now play the roles of Aphrodite or Mercury or even—God help us—Cupid will grant us our fondest hopes, release us from grief, find our lost loves, carry us away—sound the trumpets for the finale, the processional, the full orchestra announcing our exit.

But look.

Look at me!

I've served those divinities all my life—the demigods of Versailles and the Palais-Royal—of history. The Muses. But they have abandoned me now, finally.

I don't blame them. Not really. I've demanded a great deal of them over the years. They've granted me redemption—absolution—any number of times. If I were someone else, a lesser being, I might still hope for Pallas Athéna to sweep down from the clouds in her chariot, her intricate machine.

But I look to the skies and see only myself. Alone. Hair down around my shoulders. Not smiling. Not even holding out a hand. I am truly forsaken.

Sometimes there is truth in a tale. Sometimes there is a dream.

Now—dear God, I must indeed be dying—I see both, darkly, clearly.

Act 3, Scene 6

Divertissement

'HAVE YOU HEARD?'

'Whatever it is, no doubt you will tell me.'

'That new singer, Mademoiselle de Maupin—'

'I have heard of nothing but Mademoiselle de Maupin for weeks. Pray tell me of something else.'

'But you won't believe the latest ...'

The Comtesse smiles to herself. Julie's name is on everyone's lips, just as she planned. Even here, in her own salon, where the most discreet, the most discerning people in Paris gather. How delightful.

'The young Comte d'Albert is much taken with her, so I hear.'

'He'd do better to find himself an heiress to marry.'

'Surely he can do both. Everyone else does.'

The Comtesse glides past the card tables to greet more guests. She motions to a footman to bring Madame de

Sévigné a chair. Hears carriage wheels clatter in the courtyard. Calls for more wine. Listens again.

'D'Albert has no money of his own, you know.'

'Don't worry about him. He'll do well enough. A war hero now, so the story goes. The darling of Paris society. He'll be betrothed within a month. Mark my words.'

'Not if Mademoiselle de Maupin can stop it.'

It's not often that the Comtesse is seen without a smile—it is one of her most vital assets, after all—but anyone watching at this moment would have seen it vanish. Just for a moment, a heartbeat.

She can't help it. She glances at the door again, waiting for her darling, her goddess. It is time, she knows, to let Julie go. The grooming, the teaching, the secret love, is over. But it turns out it's not such an easy thing, after all. Not like the others. You send them on their way, like fledglings, like blessings, and wish them joy.

Not this time.

But she must. She must. The smile returns, if not quite as serene as before.

The footman is at the door again with an announcement. 'Le Comte d'Albert.'

Ah.

The Comtesse accepts his greetings and his compliments with grace. He bends low over her hand, his yellow hair falling loose, but his eyes glance around the room. He has come for Julie. Of course. So has everyone else.

By the time she arrives, everyone is watching the door. Mademoiselle de Maupin prefers it that way. She lingers on the threshold, gazing around the room for familiar faces—

enemies, lovers, former lovers, their husbands or wives—and finds the Comtesse.

A deep bow. Almost extravagant. But before she even straightens up, d'Albert is there.

'Émilie.'

'Sieur?'

'Imagine my surprise at seeing you here.' It's pathetic. They both know it.

'Yes. Imagine.'

The Comtesse feels all the card players and gossips and even the Bishop watching.

'Forgive me for interrupting, Comte,' she says, always polite, perhaps dangerously so. 'Julie, my dear, I want you to meet Madame de Sévigné.'

She puts one hand gently on Julie's sword arm.

Julie smiles. 'As you wish.'

But d'Albert won't go away, follows them across the room, whispering in Julie's ear so loudly the whole room hears. 'Meet me tomorrow. Promise you will.'

'I'm singing tomorrow.'

'In the morning then. Or afterwards. I will collect you from the theatre.' He can't quite keep stride with her. Falls behind.

'There's no need.'

He doesn't bother to pretend whispering now. 'It's that man, isn't it? That singer?'

'God, give me strength.'

'Shall I challenge him? Is that what you want?'

Julie stops halfway across the Comtesse's elegant rug. Turns. Grabs d'Albert by the arm.

'Please excuse us, Comtesse.'

'Of course, dear.' This time the smile is genuine.

D'Albert finds himself shoved into a small blue room, collides with a table, knocks over some glasses. Straightens his collar. Turns to her. 'That's better.'

'What are you on about?'

'Don't be angry with me, Émilie. All I want is to see you again.'

'Really? That's all?'

'Perhaps not quite all.' He grins. 'But I'm willing to negotiate.'

'You're a stupid boy.'

'I know.' He takes a step forward. Then stops. 'You have to be polite to me. I'm a celebrated war hero. Ask anyone.'

Julie leans back against the door and crosses her arms. He can't tell whether it's nonchalance or defiance. 'I have. You know what they said?'

'Oh, I expect they told you how I swam ever so bravely across the canal with a knife between my teeth to attack the enemy. How I was wounded. Gallantly. Famously.'

'They told me you are a wastrel,' she says. 'A hothead. A womaniser. But charming.'

'No war stories?' He looks genuinely crestfallen.

'There might have been some mention of it.' There's the beginning of a smile on her lips. At last.

'Gallantly wounded? Anybody say that?'

She shakes her head. 'Don't think so.'

'Or how my regiment has the finest uniforms in the army?'

'No. Though someone did say you were dreadfully vain, so the two things may be connected.'

'I see.' He glances down at his impeccable boots, his gold-embroidered jacket.

'Do you? I wonder.' Julie strides across the room and sits in the very place where she sat when she first met the Comtesse. One of her hands brushes gently against the silk cushions. 'I love this house.'

D'Albert feels, not for the first time, as if it's one of those awkward interviews with his father, as if he can't quite control what's happening, as if the whole conversation—which he practised for hours this morning—has gone terribly awry. He tries again. 'Listen—'

'No.' She looks up. 'You listen.'

'People don't usually speak to me like that.'

'I don't care. Sit down.'

He does. He wishes he hadn't. But somehow she made him.

'I could give you what you want—' she begins.

'Truly?' He jumps to his feet. 'Why, that would make me the happiest man alive.'

'Don't interrupt me.'

'Sorry.' Sits down again, but a little closer.

'I could give you what you want. But I won't.'

'Oh.'

'You want a mistress,' she says. He's not sure if it's a question—it sounds more like a challenge. 'You want me. True?'

'Of course,' he says quickly. 'Those weeks in Villeperdue—'

'Are gone. Long gone. I am not a mistress. Not anybody's.'

'You were once, so I hear.'

'Mention that again and I'll kill you.'

'I'm not as rich as d'Armagnac, but I have money.' The plea is out of his mouth before he realises how it might sound to her.

'I really might kill you.'

194

'Please.' Perhaps he should fall to his knees. But he's a nobleman. And she might just kick him aside. She stands, towers over him, and he can't seem to do anything but sit there like an idiot.

'Yield, Joseph. It will never happen, no matter what you say. But you were a sweet lover and I am willing to give you something much more precious than my body.'

'What could be more precious than that?'

'Silly boy.' She is definitely smiling now. She might even be laughing. 'If I don't take you in hand you'll get yourself killed in some idiotic duel.'

'You mean ...?'

'Yes, you fool. I will teach you to fence properly.'

Act 3, Scene 7

Recitative

THAT'S THE THING, YOU SEE? Everyone wants you. It sounds like a dream, but it's not. Far from it. People grab at you—men grab at you. Women smile. It's the same. Not even desire, really, just wanting. Just some game, some lack in their little lives, something to brag about. A hunt. Not everyone, sure. But many. Too many.

There were the men with wandering hands, men with wandering pricks.

'Didn't mean anything by it,' they say. 'Just being friendly.'

An odd euphemism, that, don't you think? As if there is anything remotely friendly about being shoved up against a wall with some moron's hand at your throat.

Men with wandering wives. That's who should look out for me.

But they rarely did. They couldn't believe their cuckold was a mere girl. Or by the time they noticed, by the time they heard the jokes and the songs in the streets or read the gossip sheets, it was too late.

Then there'd be nothing for it but a fight.

Even if I was a mere girl. Even if I was, after all, just being friendly.

There was that fool, don't even remember his name now, who challenged me in front of everyone at one of the Comtesse's salons. Well, what can you do? He accused me of making eyes at his wife. God knows, I'd done much more than that. For weeks. But he was too stupid to realise it. She was lovely. Really lovely. I forget her name, too. Red hair. Dyed. Don't ask how I know. Three children, but you'd never think it. Her breasts were as firm as—

Yes. Of course. As you wish.

So he challenged me. I could have killed him. I could have killed any of them. Just a flick of the blade, that's all it takes—not even a second of one's life to take another. But I never did. You may suspect whatever you like about me, but I've never killed a man, sorely tempted though I have been at times. Humiliation is a much more lasting and effective weapon, I've found.

There was a man—there were so many—but this one, this creature ... I put up with him for years. We all did. He'd been a singer long before I came to the Opéra, a favourite with the crowd but not with the company. Duménil.

Imagine. He was one of the first singers I ever saw on stage. He played Persée that night when I stood, an open-mouthed child, there in the stables, and felt my heart explode with delight. He was Lully's favourite *haute-contre*, sang with Le Rochois for years before I came along.

He could sing, I grant you that. But he felt like a weakling on stage—how to explain it?—as if the air and noise that came from his lungs was all there was of him. That, and a wig. A pair of fat thighs. Piggy little eyes. His acting was *fêted* by all of Paris, but I could never understand it—to us, he was all annoyance and nasty smells.

He was famous. The butcher who became a star. Lully's muse. I had loved him—had loved every single one of them—from a distance, from the time I was nine years old.

But the moment, years later, when I met Duménil man to man, as it were, I hated him. He hated me, too. We saw each other for what we were, perhaps—I knew him for a primping fraud, and he knew I could threaten his happy, sweaty little life of ballet dancers and outrageous demands and tantrums.

I kept out of his way most of the time. He was a pest backstage. Hands everywhere, including our purses. Prick always finding its way out of his breeches. He grabbed at the girls while they stood waiting to go on stage. Fingers down their bodices, up their skirts. It's not easy to fight off a libertine when you're trussed up in corsets and helmets and Heaven knows what else. They'd laugh and move out of his way. Flutter a fan. Accidentally stand on his slipper.

Never laid a hand on me, mind you. I'd have cut it off for him.

But one night, he stepped just a little too far beyond the border of decency. One night, I decided to teach him a lesson in humility.

In power.

Act 3, Scene 8

Ensemble

PLACE DES VICTOIRES. It's dark. Late. The performance went on far too long and Duménil is tired. He's spent weeks trying to seduce that little bitch Fanchon and now she's slipped out of reach. Again. He can wait. She can't avoid him forever. Next time, he'll have her. Whether she likes it or not. Next time.

His mouth is wet. His shirt damp against his skin. His breeches tight against his—his manhood, that's just the right word—his mighty manhood—he'll rip Fanchon apart, one of these days, ride her until she screams. Delicious. Sometimes they do scream. He wonders why. His manhood. Yes. His left palm slides down along smooth silk towards his mighty—

Here? Does he dare? Nobody about. It's darker under the arcade. Perhaps …

A shadow slips from behind a wall. A tall, slender figure in a cloak. A shimmer of steel.

Ah. Perhaps not.

The big man halts. Glances behind him at empty streets. Feels the pulse in his wrists flicker and flow. His tongue on dry lips.

Ridiculous. Walk on as if—

'Don't move.' The shadow's voice is soft.

'I beg your pardon?'

'You heard me.' It's a familiar voice but he can't quite place it.

'An outrage, sieur,' says Duménil in his best stage manner. 'Move aside.'

'No.'

'Why, you—'

'You are the outrage, not me.'

Duménil gasps aloud. 'How dare you?'

'Slug. Vermin.'

Surely this cannot be happening. Not to him. 'Do you have any idea whom you address, sieur?'

'Oh, yes,' says the shadow. 'I am quite sure of that. Duménil—mediocre singer, dreadful actor, lascivious cad, petty thief, molester of young ladies. That's you, is it not?'

'I am none of those things.' It must be a mistake. A trick. A little joke played by one of those layabouts in the orchestra. 'Except—the name is mine.'

'Allow me to expound your biography. You are the festering scab on the arse of the Académie. The low-life who insulted Marie Le Rochois and threatened Fanchon Moreau. You are the heavy breather in the wings, the sweaty hands on a garter, the foul jests that make every woman's skin crawl. That's you.'

'I have no idea what you mean.' Duménil looks around again but there's nobody nearby. Perhaps if he screamed ... But no. 'Move aside.'

The shadow raises an arm. A weapon. A cane.

'I am an angel of vengeance,' it says.

'You're a pest,' says Duménil. 'I will sweep you aside like ... like ...'

'Shall we pause while you finish your sentence, or will I beat you now?'

'A duel—is that what you want?' He's never fought a duel but how hard can it be? Might delay this nastiness until dawn, anyway. Plenty of time to hire a carriage and flee to the countryside. Or find an assassin. Or both.

'I won't sully my honour or my blade with your blood, you louse.'

'Money? Is that it?' Duménil reaches for his purse.

'You will pay, certainly, but not in coin.'

The first blow lands on his shoulder. He cries out. Another blow, this one across his head. There's blazing pain in his ear and the warmth of blood on his neck. Another—this time not with the stick, but a fist in the face, a knee in the fat of his gut, and a back-handed slap across his eyes that sends him sprawling in the dirt, hands first, tearing the skin from his knuckles, nails from fingers.

'Please. Please.' He's squealing now and he can hear himself—hates the sound of it—but he can't stop. 'Please, God.'

'Do you really think God listens to lice like you?'

A boot in the belly.

'I'll give you anything. Anything.' He gurgles blood. Maybe teeth. Hears the shadow laughing softly.

'Everything. I want everything.'

Scrabbles at his purse strings. There's not much. A gilded snuffbox he pretends is a gift from a mysterious lady. He picked it up at the market in Aix on a tour of the provinces. Pearls stolen from one of the dancers. A silk kerchief with Le Rochois's initials embroidered in one corner. A few coins. The watch he bought for next to nothing from an old man in Montparnasse.

'Here. Take it all.'

The shadow bends, scoops it all up in one hand. Brings the other fist down hard on his head one last time.

'You disgust me,' it hisses. And is gone.

The violins scrape together a few notes to set a tone. It's an hour until tonight's performance and the crowd is arriving already, people muscling each other aside for the best spots. The quality arrive late, sometimes well after the Prologue, which, after all, is only written for the King, and the King, these days, is never present to hear it. Even Monsieur doesn't care for the Prologue. The young ladies like to enter earlier, so they have time to properly discuss the events of the day and admire each other's wardrobe.

In the warren of smelly rooms and hallways behind the stage, the gentlemen of the chorus smoke and chatter, Thévenard waxes his beard into a point, dressers race from room to room with sewing needles and ribbons. In a dark corner of the rehearsal room one of the lesser-known tenors tries to breathe quietly while a boy from the ballet takes his cock down his throat and sucks hard, the tongue soft and willing, the sensation so exquisite it's almost pain.

He comes, violently and with a moan that's far too loud, in the boy's mouth, in the same moment as Duménil knocks on the leading ladies' door.

'My darlings? May I come in?'

He breathes in the scent—musty silks, stale sweat, powder, perfume, singed hair, face paint, the juices of half a dozen whores.

A couple of them turn to greet him. There's a satisfying gasp.

'What happened to you?'

'Ooh! A scrap with a jealous husband?'

He waves a hand. 'Please, don't pay any attention to me.' Pauses for effect. They all know the trick, play it themselves every night, admire his artistry. He seeks out Fanchon Moreau's half-painted face and focuses on it. 'I was attacked. Last night. By bandits.'

They all stop the powdering and hair curling. Gasp again. Put on their sympathetic faces. Clamour at him with questions.

'Where?'

'Just at the corner of the rue d'Aubusson and rue de la Feuillade. You know it?'

'Yes! It's not safe there. So dark.' Fanchon Moreau comes close, very close, gazing at his bruises.

'The Place has gone to the dogs,' says one of the prettier dancers. 'I told you so.'

'What happened? Sit down. Poor creature.'

'I'm all right.' He sits down on Fanchon's chair so his face is level with her breasts. 'Don't fuss. Please.'

'But what did they do to you?' she asks. 'How many were there?'

'Six or seven, maybe more. Evil-looking characters, too. Pretending to be gentlemen, but obviously street scum. Thieves.'

'They threatened you?'

'Of course.' He has spent half the night seeking consolation in various taverns but every part of him hurts. 'But I was having none of that. Told them to retire and nobody would be the wiser, but they wouldn't listen to reason.'

'Desperate sorts, then. Probably southerners. A lot of them hanging about lately.'

'I fought them off as best I could, but they were too many.'

'So valiant.' Fanchon's voice has an odd tone to it.

He checks her face to see if she believes him. She is gazing at him, heart filled with compassion. She is nothing if not a superb actress.

'I threw one to the ground, dashed another's head against a stone,' he says. 'You see my hand?' He holds out his bruised knuckles. 'That's from punching the leader, the brigand, and bringing him to his knees.'

'You fought like a lion.' It's a girl from the ballet he's never noticed before. Must pay more attention in future.

'And yet, I'm afraid ...' He lowers his head, disconsolate, brave but beaten. 'I was unarmed. One against many. Ah, well. One does what one can.'

'Did they steal anything?' asks Fanchon.

'My watch. My snuffbox. Nothing of value. Except—' his face saddens '—my father's gold watch. All I have to remind me of him. Gone.'

'Oh, you poor thing.'

They crowd around. He smiles courageously as they touch the bruises, black against his flaccid skin.

The tall one, the pretty contralto, stands right in front of him. Tips her head to one side and surveys his wounds. 'Enough of your lies, Duménil.'

'Eh?' He looks up. That voice.

'It was me.' Julie can't hide her disgust. She leans down and spits the words into his pathetic face.

'What are you saying?'

'Your mob of assailants, those legendary bandits against whom you fought so bravely. It was me. This is the very stick with which I caned your pathetic arse.'

'You lie.' The woman is a harpy. A menace.

'Here.'

The snuffbox clatters to the floor but he doesn't look at it. He knows she's telling the truth, knows his own cowardice better than she could ever imagine, knows that the other women know, too.

'You poltroon,' she goes on. She stares into his face—as if he doesn't exist—as if he's the only soul left on earth. 'You make me sick. Lay another hand on any of my friends and you will not live long enough to regret your baseness.'

His face beyond fury, beyond pale, the blood in his veins alternating between fire and water, he stares right back as long as he can manage—longer, in fact, than she'd ever believed he would—until his fury is swamped by shame. He falters. Stumbles. Turns. Weeps. Scrambles somehow out into the hallway, out into the street and the night and the cinder smoke of Paris.

His understudy watches him go, smirks, and brushes his wig.

In the dressing-room, the women turn as one—on one.

'You've really fucked it up this time, Julia.'

'What on earth possessed you?'

'But he steals from you.'

'Oh, please. Who anointed you Queen?'

'You Sapphists. No sense of humour.'

'He threatened to rape Fanchon,' Julie shouts over the racket.

'Have you seen his prick?' Fanchon turns back to face the mirror. Checks her painted lips. 'It wouldn't hurt much, believe me. Anyway, I can look after myself.'

'But he's a poltroon.'

'We heard.'

'What's a poltroon?' asks the youngest dancer.

'Thing is, he's a very rich one,' says Fanchon. 'And well in with the *directeur*.'

'Oh, come on, you can't really—'

'I should go after him. Make sure he's all right.'

'Fanchon, you can't,' says Julie. 'Please.'

'I suppose he'll be getting drunk at the Lion.'

'But it's half an hour to overture.'

'Leave it to me.' Fanchon winks. 'I know how to deal with him.'

The others laugh, go back to their makeup, keep talking about him, about her, about rubbish, while Fanchon slips out the door, calling his name.

His first name.

Like an old friend.

Like a lover.

Julie sits and stares at the snuffbox until her dresser comes with her goddess's gown.

Act 3, Scene 9

Recitative

HE GROVELLED AT MY FEET. Just think of it. Six feet of quivering *haute-contre* on the floor before me, begging forgiveness and filled with remorse. How he apologised. How he begged their forgiveness—and mine. Oh, how they marvelled at my audacity, my power, my sheer—there's no other word for it, forgive me—brilliance.

No. That's what I told myself, what I told everyone. But now—the truth. You speak of forgiveness. Why is it that men can be forgiven so much, in life and in death? When I was little, I forgave my father, time and time again. I suppose I even loved him in a way.

I can't forgive Duménil, not even now, for all his petty lies and crimes. He deserved a good beating. From that day on, I swear to you, the braggart didn't dare lay his cowardly hands on any of those women. Unless, of course, the women wished it. Which, I must admit, they sometimes did.

Even Fanchon—sweet Fanchon. Well, she went on with her life as if nothing had happened. They all did.

But I was her champion. Surely. Like the knights in the old tales, in the ballads. I wore her handkerchief at my breast, I defended her from evil, I kept her safe from straying hands— although I can admit now that sometimes she might have preferred if I hadn't.

She was a bit of a flirt. I can admit, too, that I was as susceptible to it as Duménil, as the Dauphin, as half the men in France. I thought—I imagined—that her smiles were meant only for me, and that my own charms were irresistible. I see it now. All of it. But I'm not ashamed. Not of that.

It's funny, but it appeared to me then that I could have anyone I wanted. Indeed, I did. Too often, I had lovers I didn't even want. A pretty smile. A strong thigh. The most handsome man, the loveliest woman. Whoever. If there was someone who seemed untouchable, I wanted to be the first to touch them. If there was a girl begging to be kissed, then let my lips be her first. I confess my choices weren't always wise—if I was a little drunk, or a little foolhardy, I might wake up next to someone I barely even liked. Or remembered.

True enough. Sad, even. For them. Sometimes for me. I couldn't love them. None of them. Not really. They couldn't touch me, I wouldn't allow it—but that's enough. I'll say no more about that.

I'm not proud of it. Well, not all of it, anyway. But that's how it was, in those first few months, the first year or so, of being me—of being La Maupin. Heady times. Perhaps a little too much so.

I was too fabulous. Too young. Eighteen years old, with the world throwing itself at my feet—sending me flowers and wine and sides of pork and daughters and more wine and ... It's a wonder I ever got out of bed to go to rehearsal.

I don't recommend it.

People were envious of me, too. Even Thévenard. Even d'Albert—strutting back into town after some battle or other, a war hero—a darling. Told everyone I was his woman. Again.

Sorted that out soon enough. I threatened to run him through again, and heard no more about it.

I'm nobody's woman. Never was. Never wanted to be—not since Avignon, since Clara. Had refused plenty of offers, some very lucrative—as if I care about that. I don't mind someone looking after me, don't get me wrong. I won't turn away the odd bouquet, a trinket, a fine mare. I'm not an idiot. But I do get fidgety. Hate obligation. I am likely to lash out, like a horse unused to traces.

There did come a time when I gave myself up, freely, to be possessed, to be as one. But, no. I can't tell you about that. Not yet. I will. I have to. Or there will be no-one to bear witness, no-one to remember her, and me, and one moment in a ballroom.

But what am I saying?

Half of Paris was there.

It's not something any of them will ever forget.

Act 3, Scene 10

Divertissement

THERE. IN THE MIDDLE OF THE ROOM. A girl. Of surpassing beauty, as they say in the romance novels. Of heart-rupturing beauty. She's listening to an old man talk as if he were the most important person on earth.

Julie knows that trick, knows it well.

The girl is a master at it. She's smiling now, deep into his eyes, nods as he bows, takes his leave, and relinquishes her to a crowd of impatient young men.

Then she looks up.

Does the earth really shatter? Julie hardly knows. Her pulse, her lungs, her life, contract to nothing, so that she dies, right there on the polished floors of the Palais-Royal ballroom, and nobody even knows, nobody sees it, nobody realises except her and the girl, who is also dead, who no longer breathes or feels her heart or her body or anything except a flaming certainty that her life has, in this moment, altered forever, and the room and the chatter drop away and there's nobody there, just the two of them.

Someone dances through—slashes through—the shaft of light that connects them, and they both jolt back into breath, into life, like drowning men brought ashore, panting and sick and frightened and more alive than anyone, ever.

Then the girl is out of sight, lost in the crowd as Monsieur and Madame enter the ballroom. Everyone bows to Their Highnesses, shuffling in their slippers, a million yards of silk rustling at the same time, a cloud of butterflies, but where—where is she?

Julie is the first to move. She can't help it. She pushes someone aside. Apologises. Sidesteps a dowager sunk in a deep curtsey. So many people. What are they doing here? Why are they in her way, in her world, when all she wants is the girl? Even a glimpse, even a—

The orchestra strikes up a *coranto*. Monsieur loves a *coranto*, although he always wishes—always—that just once he could dance it with his love instead of this princess he married. But instead he takes her hand and leads her onto the floor and simply pretends, as he always does, that he's dancing with Philippe. He reminds himself that it's Philippe's body he will feel against his tonight—the hard backbone, the rough skin on his throat—and not his wife's fleshy thighs.

But her hand is in his, and he can feel the sweat in her palm as the dance picks up tempo, and it's all he can do not to walk out right now, with the whole of Paris watching, down the mirrored hallways and marble stairs, past the tapestries and the oblivious footmen, across the forecourt and home to his bedchamber and his man.

But he knows his duty. He is the brother of the greatest king in history. He is a radiant ornament in the court of the Sun. His duty is to dance. So he does. Smiles and applauds the orchestra. Nods to the senior courtiers. Winks at his friends. Notices that the tall contralto from the Académie is wearing men's clothes—crimson silk amid the gowns and petticoats and fluttering fans. Her sword doesn't look entirely ceremonial, and she appears to be either ravaged and desperate or badly hungover.

This—she—could be fun.

Monsieur makes himself comfortable on what passes for a throne at these things and motions for a glass of wine. A footstool. Perhaps some ice-cream. He's ready to watch the show.

There's a black-haired page whose breeches are far too tight for his own good, and who dances the next set so obviously in Monsieur's sight that even the prince himself is slightly repelled.

If they present themselves as meat, they cannot complain if they are devoured.

The opera singer creates a flurry in the corner, pushing someone out of her way like an old woman at a market stall. She's so tall, so—well, remarkable—Monsieur can't stop watching her, even though she's moving fast through the crowd. She seems to have lost something. Or someone.

There.

A girl. She and the singer stand and gaze at each other from a distance for what feels like an hour.

Monsieur waves to one of Madame's ladies. 'The girl with the green eyes. The blonde. Over there. With Abbé Noye.'

She glances over quickly. 'That's the Marquise de Florensac, Your Grace.'

'Ah! The young bride. We've not seen her at court a great deal.'

'They spend all their time at the chateau. Her husband abhors company.'

'Understandably.'

'She is the daughter of Saint-Nectaire—you see, she has his eyes.'

'She's pretty.'

'Very, Your Grace.' She lowers her voice to a whisper. 'And wealthy, so I hear, in her own right. Do you wish her to be presented?'

'No.' He waves her away. 'No matter.'

The young Marquise is standing perfectly still among the swirling dancers. She has forgotten the steps, ignores Noye, who stands embarrassed by her side. She has forgotten everything but that extraordinary, beautiful, wild creature in breeches and sword belt.

Monsieur stares. He knows—sees who they are—two souls who recognised each other's essence in an instant. This instant.

He feels for her—for them.

What a *tragédie* they perform. Each of them, no doubt, dressed this evening with care, admired her brilliant face in a looking glass, smiled at the thought of the evening ahead, of the flaring candles and swish of silk and laughter, but with no idea that tonight she would meet the one person in this world she cannot—and inevitably must—live without.

Monsieur moans softly.

The pity of it.

But look!

Julie walks through the empty spaces on the dance floor. It's a trance, perhaps. A spell. Her body is drawn forward, beyond her control. Bewitched. The dancers move around her, sweating and giggling, but she doesn't hear them, and the girl waits for her, still as a stone in a stream, in the centre.

Where she stops. Takes the perfect face in both hands, the blessed, magical skin against hers, leans down and kisses her own soul, kisses lips that are soft, are hers, are home.

There is a moment of complete silence.

Monsieur holds his breath.

Madame gasps.

Then all the fury in the world erupts.

Julie staggers back, shoved away by Abbé Noye. He raises a fist and she lets it land. Nothing hurts except her heart.

Someone grabs the girl and drags her away through the crowd, but Julie cannot move. Not because of the men that stand in her path but her own, stunned, self. Her life is over. That's all there is.

But they will not leave her in peace.

Men are shouting at her, everyone at once, and Monsieur watches as she shakes her head like a boxer staggered by a blow, stares around her, and tries to walk away. They won't let her.

Noye grasps her arm. She shrugs him off but he grabs at her again.

She blinks. 'What?'

'You have insulted the Marquise de Florensac.'

'Is that her name? De Florensac.'

Perhaps she's married. Pity. But no real obstacle.

'Don't you dare let that name pass your lips.'

These lips, she thinks, have done more than speak the name. They have sealed a pact.

The lips part in a smile.

Noye hisses at her, 'Mademoiselle de Maupin, you wear that sword like a man. I hope you're ready to die like one.'

She shrugs. 'You don't want to fight me.'

'No, I want to grind your face into the ground.'

'An unlikely outcome.'

'I want to pierce your sinful heart—'

'Enough threats.' Julie pushes him away. 'I understand. A duel.'

'I will not honour it with that title,' he says.

Another smile. 'Call it what you will. Meet me at midnight in the rue Saint-Thomas du Louvre.'

She turns away from him. Before her stands that pup from the house of d'Uzès. She knows him from long ago, carousing with d'Albert. 'Move aside, sieur, if you please.'

'What kind of demon are you?'

She sighs. He's not going to shut up.

'Are you a man? Or a devil?'

'Neither. Idiot. You know who I am. Out of my way.'

'You have sullied the reputation of my brother—his wife—'

'Let me guess,' she says, peering over his shoulder in the direction of the spot where once an angel kissed her. 'You want to challenge me?'

'Challenge you?' says d'Uzès with a sneer. 'So you do declare yourself to be a man?'

'Not at all. But I'll fight you, since you will insist and I don't care.'

'My seconds will call upon you to make arrangements.'

'Don't bother, d'Uzès. Meet me at midnight in the rue Saint-Thomas du Louvre.'

A tap on her shoulder. She turns. A young man looking as terrified as Thévenard on opening night. He tries to speak. Fails. Then splutters. 'You insulted my cousin—'

'You know her?'

'Marie-Thérèse? Of course.'

She lifts her head and glares around the room. 'Is there anyone here who is not her relation?'

The boy blinks. Tries again. 'My family's honour ... it's impugned ... and I—'

'Midnight. Rue Saint-Thomas du Louvre.' She shouts it. 'Anyone else?'

There's silence. Always silence.

'Very well.'

Then she is gone.

Midnight in the rue Saint-Thomas du Louvre. She stands waiting, sword drawn. A full moon. Clouds. Shadows. The river.

The cousin is the first to arrive. His chaise halts near the corner. His friends hang back, not sure of the protocol. They are young. None of them has seen a real duel before. And this—this is perverse. A duel with a woman.

A clatter of heels on the stones.

Abbé Noye has come alone. He told no-one of the duel—challenged too hastily, didn't consider the dishonour. There'll be no end of trouble if his father hears he's been fighting a woman—a whore from the Opéra. His temper gets away from him sometimes. It's the wine. Must stop that. Next week. But now—

'Let's get this over,' says Noye.

The woman smiles. 'Gently, gently! A little patience, my lord.'

'You wish to withdraw?'

'Not at all,' she says.

'Then?'

'I'm waiting. There's another.'

'Another what?' The impudence of her! Noye notices the cousin for the first time. 'What are you doing here?'

'I challenged him,' says the boy. 'Her, I mean.'

'For the love of God.'

'So did d'Uzès.'

'Three of us?'

'So it seems.'

D'Uzès arrives, borrowed sword in hand. He nods a greeting to the other men. 'You, too?'

'I challenged first,' says Noye. 'I'll kill her.'

'Good. Then I won't have to.' The cousin sounds hopeful. He likes this duel idea less and less. It seemed so obvious at the ball, as if he really had no choice. But nobody's ever challenged a woman before. Now everyone's done it at once. He glances quickly at her. She seems too unearthly, too still. Not afraid. Not in the least.

'It's terribly dark,' he says. 'Why aren't the lamps lit?'

Noye looks around and shrugs. 'What difference does it make?'

The damned woman raises her sword.

'We commence.' Julie salutes, the blade gleaming in the darkness.

Noye won't salute, but he steps forward. 'Stand aside, my friends.'

'No need for such delicacy,' she says. 'I can take you all at once.'

They laugh, then. All of them, even the boy.

She doesn't smile. 'This is becoming tedious.'

She lunges. They don't see what happened, her sword is too fast, only that Noye staggers against a water trough and slumps to the ground.

D'Uzès doesn't hesitate, doesn't salute. He moves quickly, throwing himself into a *flèche* intended to knock her off her feet. Instead, she sidesteps, thrusts as he passes, and he crashes into the wall opposite, blood swelling through his shirt. There's a shriek then nothing, but he's not dead, just quivering in fury and shame and filth.

Further along rue Saint-Honoré, the young man's friends leap into his chaise and whip the horses into a gallop. Then they're gone.

The woman turns. 'Now you?'

She salutes the cousin, who wishes with all his heart he had never been born into the same family as Marie-Thérèse, decides he never really liked her, anyway—remembers that one summer she pushed him off a chair and everyone laughed.

But he's a nobleman. This is the first of those moments he has trained for all his life.

He salutes. '*En garde.*'

Now the woman smiles. 'You've never done this before, have you?'

'That's of no consequence.'

'You're scared. That's sensible. And a better man than those two. I see no arrogance in you.'

He clenches his fingers even more tightly around his sword grip. He notices that the tip of his blade is quivering.

'I will do my duty.'

'Yes, you will,' she says. 'I see that. *En garde.*'

She doesn't aim for his body. He is Marie-Thérèse's cousin, after all. He even has her eyes, not quite the green of a sultan's emerald, but a shade lighter.

When the blade pierces his arm he barely notices at first. A slight tearing sensation. He looks down.

'Oh,' he says. *'Touché.'*

'The contrary would have surprised me.'

'I'm bleeding.'

'Just a little. You'll recover.'

He falls sideways. Curls up on the cobblestones.

She wipes the blood from her sword with a scarf. Looks down. 'You were brave. I'll send someone to take care of you.'

He gazes up at her. So beautiful. For a monster. 'Thank you.'

She bows. 'An honour.'

The boy sees only a flick of her cape as she vanishes into the dark.

Monsieur can't hide his smile when she returns to the ball. Everyone gasps at once. One woman faints. The orchestra falters. The singer is looking for the girl. Of course. But the girl has been taken home, locked in her room, no doubt, perhaps whipped by a humiliated husband.

The three men are nowhere to be seen, which means— well, it couldn't possibly mean … could it?

An evening of gasps. Wait until he tells Philippe. The two of them have always secretly enjoyed La Maupin's extravagance, her dramatic performances, her disdain for the witty tongues and tearing teeth of the salons. They've loved her more than most, because her every outrage causes d'Armagnac pain and he—Philippe's older, contemptible brother—has created nothing but anguish for the lovers. Tomorrow morning, when d'Armagnac hears the news, he'll be apoplectic. How wonderful.

A horrified whisper sweeps the room.

Word has reached them. Three duels. Three victories. Even the noble d'Uzès lies dead in the street. Or the gardens.

Or perhaps they aren't dead, but mortally, treacherously wounded. Treachery is certain, or possibly sorcery, for who can believe that the opera singer could defeat the court's finest hotheads?

Monsieur waves to a page. 'Bring her to me.'

The young man gapes at him, mortified. What next?

'Now!'

The woman in breeches bows before him, lifts her face, and looks into his eyes as no-one but his beloved Philippe is brave enough to do.

'Your Grace,' she begins. 'In the rue Saint-Thomas du Louvre three gentlemen lie stretched on the street. Less than an hour ago they were excessively hot in the head, but the night air might perhaps chill them. Kindly give orders that they be attended by a surgeon.'

He raises a finger, and it is done.

'You are a chevalier, after all, I see,' says Monsieur. 'Your name, sir?'

'I am no chevalier, but Julie—Mademoiselle de Maupin.'

'I knew you, of course. Still performing your old tricks? I have heard you sing. Your debut was as Pallas Athéna, I recall, and here you are, come among us as an Amazon.'

Her head bows.

'Rise,' he says. 'Look at me.'

She does. His heart is still sore for her, for the girl.

'My brother the King has banned duelling. You must know this.'

'Forgive me. I was challenged.'

'By three men? How can that be?'

'I provoked them,' she admits. 'I didn't mean to. They took exception to my—'

'I saw it.'

She presses her lips together.

'You are wounded?' he asks.

'Not by a blade. Your Grace knows that I do not kill His Majesty's subjects, and that there are sweeter meetings than are found at a sword's point.'

He can't speak of it. His chest constricts with something like sorrow, something like love, like the ferocity he felt when he first held his son: a murderously protective, incomprehensible ache.

'But you fought. In the street. With three men.'

'Not all at once, Your Grace. Although I could have.'

'I have no doubt.' Laughter bubbles in his throat and he fights it down. The courtiers are watchful, will report it all to Louis, and he'll get all righteous and kingly and there'll be a scene. So Monsieur hides his smile behind one gloved hand.

'Be still, gadfly. Consider yourself chastened. I reprimand you, on behalf of the King.' He says it aloud so they can all hear.

She drops to one knee. She's seen the baritones do that many a time on stage, offering themselves up to some god or other.

Then Monsieur leans forward and whispers, 'If I were you, I'd leave the city for a while. Months. My brother will be angry, and your victims—the girl's family—they'll be crying out for blood. The house of d'Uzès is prickly enough at the best of times. You'll be safer elsewhere. Anywhere.'

'I only just found her.' She sinks further down, onto both knees.

'I know. But you will find her again. Believe me. Do you need anything? Money?'

Julie looks up, surprised. 'Your Grace's friendship is enough.'

'You have it. Ask my brother, the King, he will tell you: I have a soft spot for circus performers, stray dogs and contraltos in breeches. I forgive them any trespass, and I celebrate their goodness, their uniqueness, with all my might.'

'You are very good, Your Grace.'

'Yes. I am.' Monsieur smiles. Julie sees the bad teeth, the thinning face—the humanity of him. 'Go now. Return only when it's safe. One day, you will appear again on stage with the Opéra and all will be forgiven. I promise.'

After she leaves, he sits and watches more dancing. Fidgets. Drinks too much. This is his world, the alternative court of France. Some say the more civilised court. More cultured. More circumspect than Versailles. More fashionable.

Monsieur holds court just as theatrically as his brother, but he allows his subjects closer to him. Too close, it is thought in certain quarters. He likes people, which his brother does not. He likes talking with women, adores sleeping with men, loves watching them all, dancing, loving, fighting—being human.

Some of them he likes more than others, he cannot lie. He feels too much, loves too deeply. His real vice.

Madame chatters with her flock of ladies, all pretending not to be thrilled at the evening's unexpected excitement and desperate for the night to be over so they can discuss it all again in the morning in the comfort of the boudoir.

Monsieur imagines the dark hours ahead, in bed with Philippe; the tales he'll be able to tell, in whispers—Philippe's face when he hears about the kiss, their stifled laughter when they think about those three buffoons falling to the sword of

La Maupin. The idiots. Can't they see the fire in her? Can't they see past the breeches to the fine porcelain heart?

No.

But I see her. And she sees the truth in me. In her I am purified, Philippe is purified, for now we know that our love can be as perfect as that one kiss I witnessed this evening. We are not evil. We are drenched in sunlight. By those lips we were blessed.

Monsieur smears tears across his face, wonders what La Maupin would say if she knew his thoughts.

I'm an old fool.

There's a flurry of fans. He sighs. His wife is waving at him.

'Monsieur! I'm bored. Nothing interesting ever happens in Paris.'

Act 4, Scene 1

Recitative

INFATUATION IS A STUPID THING, ISN'T IT? We know it makes us silly, sleepless, impatient with our friends, rude to our servants, rough with the horses, careless of our own health—and yet—and yet. We can't help it—can't help ourselves. Can we? Any of us?

None of us is exempt. Even the greatest men in the land are prey to the whims of their hearts. Poor Monsieur had the boy, Philippe. D'Armagnac's brother. A spiteful little wretch, but Monsieur adored him, and that's all that matters. Both the younger brothers of great men. Perhaps that's what it was.

Louis himself spends more nights in Madame de Maintenon's apartments than his own. That's just how it is, in this world.

Even the great Jeanne d'Arc had her infatuation with the Dauphin. He was unworthy of her—history has proved that.

Our Dauphin—yes, it's true—was once infatuated with the most beautiful woman in Paris—in France.

No, not me. Although I thank you for the first compliment you've ever paid me. No. I've never been on good terms with the Dauphin. He's a fool. Why is that so often true of Dauphins, eh?

He was obsessed with Madame de Marquise de Florensac. Can't blame him for that. I'll speak more of her when I am able. She was no Maid of Orléans, though, let me tell you. Nobody knows it better than I. But her beauty was almost a sacred thing. You wouldn't be in any doubt, if you'd seen her, that her face was a gift of God.

The Dauphin was besotted, and that's always dangerous—for him, for the girl, perhaps for the whole court. So Monsieur stepped in—the King was no use by then, so that dear man decided to do what only someone in the royal family could do or risk incurring the Dauphin's wrath—and he sent her away.

To a convent, and then to Brussels.

You see? It's always Brussels.

That's where I went, too. After the famous three duels.

No, she wasn't there. Not then. That was later, the thing with the Dauphin. I forget the details. After the ball, she stayed in Paris. With her husband, who didn't let her out of his sight again for several years. And then look what happened.

But in the meantime, I was in Brussels. Alone. Although not for long.

I sang *Amadis* there. Speaking of great romances. I was always fond of *Amadis*—I sang it many times, in Paris, in Brussels. The music itself is so-so, except for that one glorious air. But the story—it's a silly tale, really. D'Albert once showed me the book—an immense row of volumes in his library, all in Spanish. The *tragédie* I knew, it turned out, was just a small fragment. It was the King's favourite, and he had Lully write the music. So you see, even a king approved of the story—he fancied himself as a knight errant, I think—but the whole story, *Amadis de Gaule*, goes on and on, longer even than my own. I haven't read the whole thing—dear God, it has more pages than the Bible. But in there I read of a woman who goes about dressed as a man—a brave woman—and falls in love with another. You see?

I memorised the lines—I nearly wept when I heard them first, there in d'Albert's library. He read them aloud to me. Sweet, darling boy. She says: 'For a girl to love a girl, alas, what is that—except to be in love with the moon, and try to take it between your teeth?'

She breaks my heart, the Amazon in that book. I wish Lully had written music for those words. How I would have sung it—the whole of Paris might have sobbed at my feet.

Perhaps it has. Perhaps it will, one day—weep for me. For my kind.

Having Brussels sob at your feet is not quite the same feeling, but it's not so bad. Exile. There are worse places. Worse things. Just look around you, look at me.

The pamphlets, the street songs—they relate some of the tales truly enough, as true as my words to you. Others invent and embroider and twist my life like toffee, into scandal or bawdy. You'd never believe the number of men I've killed, the dozens of women and men I've bedded, according to them. Well, perhaps you would, but please don't. The tradesmen, the shopkeepers, the street sellers—they believed it all, embellished the tales themselves, no doubt. It's as if they imagined the streets of Paris to be scattered with the corpses of those who had faced me, as if they believed every woman in France would open her boudoir door to my knock. Ah, if only it had been so.

I wonder what they're saying now. Are they singing of my death? I don't begrudge them that. But I hope it's a dirge, not a ditty.

Why did Paris wish it to be so—all the duels and all the infamy? Why did the city envy me for it, hate me for it, and then wish it again? How could those who invented the tales and composed the ditties come to believe their confections were true?

I can't comprehend it, myself. At the time, I laughed aloud at every outrageous broadsheet, sang the songs backstage to annoy the others. But there were days when even I could find no humour in it. There are days when you want to climb into a bathtub and open your veins like Seneca, or burn every pamphlet in a great bonfire in the Tuileries.

But I learned. Instead you keep your face veiled—you stay off the streets, off the stage, for a while. You eat at home, frugally. No duels. No affairs. You wear brown. Pay your servants a little extra something. Rehearse. Drill. Work hard. Laugh heartily at every joke told at your expense. After a while, the stories change, the songs are in someone else's honour. At Louis's court, there's always somebody doing something scandalous or stupid, and soon enough the wits of the palace and the city will learn of it. Off they will go, sniffing after a new scent.

Then I emerge, to appear in the next show. Everyone remembers why they loved me, and all—or almost all—is forgiven. There are songs instead about Thévenard, or the Dauphin, or that sour-faced Madame de Maintenon. I sing along. We all do.

So that time, after the duels, I took to the road—to the air. I vanished from sight, or at least out of view of those sharp-eyed gendarmes. I rode again through the night, through the damp forests, forded nameless rivers and braved the local bandits. Just a horse, a cloak, a blade, a song. Perhaps a loaf of bread and a jug of wine. I was a troubadour—perhaps what the Spanish would call a *picaro*. A *picora*, in my case. Spain. Bah! I will get to that, by and by. Patience. But first—you recall—the night of the duels, the night of the kiss, I rode north.

In my exile in Brussels I was treated like a queen. Literally. But it was an odd, bereft feeling, at first. I felt as if, that night at the ball, I found my lost—or maybe fractured—soul. In her eyes. Her face. Thérèse. Marie-Thérèse.

A kiss. That's all. Not even a dance. Certainly not a courtship. Then she was bundled out of sight and I found myself on a fast horse, fleeing the gendarmes and their righteous grasp.

They weren't after me at all, as it turns out, but I didn't know that. Monsieur had seen to it. Still, I was better off well away from the city—out of mind, if you like. Out of Paris. Into the fog and the heavy air. Not good for your chest, you know. For your throat. Riding at night, missing someone I didn't even know—had barely met—as if my heart was broken all over again. How could I know, then, what she would—could—become to me?

I knew nothing. I was wrong. So hilariously, pathetically wrong. But never mind. You can't change history. At least, not much. You can elbow it out of the way from time to time, but it comes back to its true course, like water—like love.

Act 4, Scene 2

Ensemble

BRUSSELS. THE CITY GATES. Dusk. Four guards. Two pikemen. All arguing with a farmer on a dilapidated cart. At once.

A horseman approaches at a canter. A fine black horse. French saddle. A chevalier, perhaps, in a great cloak and feathered hat and ready sword.

Reins in. Halts.

'Good evening.' The voice—it's not quite—could it be? 'Do you speak French, my good men?'

'Of course we do. Where do you think you are? The moon?'

It is a woman. In boots. She's laughing. She's—why, she's beautiful.

'I beg your pardon. May I pass?'

'Your papers?'

A flourish. A fine leather glove. A smile.

'They are all in order,' Julie says. 'Authorised by the King's brother. Signed by the Cardinal himself.'

'Let me see.' A sergeant pushes the others out of the way. 'Madame de Maupin?'

'Yes. Why?'

'We were told to expect you.'

'Really?'

'There was a letter yesterday. From the palace.' The sergeant takes hold of the reins.

Julie resists the temptation to drag the horse's head around out of reach. 'From Versailles?'

'No, no. From our palace—from the Elector's secretary.'

'Please. I can explain.'

She tries to take the papers back. Can't quite reach. Her hand goes instead to her sword.

The sergeant holds his ground. 'We were told to escort you to the Quai.'

'What is that? Some kind of lock-up?'

Laughter.

'No, no, madame. It's the opera house.'

They are all waiting for her. The musical *surintendant*. The *directeur*. Two sopranos. A dozen secretaries. A baritone even taller than Thévenard. A handsome *haute-contre* with charmingly slender ankles.

They greet her with cries, welcoming smiles, a smattering of applause. They were in the middle of rehearsals, someone explains, when the news came. They are saved. It's a week since the girl playing Minerve came down with a fever. They had hoped—but, no—it's no use. She can't perform. Nobody else can carry it off. It's a big sing.

But now, their saviour—if it's not blasphemous—that's how it feels—a sign of God's favour—the great good luck of the company—and here she is, among them—as majestic as everyone says—as brilliant as—yes, let's not pretend—she is indeed wearing breeches and sword, just like the rumours— the tales spread from Paris and across Europe—La Maupin. Here. Now.

Singing as if her heart might break.

If they fear her a little, so be it. In the days that follow, while she spends her days in rehearsal and her nights sitting alone, the incredible news arrives in houses all over Brussels, in letters from family, friends, mere acquaintances from Paris. There was a duel—she kissed a girl—tried to abduct an innocent maiden—no, a married woman—dragged her screaming from the ballroom. No, she fell in love. That's all. She fought dozens of men. Three are dead. Four. Possibly seven. On the ballroom floor. In the streets. On the steps of the Palais-Royal. A frenzy. No, a cold-hearted assassination. No, a misunderstanding. She's a monster. She's mistaken. She's Monsieur's favourite—and you know what they say about him.

Now she's here. Striding across the stage on the opening night of *Thésée* as if she was born for this moment, born to astonish, to entertain—to enthral. She is a goddess, dwelling on high, intervening from the heavens in the pitiful affairs of humans—Minerve the wise, the magical. Minerve the goddess of music, of poetry, of war. Minerve—La Maupin? Who else could La Maupin be? Who else could possibly play Minerve? Impossible to imagine, ever again, that a mortal singer, a mere woman, will sing these words.

She wrings every tear, every ounce of pity, from the *parterre*, even from the benches above. She is enough, almost, for the crowd to forgive her the duels, the outrage, to forgive the French for the wars, the siege, the many deaths. But not quite. Instead, they forgive her for being French. After all, she can't help that.

In the royal box, the Elector, the great Maximilian Emanuel himself, God's representative on this earth—or, at least, the Emperor's representative in Brussels—feels his chest flutter like a girl's. His breeches tighten uncomfortably. He can hear his own breath, loud and jagged. He watches as this woman—this deity—from Paris holds the hearts of the good people of Brussels in her warm hand and squeezes.

Beside him, his Polish princess sits as open-mouthed and amazed as everyone else.

The next morning, once Maximilian has recovered his composure and eaten his breakfast, he summons La Maupin to the palace. To his bed.

Act 4, Scene 3

Recitative

HE'S A GENTLE MAN, Max Emanuel. For a soldier. A little too fond of his own greatness, it's true, and of his own reflection in the glass. A slightly elevated opinion of his prowess as a lover—but that's not uncommon, I've found. Ambitious, yes—but why not? He's the son and grandson of kings, emperors. At war with everyone now, you know—always did hate those Habsburgs. He's fled to Versailles, so I hear, to hide behind Louis's coat-tails, just as he has hidden so many of us in his court over the years.

His weakness—well, frankly, he has several (including an unfortunate chin), which no doubt our own King has now discovered for himself, but his greatest weakness is women. Mine, too, of course, so we had a lot in common.

He has a wife—the daughter of kings herself, so I understand, though I never can keep track of these things. This war they're having now, this nonsense about the Spanish succession, the business at Blenheim. Who cares? Louis and

Max Emanuel, certainly. But who else understands why the Austrians and the French are killing each other over the Spanish crown? What does it have to do with us? With England? You have to be of the Blood, I think, to know who's related to whom or to care which of your fifteen titles derives from what branch of the family tree. I'm not. I don't.

But Max Emanuel does, and with good reason. There are endless thrones and titles for him to claim, to inherit, to take by force or charm or espionage. It was an education, I don't mind telling you, just to be near him—watching how the wheels turn in such a mind, such an empire.

He's not so different from d'Armagnac, of course. Much younger. Better looking. But they both had armies at their disposal, and hundreds of horses, and mistresses galore, and gold plate, and me. I wonder how he fares now, trapped in the costume party that is Versailles. The third circle of Hell for men like him, like d'Armagnac.

Funny, isn't it? I'd thought when I left Paris my life would be over. I pictured myself living out some horrid existence in exile. Well, that was to come, sure enough. But in Brussels, I fell on my feet. Or, to be more precise, on my back.

Onto a goose-down mattress.

He looked after me, it's true. He gave me an apartment in the palace—in the opposite wing to his wife's, naturally. I had the pick of the stables whenever I wanted to ride, and a new pair of gloves every month. There were servants, dinners, salons, the occasional ball.

So life went in Brussels—singing, mostly, and being polite to old men in drawing rooms on Saturday afternoons, and waiting around in my rooms in case Max Emanuel decided to look in. At first, I thought it was the least I could do. After eight months, the palace felt like a prison and no number of fancy gloves would keep me within those walls on a fine day.

Did I love him? No. Never that. But he was mine, and I defend what is mine. I was like one of those enraged animals in the King's menagerie, pacing, growling—howling, even— desperate for attention, just as desperately hating every moment of it.

He felt the same. He's a man of war, of power, like an old charger trapped in the stables. He needs air, blood, cannon and marches. Trumpets. Not harpsichords and lace fans. He needs problems to solve: forage shortages and artillery trajectories. Sieges to raise. Bridges to build. So do I. In my own way.

I'd imagined I'd never again need to be anyone's mistress. I'd been rich and beloved and thought I'd never have to ask a man for anything ever again. Ingratitude has never been one of my failings. I am only too aware of the thin veil that separates me from hunger, from poverty, to underestimate the value of friendship. But there I was. All because of a kiss, kissing someone else, pleading his indulgence, begging for an afternoon in the sun, a ride in the forest, a moment, a hint. I wanted blood. His, mine—I didn't care. I wasn't in my right mind. Fractured, somehow. Furious. I see that now. I hated him, I hated myself, I hated what I had become.

They say I tried to kill myself. What nonsense. I know where the heart is. I never aim for it—not my own, not anyone else's. If I did, I wouldn't miss, believe me. But I made a fuss, it's true. It wasn't my finest moment.

Act 4, Scene 4

Ensemble

T HE CURTAIN RISES on a row of flaming candles, another dazzling evening. The opening night of *Aeneas*. Everyone in Brussels—the quality—is there. The Elector is in the royal box, as he has been so often over the last few months, because of the singer.

But all is not well between the goddess and the prince, or so the story goes. It swirls around the theatre, the foyer, the streets beyond. The rakes in the *parterre*, the *duchesses* on the benches, the stagehands, the chorus, the flower-sellers outside whisper it to each other.

'The Elector has taken a new mistress.'

'I heard. The dancer. Mademoiselle Merville. Is she beautiful?'

'Pretty. But not prettier than Mademoiselle de Maupin.'

'Nobody is.'

'But more ...'

'More feminine.'

'She's jealous? I wouldn't like to be that dancer.'

'But is the Elector mad? To give her up for some plaything?'

'True. If she were mine ...'

The singer is distraught. Everyone knows it. What will become of her? What will become of us if she leaves? The new mistress is French, is English—perhaps German. A distant cousin. A lady. Beautiful, yes. But not beautiful enough. And married.

The music begins. It doesn't stop them talking. A German opera, in Italian. That's modern life in Brussels. It's mournful, gently moving. As Dido, Queen of Carthage, the French singer struggles a little with the lyrics, but it doesn't matter; her tone, those long, soft, expressive notes, the breath, the silence between the sounds, the purity, the sorrow—ah!

They are spellbound. They are silent at last. Dido weeps, they weep.

The last scene. Dido must sacrifice herself—for her city, for love. She holds the knife aloft. Four hundred people hold their breath. She stabs at her breast, and again, then falls to the stage.

Stops singing. There's blood. Nobody has ever seen such brilliant acting. Such special effects. So realistic. So gripping. The other cast members stand in awe. Or something. The crowd is on its feet, applauding, calling out for the final aria.

Until a stagehand runs across to the singer, turns her onto her back. Her head lolls to one side. He waves his arms. A baritone vomits into his helmet. Someone screams.

The curtain falls.

The Elector is furious, it's said. He has so many mistresses—what harm can there be in another? The singer recovers enough for them to have another blazing row, so violent you can hear them in the guards' hall. In the chapel. The Chancellor, the kitchen boys, the sentries on the gate overhear.

'How could you do such a thing? And in public?'

The Elector glares at his attendants and they scamper for the door.

Julie waits until they leave, but knows they're listening just outside. 'Don't pretend that you care.'

'I see. So it was a test of my regard?'

'At least you noticed.'

'Everyone did, you idiotic woman.'

Julie is propped up in bed on a dozen silk cushions, her throat and shoulder tightly strapped. The pain is visible on her face, but it doesn't stop her shouting. 'Your mistress—the other one—was she there with you?'

'Even worse.' The Elector paces the room like a captive lion. 'Some paltry attempt at revenge.'

'Did she see?'

'Why do I bother with you? I, who can have any woman he wants?'

'So can I.'

Julie manages to struggle out of bed and throws a set of dinner plates, brought all the way from China, at the Elector's head. He shouts gutter words, filth, soldier's curses.

The reconciliation is almost as violent. She cries out, he cries out, their voices rise and fall in duet. The doctors fear for the singer's wounds. For the Elector's soul. She heals fast. Is back on stage within two weeks, lamenting Dido's tragic fate as if nothing happened. He meets his other mistresses with more discretion.

The Comtesse d'Arcos, for example. Perhaps a little less interesting but a great deal less trouble than the singer. She

plays cards in the evening, waits in her boudoir for his visits—
her body, her mouth, her smile available to him at any time.
She lets him do whatever he wants, doesn't fight him, straddle
him, insist on her own pleasure. Like some. At least, those are
the cards she has laid out for him, for now. The stakes are high
and she understands, better than the singer, how to play.

Her husband knows not to visit his own house at certain
moments. His drivers, his footmen, alert him to the presence
of the regal carriage in his own courtyard and he drives on,
to an apartment in town, to his own mistress. All so civilised.
Circumspect.

So the Comte d'Arcos is not surprised by the summons
to the palace, nor by the private interview with the Elector's
personal secretary, and although he is a little nervous about the
task he is given, the request so politely made can't be refused.
But he understands. These are delicate matters. Need to be
handled with care, with diplomacy, at a distance. There need
be no plate-throwing, no stabbing. No dramatics. He hopes.
Still, it must be done. One does not decline the honour of a
commission from the palace, even if it may seem, to outside
eyes, perhaps a little perverse, perhaps a little insulting.

So d'Arcos finds himself backstage at l'Opéra du Quai
au Foin late one night after a performance. *Amadis*. He
imagined it would be the perfect setting—a private dressing-
room, a rowdy atmosphere beyond so they can't be overheard.
Instead he finds the singer surrounded by women in various
stages of undress, some still in face paint, some slightly drunk,
all laughing and singing, and two in the corner who look as if
they might be fondling each other's breasts.

She is laughing with the others, a grubby towel around her
neck, her beautiful face wiped clean of paint—though there's

a smudge of it on her throat—her hair hanging in ringlets down her back. Here, she is the *prima donna,* as the Italians say, the one who chooses her roles, who receives the most flowers, who kisses the dressers and consoles the chorus girls and teases the dancers. It is she the crowds come to see, to hear. She will not give it up easily.

She sees d'Arcos waiting—knows all too well who he is, what it means. Ignores him. Nothing less than a regal decree will rip her out of this place.

It is nothing less that he carries.

'Madame, if I may ...' he begins, with a bow.

'Have we met?'

'No. Sadly, no.'

'Do I wish to meet you?' She faces the mirror, watching his reflection.

'Probably not,' he admits. 'And yet here I am. Comte d'Arcos, at your service.'

'Are you really?'

'Forgive me. No.'

'In whose service are you, then?'

'I cannot say.'

'I understand.'

D'Arcos glances around him. 'Is there somewhere more private we might speak?'

'Forgive me. No.'

'It might be more pleasant.'

'I doubt it.' The damned woman still won't look at him.

'More discreet.'

'These are my friends, my sisters,' Julie says. 'I have no secrets from them. Well, not many. If you have something to say, out with it or be off.'

D'Arcos swallows. 'As you wish.' But then the words won't come.

'You were saying, sieur?'

'I have …'

'A message?' She smooths oil into her forehead, her fingertips circling, massaging, entrancing.

'Yes. That's right.'

'I don't wish to hear it.' She stands and turns to face him at last. She really is very tall.

'I'm afraid I must insist.'

'I see.'

She doesn't appear to have a sword to hand, but looks as if she could snap his neck in an instant. Her robe falls open. He sees Dido's scars, only just healed, near her heart, her breast.

He has never wanted any woman as much as he wants her at this moment. He struggles for breath, for words.

Gives up. Holds out the purse.

'What's this?' She stares at his outstretched hand as if it held a viper.

'Two thousand *livres*.'

'That's my price, is it? It's not much.'

'Two thousand every year.'

'Ah! My pension?' She lets go a laugh.

'Your recompense, madame.'

'For what?'

'Travelling expenses.'

'Really?' She moves closer. 'Where am I going?'

'I don't know. I don't care. Nor does the Elector.'

He realises too late that he's lost, he's failed, he's in mortal danger. She snatches the purse from his hand and flings it at his face. He feels his nose smash into fragments, a spurt of blood, cries out. But she's shouting at him now.

'Pay me off? Is that the plan? Pathetic. How dare he send you to deal with me?'

'I was ordered.'

'A man like you, a weakling like you.'

'I'm bleeding.' Is he weeping? Is it possible?

'D'you think I care?'

'I'm sorry.' Now begging. In a moment he will bow at her feet, he knows it. She knows it.

'I cannot be bought.'

'It's a gift, that's all. I swear.'

'You have it then,' Julie says, almost snarling. 'It's your reward for being an arse-sucker. If you were even half a man you'd take it back and throw it in his face.'

'I can't. My wife—'

'As if I would stay here, in this cesspit of a city, after this insult.' She throws her robe wide open and he shouldn't look at her, but he can't help himself. 'Let's see how your precious Opéra gets on without me. You'll be sorry. He'll be sorry. Imagine how dull your lives will be now. Without me. Without La Maupin.'

'It's true.' D'Arcos hears his voice as if it's someone else's. 'You must stay. I'll talk to him. Beg him.'

'You tapeworm. You flea. You cuckold. Get out before I kill you.'

He stumbles from the dressing-room, his sleeve across his face, blood everywhere, tears. Behind him, she stands at the top of the stairs, naked now and still shouting, and he can hear the uproar—fifteen women on their knees scrabbling for gold coins.

Act 4, Scene 5

Recitative

I'VE READ CERVANTES and the great romances. I thought that after Brussels, Spain would be—I don't know—picturesque. It may well be, but picturesque is not what you need when you're as poor as a rat-catcher.

I rode like Amadis—or perhaps Don Quixote, it seems to me now—for weeks, through dry mountains and great plains, past towns walled up so tight that not even one of their famous conquistadors would bother with a siege. Yes, there are windmills and herds of goats, just as you read in the books, but there are orchards, too, and orange-blossom fragrance in the air, pilgrim pathways and rivers too fast to ford.

I tell you this—Spain may be under the thumbscrews of the Inquisition, but they have a fondness for an Amazon. Who can blame them? They were good to me, in the countryside and the villages. Just as well, or I might have starved—or, worse, gone crawling back to Brussels begging forgiveness and coin.

But where was I? Ah, yes—hoping to find my fortune in Madrid, and finding nothing but hunger and boredom. The local opera companies performed the Italian stuff mostly, and a few Spanish pieces—we agreed early on that we were not suited to each other.

I kicked around the city looking for trouble, it's true, making what I could from a duel here, a song there. Sold my horse to pay the bills—stupid of me, of course, because all I wanted by then was to ride back to Paris and see if the fuss had died down. But I was stuck.

I'd seen enough of the world—it's not to my taste.

I had no coins for a room, few enough for food—a bowl of slops from the cookshop, a pie. Half a cabbage. I sold my boots. My cloak. Then I gave up. I needed a job, and anything is better than nothing—or so I thought. But I should've known by then that when your choices are starvation or humiliation, your decisions will always be regrettable.

So I went to work for the Countess Marino. She spoke French. That was her only redeeming feature. Her husband was the Minister for something or other—hunting, probably, or shipwrecks. Who knows? Very high up at court, anyway—a fact none of us were ever allowed to forget. He was rarely at home. Not surprisingly.

Months I worked for that bitch, dressing her, complimenting her, painting her face white so nobody would see the age spots or the bruises her husband left. Or at least, that's what she imagined.

She bore a passing resemblance to the Infanta, or so she said. In fact, it was more than a passing resemblance to a wild boar—all bristles and crooked teeth. She delighted, so I heard, in telling people that she had an Académie star as her maid—

that she had reduced me, tamed me, that I had given up the stage to serve her every need.

No, not every need. I wasn't that down on my luck. Mercy, I feel sick at the thought. Let's strike that from our minds this instant.

So. To the point of it. Revenge is simply God's way of righting the world. He uses us as His instruments when His plans go wrong. When, for example, a woman of great beauty and talent is abused and defiled by a creature of warts and crashing stupidity. Such things cannot be borne by the universe. Such wrongs must be righted, and revenge is one simple way of doing so, of correcting—of eliminating—the evil.

She was evil. Believe me, if you'd seen that face there would be no doubt in your mind. Perhaps not Satanic evil, I grant you. But the flaccid evil of the weak, the cunning—those with inherited wealth and hereditary folly, those with no redeeming qualities beyond the entitlement of rank; the bullies, the petty thieves, the body snatchers and swindlers and bureaucrats. All of them. They may not be instruments of the Beast as such, but they torment us in this world. You know the type. You may even be one of them.

But the Countess Marino—oh, my, she was a piece of work.

Day after day, night after night—whining, carping, squabbling with her husband, cheating even her daughters at cards. She was mean. I slept on the kitchen floor with the rest of the servants. They were a dull lot, and no wonder. The Countess once had her footman whipped because it was raining when she alighted from her carriage. Whipped. Right there, in front of everyone, before Mass at the cathedral. A pious Catholic, indeed.

A wretch. A cow. Devoid of—

Very well, I will come to the point, to my glorious retribution.

Every winter in Madrid there is a grand ball. The Cardinal, the Duke, everyone attends, apparently, and all the fancy titles come in from their country estates and their palaces and spend three weeks talking about what everyone else is going to wear. Everyone has a title in Spain, by the way. There are more princes there than in Heaven.

Countess Marino ordered a gown from Barcelona—I don't know why, since the couturiers there have never been to Paris—and gloves from Rome, and I don't know what else. All hideous as sin, anyway, and let's face it, no amount of imported silk was ever going to conceal that ugliness.

But the hairpiece! The hairpiece was my own special creation. I slaved over it for days. A pale blonde wig, hair of a virgin from the mountains of the Swiss or some such nonsense, laced with gold thread and tiny pink rosebuds of softest silk. A thing of blessed beauty. I might have worn it myself. Or Fanchon—it would have suited her perfectly.

But not the Countess. Oh, no. She hated it. Too young for her, of course, and she knew it, but I'd forgotten—mercifully—in the afternoon hours of braiding silk and flaxen tresses, that this floating wisp of hair was to crown a warthog. I'd wanted to create something fine, to help me drift away from my repulsive life of patting powder on that wrinkled neck and whispering compliments into the ugliest ear in Christendom. I'd sat in my workroom, singing softly, sewing and weaving and smiling to myself, as if I were elsewhere—as if I and my voice and my delicate fingers were drenched in sunshine and rosewater, instead of sweat and despair. I poured into it all the skills I'd learned watching the dressers at the Opéra, all of the grace I'd absorbed from the Comtesse. So it was my own fault, I suppose. I made something too beautiful to be worn, except by the beautiful.

On the afternoon of the ball I presented it to her proudly. Perhaps pride was my sin then, too.

She glanced at it for only a moment, then snatched it from my hands, tore it to clumps, and threw it on the ground. She raged and cried and threatened to dismiss me on the spot.

I said nothing. Nothing at all.

Unusual, I know.

Her chambermaid came and took her away for a bath. You see? My lot could have been worse. At least I didn't have to see her repulsive crocodile skin all over, or empty her chamber-pot.

She was returned to me in her undergarments, praise God, and we squeezed her into the corset and gown, the stockings and slippers, the favourite black wig. I painted her face until she looked like an ageing courtesan, which was just how she liked it, and dressed her wig.

I admit it was not as exquisite as my first attempt. But stunning in its own way. Crimson ribbons set against the black hair, her ruby nestled on the forehead with a gold chain woven through the curls. White marabou.

She was radiant. She was as pretty as a suckling pig. She even condescended to compliment my work.

'Ah, my dear, my hair is lovely tonight—you have excelled yourself.' Her very words.

I assured her that the true glory of her hairstyle would only shine through at the ball.

I feel sure it did. But by then I was on the road to Paris—on my way home.

Act 4, Scene 6

Divertissement

THE CARRIAGES WAIT in a long line before they can reach the portico. The Countess Marino hates every moment of it, would scream, would get down from her chaise and be carried in a chair if she could. But it isn't done. One must wait. Even when one feels like scratching out the eyes of one's driver.

Finally, the carriage door opens, the Cardinal's footmen greet her with a bow, help her down the stairs and into the foyer, the maids take the cloak from her shoulders, the mantilla from her perfect hair.

'Careful, you fools!'

The Count is there to offer her his arm and lead her into the ballroom. He's smiling, almost laughing. The excitement of the evening must be affecting him—even him, when he's grumbled for days about it.

The Cardinal stands in the doorway to greet his guests, who bow low, kiss his ring. The Countess sweeps into the room as if she were a queen—which is just how she feels for this evening, this moment. Gloriana. Triumphant. Beautiful.

Across the room, the Grand Duchess waves a fan. Her sons, handsome in their uniforms, bow. The Italian ambassador and his plain daughters come forward to offer a few words, a greeting, a compliment. The dancing begins. The Count leads her to a chair where she can watch it all and be seen by everyone. He is attentive—waving to a footman to bring supper, a little wine, introducing her to several charming gentlemen new to the court, their daughters, their wives. They are all extremely complimentary, especially about her hair. There is—yes, there is—a queue of people waiting to meet her, to talk with her, to admire and flatter her.

'My goodness, madame, what a delightful spring hairstyle!'
'You are a vision this evening, Countess. Quite a vision.'
'Pretty as a picture—a painting, perhaps, of a garden.'
They all agree. Nobody has ever seen such a hairstyle, such a delicately wrought combination of curls, and marabou, and precious stones.

And at the back, just so, faultlessly matched to the ribbons and just out of her sight but placed so that everyone else can see them, a dozen or so small, perfect, pink radishes.

The perpetrator of this outrage is miles away by dawn, heading for the pilgrim route through the mountains to France.

In an old Castilian city filled with monasteries, she stops for a few days to rest, to sell her stolen mare and buy a horse less likely to attract attention. She, too, is conspicuous, in her breeches and sword, a head taller than everyone else in town—even the men. She must keep moving, keep riding. Someone will hear, someone will know. Instead she goes to the theatre.

The play is famous, the story remarkable and, even more remarkably, true. Once there was a woman—a nun—who, in breeches and armour, sword in hand, helped conquer the New World. Catalina, *La Monja Alférez*. The Lieutenant Nun. The audience cheers her on, through her wars and her duels and her loves, to her triumphant return home.

In the crowd, only half comprehending what is said on stage, stands the Frenchwoman in breeches, hands clenched so savagely that later she will find her nails have drawn blood. Her own. She watches Catalina on stage. A conquistador, a chevalier. A hero. The audience gasps: that poor maiden doesn't realise her love is really a woman. The conquistador, brawling and drinking, deceives innocent virgins and comrades in arms—one moment he's a man, then next she's a woman, hiding in a convent. The shocking truth is known only to the sixty people in the theatre, even the singer, whose Spanish is sparse. She knows more than all of them.

Her face is in darkness, her breath oddly jagged, as if she is sobbing. As if she has seen a ghost. Or a mirror. She feels the people around her touching her sleeves, her coat-tails—is she real? Or one of the performers? She isn't sure herself. There are more of us, she knows it now—of course there are, just not as famous as me. For every great chevalier there must be a dozen gutter imps and farmers' daughters and restless milkmaids who can only dream of the lives we lead, Catalina and me. Not the myths of the ancients. Not the imagined romances of the books. Real women. With other women.

Oh, Clara. If only you knew.

Oh God, if only I'd known.

Act 4, Scene 7

Recitative

IT WASN'T STEALING. NO. The story of the radishes was about vengeance, not other worldly crimes. I am not a common thief. I am not a common anything. Retribution was exacted. The money, the horse, it was owed to me—that and more—for my months of work and my many humiliations.

Whatever penance I owed to Paris had been well and truly paid and the city welcomed me home. With open arms. More or less.

My duels were forgiven. Not another word was uttered on the matter—not officially, anyway. The gossips still fluttered on about the night of the three duels, and there were songs in the streets, little ditties in which I always came out the heroine, even if the lyrics were less than kind. But there was no official trouble. Monsieur had seen to that.

See how far I had come? No need to ask d'Armagnac to intercede for me this time. From then on, I knew that if ever the need arose, I could whisper into the ear of Monsieur myself. Give the lobe a little nip, even.

Monsieur knew, too, that I was his champion, just as everyone at court and the Académie knew he was my protector. So I might have whispered in any ear, at any soirée, and any courtier would run to do my bidding.

Tell you a secret, Father, though you'll never have need of such precious knowledge. But any lady of the court knows it. The secret of whispering successfully to a powerful man is to wait until he is seated. He is at your mercy. Then you bend over him, low and close, so that all the time your breath is on his skin, his eyes are mere inches from your throat, your décolletage. He imagines—well, whatever he wishes—and he is utterly yours.

Men whisper from the side, or even from behind, because to do otherwise would be too threatening. But women who do the same are fools. Or wives who have grown complacent.

You see, the other secret about powerful men is that they all grow tired of being masters of their world. They can't let anyone have any more power than they possess, or they will lose prestige, land, maybe even a kingdom. It wears them out. So they dream of a few moments of being subject to someone else, of losing themselves in the joys of submission, of surrender.

That's what they imagine when you bend over them.

Well, not you, obviously. That would be anyone's nightmare. But if I do it, then whatever I wish for is mine. A pardon. An invitation to the next ball as if nothing had happened. A private dinner. A solo performance in the next concert at Trianon. Jewels, I suppose. A minor title. Anything.

But I asked for little. Just to be left alone and, on occasion, to be forgiven my trespasses.

All that didn't work on Monsieur, of course. He and I saw eye to eye. Breasts and breathing had no effect on him at all. He couldn't be swayed by a pretty smile unless it was worn by one of the palace guards.

Too much for you? I don't care. This is my story. Whether or not you listen, whether or not you care, or cry, or applaud, or snigger into your sleeve—that's up to you. It won't stop the telling. Only death can do that.

I've been thinking about what happens after my death. Not to me. To you. All of you.

You won't weep. That would be asking too much. You will pray for me, though, won't you? I've already paid the Abbess for it. I want a proper *Requiem* sung for me, every night for a week. Perhaps a month. I can afford it. Even a *Te Deum*. Charpentier's. I always liked it. I don't want you saying the Mass, either. Bring in someone from the city. Someone good. I deserve that, at least. A choir. Heavenly or otherwise.

I never sang much sacred music myself. Not in public. Pity. They wouldn't let me, most of the time: fearful, I suppose, that I'd do something outlandish or act the jester. But I wouldn't have. I promise you that.

I did sing a Mass for the Duc d'Orléans once, you know. For the King. But there weren't many voices that night. Louise Couperin played spinet, bless her, and Thévenard shouted a few choruses. I was brilliant, naturally, but it's not quite the same thing.

Outside bed, I'm never so transported as by a choir. Especially nuns. Women's voices, you must admit, bring one as close to God as is possible on this earth. Even the monks— there was a *Stabat Mater* by one of the Italians—Palestrina, perhaps—I heard in Saint-Germain-des-Prés one evening that left me howling. I hadn't heard anything so sublime, so crystalline, ever.

But to the priests, opera singers are little better than prostitutes. I can see their point, but still—imagine if Fanchon and I had been allowed to sing with Le Rochois in one of those holy places where any music swirls and ascends. Even in the Palais-Royal, with all the noise and smoke, our voices melted together like a heavenly chorus, like a harpsichord and trumpet and viola. Me being the trumpet of the trinity, I suppose. When I sing with Thévenard, on the other hand, with our voices low and sombre, we sound like a *basse de viole* and a *flûte à bec* in duet. You can hear our friendship in the notes—sometimes furious, sometimes hilarious. Sometimes smiling into one another's eyes.

How we might have soared, we three women together, with the Holy Mother looking down on us from atop the altar. We would have turned men's hearts to butter. Or gold. Or sunshine.

Le Rochois was often invited to sing sacred music, being somehow free from the stain of the Opéra. I can still hear one of her solos in a *Magnificat*—I don't remember the occasion, but the Dauphin was there. There were several sopranos, but it's her voice that lingers in my ears, she of the impeccable morals and an uncontaminated heart of the sort one doesn't often meet on the stage. We are a pack of sinners, as a rule.

Yes, all your prejudices are well-founded, Father. You can rest easy there. I know only too well that no matter how completely I confess to you, the Church will never allow me to be buried in consecrated ground. You think we are whores. Painted ladies. It's true, the women of the Opéra all have lovers and sometimes husbands as well, and the men drink too much, and everyone—well, it's intense, you see. There is rivalry, of course. But mostly there are long hours of gesture practice, endless rehearsals, costume fittings and voice exercises over and over. Rituals and rules.

Like the fencing halls. Like this place, come to think of it. Yes, that's what I said. The Opéra is in many ways just like your precious sisters of the Visitandines.

Funny, isn't it? You think of me as some kind of wastrel. Don't you? Admit it. Yet I've spent most of my life—hours, every single day—driving my body and my mind towards a kind of perfection you can't even imagine. Drills. Exercises. Lunge after lunge after lunge. You have no idea how it hurts. Scale after scale after scale. I am more disciplined and regimented than you, and have been since I was seven years old. Granted, I've had more fun in my hours of leisure. But those hours were few.

Yes, there were more duels. More reasons to keep up my guard, to perfect my aim. I've always worked hard. Like my father—except sober. Well, mostly. Early mornings in winter, legs burning with pain, fingers almost frozen to the sword's grip. Late nights in the rehearsal room with a drunken baritone—there is always a drunken baritone, usually Thévenard—a tyrant for a *surintendant,* and the women always stuck there until the last bell. We challenged each other, it's true. We fought and almost sobbed with frustration and laughed heartlessly at each other's mistakes.

But it was worth it. On those nights, opening nights especially, when the crowd is spellbound, when our voices weave and circle and embrace each other, they soar and hover over the stalls and the sound—ah!—a sound like the passing of angels' feathers. You'll think it sacrilegious, I know, but we were a heavenly choir and, above us all, like the Mother, flew Le Rochois.

When she retired—the year '98, it was—I'd just returned from Madrid. She was tired, she said, worried that her voice was wearing out. Now I understand what she meant. She performed one final, miraculous Isis and bowed out, graceful to the last curtain. All of Paris was desolated. We were bereft, those who were left behind. There was an empty space on the stage at the Palais-Royal, a blackness that could never be made light, a rent in the fabric of the Académie—or so it seemed at first. Then I realised, a heartbeat before the others, and probably an entire month before Fanchon, that it wasn't a blackness at all.

It was a brightly lit spot in the centre of the stage in the greatest theatre in the world.

So I stepped into it.

And I shone.

I glittered. I was radiance and majesty. I would never be Le Rochois, but I was something else, something they had never seen—and will never see again.

La Maupin.

Act 4, Scene 8

A ballet

THE PALAIS-ROYAL. THE SHOW IS OVER. The crowd spills out of the rue de l'Opéra and onto the forecourt. Someone falls—someone else shoves the guardsmen back. But there's no room for a fight. It's always like this. Hundreds of people funnel through a dark passageway. They hold their noses, try not to slip over on the slimy flagstones, and push until they reach the air.

Another evening of *Thésée*: the poetry of Quinault, the magic of Lully. Everyone agrees the Académie was in fine form this evening. The women confer, heads close together, about the costumes, the singers, about Thévenard's thighs, the magnificent theatrics of La Maupin, Fanchon Moreau's freckled arms. The men place bets for tomorrow's wrestling bouts at the Montmartre fair. There's a great deal of money on a lightweight from the Midi called Séranne. He's a beast, apparently. Broke an opponent's neck last month in Lyon. But the money says he'll be no match for the local lads.

In the corner of the terrace, someone's talking far too loudly. A man. An enormous man. Dressed as if he's the richest king in Christendom. Perhaps he is. Who knows? The young blades cluster around him in the hope of a little sport, of an invitation to supper, to cards, to drink.

The Baron de Servan feels their eyes on him as he speaks, knows they are admiring his shoes (too new and pinching a little, but worth every *sou*), his gold-braided coat and the finest silk cravat money can buy. The rings on his fingers. His wig, higher than almost everyone else's—except, perhaps, Monsieur's. His cane. His buckles. They admire him. They must. He has spared no expense. He also has a great deal to say.

'The opera in Venice is paltry compared to ours. I'd give you one Lully to ten Monteverdis. Ten! And the singers there—let me tell you—they have nothing, *nothing*, on ours. Thévenard is the finest baritone on earth. Without doubt. Ugly brute, of course, and not a gentleman. Not at all. Peasants. They are all peasants, of course, these singers.'

The young men laugh. Not at him, surely?

'Some of the ladies, I grant you, are pretty enough,' he goes on. 'I've had them all, of course, every one of them— singers, dancers, even the plain ones—sometimes several at once. It is my great fortune to be—not to put too fine a point on it—and that, my friends, is the point, if you take my point. Ha! I am, for reasons, shall we say, of anatomy, irresistible to women. Especially to the women of the Académie. For they have no morals. Only lusts. I am the only man who can satisfy them. So I can assure you, gentlemen, of their peasant nature, their animal tendencies—you have no idea.'

The young men glance around, check who's listening. A few snigger. It's gone too far now. Some of the older fellows shout a protest.

'Good sieur, mind your tongue. Please.'

'There are ladies within earshot, Baron.'

He doesn't hear them. He has an audience, a title, new shoes and gold braid and, by God, they will listen to him.

'The Desmatins sisters are too coarse for my tastes. Goblins. Fishwives. But there is a new face this season who has caught my eye. Oh, yes. The dancer Pérignon. A fine figure, don't you think?'

'Oh ho, Baron,' says one man, slightly more drunk than the others. 'You set your sights very high. Mademoiselle Pérignon is a good girl, from an old family.'

'There are no good girls in the Académie.'

The young Comte du Saint-Rémy steps forward, whispers, 'Take more care in what you say, sieur.'

No hope of that. Not tonight. Not ever.

'I am rich,' says Servan. 'I could buy her—any of them— like that. But I'm a hunting man, my friends. I like a chase, and that filly Pérignon—'

'Enough!' The shout comes from the shadows, from the portico. 'You have said enough, filth.'

Baron de Servan waves impatiently at the interruption. 'That gentleman does not appreciate my humour.'

The shadows ripple and a figure steps into the half-light. Someone tall, lithe, sneering.

'Really, I admire the patience of these gentlemen.'

'Are you speaking to me, sieur? You dare to disagree?'

'You are a foul liar, I say!'

'What?' says the Baron, peering closer at the stranger. 'Who are you, to speak to me in this manner?'

'The Chevalier de Raincy, more gentleman than you are, and ready to teach you a lesson. And you?'

'I am the Baron de Servan.' He will not bow in the face of such impudence. 'No doubt you have heard my name.'

'No, never.'

'It will be written on your headstone.'

'Such fantasies!'

Servan feels the circle of men sidle away from him. He has no choice but to accept the challenge.

'You have declared yourself my enemy, Chevalier. My seconds will call on you in the morning to make arrangements.'

'I will await them eagerly.' The Chevalier de Raincy bows deeply and slips back into darkness.

Baron de Servan snaps his fingers at the man closest to him. 'Saint-Rémy! Will you act as second for me in this matter?'

'But, Baron, we are barely acquainted.'

'You dare deny me this? Will you, too, insult me in front of so many?'

'Forgive me. I will act for you, if that's what you wish,' says Saint-Rémy. 'But, Baron, you should know—'

'I have heard enough. Find out where that scoundrel lives, then come to me to set the terms for this duel.'

Saint-Rémy can do nothing but bow and take his leave. He knows perfectly well where the Chevalier de Raincy lives—and it's nowhere near the Château du Raincy.

In a tavern in the Marais, two people argue as if they are husband and wife. Both handsome. Both armed. Both just a little drunk.

D'Albert slams a fist into the table. 'Chevalier de Raincy? What were you thinking?'

'It was the first name that came into my head.'

'An odd choice, Émilie, you must admit.'

'I sang there once. For the Princess Palatine. Monsieur arranged it for her birthday. I'd just been thinking about it during the afternoon. Gorgeous gardens.'

'We need to discuss this challenge of yours.'

She's not listening. 'You know the stables at Raincy are almost as fine as Versailles?'

'You judge all chateaux by their stables?'

'Of course.' She takes another swig from a bottle. 'It's what I know best.'

'Stop changing the subject. This oaf Servan obviously doesn't realise who you are.'

'All the better.'

'For whom?'

'Everyone.'

'Please.' D'Albert leans forward. He tries to catch her eye but she looks away. 'Let me tell his seconds. They'll call it off.'

'I don't want to call it off. I challenged him. I'd do it again, too.'

'But, Émilie, apart from anything else he's a Goliath.'

'That doesn't matter,' she says. 'I'm not wrestling him.'

'But his reach—his sword arm is twice as long as mine.'

'You think I'll lose?'

D'Albert is silent.

She puts her hand on his arm. 'Joseph? Do you?'

'Of course not.' He doesn't sound sure.

Julie sits up straight, puts the bottle on the floor. 'He's a rich, loud-mouthed brute and someone has to teach him a lesson.'

'But why you?'

'You weren't there,' she says. 'You should have heard him. Wait until I tell Thévenard. He'd rip him limb from limb.'

'Servan has a mouth. Everyone knows that.'

'The things he said. Nobody else would speak. Well, not many. To them, Mademoiselle Pérignon is just another whore from the Opéra. Like me. Like Fanchon.'

'She's not like you,' says d'Albert. 'None of them are.'

'They are exactly like me. Women. Girls. Trying to get through our lives. Make a penny or two. Fend off disease and hunger and bastards in our bellies for long enough—just a couple of years—to save a few *sous*. Marry well, if we're lucky. Poorhouse if we're not. Our only options.'

'Not you, Émilie.'

She struggles to her feet and stands there, swaying slightly. 'Yes. Me. All of us. Marie-Louise fluttering her eyelashes at the Dauphin. Fanchon flitting from man to man. Ballet girls letting that prick Duménil put his filthy hand up their petticoats. Me—'

'You never let me give you any money!' D'Albert reaches out to steady her, tries to pull her back onto the seat.

She shrugs him off. 'I'm not talking about coins changing hands.'

'I'd give you anything you asked. You know that.'

'I do. That's why I never ask.'

'What's any of that got to do with Servan?'

'He insulted us all.' Another gulp of wine. 'Not just Mademoiselle Pérignon.'

'He's a cretin. I could kill him myself.'

'After I'm finished.'

'He's not a gentleman, certainly,' says d'Albert. 'He must have bought his baronetcy.'

'Not the first to do so.'

'Émilie, he's not worth the risk.'

'He may not be,' she says. 'But Mademoiselle Pérignon is.'

'You are determined?'

At last she lowers herself down onto the chair, almost misses, straightens up in the hope he didn't notice. 'Speak to his people. Thévenard will act as my other second. You two can make all the arrangements. I don't care what you decide. Just make it soon. He has the look of a coward about him and he may vanish before I can fight him.'

'But, Émilie—'

'Go now.'

Elsewhere in the city, the Baron plays cards by candlelight.

Jacob du Saint-Rémy paces the room until Servan snaps, 'What's wrong with you? You're acting like an old fusspot.'

'This Chevalier de Raincy ...'

'He's a fool, obviously. Soon to be a dead fool.'

'In fact—well, it will sound silly—but ...'

'Out with it!' Servan gives up on his game and slaps his cards down on the tabletop.

Saint-Rémy stops pacing, takes a breath. 'It's not a man,' he says. 'Not a chevalier. It is the singer, Mademoiselle de Maupin.'

'A woman?' Servan laughs. 'Insulted me to my face, then challenged me in public?'

'Yes. So it would seem.'

Servan's laughter fades. 'Does everyone know?'

'Probably.'

'Then what am I to do? I can't fight a woman, surely.'

'It's not unheard of, at least in her case.'

'Really?'

'There was an incident …'

'Extraordinary.'

'A few years ago now, at a ball at the Palais-Royal.' Saint-Rémy will never forget it. Nobody will.

'A precedent?' Servan takes up his cards again and starts shuffling.

'Yes, although in that case she—'

'And her opponent was a nobleman?'

'Yes. In fact—'

'Excellent. Then we proceed.'

'My dear Baron, I should warn you—'

'We need to make arrangements. Duelling ground. Weapons.'

Saint-Rémy bows his head. Nobody can say he didn't try. 'Yes, of course.'

'I choose pistols.'

'I see.'

There is a long silence.

'You don't approve?' says Servan, although it's clear in Saint-Rémy's face.

'Forgive me, but it may appear churlish. Everyone knows La Maupin is a swordswoman, not a marksman.'

'In that case she shouldn't have insulted me. She took the risk.'

'But she would never have dreamed it would be anything but swords.'

'Then she can apologise,' says the Baron with a smile. 'Back down.'

'She can't do that. Everyone knows what happened. She would be dishonoured.'

'So? Honestly, Saint-Rémy, you talk about her as if she was a gentleman. She's a whore from the Opéra.'

'Very well, I'll try to talk her out of it.' Saint-Rémy could not sound more reluctant.

'Don't tell anyone I said that.'

'Of course not.'

'Anyway, I don't care if she can't shoot. I'll happily blast her smiling face off.'

'Servan!'

'What?'

'This is a woman you're threatening.'

'I'll shoot you, too, if you don't stop nagging me.'

'If you prefer, you may choose another second.'

'Oh, shut up. Dawn. The riverbank, near the Pont Neuf. Pistols. Or an apology.'

The woman does not back down or offer an apology. Her second, d'Albert, argues for a few minutes on the subject of the pistols but it's no use. The challenger forfeits the right to choose the weapon. There's no way around it. Tradition must be followed. Honour must be upheld. Pistols must be used.

When Julie hears of it, she simply nods. 'You'll have to lend me some, Joseph.'

'You don't even own a pair of pistols?'

'Why would I? Nasty, noisy things. Never had any use for them.'

'Never?' D'Albert shouts it. 'D'you mean you have never duelled with pistols?'

'I know how they work. I used to clean my father's musket.'

'Émilie, please, an apology.' He grabs at her hand. 'Call it off.'

'Don't be absurd.'

'He's a famous marksman. Hunts all winter. Deadly.'

'So you keep telling me.' She slips free of his grip.

He sighs. Loudly. 'That's because you won't listen.'

'It's boring.'

'I just don't want you to get killed.'

'Oh. That.' She shrugs. 'It doesn't really matter.'

'It does to me.'

'You're sweet,' she says. 'Now, lend me some pistols.'

Almost dawn. The river's low, edged with sludge and vile as a cesspit.

D'Albert groans in the darkness. 'Absurd choice of duelling ground. The man's a fool.'

'I told you so.' Julie gazes up at the outline of the city against a softening sky. Her city.

'The gendarmes at the Conciergerie will be here in minutes,' says d'Albert. 'As soon as they hear a shot.'

'At least the blood will run away quickly, into the water.' She kicks aside a plank of rotting wood.

'Émilie, in the name of God—'

'In fact, you can just roll my body into the river and save on the expense of a funeral.'

'That's not funny.'

'It wasn't a joke,' she says, and he knows it. Feels it.

A carriage pulls to a halt on the bridge.

'Remember what I told you—'

'Yes, Joseph.'

'Fire as soon as you see my hand drop.'

'Yes, I heard you the first twelve times.'

'And if he fires first—'

'Fire anyway.'

'That's right.' He attempts an encouraging smile.

Footsteps sound in the square, on the stone steps.

'Don't be nervous, my darling boy.'

'Me?'

'You're trembling.'

'It's the cold,' he says. 'But I do fear for you.'

'Is it cold? That's funny. I can't feel it.'

He doesn't remember ever hearing her sound so ethereal, so defeated. Shadows—men—make their way across mud, flotsam, filth.

'Sometimes I wonder if I'll ever feel anything at all,' she says. 'Again.'

'How can you say that?'

'Forgive me.' She grabs at d'Albert's arms. 'Forgive me everything.'

'Émilie. My friend. There's nothing to forgive.'

'I wasn't talking to you.'

There's no time to ask her meaning. The others are there: Thévenard looking as if he could kill, Servan scowling, Saint-Rémy unpacking a set of expensive pistols from a leather case.

Julie calls out a greeting. 'Lovely morning for it.'

Servan's eyes narrow. 'Do you continue to mock me, madame?'

'It seems so.'

'We'll see who's laughing soon.'

Jacob du Saint-Rémy steps forward. 'Madame de Maupin,' he says, 'do you offer an apology?'

'I do not.'

'Will you retract your challenge?'

'No,' she says. 'That is impossible.'

'Very well. Baron de Servan, do you wish to continue with the—'

'Yes, yes. Hurry. The sun is coming up.'

'I ask again, do you wish to continue?'

'Of course. My honour has been sullied.'

The blasted woman laughs at him. 'This vicious pettiness has nothing to do with honour, nothing to do with me. You fight because you can't have the woman you covet. Simple.'

Fury writhes across Servan's face. 'You have impugned my reputation enough.'

'It is you who does the damage, sieur. Your every word renders you less of a gentleman.'

He lurches forward. The seconds step between them.

Thévenard shoves Servan along the bank a little. 'You behave,' he growls, 'or I'll shoot you myself.'

'Gabriel.'

'Sorry, Julia. But really.' He moves to stand close by her.

Julie pats his arm. 'Get out of the way, dearest.'

Her seconds take their places. D'Albert stands next to Saint-Rémy, with signal arm raised, Thévenard to her left with a spare pistol. She smiles at them—her bearded giant, her golden boy.

'My two friends. I love you.'

'Stop acting like this is the Ascension, Julia,' says Thévenard. 'Concentrate.'

'Bless you. You worry so.'

Saint-Rémy clears his throat. 'You know the rules?'

'Get on with it,' says Servan.

'Very well. Commence pacing.'

They stand back to back and pace away from one another, their seconds counting the steps.

'Nineteen, twenty.'

Saint-Rémy allows a moment of silence. 'Now turn to face each other, salute, and when you see Comte d'Albert drop his arm, you may fire.'

They turn.

Servan's impatient. Feet placed precisely, his gun arm up—a model of perfection.

'Get ready, Julia,' says Thévenard. 'In the name of God.'

'Oh, I am ready. Believe me.'

Her wrist is languid, the pistol barrel pointing down towards the riverbank.

Some part of Servan knows it's a ploy—she can't possibly be so relaxed or so inept. But the greater part—the roaring bluster, the utter certainty—tells him this is a woman, this is a peasant, this is easy. The target is too wide, too open, to resist. He readies his nerves, his legs, his arm. Waits for the signal.

Then he's on the ground.

His supporters tell him later it was impossibly fast. As if it matters. He's beaten and she's gone, striding off along the quay with her arms around her friends, as if nothing has happened, as if he—he!—is nothing, as if—

She leaves him without even the dignity of a flurry, an exchange, that brilliant shot he'd planned—not really a duel at all but an assassination. But he's not slain. Not even wounded badly enough to attract sufficient sympathy in the salons.

'She cheated,' he shouts, blood pouring through his fingers.

'No, Baron. She's just very fast.'

'She fired before the signal.'

'I'm afraid not,' says Saint-Rémy, bending over him. 'I'll call the surgeon.'

'Did you see?' Servan clutches at Saint-Rémy's cloak. 'She cheated.'

Saint-Rémy motions to the waiting servants. 'Fetch the carriage. A rug. Quickly.'

'She must have. Dear God, I'm dying.'

'I doubt it,' says Saint-Rémy. He's quite calm now this unpleasant duty is finished. 'La Maupin never duels to kill.'

'Who says?'

'Everyone.'

'Everyone?'

'She's famous for it.'

'What d'you mean, famous?' Servan's servants bundle him up in a quilt.

'I thought you knew,' says Saint-Rémy. 'Everyone knows.'

'Fuck everyone. Get me to a surgeon.'

Later, they tell him he'll survive the amputation, if not the shame.

In an inn just off rue Saint-Séverin, there's a woman eating. A great deal. She sits at a long table between two men—one as tall as a mountain, one as pale as winter sun, both laughing and shouting at once.

'Did you see his face, Émilie?'

270

'I didn't care to look. Pass the bread.'

'He didn't know what had hit him.'

'I would have thought it fairly obvious,' she says. 'Are you going to eat that chicken?'

'A fine shot,' says d'Albert, 'for someone who's never fired a gun.'

'Don't be ridiculous. My father was a *mousquetaire*. I learned to shoot at six.'

'But everyone's been saying—'

'Everyone else. I said no such thing.'

Thévenard throws his head back and roars. 'Ha! The fool.'

'Pompous, festering arsehole.'

'Joseph, I've never heard you talk like that.' Julie grins at him.

'What do you expect?' says d'Albert. 'It's true.'

Thévenard thumps d'Albert on the shoulder. 'First sensible thing you've ever said.'

'Thank you. I think.'

'You two behave yourselves, please,' Julie says through a mouthful of roast chicken. 'There's been enough nonsense for one day.'

'You're right.' Thévenard slaps the tabletop. 'We'll get drunk instead.'

'Gabriel, it's only just past dawn.'

'You see? We've missed at least an hour of drinking time already.'

'Is he always like this?' asks d'Albert.

'Only on work days.'

They laugh—the cook's son, the prince and the singer with the sword—and get so drunk that the gods Minerve and Egée can barely stand upright on stage that evening, and Minerve clutches tight when her machine lurches up into position above the chorus.

The next morning, the goddess of the Opéra wakes with a sick stomach, in a bed scattered with flower petals by every ballet dancer in the corps.

Act 4, Scene 9

Recitative

GOOD MORNING.

Sit down. Hurry up. Time is short, I feel it. My voice, my breath, are wasting away. You should see my legs. Bones. That's all. I won't show you. I still have some pride.

I will try to tell you a little more of my story. But I'm fading. I never thought this would happen. Not to me. My forehead burns, and all the potions in Avignon can't ease this fever. Sometimes it feels as if my eyeballs might melt. Ah, well.

You are not my first visitor this day. Christ came to me in the night. He visits me quite often nowadays, Father. He speaks to me—our Lord—stands by my bed, places His hand on my brow.

You doubt me. Well. Does He speak to you? Directly, I mean? Say your name and command you to Him?

No.

I thought as much.

The first time it happened, I told the Abbess. As one should. Doesn't happen every day, after all—or at least, it never had. Not to me. Did she tell you? She blames the fever. Wild dreams. Hallucinations.

I know what she thinks, what you all think. But if I were a real nun, those dreams would be called visions. You'd rejoice. Write to Rome. In fifty years' time, widows would pray to me, pilgrims journey on their knees to my grave.

But not me, not this sinner.

That's what you say to each other in your scrubbed hallways and nasty little offices. It wasn't a dream. I don't sleep. Not anymore. I lie here, sweating and thinking and deciding what to tell you and what to keep safe inside.

But He doesn't care, He who loved another sinner—that Magdalene, whose sins were like mine. He forgave her. He forgives me, even if you will not, you and your Abbess. But His opinion is the only one I care about at this stage. The hour of my agony approaches.

You remember, Father, the parable of the lamp under the jar? I do. Funny, I remember more of the Gospel now although it's years since I learned it, by heart, reciting it back to Papa every Sunday morning while he nursed his sore head and first bottle of wine. In that story—Luke, isn't it?—Jesus said, 'Then pay attention to how you listen; for to those who have, more will be given; and from those who do not have, even what they seem to have will be taken away.'

You'd do well to dwell on those words, next time you feel the need to contradict or interrupt me.

But I wonder—my God, I do nothing but wonder—why would He want such a thing? *From those who do not have, even what they seem to have will be taken away.* I always thought that a little harsh. Coming from the God of love.

I mean, those who are born into a life of grandeur understand that the world is arranged to suit them. Those who make their own wealth assume they can rearrange the world the way they want it. Both are terrifying, close up.

I'm not like that.

I'm a freak. A queer creature.

All I can do is put on a show—all day, every day—and wait for the applause. Or hisses. In a way it doesn't matter which. It's the show, the performance, that matters to me. To everyone.

Although two thousand *livres* a year doesn't hurt.

But I find, to my great surprise, that I am one of those who do not have, and that everything has been taken away. Just like Our Lord predicts. And I hate it. Hate it. There are moments when I hate Him, too, for saying it, for making it so. If indeed He does.

For a brief moment in the span of my life, I was truly happy. For months, even years at a time, I was adored, wealthy—other years, everything vanished. I fought with my friends, I hurt people who did nothing more than irritate me. I soared and then I fell. Are those moments of my life—those memories—as random as they seem now? Or does God really have a plan—for me—for anyone? Some people never leave the ground, and still they fall.

I ask you, O utterly useless spiritual adviser, how can that be right? How can that be just? Why would God allow it to be so?

Don't give me any of your platitudes. My time is too short to waste listening to you. I will ask Him myself when I see Him. Soon.

But I do understand, in a way. It's not about money, about riches or carriages or pretty clothes. It's about our souls, our hearts, isn't it? About love. About the people around us. And how easy it is for them to be swept away, no matter how you cling, no matter how many tears you shed. Yes, even me.

Look at me. Here. In a building full of people. Alone. Except for you, of course, and you don't count. But all these women, all these faces. None of them any use to me, none of them the face I want. Love.

When I was younger—then—I didn't understand the difference between desire and love. How could I? Desire was the only thing I had known, and it felt so strong, so consuming, that I thought, I assumed—especially after a few bottles of wine—that feeling must be the romantic love of the ballads and the stories.

But it wasn't. I see that now. Don't get me wrong. Desire can be a fine thing. Desire is enough, sometimes. It will send armies to conquest, inspire the poets—pathetic lot that they are—make friends aim pistols at each other in the Place Royale.

It was enough for me. For years.

What do you say, there? Muttering at me like that. What would you know? Keep your nonsense to yourself. I have no use for it.

I am trying to reconcile myself to my own life here. You can help or hinder. But remember, those who hinder me inevitably find themselves bested.

I've had few friends but loyal. I've had many romances— are you keeping some kind of tally, Father, in that book of yours? Double it. I can't be bothered to tell you of the boring fucks and the odd momentary madness.

I've had great love. Felt it. Lived it. Lost it. Truly great love, biblical love, a romance worthy of a thousand books, of an opera, of a broken heart.

There is passion in all of it, even in the anger, even in the curses and spitting fights and long nights staring into the embers. Passion isn't a sin. Passion is godlike. But so human. Passion is the link between all of those things—desire, love, friendship, sin; between all of us.

I have been lucky in my friends. D'Albert, Thévenard—silly bastards, both of them. Fanchon, all the girls. The Comtesse. And Maréchal. Many more. More friends than enemies. That's something, eh?

Though there have been times, I confess, when it's been hard to tell the difference between the two. Take Thévenard. There was a time—a few years ago now—it wasn't my fault, so this is not so much by way of confession as providing you with a few morsels to write down on that growing sheaf of paper—he got a bit full of himself—puffed up, you might say—slightly too intoxicated with his own heady perfume.

Francine promoted him to *primus bassus*—the world wondered at it, with Gabriel still so young and not long with the Académie—but I can admit now that he did deserve it, and since he's had a few more years to prove his worth, there are few in Paris who'd disagree.

But then—then—he was a pigeon promoted to peacock. He ordered four sets of clothes, a new cane with a silver handle, hats and shoes and Lord knows what else. Hilarious. Had to have his own wig-maker present at each performance to ensure the sanctity of his tresses. Another boy in attendance to apply his makeup, because doing it himself was beneath him. And he never, ever, stopped talking about it. Every sentence began with 'Now that I am the *primus bassus*', until I and everyone else was ready to turn him into a *castrato*.

Perhaps he even felt guilty about being so favoured so soon—I don't know. But he became extremely tedious.

I played a little trick on him—or maybe two—and instead of taking it with his usual good grace, he exploded.

I suppose I exploded right back at him.

Act 4, Scene 10

Comédie en vaudeville

'GABRIEL, IN THE NAME OF GOD, shut up.'

'I will have a new cloak made. Ermine trim. That'd look fine, don't you think, Julia? Very fine, in fact.'

'If you want to look like some *abbé*. Why don't you find yourself a nice altar boy to go with it?'

'Stupid girl.'

'Remind me why I have to listen to this?' Julie stands up and heads towards the door.

Thévenard shouts after her, 'You could at least pretend to care about my career. After all, it was I who—'

'Don't say it.'

'—talked Francine into letting you audition—'

'I warned you.'

'—into taking you on, that very first day in Paris.'

'But you won't stop. Never stop. Talking. Always talking. Dear God.'

'It was I who made you who you are,' he shouts even louder. 'What you are.'

'Enough.'

The *primus bassus* looks around. She has disappeared. He hates how she does that. Somewhere a door slams shut.

The next night, he's on stage, as always. Declaiming. She's on stage beside him, as she so often is these days.

He is a king, a hero, an adventurer. She appears to him in a dream. A goddess. A vision in white silk and gold paint. Between them they hold the audience in a web of rapture, of breathless wonder. He flashes his dark eyes at the crowd. The women sigh.

The goddess whispers in the king's ear as he sings. Appears to—did she really? The king howls, grabs at his bitten ear. Resumes the song. The goddess grins. They both sing.

The people in the expensive seats at the side of the stage see the king pinch the goddess extremely hard on the buttocks. The goddess, mid-note, squeaks. Stomps a sandalled heel on the king's toe.

He wanders in front of her as she winds up for a difficult note. The audience leans this way and that, trying to get a glimpse of her behind the big man. But he seems to be in the way. All the time. Until he is pushed or kicked aside, gasping for breath, so she can stand centre-stage alone and finish her song. The people in the *parterre* applaud until they fear their hands will break.

By dawn the next morning, the city is filled with ditties and poems and broadsheets about the great duel between Thésée and Minerve, the battle of the ancients. La Maupin hears the water-sellers singing as they drive past.

Who is the bravest?
Who is the mighty?
Troy fell before him
La Maupin falls nightly.

Thévenard overhears his washerwoman, as she pounds his new linen shirts in a tub in the courtyard.

There was a primus bassus
Beaten by a woman
Bitten by a woman
Oh! What a woman—la!

Francine shouts at them for nigh on an hour before the next performance.

'The crowd noticed. Monsieur noticed. Everyone's talking about it. There will be no more of this. You will stop this duel now. Both of you.'

Over and over he says it, and over and over they pinch and bite and kick and block. Every night. Ticket sales soar.

One night, a dead mouse is hidden in La Maupin's wig with a little note: *With compliments.* She laughs and throws the tiny corpse at her dresser.

Thévenard wakes up the next morning to find the city plastered with posters making outrageous claims about the size of his cock, or lack thereof.

Have you seen THÉVENARD
Up close?
All beard and manliness

Muscles and moustaches
But NOTHING to show for it
Down there.
Nothing at all but NOISE.

He spends a fortune paying a gang of men to take them all down. By nightfall, another poster has found its way onto every wall and door.

Beware the *primus bassus*, my friends,
The lowest of the lowly,
The fattest of the fat,
The thickest of the thick.
Beware the *primus bassus*, my friends.
Beware the noxious vapours,
Beware the endless rumble,
Quake in fear before the *primus bassus*,
My friends!
Beware his *primus* anus.

A week later, La Maupin discovers her horse's stall is empty except for a sign that reads: NOW THE PROPERTY OF THE PRIMUS BASSUS.

So Thévenard is not really surprised to find his dressing-room floor covered in horse shit.

Julie hears rumours that an anonymous person has commissioned a *comédie* about her life, in which her character will be played by a cow from the Carnival.

It's the last straw. She's ready to draw a sword. A pistol. Anything. She issues a mock writ, asking the good people of Paris to arrest him on sight.

Thévenard won't leave his house, no matter how piteous Francine's pleas. He hides inside for three days. He may be huge, but he's not stupid. He remembers what she did to Duménil. To Servan. At last he opens his door, slowly, to see workmen dismantling the staircase below him. Has to climb out the window, roaring curses.

Finally Francine brokers a truce worthy of the Edict of Nantes.

Palais-Royal. Foyer. Just before curtain. The big man stands on the fourth stair so everyone can see him. Holds up his hand until the crowd falls silent.

'My friends, I have an announcement.'

'You're retiring?'

'You're getting married?'

'To La Maupin?'

He keeps his face as tragic as possible while the laughter fizzles out. The tragic face is his area of expertise.

Then he speaks. 'My friends, I have wronged, unjustly and foolishly wronged, the greatest singer on this earth and this—bear with me—this is my modest apology.'

He takes the letter from inside his ermine-edged cloak. 'Please allow me to read it to you, so that you may witness my humility.'

He pauses. Gazes around the room. Pauses again, then reads.

'*My dear Julia—*'

The crowd shouts with delight.

He ignores them and waits again for silence before continuing.

'*My dear Julia, everyone in this world has his good points and his bad. I am quite ready to admit that you handle a sword a*

283

great deal better than I do. And you must agree that I sing better than you do.'

More shouting.

'Well, then, that being so, you must please recognise that if you only ran me through the breast three times, my voice, supposing I did not die, might be very seriously impaired, and I am bound to think of what my voice means to me, not to mention the bliss of gazing into your eyes when we play together and you don't fire off those ferocious retorts which rob your expression so completely of its sweetness.

'So let us make peace. I come to you bound hand and foot (in writing, however, for an interview with you might be dangerous). Forgive me for a jest for which I am unfeignedly contrite, and be merciful.'

He knows that by noon tomorrow, versions of his letter will be printed up and pasted on walls all over the city, that wherever La Maupin goes, people will stop her and ask her about his apology and whether she will forgive him. He knows her too well—as she knows him.

That's the only danger. He has backed her into a corner but he knows, better than anyone in Paris, how she loves a fight when the odds seem to be against her.

Sure enough, a few nights later, after the show and in the same foyer, with many of the same faces milling about, La Maupin stands on the same stair with a piece of paper in her hand.

She doesn't need to do anything at all—everyone stops talking and turns to her.

'My friends, I have an announcement.'

The cheering is almost as loud as it was after the performance. She smiles. She doesn't need to read from the paper, but she holds it aloft, for effect, as she speaks.

'*Since Monsieur Thévenard so frankly admits the distaste he entertains for a meeting with sword in hand, even with a woman— which leaves me no other course than to congratulate him upon his prudence—I consent to forgive him his offence.*'

A man down the front laughs so much he spills ale onto his boots. The others clamour for an encore. She inclines her head graciously and goes on.

'*But I wish that, with this pardon granted, he ask me forgiveness before those who witnessed the injury; if he takes care to reunite them in my presence, I will keep my word.*'

'Ooh!' the crowd exclaims as one, and as Julie turns her back to them and climbs the stairs, two-dozen white wigs lean towards one another.

'How extraordinary.'

'So the apology is accepted.'

'Without a doubt.'

'But Thévenard faces further humiliation. Tomorrow night, perhaps?'

'He won't mind. It's better than a duel.'

'What on earth caused it, do you know?'

'I heard he insulted the Comte d'Albert.'

'I heard he seduced Fanchon Moreau.'

'Yes, La Maupin is jealous, that's all.'

'Rubbish. She upstaged him one Sunday, and he was furious.'

'No, no. It was nothing like that. I heard ...'

Act 4, Scene 11

Recitative

OF COURSE, THEY WERE ALL WRONG. I can barely remember now what the precise cause of all the fuss was, but the fight and the apology were well worth it, whatever the grounds.

Why aren't you laughing? Not even a hint of a smile.

Honestly. You aren't much of an audience, Father. A tough crowd, as they say in vaudeville. This is a tale of penance. You should enjoy it.

Gabriel learned the joys of humility, and I experienced the pleasure of public vindication. Of sorts.

It was just as well, really, as our destinies were so closely entwined, and we had to see each other every day, sing together every night. For me—for him—singing is an act of love. It always has been. We can't sing easily, readily, with someone we detest. Singing with Duménil was torture. I wanted to spit at him. I did, once or twice. But with an old friend, it is a pleasure.

So long as you're talking to one another.

We made up. Just in time. For our next show was something very big, very important—to me, at least.

The piece itself was neither here nor there—oh, no. *Proserpine,* it was, one of Lully and Quinault's; rather lovely in itself but adored by the King, who promised to attend if we performed for him at Versailles. His home and mine.

So I returned. Not as the urchin. Not as the great man's mistress. Not as the lover of a swordsman from the Midi or a runaway nun or the Madrid maid—but as a princess of the Académie, a star in the heavenly firmament, the woman with the sword who would make them all forget about Le Rochois or the blonde sopranos.

As me.

La Maupin.

There is no woman on earth, or in Heaven for that matter, like me. Perhaps there never will be. Although you never know.

We played—not in the stables this time, but in the forecourt—to the King and Dauphin on a dais in the centre, and their children and mistresses arranged like shop goods about them. Hundreds of courtiers—muttering, chattering, shimmering like schools of fish in the Grand Canal.

It was a beautiful moonlit evening. Part of me longed for a sudden downpour upon all those feathers and jewelled slippers, so we'd have to sing in the Grande Écurie. You see? I do have my sentimental side.

I played Cérès—another deity, another Olympian—the vengeful mother, the source of goodness. Gabriel was Pluton, against whom Cérès vows revenge. Appropriate, don't you think? The irony was not lost on us. On anyone.

D'Armagnac was there, of course, and Monsieur, who sent flowers to me during the ovations. Many, many ovations.

You don't believe me?

I don't care. I can hear the applause, the cries, even now, echoing around the palace—off the walls of the Grande Écurie, through the hallways and kitchens, the dark dormitories, the orchards and potager—through my father's musty bedchamber and the cemetery where he lay rotting—through my skin and bones and teeth, stinging my eyes—thundering in my chest like redemption.

Act 4, Scene 12

A minuet

WINDOW PROPPED OPEN. AN apartment looking out on rue Traversière-Saint-Honoré. Another sunset over the city.

It's a bedchamber like any other. Swept clean. Tidy—extremely tidy. That's how she prefers it. The woman is practising her parries and her arpeggio at the same time. Parry *quarte*, riposte, parry *sixte*, riposte. Lunge.

'Fa, la, la, la, la.'

Lunge again. Simple thrust. And again. Again.

'Fa, la, la.'

The blunted sword tip spears into the soft pine of the wall, over and over—the same spot, the same precise motion.

A knock. Her supper. Julie leans her sword against the bed, throws a blanket around her shoulders, and opens the door.

'Good evening, Madame Foré.'

Silence. The maid pushes past, glances around the room, at the hole in the wall. A clunk as the tray is set down on a chair.

'Thank you.'

Silence. The maid turns to go.

'Wait.' Julie peeks at the food on the tray. 'That's not what I requested.'

A shrug.

For a moment, Julie feels like a guest in her own room. She circles around the maid and looks right into her face. 'Madame Foré, have I insulted you in some way?'

'Pardon?'

'You never speak to me, and if you do, it's as if demons have forced your tongue.'

The maid crosses her arms. Wrists as plump as a thigh of pork. 'Perhaps that is so.'

'Nor do you address me properly. Not as madame—not as anything.'

'But what are you?'

'An odd question. Impossible to answer.'

'Yet you expect me to call you madame?'

Julie pushes a stool sideways with her boot. Sits. 'Politeness. It's all I ask. Manners. In my own apartments.'

'Manners are for those that deserve them.'

'But surely I have treated you well? I pay you more than enough for your trouble.'

'For my work, yes. But not enough for conversation. And not for some weeks.'

'Is that it?' Julie asks. 'Don't worry, Madame Foré. There will be money enough, soon. Next month, the new season begins, and my contract—'

'I don't care about the money. I know what you are.'

'Yet you show me less respect than a fishwife or a beggar.

I, who have performed before the King, only last year—sung for the greatest courts in Europe. I am—'

'You're a whore.'

The word blasts—a cannonball, an exploding shell—through the air.

She should stand—should reach for a sword—run the old bitch through. But instead she sits, staring.

She's heard it whispered in the streets. She's heard the muttering in the hallways. But nobody has ever dared—

'Devil!'

She gazes at the woman's face—her fat lips glistening, her tired eyes—and feels strangely still, as if the anger—there must be anger, surely—is too poisonous to be borne. She senses it, just an edge, and retreats from it, all in an instant. She understands for the first time the impulse to murder and the darkness from which it strikes—the deep, fluid—

'Monster! There. I have said it.'

So now everything is clear.

'You have said enough, Madame Foré. Fetch the landlord.'

It's a whisper—barely a sound at all—but if she speaks aloud she will scream, and never stop screaming. She knows that all the years of discipline, of training, have been for this one moment—this agony of not killing someone, of not unleashing the demons within, of not burning the house to coals, of not dragging the stupid cow by the hair all the way through the streets to the stocks in front of the Conciergerie, of not crushing her skull beneath a boot—between two hands—not tearing the veins from her throat—not—

'I am frightening even myself.'

Did she really say that out loud? She is alone now.

She waits for the landlord as if he was Richelieu. Smooths the creases from her blouse. Throws a rug over her pillows. Picks up her swords very slowly and deliberately, and locks them in the weapons chest so she can't—won't—hurt anyone.

And she waits.

The landlord doesn't come. Nobody does.

She waits until the food that she didn't order is congealed into yellow lumps on the tray.

Downstairs in the kitchen, there's a whispered argument between maid and landlord that's been going on for hours.

'Then throw her out in the street,' says Madame Foré. 'What of it?'

'She's a good tenant, that's what. Pays on time.'

'Not lately.'

'Even so.'

'She's a witch, monsieur.'

'She means no harm.'

'You haven't seen it—her room, her bedclothes after visitors. Disgusting. All sorts of men she has up there. Even women.'

Monsieur Langlois snorts. 'Don't be stupid. She's so orderly. So neat. Military training, so she says.'

'I'm telling you.'

'It can't be. Perhaps when visitors come—'

'She's unnatural.'

'You're dreaming.'

'The men are bad enough,' Madame Foré says. 'Filthy boots everywhere—stomping away.'

'They are gentlemen. Real gentlemen. Rich. Practising their swordplay.'

'So they can go off and get into scrapes with *duchesses*. Do you think I don't know what's going on? It's the talk of Paris. Duels. God knows what else.'

'But that's not her fault,' says Monsieur Langlois.

'She's a monster.'

'Please. Leave her alone.'

'I cannot, in all Christian conscience, serve her a day longer. It's immoral.'

'I can't believe you said those things. She'll kill us.'

'All the more reason to—'

They hear boots on the stairs.

'Don't you say a word, Marguerite. Not another word. You hear me?'

'I'll do my duty as a Christian.'

'Please don't. It will only make things worse.'

He pushes her into the scullery.

A rap on the kitchen door.

'Monsieur Langlois? May I come in?'

'Mademoiselle de Maupin. An honour, as always.'

She's not armed. That's good. But there's an uncanny, unnerving smile fixed onto her face.

On most days, Monsieur Langlois can't look at her. She's so very beautiful. He fears he might throw away his pride and cast himself at her feet. Begging. Weeping. She has that effect on every man he knows. They all ask him about her—all the time. He has earned a reputation for discretion, but in truth, it's only because he can't bear to speak of her. He can't abide the thought of any other man feeling the way he does. Not for her.

Now here she is. In his kitchen. And that Jesus-fucking Marguerite hasn't done the dishes.

He shuffles a few steps forward. Bows.

'I've heard about your misunderstanding, madame. Please. Forgive our—'

The goddess raises a hand. 'All is forgiven,' she says.

'A thousand apologies.' He's babbling, he knows it, but he can't stop. 'Madame Foré—she's not been well lately, her duties tire her. I'm sure she would apologise herself if she was here.'

'There's no need.'

He hears a grunt from the scullery. She hears it, too.

'Do I ask too much of you, Monsieur Langlois? Of her?'

'Not at all, madame. Far from it.'

'A roof. A bed. A few sticks for the fire. Two meals a day and wine. It's not a great deal.'

'No, madame.' He bows his head so she can't see his face, his shame.

The goddess goes on. 'I see how my wine bill and my own thirst don't quite match up. I look the other way. I reason that a landlord might need to finish off the odd half-bottle from time to time. I ignore the fact that your other tenants have screaming babies and children jumping outside my window at dawn. I forgive everything.'

'You are gracious. So gracious.' He bows again. He can't help it.

'But I do ask two things.'

'Yes, madame. Anything.'

'When I request fish for my supper, I do not expect pork.'

'It will never happen again.'

'Very good. Then you will deliver fish to my room for my supper this evening, as requested.'

'Fish?'

'That's right', she says. 'Tonight. Immediately.'

It's so gloomy down here she can barely see him. He was once a handsome devil. He's told her so himself. That must have been before the smallpox and thirty years of drink. She tolerates his longing gaze, his speechlessness in her presence. It happens to so many men when she's around. She knows that sometimes he follows her along the street. Still, the rooms are big and light. The food tolerable. Normally. But she bars her door at night. Just in case.

'And the other subject.'

'Yes, of course. What is it, madame?'

'Manners. It is all that matters. Civility. The only thing that differentiates us from the beasts.'

'I agree completely.'

'The only thing that stands, at this moment, between me and murder.'

He gulps. Noisily. It sounds like fear.

'Do you hear me, Langlois? Manners. Fish.'

'Yes, madame. I heard you quite distinctly.'

She turns to leave.

'The only problem—'

She halts. Doesn't turn back.

'There is no fish,' he says. 'There was none at the market, and it being the weekend I thought you wouldn't mind if—a little pork now and then is no problem for most people—so I bought it and—and—and—there is no fish.'

'I see.'

She is still facing away from him as she pauses, breathing deeply, blinking back fury.

He watches her, senses her, breathes her in. Marguerite is right. It's the scent of a whore. All those men. Even women.

Of course he's heard the stories. Everyone has. She's lied to him. That woman who visits every week. That's no sister. His friends would laugh if they knew. She would laugh if she knew what he feels, what he needs.

She has never been so close. Within an arm's length. He could touch her, if he tried. If he just reached out one hand he could feel the skin on her throat.

He could grab her arm and pull her towards him. He could have her. Right here on the kitchen floor.

So he tries.

His hands tighten around her wrists but she twists clear and lurches for the door. Reaches for her scabbard but there's no sword. She spins around, and it's as if the heavens had burst into flame—as if lightning had shattered the clouds on high—and now she races towards him—bellowing—reaches for something—anything—a key—a frying pan—the poker—and there's blistering, exquisite pain in his skull as she bashes into him—smashes the dishes on the table, on the mantel—his mother's wedding platter—that ugly milk jug—and Marguerite is screaming for the gendarmes even though it's all her fault and Monsieur Fouineur from next door is running in and out and the upstairs children—he sees them, through a veil of his own blood, peeking around the doorframe—and the goddess—the blessed one—is a monster, shouting even louder and striking anyone who comes near, even the gendarmes who drag her, poker in hand, out into the courtyard and off to God knows where.

Act 4, Scene 13

Recitative

ANOTHER SIN. I JUST REMEMBERED. Anger. There. I confess it. I do. It may not be a mortal sin, but it is a failing of mine. From time to time, I have been guilty of slightly precipitous behaviour.

Oh, I've been scolded for it, don't worry. Punished. You're not the first to knit his eyebrows and scowl at me as if I was, once again, a scamp in the King's stables. D'Albert will do it at the drop of a hat, nowadays, since he has grown complacent and flabby.

It was sometimes his fault, anyway. I swear it. Ridiculous boy. He can't look after himself. Someone else has to step in—me, usually, or d'Uzès. Or both, God help us. So many scrapes. The worst, the darkest time, was when he took up with the Duchesse de Luxembourg. It wasn't as if he even loved her. How could he? She was a plaything, nothing more. It was one of those affairs you have when you are bored, and everyone is out of town for the season, and the world seems just a little ordinary. How could it have been anything more? He wasn't betrothed then and she was only a little bit married.

I had other matters weighing on my mind—a small legal entanglement with my landlord, nothing to bother you with—and hardly took any notice, though I'd never liked her much—such airs and graces, such a fiendish tongue in her; after a few weeks, I'd have happily ripped it from her mouth.

But then—I don't know all the details—it all got out of hand and the whole world knew, even her mad husband, and they were all at a ball—d'Albert and d'Uzès and Luxembourg and her husband the Duc, and some friends of theirs—some fools, I should say—should have known better, all of them, but the nobility just don't think like you and me. There was a fight, and a challenge. A duel. D'Albert and d'Uzès, together as always, against Count Rantzau and that tedious Schwartzenberg, who decided to defend the lady's honour, even though that was long gone.

We've all done it. Tempers go missing. Manners escape us. Before we know it we're trying to skewer some fellow with any blade that comes to hand. We risk everything for that one moment of fury—or obligation—or sometimes just a tepid dislike. I know—I festered in Brussels all those months, paying penance for a few moments of swordplay, legendary though they may be, or so I hear.

But of course Schwartzenberg got himself killed. Some toady told the King about it. He lost his royal temper. Called for d'Albert and d'Uzès to be clapped in irons and disinherited and stripped naked and flogged like mules and whatever else popped into his aged head. Louis may turn a blind eye to affairs and bastards and even fraud, but when it comes to duelling, he's livid. Takes it personally. The highest standards apply, after all, to the great men of the realm. And their sons. Decrees go out. The Hôtel de Ville is notified.

D'Uzès surrendered to the Conciergerie. His brother talked him into it. D'Albert should have given himself up straight away, too. But, no. He hid in a bolthole in the country—out near Montmartre.

But I knew who to blame, even if the King didn't. So I went hunting that vixen Luxembourg.

Act 4, Scene 14

A minuet

ORNING MASS. IT'S GLOOMY as ever inside Saint-Roch—winter sun falls chilled on the flagstones. The priest faces the tabernacle, intoning the Sacrament. It's his favourite moment. The perfect union with Christ.

Someone snores. It echoes through the church. People sit scattered across the nave on spindly chairs, staring or praying or talking in hushed voices. In one of the chapels, in an old family pew, there's a pretty young noblewoman in black lace. Alone. No husband. No children. Not today. Not for a while. Some of the parishioners have noticed it's a long time since they saw her going in to Confession, too. They pretend not to stare. What Her Grace does is her own affair. Literally.

Another woman—tall, and in a dark cloak that sweeps the floor—slips in through the side door. Dips a dutiful knee, crosses herself, takes a seat in the second row. It's reserved for the nuns from the convent next door. She doesn't care. She shuffles along slowly, sideways, until she can lean forward and whisper into an ear enfolded in black lace.

'Stay away from him.'

The Duchesse de Luxembourg sits upright, not breathing. She knows the voice well enough, even as a disembodied whisper.

'How dare you come here, to threaten me in God's sight?'

'In God's sight, I'll blow your brains out if you go near d'Albert ever again.'

'Blasphemer.'

'Bitch. I'll cut your throat, I swear it. You understand me?'

The Duchesse nods ever so slightly.

'I'd do it, too. You know I would.'

There's little doubt of that.

Somewhere the friars begin their chant.

The Duchesse glances around. People are watching but nobody can hear—nobody will be able to help her until it's too late, until her blood runs across the flagstones, until her lifeless body falls—

She dares to look behind her.

There's nobody there.

Montmartre. An inn. Outside, the apple-growers bring in the harvest. The horses' heads hang low as they strain against the leads, the load. Their forelegs are thick with mud. Clouds pile onto the tops of the hills around.

Inside, in the gloom, they argue. Again.

'Émilie, what have you done?'

'I don't know what you mean.' Julie bites into an apple. It smells of autumn in Provence.

'You've made it worse, you know.'

'For whom?' she says. 'Your *duchesse*?'

D'Albert runs his fingers through his hair. 'Why would you do such a thing?'

'Why not? She has caused you nothing but pain. I thought I'd return the favour.'

'She's told the whole of Paris.'

'That's priceless.'

'Even my mother heard of it.'

'La! It was a lark.' She throws the apple core into the fireplace and it hisses in the embers. She watches it sizzle and shrink. Remembers another fire—an elderly nun, a young girl, a lifetime ago.

D'Albert frowns like a child. 'I've been forbidden to see you.'

She doesn't look up. 'Again?'

'Don't laugh. You can't go around threatening your betters.'

'My what?' Her anger bubbles so close to the skin nowadays. He has no idea. Nobody does. So tiring, keeping it in, keeping it from exploding everywhere.

'You heard.'

'I heard, Joseph, but I don't believe you said that. To me. After all these years.'

'Don't take it the wrong way.'

'I won't. That's your preference, I recall.'

'Very funny.'

'Does she do that for you, too, your pretty *duchesse*?'

'You can be so nasty. Are we going to fight now? Just when I'm about to leave Paris forever?'

'It's not forever.' She sighs. So weary. 'Don't be dramatic.'

'You don't even care.'

'God's oath! If you weren't my dearest friend I'd throw you out the window. In fact, I might do it, anyway.'

She grabs at his arms. He tries to shrug off her grip.

'You couldn't.'

'Want to bet on it?'

'I can't. I'm too poor.'

She lets go. 'You're pathetic when you're sober.' Shoves him backwards. He stumbles.

'Will you miss me, Émilie?'

'Not at all.'

'Just a little?' He comes closer, nudges her with one arm. She ignores it.

'You'll be gone six months,' she says. 'Less. I promise. Then all will be forgiven.'

'You don't know that for sure.'

'Want to bet on that, instead?'

D'Albert sits down heavily in the chair by the fireplace. 'What will become of me?'

'Your friends will die of boredom and you'll be all alone. That's all.'

'I am nothing,' he says, his head in his hands. 'I don't even have a proper title. My brother inherits everything.'

'So? He doesn't have your handsome face. Or me.'

'I wish I was dead. I wish he was dead.'

'I wish you were both dead,' she says. 'For the love of God, stop whining.'

He looks up. 'Come with me!'

'To Brussels? Never.'

'You know people there.'

'Too many.' She drags a chair close to his and sits down.

'It'd be splendid.' He smiles at the thought. 'We'd be together.'

'In Brussels.'

'So?'

'It's not quite the same as Paris,' she says. 'You'll understand when you get there.'

'I don't want to go alone.' The smile fades.

'You are never alone for long, Joseph.'

'Please?'

She shakes her head. 'Forget it.' She means it. He knows that tone.

Silence. He sighs.

She can't help but smile.

'This is for you.' She holds out a letter. Sealed.

He takes it from her slowly, as if it might be a trick. 'To the Elector?'

'Maximilian.'

'Your lover?' His voice is edged with suspicion.

'Once.'

'I thought you hated him.'

'I was a little cross with him for a while,' she admits. 'But you know me and my temper. I recovered my wits, and he remembered his manners. It's a letter of introduction. He'll take you into the army. Keep you out of trouble until the waters here are calmer. He promised.'

D'Albert smooths the paper between his palms. 'You are the dearest, sweetest friend.' He is close to idiotic, childish tears.

'And you are a fool.'

She moves towards him, reaches out a hand—both hands—and unbuckles his sword belt. Unlaces his blouse. His boots. His waistcoat. His breeches.

She is alone in the city. But everyone loves her—everyone who counts. Monsieur, Francine, the Comtesse. The oyster girls. The stagehands. Thévenard. Lamplighters. Dancers. Salon ladies. Card players. Tinkers. Everyone.

Those that don't—the house of d'Uzès, Duménil, a certain family in Marseille, a housemaid, several jilted lovers, the Countess Marino, defeated duellists, a few elderly nuns in Avignon—they don't matter. Not to her. She does not acknowledge hatred. A waste of time.

Life is music. Light. The poetry of the sword, the city. The candles, the paint, the applause.

Triumph. Again and again. *Tragédies en musique, opéra-ballets,* even a *pastorale-héroïque. Canente. Hésione. Amadis. Aréthuse. Omphale.* Role after role. Night after night. She is a priestess of the sun, a nymph, Grace. A queen, a river sprite. Each evening, each new character, she is different, better, mercurial. The crowds come week after week—she is divine, a bird, the earth, a lover, a fishwife. She is theirs. They are hers.

She works hard, too hard. Francine worries that she takes the music too seriously, that the roles consume her. Thévenard tells her to slow down, to enjoy her wealth, to rest her voice—her soul. He brings her minted tea with honey. Monsieur sends fruit from his *orangerie.* D'Albert sends letters filled with pity and pleas, and returns like a lost dog after a few months to share a cell with his friend d'Uzès in the Conciergerie, awaiting the King's justice. Julie doesn't visit.

She lives alone, just behind the church of Saint-Gervais-et-Saint-Protais, in an old pile of a house, right at the very top of the stairs. Getting home drunk is an adventure in itself. Her room is up in the clouds, almost, level with the church bells, so that in the waking hours they frighten her clear out of bed. She can see the river—her river—and the buttresses of Notre-Dame.

While the neighbourhood sleeps, before the moneylenders and duellists meet for their dawn exchanges at the Crossroads of the Elm, she slips in through the back door of the church to have a quiet word with God. Just the two of them. It's so silent she can hear the candles burn. Dark. Restful. She finds herself praying sometimes—for her father, for a girl she once knew down south. She prays for peace, seeks it everywhere, finds none.

The court composer François Couperin plays the organ in Saint-Gervais-et-Saint-Protais—like his whole family, for generations, even the women—and the cousins take turns rehearsing in the early mornings. If nobody's about, they ask Julie to sing with them. Other times she sits and listens to them, or to the monks and their chants.

She tells no-one. Couperin tells no-one. It's a world away from the palace, where he fights with other composers for the King's attention, and the Opéra, where she fights for breath.

No-one hears them, no-one sees but a few monks and parishioners crawling from station to station. No-one knows how the cold mornings creep into her bones, how black the nights seem, that she dreams of a girl in a country lane, wakes alone, walks the streets in the dark, creeps into the church, sits. For hours.

Until she buckles on her sword, sweeps a cloak around her shoulders and steps into sunlight and glory.

Act 5, Scene 1

Recitative

YOU AGAIN?

You're a brave man, Father, coming back today. I'll grant you that. Or a foolish one.

I hope you aren't falling for me. My life is difficult enough as it is. So you must try to curb your impulses, natural though they may be, at least in my presence. I suppose you've made a career out of that. Never understood the appeal of it, myself— denial of the flesh, of desire. It's not my natural state. But please do your best.

I'll pretend I don't notice. It's only polite. I'm used to it. Now.

On which sin would you like to concentrate this morning? What have I missed? I'd hate to deprive you.

Vanity, you say?

That's a little pointed, don't you think, for a deathbed? Here I am, covered in Sister Angeline's foul-smelling poultices and sweating like a blacksmith, yet you call me vain.

Since you ask, yes, I am vain, as are we all, and anyone who claims otherwise is also guilty of the sin of deception. But what is vanity, after all? Not merely a love of display. The Archbishop of Paris wears more precious stones than any woman I know. Don't give me any of that rubbish about offering glory to God. I've seen a priest snatch a pearl from a woman's ear—not because she was sinning, but because he desired it. God was nowhere to be seen, believe me.

Greed is a sin, I agree, but vanity is not. Let me qualify that. Brainless vanity, I grant you, is a serious crime against Heaven. Vanity with no basis in reality—the plain painted to look like the pure, the matron made up like the Holy Mother. I worked for a woman like that once. In Spain. Hell of a place.

If you don't mind me saying, Father, I don't think the Church has done Spain any favours. All those centuries of the Inquisition, and what do they have? Roads barely passable. No decent inns. Nobody has any teeth, for some reason. There are cities where nobody knows my name, barely recognises a note of civilised music.

Mighty good swordsmen, though, with the finest blades.

But the Spaniards would have been better off keeping the Jews around, if you ask me. Nothing to be proud of—expelling the only cultured people in the country in favour of black-bearded priests determined to keep everyone in the mud.

Gone are the days when the Church was the garden bed of civilisation, I'm afraid, when music and painting and poetry were witness to the glory. Now you lot spend all your time banning books and tut-tutting at the world's finest singers. Especially in Spain.

So, the cow for whom I worked in Madrid—

What? I already told you that? The radishes story? You sure?

Pity. It's one of my favourites.

There's no need to be quite so chronological about this, Father. I'm dying. That's clear. If I circle about, or repeat myself occasionally and lose the odd thread here and there, the polite thing to do is nod and smile encouragingly, as if it's all new to you.

Funny, lately I find myself becoming both more patient with others and impatient with myself.

But you—you should be grateful. Few others have had the privilege of sitting at my feet. In fact, no other person—at least, nobody living—knows everything I'm telling you, giving to you.

La Florensac knows—knew—everything, every snarl and sinew of me, but—well.

As for you, you can just write it all down. Every word, so others—more worthy than you, more forgiving, more interested—can read it.

I've decided. Mine is too precious a story, a moment, to be hidden away in your bishop's archives. You will publish it. I will make you famous. Celebrated. Yes, you.

You will need more paper than that—a whole book of it, I should think. I might read it myself when I feel stronger. What a laugh.

Then you will have to scribble faster. Every word, mind. I'll know if you leave anything out. You might not be interested, but others will be—one day. Mark my words.

Accept it gracefully, Father. Grace is all that's left to us, all that matters. All, now, that I seek.

You could try it yourself.

So shut the fuck up.

Where was I?

Madrid. The Countess Marino. Vanity. Yes.

She was vain.

But the vanity of youth is no such thing. We who are truly beautiful owe it to the world to display our finest plumage. D'Albert is vain, but he was so beautiful when he was young. Now, granted, he looks rather too much like his father for my liking, but his vanity has not left him. It's a lesson he has yet to learn. Vanity in a man can be draining for those around him. Vanity in a woman can be charming. Sometimes.

But we who are genuinely gifted owe it to God to parade our glories on the most brightly lit stage we can find.

Oh, don't cross yourself like that. You're boring me now.

Let me put it this way—if God gave me the gift of song, do you think He would rather I use it in the taproom of a country inn, or send it soaring into the *paradis* of the Paris Opéra?

Would He rather the possessor of that voice, this face, be clean and well-fed and dressed in silk, or tired and hungry and covered in dust from the road?

As if a little cologne behind my ears is going to damn me to the eternal flames. Believe me, that sin will come way down Saint Peter's list. I'll argue every item with him before the gates of Heaven, even though I'm fairly sure he'll take a dim view of a woman raising her voice.

I don't care what he thinks—I don't care what you think. My sins are clear enough to me. I have my own commandments.

Thou shalt not break the heart of the one you love (though you could argue I learned that a little too late for it to be useful).

Thou shalt not diminish thy life for fear of the wrath of men.

Thou shalt not curb thy tongue.

And, of course, thou shalt never wear satin in the rain if thou can help it—ruins the fabric.

What?

For God's sake, man, here I am dying and you want to argue the niceties of the law. I'm above the laws of men—I've proved that. I've got no interest in the laws of God, either—at least, not the Church fathers.

The Gospels themselves, I grant you, make for a gripping read, though I prefer the Old Testament for drama, for the pathos of it. But what are they, really? Poems. *Tragédies*. No different to those endless epics I appeared in on the greatest stage in Europe.

I have been a goddess many a time—Pallas Athéna (had to wear the world's most uncomfortable helmet, but never mind), Minerve—and on occasion a queen—doomed, usually, but terribly regal, like Médée or Dido.

But even deities can fail. Falter. Apollo was muddled by Cupid. Achilles felled by an arrow to the ankle.

It feels like half a lifetime ago. One of my very worst times, and I've had several of those. We lost Monsieur, that dear man, in midsummer. Fell into an apoplexy after an argument with the King. Some family thing. Paris mourned for weeks, and I grieve for him still—although the King, so they say, went back to his apartments and finished his game of cards.

Our lives went on, too, although the Palais-Royal seemed a solemn place without its soul, its patron. Théobalde had produced a new work. What was it now? God help me, I've forgotten. I knew it only yesterday and now... My grip is loosening.

Scylla. That's it. I have it. Yes. Why am I telling you this?

Ah, yes. Vanity. Théobalde. And he, being the excitable sort, simply had to present it first at Versailles. A mistake. I knew it would be. But nobody asks us. We just turn up, slap on a wig and a pint of paint and sing our lungs out. So there we were, on a cool autumn evening, in the forecourt, dying in front of two thousand people.

They didn't like it. Nobody did. Not the Duc d'Orléans, by whom all matters of taste are decided since the passing of Monsieur. Not the court. Not the *parterre*. Not even some of the singers.

They hissed us off the stage. A little unfairly, I thought. Théobalde—another Italian—took it badly. He'd wanted to try something new. You can't blame a man for that. God knows, we were all bored to tears by endless return seasons of this or that. He had this whacking great bass violin—made a noise like a chorus of baritones, if you can imagine such a thing.

I don't suppose you can.

I thought it was magic. Gave the strings depth, feeling, a sort of earth from which they could fly. But, no. Too radical for Versailles. It was, above all, categorically not Lully—not in any way, except for being written by an Italian pretending to be French. The King didn't hiss, of course. Wasn't even there. It would have been worse, probably, if Louis was present. We might have been locked up or banished.

It was a blow to my pride more than anything, but at least I wasn't alone. We all knew we'd sung well enough—the *haute-contre* was in fine voice. Chopelet, I think it was. Couldn't have asked for more. But it didn't matter. They hated the music. I don't think it's been heard since. It never opened in Paris. One night. One performance. Not even that. We left the stage in the third act.

Thousands of *louis* spent on machinery and scenery and not a single *sol* taken in tickets. Not that I care. I get paid for the season, not each performance, and handsomely, too. But the others, the lower beings, as it were, found themselves cast back onto the streets or the fairgrounds or the whorehouses or wherever they'd come from, for months until the next show.

But it wasn't a complete waste.

For at the party afterwards I met the vainest person on earth, and one of the sweetest—the Chevalier du Bouillon.

Did you get all that down?

Do I speak too quickly for your pen?

Then you will simply have to write faster.

Act 5, Scene 2

A minuet

FANCHON MOREAU NOTICES HIM FIRST.

'That gentleman—there—the chevalier with the gold sash. Do you know him?'

The other women peep over the top of fluttering fans.

'No, but I wish I did.'

'My goodness. What a fine pair of ankles.'

'And the eyelashes?'

'Divine.'

'He's coming over!' Fanchon hisses. 'Remember, I saw him first.'

Only one of the women doesn't look. She gazes out of the window towards the Grande Écurie.

The Chevalier du Bouillon knows as well as the singers the importance of a dramatic entrance. He throws his arms wide and advances upon them like Thévenard playing Apollo.

'My dear ladies. My heroines.'

There's a gasp from behind the fans.

He bows. 'Allow me to apologise for the unforgivable nature of my fellow human beings. Never have I seen such disgraceful behaviour. And here, at Versailles, the centre of the civilised world. You poor things.'

'You are very kind, sir.' The blonde one, Fanchon, makes a gracious bow. 'It is not we who are distraught, sir, but our poor Théobalde.'

'But of course! For his music to be so disparaged.'

'He feels disgraced.'

The handsome chevalier does not allow himself to laugh. He hated *Scylla* as much as the rest of them, despises the *tragédies* anyway—much prefers the Comédie-Française—hissed loudly himself, and cheered ever louder when the cast left the stage. But he couldn't stop staring at the girl—the tall one with the glorious hair—the infamous La Maupin. He has heard of her, everyone has, has heard all the stories, but never imagined she would be so ... But she's not looking at him. The blonde one keeps talking. They all do.

'We are but his instruments, our poor Théobalde,' says Fanchon, 'and we must weather the storm.'

'You are not deserving of a moment's approbation.' The chevalier bows again. That damned woman is paying no attention whatsoever.

By the window, La Maupin picks a ripe pear from the platter. It's one of the small mottled ones from the palace gardens. She turns it in her hands, remembering the gravel paths through the potager under her bare feet, the gardeners in their brown smocks, grumbling about the early frost, their cold toes, digging horse manure into the earth—and a young girl in breeches hiding behind the pear tree with the first of the harvest—still firm, grainy on the tongue, but sweet and even more so for being stolen, forbidden—although she realises now that the gardeners must have seen her sneaking behind the espalier frames, must have known, must have allowed her to take the first bite of the fruit they so carefully guarded.

She cuts into it, through the skin and into creamy flesh, the silver knife cold in her hand. A pool of juice gathers in her palm, drips down her wrist, onto the floor. She watches it, watches the man with the fine ankles trying to get her attention—watches the dancers, the posers, the girls with the fans laughing at nothing, Fanchon working hard at pretending that she—she, La Maupin!—doesn't exist. As if she had never existed, never caressed her so softly—so fiercely—that Fanchon wept in wonder, shouted ecstasies too wild to clearly recall, clung to her like a kitten.

So be it.

Julie swallows a slice of pear, tries to parry the pain away, but it won't work. Not here. Not anymore. Her guard is slipping. She must be getting old. Nearly thirty and weary. Too weary.

She sees d'Armagnac in the corner, bored and alone, the Comtesse and her latest protégée surrounded by elderly men, a footman yawning, that *abbé* with the dreadful Swiss accent picking his nose—and then d'Albert appears beside her.

'Émilie. Darling.' He kisses her hand.

'Here you are.' Her eyes rest on his dear, familiar face. 'Back in the good books?'

'So it would seem.'

'That didn't take long.'

'What do you mean? I've been away forever. Didn't you miss me?'

She thinks about teasing him, but doesn't have the energy. 'I did, of course. I'm glad you're back.'

'You didn't visit me in prison.'

'No. Nasty place.'

'You could have tried.'

'But you've been out for months.'

'My father banished me to the country—I've been sitting about with nothing to do. I thought it would never end.'

'Still, a few months of rural exile obviously suit you.' She raises her eyebrows, looks over his belly, his thighs.

'Do I look that fat?'

'Maybe a little.'

'So insulting. I should challenge you for that.'

'Please do. It ended so well last time.'

He smiles at the memory of nearly dying at her hands. She loves how he does that.

'Will you come to Paris next, Joseph? The city has missed you.'

'Of course.'

'For how long?'

'Until Christmas.'

'Perfect.'

'Are you well, Émilie? You look...'

'Don't you start.'

'... a little melancholy.'

'Me? Nonsense.' She waves a dismissive hand. 'Now. What mischief shall we get up to?'

The chevalier with the ankles appears beside them. They both stare at him—they had forgotten the existence of the hundreds of people in the gallery—the singers with the fans, the gossips.

The chevalier bows deeply to d'Albert—to her.

'Forgive me for interrupting, my friend,' he says. 'You must introduce me to this young lady.'

'Why?' Julie asks, without even looking at him.

'Because I am here. And I wish it.'

'I do not.'

The woman turns—walks away from him. Never happened before. He blinks.

'D'Albert—stop her! What is she doing?'

'What she wants, as always.'

'No. That's—she can't—'

'But, as you see, she has.'

'Where is she going?'

'Who knows?'

But d'Albert does know—she will go to the stables, the gardens—the shadows—a neglected grave. He sighs.

The chevalier waits another moment before sighing, too. Deeply. 'Ah! What a remarkable creature.'

'Yes.' D'Albert's smile is wary.

'Then, my good Comte—if I may be permitted to ask—the rumours are true?'

'Which ones?'

'That she is your—you are lucky enough to …?'

'She is my friend,' says d'Albert in what he hopes is a warning tone. 'My dearest friend.'

'Ah. I see. Excellent. So I may yet hope?'

'Hope is open to us all, my dear Chevalier. Paradise is more exclusive.'

They bow and part. One tastes disgust, one tastes desire.

Days later. A world away from the painted salons of Versailles—a cabaret near the river, the one with the livery on one side and the brothel on the other. Everything a man could wish. Two friends sit by the fire, pipes between their teeth, boots resting on the hearth. They don't talk much. They don't have to. The young man almost lets his tankard slip to the floor. The woman is drinking wine. A great deal of it.

She orders another bottle.

He raises his eyebrows. He's been practising that.

'You are feeling a little reckless, perhaps?' he says.

'None of your business, Joseph.'

'But it is—or it will be soon—inevitably.'

'I can look after myself.'

'Of that I am sure.'

A few minutes of silence.

'But seriously, Émilie, I've never seen you drink like this.' He glances at the empty bottles on the table.

'What of it?'

'Last night you could barely stand.'

'You've been the same, many a time.' Julie fills her glass.

'I know. But not you—well, rarely. Something's wrong.'

'Everything's wrong. Everything has always been wrong.'

'But, Émilie—'

'Let's just drink.' She stares into the fire. 'Silently.'

'My friend, if you—'

'Enough!'

Her hand is on her sword hilt.

He shrugs. 'As you wish.'

But the next day it's the same. And the day after. On the Sunday, d'Albert takes a detour after Mass—he's promised to meet her for yet another bout of drinking and fire-staring and not talking. But first he pushes his way slowly through a room crowded with young men in silk stockings, ladies at cards, a cloud of wig powder, looking for one face, one reassuring presence. There. At last.

'Comtesse.' He bows.

'Comte d'Albert. A pleasure.'

'May we speak?'

'I am at your disposal, as always.'

He takes her arm. The lace is soft to the touch. He lowers his voice, turns his face away from the room so nobody can hear him.

'You will excuse my impertinence,' he says.

'That depends on the circumstances.'

'We've never acknowledged that we have a mutual acquaintance.'

'Must we acknowledge it now?' The Comtesse smiles graciously and nods to someone on the other side of the room.

'It's delicate, I know,' says d'Albert, 'but I'm worried.'

'About her?'

'Yes. Madame de Maupin.'

'Julie? What has happened?'

She leads him to a corner of the room where the racket from the card tables will provide more privacy.

'Another duel?' she whispers.

'Nothing like that. She's just—I can't explain it, really.'

'Then what am I to do?'

'I don't know,' he says. 'But she's drunk. All the time.'

A deep furrow appears in the Comtesse's perfect forehead. 'That is odd. Unlike her.'

'And melancholy. Dangerously so.'

'I would not have thought it possible.'

'Nor I. Yet it is.'

'You must understand,' she says, although the admission causes more pain than she's willing to reveal, 'I haven't seen Julie for months, except on stage. And even then—where is she living?'

'She has rooms in the Marais but is hardly ever there. I don't know where she goes.'

'She has always been mysterious.'

'I know that better than anyone,' says d'Albert. 'But now, my father is expecting me in Champagne for the festivities. I am afraid to leave her alone.'

'It is that bad?' It's all she can do to stop herself clutching at her breast, crying out in fear. Instead she holds his gaze and keeps her breath steady.

'I'm afraid so.'

'I myself am expected to be at Versailles for Christmas, but I will visit her before I leave.'

'Thank you, Comtesse.'

She tries. God knows, she tries everything. But the singer will not meet with her, will not respond to the calling cards, the knock on the door, the letters.

And then it's midwinter and the city is deserted. La Maupin is alone in her room with a few bottles of wine, a loaf of stale bread, a mouse or two.

She wanders out one evening, still drunk, into the windswept city. Stares at the river, the boats. Up at the houses that cluster on the Pont Saint-Michel. The seagulls. Down at the greasy necks of apprentice oarsmen, sculling swiftly from the docks and across the channel. She gazes at the great cathedral on the island. Back towards the fortress towers, and the old palace. Her first home.

Then the water. It's not deep enough to drown in, she calculates. Not properly. She'd make a mess of it. Someone would pull her out and then she'd die of a chill instead, after a long, harrowing illness. No. There must be a better way. A carriage, perhaps—she could throw herself in its path. She hears one now.

Instead it slows. Whoever is in it is waving to her.

She turns back to the river. She could challenge him, let him beat her—whoever he is. But somehow that galls. She must die unbeaten. By swords, at least. Everything else— every other thing and person in the entire world—has beaten her, already. Somehow. Only the river matters, and the cathedral.

The person waving from the carriage is not d'Albert. Not the Comtesse. Or Fanchon. For one wild moment she imagines—but no—not Clara. They cannot help her now. None of them.

She whispers to the sky, to the river, to a girl she once knew, 'Forgive me, my love. Farewell.'

The lunatic in the carriage is still waving, shouting her name. An opera devotee, perhaps, or some old lover or enemy. She doesn't care. She never cares.

He is beside her now. It's that good-looking chevalier. Of all people.

'Madame de Maupin?'

No answer.

'May I be of some assistance to you?'

She doesn't even look at him.

He sees the dirt in her hair, smells days' worth of wine and a stink reminiscent of the guardhouse. Something in him falters, breaks. He grasps her arm.

'Would you do me the honour of dining with me?'

He gives her little choice and, for once—for the first time in her entire life—she doesn't fight back.

Act 5, Scene 3

Recitative

I WAS MORE OF A CHEVALIER than he was. All the women wanted him—the society ladies and every opera singer—so I ignored him completely. He couldn't help himself. He fell at my feet, begged me to adore him.

What choice does a woman have in such circumstances, eh? It's only fair, after all, to accede to such demands, such fervent pleading. If you have it in you to grant someone's fondest wish, why wouldn't you? I admit that when I met him I was in a bad way—he saved me, in a sense, in a moment, though he never knew it.

He was handsome, I'll grant you. Knew how to wear a sword with flair, although he had no idea how to use it. But I forgave him that, as I forgave him so much, so often, over those months. He was kind, restful. He looked after me as no man had ever done.

Very well. It's true. He saved me. From the river, from myself. I was weak. There is a price to be paid for being me. I get no peace—not then, not now. Demons pursue me. People want to touch me—everyone does, all the time. They want to be me or fight me or fuck me. Sometimes it's hard to tell the demons from the lovers, the admirers from the assassins.

But he—he was simply sweetness. He cleaned me up and stroked my hair and asked me no questions. He fed me bread fried in duck fat and put a sword in my hand and begged me to train with him every morning until I was ready to face the world again. And the world welcomed us back.

I must admit, since we're on the topic of vanity, so delicately raised by you, that we made a gorgeous couple. We were admired much more than we truly admired each other, but the admiration of others feeds both vanity and conviction. We believed ourselves to be fabulous, to be invincible, to be the most romantic of lovers—although after the first few weeks we went home to our separate beds quite relieved to be apart. We met for supper, attended every soirée together, danced all night at each society ball, fluttered and smirked and made a great show of manners and mischief—not for us, but for everyone else. I felt then, for the first time, how it must feel to be married to a handsome man; how it must be to have the world approve of your lover—and of you; how it must feel to wake each morning content in the knowledge that the vicious whips of gossip will be lashing someone else's back today.

It didn't last long. Of course not. We're neither of us made for constancy, and we were certainly not made for each other. We took other partners for the first dance at the ball, we arrived in separate chaises to the salons, we supped alone. We fell apart. He took up with Fanchon. It didn't matter. Neither of us grieved much.

But I realise now that his companionship—his friendship—just as much as the curve of his spine close to mine in the dark hours, kept me, for a while, from the edge of the crevice into which I was about to fall, so famously, so spectacularly, and from which I crawled, bloodied and alone, and then strode into the most glorious years of my life.

But that, as they say, is a tale for another day. I don't have the strength for that. For any of this.

Here I am talking about glory while the light seeps from my body. Sorrow drives it from me. I see only lengthening shadows.

Grief is a strange, fearful creature, isn't it? It vanishes from view, as if the world had never broken, for moments, even hours, at a time, and then pounces, more cruel than ever, when you least suspect its presence. So you live in fear of it: of its claws and its footless depths, rapier blades and tiny, tearing thorns, blankness and fury and gulping insanity.

It never leaves, exactly, although the minutes and hours without it do eventually get longer and longer until they stretch into days. But the nights are different.

Alone.

My father was long dead—an equerry found him one day flat on his face in a horse stall, apparently, cold and grey and reeking of wine and vomit. The only surprise was that he'd lived so long.

So they are all gone now—they are whispering to me from the wings.

Forgive me. The fever is in my lungs. Look at this handkerchief. Blood. Great clots of it, like liver. Like afterbirth. That's not a good sign, is it?

Do you pity me? You should, to be honest. Do it graciously, though, I beg you. Normally I hate condescension, but I can't help thinking that at this point a little pity wouldn't go astray.

You could even smile. It wouldn't kill you. Aren't you supposed to be bringing me comfort and succour on my deathbed? Put some effort into it, man.

Don't you understand anything? I have no soul. It fled my body, driven out by grief, and this thing—this wreck—before you is nothing at all. Dust. Ashes. Teeth. Hair. Not a woman. Not a goddess. Not a monster. Not the remarkable Chevalier de Maupin. Not even an urchin from the Marais.

Nothing.

Nothing.

There's not much time left to us. Turn the page. Quickly.

Act 5, Scene 4

A minuet

A BRIGHTLY LIT SALON. Saturday afternoon. The Comtesse entertains visitors, as she always does at this hour. Today, though, she sits in the farthest corner of the room with Comte d'Armagnac and fights against the tears that threaten to ruin her new silk brocade.

'Surely you must be mistaken.'

'Not at all, Comtesse. It was your protégée, La Maupin. I am certain of it. Cut her own wrists with a dagger.'

'She would not be so silly—nor so pathetic.'

'Nobody imagined so. But there you have it. Stupid girl.'

There's a squeak from the other end of the sofa. 'You say she took her own life? I assumed she'd perished in some dreadful duel.'

D'Armagnac sighs and turns to face his wife. She is enjoying this far too much.

'Please, madame. Lower your voice.'

She doesn't. 'Suicide seems unlikely. She always seemed so—well—cocky.'

'She failed to take her own life, my dear,' says d'Armagnac. 'The difference is significant. Particularly for her.'

His wife beckons her friends closer, the better to discuss this new turn of events, given that earlier in the day they had entertained a rather heated debate on whether or not the singer could be buried at Versailles. They had thought it improper. Even less so, now that it appears the woman is not even dead.

D'Armagnac turns back to the Comtesse, who is twisting her scarf into a damp ball between her hands. She can't bear this talk a moment longer, but cannot appear to care.

'It's all nonsense, Comte, you'll see. The opera season starts again in three weeks.'

'I know,' he says. '*Phaëton*—one of my favourites.'

'La Maupin is cast as Climène.'

'She would be perfect.'

'And she will be there, on stage, as glorious as ever, mark my words.' She can almost see it, hear it.

'If only that were so, Comtesse. I dearly wish you were right. But my surgeon saw to her wounds himself. At my request. I was shocked at his report. Shocked. It's a sorry business.'

'And over du Bouillon?' she says. 'Really? I can't imagine it.'

'So it would seem.' D'Armagnac's voice drops to a whisper. 'You and I, Comtesse, know that it is unlikely. He is nothing but an extremely pretty pair of legs. The cause of her great sorrow appears to be the soprano—the blonde one. Her name escapes me. Sang opposite La Maupin in the *Métamorphoses* last year. Rather vapid but a lovely voice.'

'Moreau? Fanchon Moreau?' It comes out as a hiss.

'That's the one.'

'Surely not. I can't believe it.'

'True enough, or so they say.' He appears to be enjoying the tale, the truth.

'But what happened? Why would she do such a thing?'

'Unrequited love, apparently.'

'Nonsense,' says the Comtesse. 'Julie is worth ten of Moreau. It must be something else—something ... deeper—for her to take such a step. Such a sin.'

'She is brave, certainly,' says d'Armagnac. 'But prone to the dramatic gesture.' He knows it better than anyone alive.

'Still, Comte, I cannot fathom it.'

'Do you remember the story of the ball—the three duels?'

'How could I forget?'

'I wondered then ...'

'She is foolhardy at times.'

'It's more than that. She simply doesn't care, the way we do, about the world, about herself. Never has. Believe me, I have known her since she was a child.'

'After all these years, to throw her life away over that—that—'

'A good thing, then, that she did not succeed.' D'Armagnac pats the fist clenched in the Comtesse's lap. 'You're right. She will return to the stage, triumphant. She will show them all. You and I will glory in her triumph.'

'Quietly.' She tries to smile.

'As always. The world must never know of our interest in this matter. Julie must never know.'

'But still. I should go to her.'

'I wouldn't, my dear. She's proud in her way. She wouldn't want you to see her in distress.'

'I'll give her a good shaking,' she says, with a ferocity he's never heard before. 'That's what I'll do.'

The Comtesse ends the salon early, pleading a headache. It's not a lie—not completely. She feels a familiar cramping behind the eyes, a slight fever—or perhaps fury. She can't tell. She knows Julie—the pet, the wayward child—knows her arrogance, knows what the breeches and bravado conceal; knows how impossible it is to touch that spirit, and cannot believe—not for a moment will she believe—that drudge Fanchon Moreau could be the cause of such heartbreak. But she understands herself too well to ignore the ache of longing, of jealousy, of all the hours she has spent watching Julie sing and brawl and transfix Paris, wishing she could, just once more ...

She shakes her head. No. She will not have it. She saw it from the first moment—Julie cannot be possessed. The others don't realise. That young fool d'Albert, the men who hang about the Opéra. Julie is too fine for them, too unruly. She eludes them, and they don't know why. They think they can tame her, but that's impossible—and why must they try? The only way to keep her close is to set her free. But now something has shifted. Something the Comtesse doesn't understand.

There's an answer, of sorts, waiting in her boudoir. A woman. The servants say they tried to stop her but she insisted, and she's famous, a singer, they didn't know what to do. So here she is.

The Comtesse almost runs to her boudoir. Could it be?
It isn't.

Fanchon Moreau dressed carefully before setting out. She's heard all the stories about the Comtesse—from Julie, from the street gossips. She's seen her, now and then, sweeping through the corridors at the Opéra as if scared she'll catch some disease. Which is fair enough. People do. Even rich people—and then they blame the Opéra, the crowds, the stink. As if they're better than us. As if we're dirty. Fanchon bathed this morning, just in case, and splashed scent between her breasts. Chose her favourite gown, the one she ordered especially for the reception at Versailles. Her earrings were a gift from the Dauphin, brought all the way from Venice. Or Constantinople. Or somewhere.

Fanchon is smaller than she appears on stage—her waist so tiny it looks almost as if the two halves of her body are joined by a scarlet thread. The Comtesse can't help but stare. It's not often she sees such an extravagance of colours, of satin, of face paint. In the theatre, at the Opéra, at a distance, yes. But not here, perched on one of her own gilded chairs like a parrot. The woman's scent—of rotting tuberoses and geranium—is overwhelming.

The Comtesse inclines her head ever so slightly and smiles. 'Mademoiselle Moreau. A pleasure.'

'Comtesse. You know why I'm here.'

'I can't imagine.'

The Comtesse waves her footmen out of the room.

Fanchon watches them go. 'It's about Julie. Of course.'

The Comtesse sighs. 'I understand she's unwell.'

'Cracked,' says Fanchon. 'I don't know. You have to help her.'

'Me?'

'She trusts you.'

'What could I possibly do?' Her heart might break. Right here. Now. She smiles again. 'I have no influence over your … friend.'

Fanchon leans across and grabs at the Comtesse's hands. 'Pig's arse. Look. I know what you're thinking. It's not like that.'

Her palms are sweaty, fingers gripping tight. The Comtesse sits back in her chair, but Fanchon moves closer, whispering. 'Everyone's saying that what Julie's done—they think it's about me. But it's not. I swear to you. Julie and me, we have fun now and then—well, usually, although she's been very dull lately. But that's all. She doesn't love me—she doesn't love anyone. Not really. I can't touch her. So she'd never ... it's just not like that.'

The Comtesse wrenches one hand free. 'I still don't—'

'She needs you. She won't listen to me.'

'She has committed a terrible sin.'

'But she's crazy,' says Fanchon. Tears spill down her cheeks, leaving trails of bare skin through the paint. 'She has been for months. It doesn't count if you're crazy, does it? Last week I found her weeping over a strand of my hair she found on the pillow. She said it reminded her of someone. That's not normal, is it? Crying? I mean, I'm not even really blonde.'

So that's it. Old wounds, reopened with a dagger. Ten years, at least, since that business at Avignon. Too long to bear a scar so bloody, so ragged. All this time. She had no idea.

The Comtesse blinks back sudden tears. She looks, for the first time, into Fanchon Moreau's eyes. 'I understand.'

The Comtesse calls for her footmen, her steward, her coach. She will find Julie, probably in some dimly lit, musty hiding-hole, and this time she will force the life back into her no matter what it takes.

By the next afternoon, the pale, bandaged wretch has been lifted from a filthy straw pallet in a tavern off rue Saint-Denis, carried across the city in a sedan chair, washed and fed and shouted at, and inserted between clean linen in a room where the only sound is the slight tinkling of finely cut chandelier glass.

As she falls back into a pitiful sleep the name she whispers is not Moreau's. Not du Bouillon's. Not even d'Albert's.

'Clara.'

Act 5, Scene 5

Recitative

THAT'S HOW MEMORY WORKS. It's a jumble, a jungle, of sunless paths and sudden clearings, of circles and dead ends and random shafts of light.

This is no history book. It is not a libretto. Things happen, then they don't. I remember—or not. I'll tell you some stories—others are best left untold.

Perhaps you've heard this story already. The Opéra tried to hush it up, but there was no chance of that. One of its stars is enamoured of another—a contralto falls for a soprano; how perfect a script! Her passion is rejected; she slits her own flawless wrists and yet fails—dismally—to die.

Even the simple achievement of death was beyond me, although it appears to be within my reach now.

I'm not sure which humiliation was worse—that of living in spite of my best efforts, or people imagining I would try to take my own life over a trifling infatuation. There are much better reasons to kill yourself.

Fanchon, at least, knew full well that my suicide—or lack of it—had nothing to do with her. Well, it did, perhaps a little. But not in the way people imagined. Certainly, we had flirted with one another many times, slept together on occasion, but nothing more. The gossips said we'd fallen out over a man— Frédéric du Bouillon, of all people. Someone even wrote a play about it.

People can say what they like. They imagine themselves in our slippers and dream of how it might be—him finding us in bed together, or me finding her in bed with him. Whichever story suits their tastes, their own desires. They don't even realise they do it.

But I understand. It's the same impulse that makes d'Albert act like a hero in battle, or sends foolish ladies into a swoon at the Opéra. They imagine themselves as actors in a drama of their own making—tragedy or comedy. They imagine that everyone else's desires are the same as their own.

But I'm not like everyone else. I don't fit into their stories, their corseted romances, no matter how tightly they try to squeeze me.

I was lonely, it's true. I even chased down my so-called husband and tried to make him love me for a month or so, but it was pointless. We are strangers. Always have been. Nothing in common but a vow we both made and broke in haste many years ago.

It was worse than pointless. After a few weeks, I hated him, when before I had barely ever thought of him at all. He made more money out of me—out of d'Armagnac—than I ever did, and he's such a lousy swine he kept most of it, too.

So now he's living like a burgher in town, with servants and his own chaise, and I'm—as you see. I have nothing.

Am nothing. I have given everything to the Abbess—all that was left.

Wait a moment. Wait. I need to catch my breath. My thread. My—

Ah. Yes. So I was bereft. Aimless. I thought I was terribly old, but now I see I was still very young and possibly silly.

But Fanchon—ah! She was a swan—a nightingale—both. I don't suppose you get to the Opéra often. How I wish you could see her. It isn't so much her voice, which is of course very fine—better than mine, many say, and I don't mind agreeing; I was always quite clear-eyed about my own shortcomings—but her presence. Crowds melt like raspberry ice before her gaze. Men's hearts falter. So did mine. I confess it. It was difficult enough for me to breathe in her presence, let alone sing.

She must have thought me pitiful. I was. I can see that now.

Of course I was besotted with her—half of Paris was, and the other half was besotted with me. But it wasn't that. A little besotting never hurt anyone. I'd loved Fanchon as a friend for many years. Maybe more than a friend, but only a little. Not like ... not like others. It wasn't desire so much as despair. She told me to stop moping about staring at her, and who could blame her for that?

I thought I had reached the limit of my life. It's as simple as that. I believed, as I do again now, that love—real love—was beyond me. All those years I had dreamed of finding Clara, of rescuing her again. But then—it came on gradually—I at last understood that she was lost to me, and in losing her I somehow lost myself.

Does that make sense? I don't know. I was nearly thirty years old and I thought my time was over. I was only out by a few years, it would seem. Although in one way my old life did end then.

I was a star.

I was ruined.

Or perhaps I was simply worn out.

Then I met my match.

Her husband was an old friend of d'Albert's. The younger brother of d'Uzès. Those nobles, they all know one another, they all fuck one another or each other's wives. Mothers. Who knows? Thank God d'Albert had never had his way with her—that would have been too awkward. That's why they have so many names, I expect. To cover any possible paternity. Hers was Marie-Thérèse-Louise de Seneterre de Lestrange. I called her Thérèse. Everyone else called her Madame de Marquise de Florensac. Anyway, I'd known of her for years, admired her from afar—and not so far on one occasion. Yes, Father, it was she over whom I had fought three duels at once, she over whom I had risked my neck and wrung my hands, years before, when she was a newlywed and I was a newly lit star. She was then—and always—the most beautiful woman in France.

We had only ever spoken that once, kissed that once. I'd never seen her since.

Now I've lost my way in this story—I'm lost. Dear God. Have mercy. I am not ready to reach the end. Hear that quiver in my voice? Pathetic. I had hoped, perhaps—but it doesn't matter now. None of it.

Where was I?

Who?

Thérèse.

Yes.

She was the reason I'd fled Paris, all those years before, for whose sake I spent years on the road, working for that monster Marino, singing for my supper in Brussels, fucking for my supper whenever I had to. Oh, it happens, more than you'd think.

She knew how that felt. Thérèse. Never had to sing or fuck or ask for anything, of course. Fabulous wealth protects you from such indignities. But she'd spent years in Brussels herself, in exile—had fled the court to get away from the Dauphin and his clammy hands. More to the point, she had to get out of the reach of his wife, who was murderous.

So we had kissed once. An infamous kiss. A kiss that lingered on my mouth all those years of my exile and then hers. You have to admit, it's not the kind of thing easily forgotten.

We met again. I remember every second of it. A salon. A blue room. Duck-egg blue. Yellow curtains. Early evening. I wore a deep purple silk. I wished I hadn't. It looked wrong against the furniture.

I felt her there when I walked into the room. Just like that. Had no idea she was coming—that she had returned to Paris. But I felt it, deep in my soul. A movement. Her presence. Love. I didn't know why—or who. I turned around and there she was.

Act 5, Scene 6

A duet

THE SUN IS LOW IN THE SKY, slanting in through the window at an inconvenient angle for the ladies near the backgammon table. The footmen bring an embroidered silk screen but it's too late. The entire afternoon is a disaster. The Comtesse won't hear the end of it for weeks.

She couldn't care less. She is waiting. Some people may accuse her of interfering, but really, who could resist? It's almost ridiculously simple, and such a perfect solution—salvation—for her darling La Maupin, her blade. How did it not occur to her before? So now the most beautiful woman in France sits at a card table in the Comtesse's salon, unaware—although perhaps she has some inkling—that her destiny will arrive—surely—any moment.

The Comtesse catches herself—more than once—holding her breath, like a girl before her first court ball. Isn't paying attention to the chatter or the sun melting the Duchesse de Saint-Simon's complexion or even supper being served. Her eyes are on the door—on the woman in the next room—on the door—and then—at last.

La Maupin saunters—really, there's no other word for it—into the salon, just as she always does, bows low to her very own Comtesse and smiles. 'My lady.'

'I'm so glad you could come.'

'I always do. You know that. If you ask politely.' Julie is safe here, she knows that, after all these years. This room, these windows, the Comtesse's intelligence and peerless wine. One day, perhaps, she will have such a home. A haven.

'You were magnificent last night, my dear,' says the Comtesse. 'I'm not fond of Rebel's work, but you made a splendid Penelope. Ulysses would have to be a fool to leave such a woman.'

'If I were really Penelope, Comtesse, it would be she who sails off, leaving Ulysses to pine away at home.'

'No doubt.'

The Comtesse lets her eyes do all the work—her gaze strays across towards the windows, and Julie glances that way—the Comtesse hears the gentle gasp, can feel the sudden shock as if of lightning, even from a distance, and watches—smiles—nearly weeps—as her darling walks away from her across the room, to the young woman with green eyes who moves to meet her, who is waiting for her—has been waiting for her for years.

'La Maupin.'

'Madame la Marquise de Florensac.' Julie bows deeply, theatrically, one hand on her sword. Tries to smile although she can barely breathe. 'Of course.'

'I knew you would be here.'

'The Comtesse told you?'

'Nobody told me. I knew. I felt it.'

'That's odd. Just a moment ago, I, too, felt—well, never mind.'

It's exactly the same as it was in the middle of that ballroom all those years ago, as it will always be. They don't, can't, do anything but stare at one another.

'Everyone is watching us,' says the Marquise. 'They fear for me.'

'With reason. They haven't forgotten the last time we met.'

'Nor have I.'

'No.'

They are older, it's true. But both still perfect. Still connected—Julie feels the exquisite barbs deep in her skin, her chest—as if only a few moments have passed since that kiss. That first kiss. Their voices, her face, her breath, her hair, her throat—Marie-Thérèse—all that matters—that exists—in the world.

'You need not fight any duels on my account tonight.'

'I will behave myself this time, I promise.'

'What a pity.'

Julie feels as if there are seabirds in her belly, plummeting and pitching, circling, crying out.

'You would prefer I fought a few men for you?' she says. 'I'm sure it can be arranged. Your young cousin, perhaps, could be persuaded to challenge me again in defence of your honour.'

'Poor Marcel. He was killed, you know. In the siege of Namur.'

'I'm sorry.' Damn. 'I didn't know. He was brave. That night.'

'And you?'

'I was angry. And—'

The Marquise reaches out a hand but then lets it drop. She can't touch her—not yet. 'Forgive me. My husband is beckoning me. I must go. I will see you tomorrow morning, at Monsieur le Perche's *salle*. I will be there at eight.'

'You want to watch me fence?'

'No. I want to challenge you.'

Julie's smile is a wonder, a dizzying shaft of light. 'A duel?'

'A bout. That's all.'

'You fight your own battles these days?'

'I learned fencing from a young age. It is, we were told, very good for the female posture. Did you think you were the only one?'

'Not at all. But my training was tougher, a little …'

'Less ladylike?'

'Exactly.'

'I'm not afraid of you.'

Julie tips her head to one side. It's bewildering, this feeling—unsettling—inevitable. Queer. 'Perhaps you should be, Marquise. Surely you've heard the stories.'

'Of course. Everyone has. And yet …'

'You will risk it.'

'What am I risking, really, that I could not bear to lose?' The Marquise whispers it so that only Julie can hear.

Julie steps back. It's too much. Offers a more circumspect bow. 'Very well.'

'Tomorrow, then?'

'As you wish, Madame la Marquise.'

'This is no jest.'

'I'm not laughing.'

'Bring your sword.'

'Always.'

The next day. The *salle* is deserted, the early-morning light just touching the weapons racks. La Maupin strides to the middle of the room. Turns around.

She laughs out loud. 'No jest, indeed.'

Awake all night for nothing. Dying a thousand deaths. Talking to herself in the dark.

She puts her hands on her hips. Turns around again. Shouts. 'Le Perche? Hell's teeth. Where is everyone?'

Nobody answers. Except.

There's a movement in one dark corner. A swirl of dust. Of silk.

'Here.'

La Maupin bows low to conceal her face—her fear. 'Madame la Marquise. I thought you had forgotten.'

'Far from it. I've been looking forward to this since we first met.'

Madame la Marquise de Florensac walks slowly into the light. She wears her golden hair high, so that the singer can admire the soft skin on her throat, the perfect ears. She is all in black—a thick padded fencing jacket and long skirt, one red glove on her sword hand and a flush in her cheeks.

'Now you're scaring me,' Julie says.

'Don't be absurd. *En garde.*'

Two women meet in the centre of the room. Swords raised, nearly engaged, nearly close, but not quite. They circle each other.

Julie almost smiles. 'We're lucky nobody's here. It's usually busy at this hour.'

'It's not luck. I paid them to go away.'

'You don't want anyone to see you lose?'

'I don't want anyone else's eyes on you. On us.'

The silver blades clash. Tangle. The Marquise's lunge brings them closer, but only for an instant. The sunlight catches in her hair. She doesn't blink, doesn't pause—attacks again. Close.

'Are you letting me win, La Maupin?'

'No,' Julie says, then grins. 'Yes. But you fence well.'

'As well as a man?'

'Better than many I've fought.' She circles around to her left, sword raised, her back to the light.

'Are you surprised?'

'A little.'

'Impressed?'

'Very.'

La Maupin slithers their blades together, taps one foot on the floor as if about to leap forward—then stops.

The Marquise retreats, smiles. Can't decide whether to focus on the blades or the body or the eyes—the face; whether to attack or retreat or surrender.

'Many ladies of the court fence, you know,' she says instead.

'So I understand. But none of them have ever—I've never been asked before ...'

'More fool them,' says the Marquise, but softly. 'I've learned more of the art in these few minutes with you than in years of training with Monsieur le Perche.'

'Really?'

'I will never lie to you.'

The Marquise lunges again. La Maupin parries low to *seconde*, then up to *prime* as the Marquise thrusts again, high. Takes a step back. And another. Smiles.

'So what have you learned, Marquise?'

'There's a rhythm. A pattern.'

'Yes. There's music in swordplay, if you have the mind to listen to it. Gorgeous, sacred music.'

'I never knew that before.'

'Even in the silences,' says Julie. 'In the breathing. The sound of one blade sliding along another—it's like silk, to me, like a choir.'

'And does everyone have their own song?'

'Most.' Julie disengages her blade, feints, forces the Marquise onto the back foot, into retreat, then slows, watching all the time—the green eyes, the pale throat. 'Some are discordant messes. Once I understand a man's rhythm, I know how to beat him.'

'And a woman?'

'It's different.'

'But you can still beat me?'

'Of course.'

'I don't mind. I am watching what you do. You take my measure. You slide the blade and tap your foot, move your shoulder forward as if to feint, but don't attack—not properly. Are you sensing my resistance?'

'Your control. Your patience. Everything. I'm listening to you. Feeling you.'

'And you allow me to come to you, to advance,' says the Marquise. 'But you aren't really retreating, are you? At any moment you might pounce.'

She does. It seems too perfect—too poetic—an opportunity to let pass. A simple thrust but it's fast. The blade grazes the Marquise's shoulder—gently.

She laughs. '*Touché*. That was silly of me.'

'Not at all.'

'You will not trick me again.'

'You know me too well,' says Julie. 'Already. I shall have to be more careful. I've fought dozens of men—hundreds—and they've never noticed that pattern.'

'They are too busy trying to beat you.'

'Perhaps.' Julie shrugs. 'They rarely pay any attention to me at all. They focus on the blade, as if it has a mind of its own.'

'They are fools, then.'

'Sometimes they're just scared.'

'Understandably. Your reputation is fearsome.'

'They don't look. You see through me. Into me.'

'Not yet. But I will.'

Now the Marquise moves more slowly, gliding across the polished floor with a low attack, easily parried but very elegant. It's dangerous, the Marquise knows that—she's vulnerable here, now, but feels that if she died this instant, at these hands, at this blade, she wouldn't mind so very much. Wonders, too, if any other moment in her life matters as much as the next few—if anyone anywhere in the world has felt like this—ever. Is she predator or prey? Or don't those rules apply? She has no idea, doesn't care.

She hopes only that her nerve won't fail her, that her hands don't tremble, that years of longing won't burst from her chest and betray her.

She tears her gaze away from the blades and looks directly into Julie's face. 'Are you happy, Mademoiselle de Maupin?'

'At this moment? Yes.'

'Other moments?'

'It depends.'

'On what?'

'On the moment.'

Julie glides her blade gently along her opponent's, pauses, then breathes. Beats the Marquise's blade sharply out of line and lunges. Stops short. Sword arm straight, her blade perfectly still, the point hovering before the Marquise's chest. They hold each other's gaze for a heartbeat. Julie stands, straightens, allows her sword tip to drop to the floor.

'What of you, Marquise? You are married.'

'I thought it would make me happy. I was misinformed.'

'A pity. You're wealthy. You could have chosen anyone.'

'I have. It's just taken me a while.'

'And beautiful—even more beautiful than you were at sixteen.'

'Don't talk nonsense. Tell me something that nobody else has ever said.'

Julie sheaths her sword and holds out one hand. 'Come home with me. I will devour you.'

'I feared you'd never ask.'

Act 5, Scene 7

Recitative

S HE SAID YES.

From that morning in the *salle* we were rarely apart. We slept, ate, laughed, walked, fenced, entertained, gambled, rode, dressed, bathed, even danced together. Every night. Every day. We woke up each morning entangled in each other's arms, breath, hair, warmth. I went to sleep each night breathless at the thought that the next day I would love her all over again.

We lived like normal people—you know?

Or not quite. Like goddesses together, princesses, floating in clouds, as if two of my most memorable roles had escaped the stage and eloped together—Clorinde and Athéna, perhaps.

I wore her likeness on a ribbon at my throat, alongside my mother's pendant. A miniature, by one of those fancy court painters. It didn't do her justice, but that's no surprise. There is some beauty, some wildness, which can never be captured by art. Her husband's family took it from me. Even that. Why? It was my only consolation.

My only love.

Don't get me wrong. The earthly delights were manifold. That's right, Father, spare me your blushes. We sinned. Absolutely. A great deal and in every manner known to humanity. We may even have sinned in ways the serpent never imagined. In the mornings, just after dawn, or in those hot afternoons when your skin sticks together and you can barely move and yet you do—in her boudoir, the dining room, the *orangerie*, once or twice in a carriage riding through the park.

She was no angel. Far from it. She was all gold hair and wild laughter, the fragrance of gardenias and lavender, a woman such as appears once in a century, if at all. She has— had—a brilliant mind, so accomplished they still sing of her in Paris. A fine rider. No-one was a better dancer. Stubborn, yes. Too witty, sometimes, for her own good. It's true she was ambitious, but not for wealth, not for fame—for me. That's all.

We lived in one of the new mansions on Place Royale. So peaceful. I dream of it. Our music room with the yellow walls and windows onto the terrace. Early-morning rides in the park. Late nights by the fire. Just us, a bottle of wine. Her laughter. The skin on her throat flushing crimson, her head back. Her breath. The salons. The balls. The teasing.

Those were the years of my greatest stage triumphs— *Tancrède*, written especially for my voice—never to be forgotten, so they say. The ultimate glory for a singer, that is—to have an entire work created for you, around you, about you and your voice. My voice. Shattered now, but then ... A thing of genius, of course. What else?

Then my Médée, in Bouvard's *Médus*. Francine thought I couldn't sing it, even Le Rochois said she'd have refused it—too hard, even for her, but not me. Oh, no. I was a triumph. Yet again.

People said I was the soul of France, the essence of Paris. A goddess. The sun. And so I was.

But I can barely remember any of that. I tell you these things, the markers of my life, so you can write them down. They mattered a great deal at the time, but now—if I think of those years, it's not the applause I remember. I think first of Thérèse and the Comtesse whispering in a corner. Thérèse and d'Albert dancing together, my twin, entwined hearts. My friends telling stories, Thévenard singing stupid ditties, and all of us drinking around our supper table. The parties. The songs. The carpets. The curtains. The bed. Evenings at the Palais-Royal, and me in full voice, knowing that Thérèse is there, watching me—feeling me, knowing me—and me alone on stage but with her everywhere around me. Forever. Or so we imagined.

Forever.

Dear God, help me. She is gone.

Forever.

Yes, it was adultery. No doubt about it. Endless amounts of adultery. You want to hear about her husband? The poor benighted cuckold? So. There's little to say. I barely knew him. He lived in the country, in his chateau over near d'Uzès, of course. He kept his mistresses there, and his hunting dogs, and was content enough, I suppose. A retired warhorse. A nobleman. She visited on holidays, his birthday. Easter. He came to Paris rarely—he went more often to Versailles, and sometimes she was summoned to appear there at his side, to dance and smile and flutter as if they were truly married.

I never went near the palace if I could help it.

Thérèse quite liked to visit, I think, to show off her new gowns and stare down the Dauphin. She liked the mirrors and the canals. She'd come home and tell me about the new murals in the salons or banquets in the park, about strolling through the gardens with some young rake just to annoy the Marquis, about him making a fuss over her slippers getting dusty, about dancing a gavotte with d'Albert and giggling behind her husband's back. She liked the ice-cream and visits to the stables and carriage rides around the fountains.

I couldn't think of it as grand when I'd run all over the place, half naked and sunburned, as a child. I remember instead the secret spaces, the haylofts and potting sheds, the orchards after dusk, the kitchens and the cool rooms. I remember the flagstones in winter, so cold underfoot it felt as if your toes would freeze. Stealing the first fruit of autumn. Dust. Fencing drills at dawn. Grapes in the sunshine, and flowers, and mown grass. My father's shirts drying in the afternoons. His cane smacking that soft spot behind my knees. A stableboy crying in his sleep. The spit roasts, and bread hot from the ovens with honey from the King's beehives.

I did wish I could show those things to Thérèse—wished I could walk with her, arm in arm, across the forecourt, pointing, reminiscing.

That's where I stood when d'Armagnac decided to take me as his mistress. Over there, in the shade of that tree, I sat humming to myself and played in the mud like an oystercatcher. This is where I saw my first *tragédie*, first heard Le Rochois, first saw that louse Duménil. Here, the King laughed at me one day when I fell into the fountain just as his carriage passed. I jumped my horse over the highest fence. I raced the pages clear across town to the potager. I trained with Master de Liancourt. I ate a caterpillar for a dare.

But I never did tell her. We couldn't visit Versailles together. Not if her husband was at court. Not ever.

I sang there again once or twice—at the Trianon, and once, just a few of us and the violins, after a wolf hunt in the forest. But the King's spirit had flown by then and he kept to himself, so the grand concerts belonged to the past. His Majesty spent his evenings with Madame de Maintenon, and who can blame him? Being fabulous is very tiring.

The Marquis de Florensac was no different. Just like his King, weary of wars and wives, he retired into a life of mistresses and hunting and wine and forgetting. He kept their son with him, in the country, out of harm's way. He knew about me—of course he did. Everyone in Paris knew. But what could he do about it? Challenge me? Not him. He simply chose to ignore my existence, so long as Thérèse played the Marquise when occasion demanded it. At court. At Mass. And every so often in his bed.

If that was the price she—we—owed to be left in peace, so be it. It seemed little enough at the time. It seemed, in fact, like luxury.

Ah. We sinned. Yes. Over and over and so deliciously, and I would do it all again—I would still be doing it now, if only—and you wanted me to unburden myself, so here it is, the impossible burden, the great grief.

This is what you want to hear. Me. Remembering how it was, every night, every day—remembering her mouth on mine, her—crying out in the darkness—it tears at me, like demons, like claws, like boiling pitch, every waking moment and there can be no greater Hell than this. Surely.

That Hell is eternal for me now, whether I live or die, on this earth or in any other place. You understand? There is no relief, no salvation. Only torment. Daily, infernal torment. My mind and my heart fill with the longing, the memories—her hair damp against her forehead, her skin always astonished at my touch, the force of desire, the overwhelming tide of it, the sleepless wonder of it, the desperate, sweaty clinging, the long hours of oblivious floating, a smile, a shudder, a pain in my chest so acute, so crushing, so delicious that nothing else—nothing—matters. Now or then.

These things I tell you, these other tales, exploits, sorrows—they make up my story, my life, it's true. But all they really do is fill in the years before Thérèse. Yes, there was a life before. It was interesting enough. People seem to find it so. Even you. But I am not entirely sure there can be a life after. After her.

After that. How can it be possible? How can it be true? I wake and endure every day now in this state of wondering. First, the desire, the fleeting, floating memories—then—then—the truth. Her breasts, those fingers, the fine hair, her silken skin, all gone. Rotting. Perhaps by now little more than dust. In a family sepulchre somewhere.

Not my family, no. Not hers. His—her husband's family crypt, of course, with the d'Uzès arms above the door and a dutiful epitaph in stone.

She fell pregnant after one of their visits to Versailles, and he never came near her after that. It was me who nursed her through the morning sickness, my hands on her belly ever so softly when the child stirred within her.

It was me who listened, ill with fear, to her birthing-bed screams, who sat with her every moment once the fever took hold.

It was me—me, who—dear God, have pity—I cannot speak the words. Cannot go on much longer.

It was me who ... who cradled her in my arms as the breath left her, held her close until the rigor set in and her skin was ice. I would have kept holding her, died holding her, right there. But they took her away.

Thérèse was my wife in everything but law. My love. My heart.

But it was him who gave her over to the Carmelites for burial, who ordered that poor weak child taken away, who accepted the comfort of the world for his loss.

It was me who was lost. Utterly. In a wilderness. In a desert. I know not where. In a city that no longer even noticed me.

So I came here.

Act 5, Scene 8

A duet

A DIM CORRIDOR. The windows, the mirrors, the galleries that once blazed with light are covered. The chandeliers remain unlit. A serving-girl scurries out of sight. Somewhere a door slams.

The young Duc d'Uzès hesitates. Smooths his waistcoat, sighs. The thing will be distasteful, no doubt. There'll be a scene. Perhaps a fight. It may come to blows, to a challenge. But it must be done. It is time.

He has walked these hallways many times, although not in the past few years. But he has heard—from d'Albert, from the whole of Paris—how they sparkled, how the Marquise and her precious singer threw open the doors in midwinter and danced in the snowflakes, how laughter rang through the galleries, how every gallant in town longed for an invitation here—to the Friday salon, a soirée, a discreet dinner. He was never invited, naturally, but he knows—everyone knows—all about the Christmas ball that lasted three days, and the luncheon parties in the *orangerie,* about Couperin playing harpsichord in the ballroom while the singer amazed her guests by singing every part of *Tancrède.* Even the King has heard of the dazzling days of La Maupin and her beautiful de Florensac. Everyone knows. Everyone adores them. Or did.

His footsteps sound sure as they echo through the house. It's not empty, he knows. But its light has gone. The magic. The heart.

He comes to a door—his sister-in-law's boudoir. One hand on the doorknob, but he can't turn it, can't look inside, where once there was giggling and velvet and music. Keeps walking.

Family portraits—his, hers—stare down at him. His father, the late Duc. His brother and his wife.

That's right. This is his house, his brother's house, now. All of it. The fabulous de Florensac wealth, the houses, the five carriages, the stables, the baby. By royal decree. By all the laws of humanity, of nature. By right. There can be no argument. He will not be provoked, not this time, not by her, not again.

In the south wing, there's a small salon. A music room. Another boudoir—the one they used, the one in which they hid their shame from the world.

If she's anywhere, it'll be here.

He doesn't knock. Why should he?

The singer is waiting for him. Heard his footsteps, heard the news from a maid who ran breathless from the courtyard. She sits, in a black gown, with both feet on the floor, a cushion gripped in both hands.

She's not ready. Not for this. That's not possible. But she's composed. Her fingernails are tearing the cushion to shreds but he will never know. Must never know.

He doesn't bow. Why should he?

'Madame de Maupin.'

'Duc d'Uzès.'

'You know why I'm here?'

'Of course.'

'Is the infant ready to travel?'

She blinks. 'Yes. She is being taken to your carriage as we speak.'

'Good.'

'Keep her warm. She's not strong. Not after … The doctors fear for her.'

'You need not concern yourself,' says d'Uzès. 'The wet nurse has been in the family for years.'

A pause. He looks around for the first time. It's as if every candle in the house—every candle in Paris—is here, in this room, and alight.

He raises his eyebrows.

'It's for Thérèse.' The legendary voice is strangely hoarse. 'She doesn't like the dark.'

'I see.'

'My father said—my father always lit a candle in the window—every night. He said if you lose someone—you light a candle, you see, and then they can find their way back to you.'

'I'm afraid, Madame de Maupin—'

'Not her body, of course. That's gone. I do realise.'

'Yes.'

'Her soul. You never know.'

'May she rest in peace.'

'I don't know,' says Julie. She stares into a candle's flame. 'Do you think she will?'

'I can't say. God willing.'

Another pause. Another moment.

'Madame, if you will permit me—'

Then Julie looks straight at him for the first time.

'You are a good man,' she says. 'I see that now. Defend your family, your friends. D'you remember that night, at the ball?'

'I still bear the scar.'

'The night we met.'

'No, we met earlier,' he says, 'with d'Albert, at Villeperdue.'

'Not you. I didn't mean you.'

He brushes away a wisp of sorrow, of pity. It's the gown that confuses him, pains him, the black silk, lace, dark smudges under her eyes. She is far from beautiful, far from fearsome, far from strong.

'Madame, I regret to say—'

'I am not your enemy. I hope you know that.'

'I beg your pardon?'

'We have fought,' Julie says. 'Many times. It must stop now.'

He bows, just slightly. 'Agreed.'

'You don't need to say anything more, sieur. My bags are packed. By nightfall I will be well beyond the city walls, beyond reach.'

'I'm not sure how to put this, but my brother has asked—'

'Don't worry. I take nothing with me that is not mine. Her jewels, her—everything—it's all still here.'

'Perhaps I might be permitted to—an inventory—just so I can reassure him ...' He sees her flinch as if slapped. 'Forgive me.'

Julie snarls at him, 'Do what you want. It's your house now. His house. His wife. I have no place here. Nothing.'

'It's my duty.'

'I wonder if he ever loved her at all?'

'I'm sure … when they were young. Before that night …'

'So it's my fault?'

'I meant only—'

She flings the cushion, bleeding feathers, into a corner.

'Go about your sordid business, d'Uzès. I must be on the road before sunset.'

He nods, turns to go.

'One last thing.'

'Yes, madame?' He faces her for the last time.

'Take care of d'Albert for me,' she says.

'I always do.'

'He'll miss me.'

D'Uzès closes the door quietly behind him. It's the least he can do.

Act 5, Scene 9

Finale

Now you've made me cry. I never cry. But recently it seems I can't stop. At her bedside. For days afterwards. Weeks. And now, remembering those long hours in the darkness.

Sorrow is an eclipse of love. For the truth is that I will never love again. That's it. Over. Even if I lived another forty years, I'd be alone. I am empty. Bereft. Beyond grief, beyond affection, beyond reach. I'll never be touched, never kiss, never feel a lover's hand in my hair or the small of my back. Never exchange secret glances across a room, laugh with my head thrown back in abandon, whisper in the night or dance in the dawn hours.

Not without her, without Thérèse.

I've lived through many griefs, many scars, many wounds. Until now. This—this life without her, without any point to it, without the rustle of her hem or her shadow in the candlelight—this is nothing. Nothing. I don't want it, whatever it is. It's not life. It's just grief and memory, memory and grief, layer after layer.

I have cried so much I frightened myself, slept so little I no longer know if it's dusk or dawn, prayed and sung and begged for release. Now it has come. My lungs hurt with every breath. My eyes sting—it's the sweat—the fever—yes, the tears.

I don't sleep. There's time enough for that. But now—now.

Now there is only a deep ache, a scar like a sword slash—crimson—across my chest.

I'm running. Drowning in my own blood. In hers.

Falling.

I'm dead. I must be.

I taste Hell between my teeth. I can smell the sulphur from here, but I swear to you that this life of mine is not worthy of the tar pits and the never-ceasing fires.

I can also feel the dampness of clouds on my face. I am in between.

I've returned from purgatory before this. I have come home triumphant from exile—from squalor, from despair—in finer voice, to greater acclaim, than ever.

And yet. And yet.

This time I fear it's beyond my strength. Where once there flared an unquenchable flame there is now—nothing. No Thérèse. Nothing else that matters.

I won't see her in the beyond. She's too good, too beautiful, to be anywhere but at Christ's right hand. The Apostles will fall over themselves and each other to offer her their seat—yes, even Saint Paul, who, you must admit, doesn't like any woman but the Madonna.

Thérèse will wait for me, I know—she is watching even now, as my body readies itself to release my spirit, to soar like the stained-glass dove in the chapel. She will hold out her hand to me and smile. Perhaps her longing and mine will even make the difference between Christ's pity and damnation.

What else can I do? I'm confessing as fast as I can.

I escaped the flames once. Perhaps I will do it again. My heart is pure. Not as pure as some, I grant you—I am no saint. But I was loved. I made people happy. Surely that must count for something? God is love, you recall, and he who abides in love abides in God, and God abides in him. Or her. So said an undisputed saint, and who are we to argue with him?

But there is a love of which the saints have no idea, there is a purity of being, in the stillness of the night, in the warmth of someone's arms, their breath on your neck, their skin like magic against yours—it happens rarely, but that is communion.

There lies redemption. Salvation. All lost to me now. But I felt it once. I held it close in these hands that now quiver—but not tightly enough. It slipped from my grasp in the night, in a fever, in dread and horror and the unutterable loneliness of someone who has truly loved and can do so no more.

I'm tired. The fever settles deep in my heart.

Release me, Father, for I have sinned. You can't forgive me. Nobody can—only Clara, only Thérèse, and they are gone.

But you should bring out your oils and crucifix, make your preparations. It is time.

You refuse?

Even this? Even now?

God help me.

So be it. I will make my own peace with Him. Your rites, your mutterings, don't matter. I am long dead.

But make sure they sing for me.
For God's sake.
And my own.
You should leave me now.
Hurry.
Close the book and go.

[Curtain]

JULIE-ÉMILIE D'AUBIGNY, KNOWN AS La Maupin, died in a convent in 1707. She was thirty-three years old. She has no known grave.

Que tout sente, ici bas,
L'horreur d'un si cruel trépas

[May everyone on earth feel the horror of such a cruel death]

Lully, *Armide*

The company, in order of appearance

Julie-Émilie d'Aubigny: Known as La Maupin, our heroine.

Antoine Le Bal*: Assistant to the musical *surintendant*, Académie Royale de Musique.

Gaston d'Aubigny: Julie's father, secretary to Comte d'Armagnac.

Louis de Lorraine, Comte d'Armagnac: Grand Écuyer to the King of France, addressed as Monsieur le Grand. Portfolio includes the Grande Écurie, the King's stables. Lover and protector of La Maupin.

Louis Gaulard Duménil: *Haute-contre*, Académie Royale de Musique. A poltroon.

Marthe Le Rochois: Soprano and goddess, Académie Royale de Musique.

Séranne: Duellist, fencing master, 'a gentleman from the Midi'.

A vicomte's son*: An unsuccessful duellist.

Clara**: A young woman of Marseille, beloved of La Maupin.

Maréchal: An actor and drunkard.

---

* May not exist except in this work.

** Actual name not recorded. A fictional name is used.

Louis-Joseph d'Albert de Luynes: Titled Comte d'Albert, later Prince Grimberghen. Lover and friend of La Maupin.

Duc d'Uzès: Friend of d'Albert, brother of the Marquis de Florensac. Opponent of La Maupin.

Gabriel-Vincent Thévenard: Baritone, Académie Royale de Musique. Lover and friend of La Maupin.

The Comtesse*: Lover, confidante and friend of La Maupin.

Jean-Nicolas Francine: *Directeur*, Académie Royale de Musique [Paris Opéra].

Monsieur: Philippe of France, Duc d'Orléans, brother of Louis XIV. Friend and protector of La Maupin.

Fanchon [Françoise] Moreau: Soprano, Académie Royale de Musique. Lover and friend of La Maupin.

Marie-Louise Desmatins: Soprano, Académie Royale de Musique.

Her sister, Mlle Desmatins: [first name unknown] Soprano, Académie Royale de Musique.

Madame Marquise de Seneterre de Florensac: Marie-Thérèse, lover of La Maupin. Described by Duc Saint-Simon as the most beautiful woman in France.

Madame: Elisabeth Charlotte, Princess Palatine. Wife of Monsieur.

Abbé Noye**: Opponent of La Maupin.

Marcel**: A cousin of the Marquise de Florensac. Opponent of La Maupin.

Maximilian II Emanuel: Elector of Bavaria, Governor of the Spanish Netherlands. Lover and friend of La Maupin.

Comtesse d'Arcos: His mistress.

Comte d'Arcos: Her husband.

Countess Marino: A pig.

Count Marino: Her husband.

Baron de Servan: An oaf. Opponent of La Maupin.

Comte du Saint-Rémy*: His reluctant acquaintance.

Chevalier de Raincy: A phantom.

Madame Marguerite Foré: A maid.

Monsieur Langlois: The unfortunate landlord of La Maupin.

Duchesse de Luxembourg: Mistress of Comte d'Albert.

Chevalier Frédéric du Bouillon: Lover of La Maupin.

OFF-STAGE

Father Fabrice*: Confessor, parish of Saint-Pierre, Avignon.

Monsieur Maupin: Husband of La Maupin, later a tax official in the provinces.

Louis XIV: King of France and Navarre, known as the Sun King.

Madame de Maintenon: His mistress, and later secretly his wife.

The Dauphin: His heir.

Rousseau brothers: Fencing masters.

Monsieur de Liancourt: A fencing master.

La Reynie: Lieutenant-General of Police.

Gautier: *Directeur*, Académie Royale de Musique, Marseille.

Sister Carmella**: A nun [deceased].

Monsieur d'Aubigny: A phantom.

Madame de Sévigné: A lady of letters.

Philippe, Chevalier de Lorraine: Lover of Monsieur, younger brother of Comte d'Armagnac.

Louis de Crussol, Marquis de Florensac: Husband of Marquise de Florensac, younger brother of the Duc d'Uzès. Described by Duc Saint-Simon as the stupidest man in France.

Mademoiselle Pérignon: A dancer, Académie Royale de Musique.

Count Rantzau: A duellist.

Count Schwartzenberg: A duellist [deceased].

Chopelet: A singer, Académie Royale de Musique.

Monsieur le Perche*: A fencing master.

A baby: Later named Anne Charlotte, born to the Marquise de Florensac.

ENSEMBLE

Abbess and sisters of the Order of the Visitandines, Avignon.

Peasants at a tavern in Provence.

Audience members at the Opéra, Marseille; a cabaret near Poitiers; the Opéra theatre, Palais-Royal; l'Opéra du Quai au Foin, Brussels; Versailles.

Stagehands, dressers, chorus, dancers and musicians of the Académie Royale de Musique, Paris and Marseille; and l'Opéra du Quai au Foin, Brussels.

Backgammon players, salon gossips, ball attendees, guttersnipes, secretaries, stableboys, gendarmes, court pages [various].

COMPOSERS AND LIBRETTISTS

Jean-Baptiste Lully: Composer *surintendant de la musique de la chambre du roi,* and *directeur,* Académie Royale de Musique [deceased but apparently immortal].

Marin Marais: Composer, master of the *basse de viol.* Musician, court of Louis XIV.

Philippe Quinault: Dramatist and librettist, collaborator with Lully.

Marc-Antoine Charpentier: Composer, *maître de musique* at Sainte-Chapelle, Paris.

François Couperin: Composer, harpsichordist, organist at Saint-Gervais-et-Saint-Protais and later the Royal Chapel. Musician, court of Louis XIV.

Marguerite-Louise Couperin: His cousin. Soprano and harpsichordist—first female musician to appear in the Royal Chapel. Musician, court of Louis XIV.

Théobalde: Composer, master of the *basse de viol*, player in the orchestra of the Académie Royale de Musique.

François Bouvard: Composer, singer, Académie Royale de Musique. Master of the violin.

Molière: A playwright. Collaborator with Lully.

Author's note

Y OU PROBABLY THINK I made this up. I didn't.
This novel is an interpretation of the life of the
very real Julie d'Aubigny. All of the episodes described
in this novel are based on documented events in her life. That
doesn't mean that they really happened, because there are so
many different accounts of her life it's now impossible to sift
fact from what my grandmother used to call 'romancing the
truth'.

One of those biographers, Bram Stoker of *Dracula* fame,
wrote in his book *Famous Impostors* (1910): 'In truth the
story of La Maupin is so laden with passages of excitement
and interest that any writer on the subject has only to make
an agreeable choice of episodes sufficiently dramatic, and
consistent with each other, to form a cohesive narrative.' If
only it were that easy.

Julie d'Aubigny was born some time in 1673, probably in
Paris, the daughter of Gaston d'Aubigny, secretary to Louis

XIV's Grand Écuyer (Master of Horse), Comte d'Armagnac. Her father was an accomplished swordsman and trained the court pages, and so his only child was educated alongside the sons of the aristocracy. She dressed as a boy from an early age and quickly surpassed the pages in fencing, learning from some of the great masters of the era. I believe she spent the years from age eight to fifteen at Versailles with the court. By the age of fourteen, she had become d'Armagnac's mistress and he found her a husband, Monsieur de Maupin, who was promptly dispatched to the provinces to a job as a tax collector.

After that, events in her life happened very quickly: the duels, the convent fire and escape, the many affairs, her lifelong friendships with Comte d'Albert and Gabriel-Vincent Thévenard, her debut in 1690, the exile, the many triumphant performances and fame, and her final grief. It's all true. Apparently. Distraught after the death of her lover, Madame la Marquise de Florensac, La Maupin entered a convent where she died two years later in 1707 at the age of thirty-three.

These incidents were either noted at the time by diarists or chroniclers, or described by eighteenth-century theatre historians or biographers. Details often differ, and I have tried to sort out the most logical or historically likely scenario. I have added as little as possible. There is really no need to insert any further drama to such a life—the fictional elements lie in the motives, the thoughts, the emotions and the words spoken by these characters.

I have managed to trace many if not all of her opera performances, and episodes such as her attack on her landlord are documented in court reports. The extract of the letter from d'Albert is from the original (published by him after her death, in 1758), and the notes passed between La Maupin and

Thévenard in their famous duel of wits are also apparently in their own hands (I admit I have exaggerated some of the tricks they played on each other). The description of her meeting with Maréchal is based on a memoir sighted by her early biographers, the Parfaict brothers (*Dictionnaire des théâtres de Paris*, 1756), but the manuscript is now lost—hopefully it will turn up one day.

We don't know exactly when she was born, where she died or where she is buried, although as an actress she probably wouldn't have been buried in consecrated ground. Some biographers claim she died in a convent, but nobody knows where—I have brought her back to the convent in Avignon she had once tried to burn down. Most biographers are coy on the question of which convent was the site of her youthful crimes, but several suggest it was the Convent of the Visitandines in Avignon.

Even her name varies. She is now usually known as Julie d'Aubigny, but in her lifetime she was most often called Mademoiselle Maupin. In some cast lists her name is given as Julie-Émilie de Maupin. D'Albert addressed her as Émilie in his letters, while Thévenard called her Julia in his famous note. Although her married name was Madame de Maupin, opera singers were traditionally addressed as Mademoiselle. Biographers and writers have used all of these names. After the publication of Théophile Gautier's novel *Mademoiselle de Maupin* in 1835, in which the character based on Maupin was called Madeleine, that name too has been used.

Most of the characters in *Goddess* were real people: the only major character I created is the Comtesse, a composite of several of the highly intelligent, well-educated and sophisticated women of the era. In the case of Clara, the name is invented but the real person and her involvement with La Maupin were widely reported—her name was never given in any of the accounts, for obvious reasons. The name of the young woman La Maupin kissed at the ball is also not recorded—I have chosen to connect that incident and her relationship with La Florensac because, frankly, I just couldn't resist. A few other minor characters, such as Le Bal, are also fictional, but based on real people in the Opéra or the court.

If you'd like to read more about La Maupin's life, two of the more sensible biographical pieces in English are chapters in Oscar Gilbert's *Women in Men's Guise* (1932) and Cameron Rogers' *Gallant Ladies* (1928). An extensive biography (in French) is *La Maupin, sa vie, ses duels, ses aventures* by Gabriel Letainturier-Fradin (1904). There are many other accounts written in varying degrees of outrage or awe, some completely scurrilous or hagiographic. One of the most famous interpretations of her, Gautier's influential novel *Mademoiselle de Maupin*, is not so much about the life of the real woman as the essence of her: the cross-dressing, the ambiguous sexuality, the spirit and beauty. It was one of the books most often banned in the nineteenth and twentieth centuries and helped ensure La Maupin's continued celebrity.

La Maupin's fame and infamy wax and wane—sometimes it seems she's been forgotten but she comes back fighting, notably in times of social change and debate around women's lives and sexuality. During her lifetime her exploits were recorded in diaries, gossip sheets and letters, plays and songs and stories; and later in dozens of almanacs and biographical encyclopaedias, books on the history of opera and fencing, biographies and novels, a ballet, feminist theory, at least one movie and even a French television series. Quite recently she was named 'Badass of the Week' online, leading to a flurry of interest and an outpouring of fan illustrations and blog posts—even a skateboard design. She fascinates and defies her audience and her biographers. What is it about her? This novel is only one answer.

It has been a delight to spend several years in her company. I'm not sure what I'll do without her voice echoing in my ears. She is an exhilarating, often challenging, companion and I hope I've done justice to her life and her voice. She deserves it.

Acknowledgements

THIS BOOK HAS TAKEN several years to research and
write and many people have supported me along the
way. Any errors in historical fact are, unfortunately,
my own.

I finished the first draft during a two-week Writing
Fellowship at Varuna, the Writers' House in Katoomba,
a place of peace, bounteous food and endless inspiration.
While there, I also had the opportunity to receive invaluable
feedback on the initial manuscript from Carol Major.

Rob and Marlene McPherson provided me with the
perfect place to finish my final draft—the house in Anglesea
where I spent childhood summers.

The novel was part of my PhD project, undertaken in
the English program at La Trobe University. I'd like to
recommend the warm and supportive environment that
postgraduate writing projects can offer. In particular, I
benefited from the advice and feedback of my supervisor,

376

the lovely Catherine Padmore, and my co-supervisors, Paul Salzman and Lucy Sussex; the generosity and wisdom of Alison Ravenscroft; and the support of Christine Burns and Loretta Calverly in all things mysterious and administrative. The faculty also provided a grant towards the costs of a research trip to France in 2011.

At La Trobe I also met my two companions in arms, Paddy O'Reilly and Fran Cusworth, who read and scribbled all over the first draft, and with whom I drank coffee, wrote in comradely silence, ate vast amounts of cake, and laughed far too much and too loudly in the library's not-quite-soundproof-enough meeting rooms.

Speaking of which, my research would not have been possible without the resources and people of the La Trobe University Library, the State Library of Victoria (especially the Arts Librarian Dermot McCaul, fount of all opera knowledge), and the Bibliothèque nationale de France, where I spent blessed breathless hours in the Opéra Library. I have accessed digitised primary sources and resources from countless museum and library collections in France and all over the world, from photographs of extant swords and slippers to original *libretti* and costume designs. In the Musée Carnavalet in Paris, I walked up a marble staircase rescued from d'Albert's family mansion. At the top, I entered a gilded room that was once in the home of his best friend, d'Uzès. I had no idea either still existed. Such are the joys of field research.

The former chapel and convent of the Order of Visitandines in Avignon still stand, in spite of La Maupin's best efforts, and the current owner, Madame Cherée, graciously allowed me to inspect both the chapel and the convent gardens and kitchens.

Thanks to my colleagues at the State Library of Victoria who put up with a part-time person to allow me time for writing, and to the many people from all over the world— some of whom I've only ever met online—who cheered me on. One of them is Jim Burrows, whose original website on Julie helped me find my way to key references in the early stages of the research.

My publisher, Catherine Milne, understood what I was trying to do with both character and text: she's a perceptive reader and all-round delight. The book has been ushered on stage by editors Ali Lavau, Nicola O'Shea and Amanda O'Connell, who asked sensible questions about obscure Paris street names and reminded me when my accents were facing in completely the wrong direction. Darren Holt designed the sumptuous cover.

Susannah Walker yet again supported me throughout this lengthy process and this book is dedicated to her with gratitude and love.

You'd never know it from most history books, but La Maupin was not the only queer, cross-dressing or adventurous woman during the Baroque (or any) era. There were many real women who wore armour, fought battles or duels, secretly joined the army or navy or pirates, worked in male professions, took lovers of either or both genders, and wrote music or books, as well as those imagined in stories and on stage. I hope this novel sheds a little light on one extraordinary life, and in doing so helps us to remember or rediscover history's legions of legendary and very real Amazons. So let's acknowledge all those who came before—the spirited, brave women like La Maupin who shook up the world, and still do to this day.